Heather Hay was b[...]
Scotland and Englan[...]
and two sons and liv[...]
kept pigs, goats and [...]
marketable pies and [...] that led to her catering for Orient Express tours on their trips to Penshurst Place, the stately home of Lord De L'Isle in Kent. During this time she started work on her first book, *Country Enterprise*, which was published in 1983.

By the same author

Country Enterprise
The Business
Heritage
Honour

HEATHER HAY

Heroes

GRAFTON BOOKS
A Division of the Collins Publishing Group

LONDON GLASGOW
TORONTO SYDNEY AUCKLAND

Grafton Books
A Division of the Collins Publishing Group
8 Grafton Street, London W1X 3LA

A Grafton Paperback Original 1990

ISBN 0-586-20807-0

Printed and bound in Great Britain by
Collins, Glasgow

Set in Times

For my mother and father,
because they were there.

Acknowledgements

My parents met serving in the RAF during the Second World War. Their memories, and those of many other friends – old and new – of that generation, have been of inestimable help to me. I would like to thank them all. As my children, Joanna, Alex and Rex, grow, so their contribution increases. As always, my husband Jonathan, agent Jane, and now my new editor Nancy have given me help and encouragement.

I would also like to thank Wendy Nash of the RAF Benevolent Fund Appeal (and her aunt for the 1940s cookbook!) and Wing Commander Alan Jones AFC Station Commander, RAF Biggin Hill.

Finally, the Montford family, who exist only in the *Heritage* trilogy, will always owe their beginning to Penshurst Place, Kent, the beautiful home of Lord De L'Isle.

*O tell her, brief is life
but love is long.*

Alfred, Lord Tennyson, 1809–1892

Honour stared listlessly out of the window. She wasn't touched by the beauty of her view, or how the soft May morning light had warmed the honey-coloured stone walls of the rose garden. Splashes of pink and yellow shone amongst the deep green foliage. It was her nineteenth birthday, and the weather couldn't have been more perfect.

She slowly crumpled the half-finished letter in her hand. She couldn't think what to write, what words to commit to paper. It didn't matter, anyway. None of it mattered, none of the past. What was important was the future. The drone of an aeroplane broke into her thoughts and she opened the window and leaned out. She scanned the sky, not relaxing until she saw the roundels and could recognize friend, not foe. As always, she wondered if it was someone she knew flying over the house. It could be Neil, or Nigel, up there in the clear blue sky. They were so handsome in their uniforms – almost identical with their bright hazel eyes and thick dark hair. Nigel was just under six foot tall and Neil an inch or so shorter; the family said that was because he had been born second. They were her cousins, Victoria's twin sons. Victoria would have known what to write, she would have penned a few short lines to tell a childhood sweetheart that he had been forgiven, and that he was, like the rest of Honour's childhood, now part of the past.

'Damn!' She banged the window closed and the diamond leaded panes quivered in their frame. The plane was out of sight, almost out of hearing. It was a waste for her to mope – time was precious. It was almost a sin to squander it. She turned and checked her reflection in the mahogany-framed cheval mirror. Her fair hair was pulled back from her face, restrained in a ribbon tied low on her neck. Rebellious wisps curled on her temples and she pushed them irritably off her face. Her dress was a soft mixture of pinks and blues, a floral Liberty print, one that her mother had chosen. Her face softened at the thought of her mother.

The fuss that had been put into celebrating Honour's birthday was very unlike the usual unflurried yet effective style of Lady Montford. Since her husband had been confined to bed, Isabella had become a formidable matriarch. Her one soft spot was for her daughter, Honour. She had been a late child, her brothers William and Eddy were in their thirties, and Honour was especially precious to them all. Honour's slight figure and fair colouring were deceptive, hiding a strong, independent spirit that she'd inherited from her mother.

She threw the crumpled paper in the waste-paper basket, then left her room quickly, closing the door firmly on a chapter of her life that seemed already far in the past.

'And this, Honour, is my gift to you.' Lucinda Cade held a showily wrapped box towards her niece. 'It's not quite what I wanted, something from Paris would have been just that little bit more stylish, have that certain, *je ne sais quoi*.' Her withered lips wrinkled. 'But this damned war . . .'

'Thank you, Aunty. I'm sure whatever it is, it will be perfect. You have such inspired taste.' Honour was pulling the wrappings quickly apart, keeping her head tipped forwards, her face hidden. She had a premonition it was going to be a hat. It would be something embarrassingly flamboyant. 'Oh, it's lovely.' She held out the bottle-green, feather-decked offering for them all to see. Her mother smiled. She was pleased at Honour's ability to appear delighted with a gift that would never see the light of day. Her father's eyes followed his daughter's hands. He was thinking how pretty they were, fussing over the piece of nonsense that his wife's sister had produced. Typical of the silly woman, he thought, as his left hand plucked nervily at the bedcovers. Lucinda had aged over the last few months and felt personally aggrieved that the war had curtailed her shopping expeditions to France, her visits to friends in America. He struggled to keep his mind on the reason for them all to be gathered in his bedroom. It was Honour's birthday, the girl was nineteen. God, he could remember being nineteen himself. He'd been full of energy and bursting with zest for a life that stretched so far ahead of him. Now he was confined to this room, confined to his bed. He would die here. A deep sigh shook his gaunt frame. He had so much still to do.

'Are you all right, darling? Is it too much for you, having us all in here?' Isabella reached over and squeezed her husband's hand. It was difficult to tell how Michael felt. The series of strokes had left his face frozen in an everlasting calm. He was lucky, though. They all were. As the doctor said, it was more usual for the muscles to tighten and distort; Michael could have been left looking like a soul in constant torment. As it was, only his pale, watery blue eyes portrayed his feelings, and his slow, difficult speech.

'No, I'm fine.' He vainly struggled to smile. He wanted to show all of them he was happy. Lucinda's sons, Tom and Albert, were standing well back from the bed as if

11

frightened of contagion, their ruddy farmers' faces creased in concern. The airless life that Michael led filled them with horror.

Albert's wife Maggy clutched her husband's arm. 'Margaret was sorry she couldn't get time off to come down. She loves a party. But they keep her very busy in London. Being a typist at the War Office is a very demanding job,' she said proudly.

A party – Honour smiled at the sickroom gathering of her elders being referred to as 'a party'. Last year had been so different, last year she had had a dozen friends of her own age to dinner. They'd had a real feast, then played silly parlour games, and she'd fallen in love. Impulsively she pulled Lucinda's hat on to her head, and turned, giggling to show them all how happy she was. She was working hard at keeping the atmosphere jolly. If they thought it was a party, then all well and good. They weren't to know of the letter she couldn't manage to write, not now, not ever. So long ago, she thought suddenly, and her mouth, despite all her efforts, turned down at the corners. So long ago I thought I loved you, James. How dared he write to her, how dared he. 'Shall I cut the cake now?' she asked. 'It's such a wicked treat, all the butter and eggs in it. Shall I cut it now?' And with a supreme effort she smiled again.

'Surprise!' The door to the drawing room burst open with a bang, revealing the urbanely elegant figure of young Eli Bradbury.

'Eli, how lovely.' Honour jumped up from her seat. The prospect of a visit from her divinely extrovert uncle brought a genuine smile to her face. 'I never thought you'd make it.'

'What, not come to my favourite niece's birthday bash?

12

Couldn't be such a cad, my dear.' He bestowed a hearty kiss on each of her cheeks as he squeezed her in a bear hug.

'I wish you wouldn't sound so theatrical, Eli. And it's not nice to say Honour's your favourite.' Lucinda's voice was high and irritable. 'My Viccy's your niece as well, so it's unkind.'

'All hail, sister Lucinda. I see the fine weather's done nothing to change your mood. Still glacial, eh?' He made his way to Isabella, kissing her in greeting, then to Maggy, who blushed – she had never got used to his town ways. 'So, Lucinda, do I risk a kiss, or might I catch frostbite?'

'Don't be any more absurd than usual.' Lucinda inclined her face towards him.

'This tea's still hot.' Isabella lifted the lid of the silver pot, and looked inside. 'And there's plenty of it. Have a sandwich.' She lowered her voice and almost whispered, 'They're smoked salmon.'

'Needn't feel guilty, Issy.' Eli began piling his plate. 'Got to keep fuelling the troops. And I must admit, much though it amazes me, it seems the powers that be actually find me useful. Which just goes to show that it's never too late to become a reformed character, never too late at all. There you are, Honour, that's my birthday gift to you, an illuminating thought to carry you through life. Oh, and of course . . .' He reached inside his jacket. 'I nearly forgot.' The box he held towards her was small, square and covered with blue leather. 'Happy birthday to our little Honour.'

She reached out almost hesitantly. The atmosphere in the room seemed suddenly serious. 'It's not a trick, is it?' she laughed nervously. The catch was awkward and she fumbled with it for a moment, then the lid flew open with a loud snap. She drew her breath in sharply, and at the sound Isabella stood up abruptly. 'But it's beautiful, it's . . .'

Her mother's voice said what Honour was thinking. 'It's the centre stone of the Montford necklace. The stone is my gift to you, and your father's, of course. But it was Eli who had the idea and had it set for you. The inspiration was all his.' Isabella's voice was trembling. There was so much in the bright blue stone that Honour was lifting from its velvet cushion. So many years ago, so long, a lifetime away, Michael had given her the original necklace. Like ice fire, diamonds and blue topaz set in white gold, magnificent, but its very opulence was something that belonged to the past. Living in wartime Britain, a girl required something simpler.

'It's beautiful,' Honour whispered.

Eli went forward to fasten the fine golden chain around the girl's neck. He too had memories, the past seemed to rise up, to want to intrude. 'And so are you,' he said loudly, dismissing the unwanted pictures from his mind. 'Now, more tea, more sandwiches. I'm famished. I spent the morning out on the water.'

They all rallied round, talking brightly, even Lucinda tried a little. It was a day to live for the present; the past was gone and the future – who knew what the future would hold? When the glasses of champagne were passed round – another present from Eli – Honour's birthday toast was followed by another, 'To William and Eddy', and they held their glasses high. Honour's two brothers were with the British Expeditionary Force in France and reports said the situation there was worsening daily. As always, the family would listen to the nine o'clock news on the radio. Perhaps tonight, Honour asked as her birthday wish, there would be a little hope.

* * *

'So, my darling, another year older. Do you feel any different?' Isabella sat down on the edge of Honour's bed. Automatically she began straightening the thick white linen coverlet. She found it hard to sit absolutely still.

'You ask me the same question every year, Mummy. As far back as I can remember. And I've always said the same thing – no, no I don't feel any different. Only this year it's not exactly the truth.' Honour was watching her mother in the mirror as she rhythmically brushed her hair. The routine was the same as on every one of the countless nights of her life that had all been leading, she suddenly felt, to this moment. 'I feel I've crossed a divide. Some kind of gap between being a child and being a grown-up. Please, please don't smile like that.' She laid the silver-backed brush down gently. 'I know you still like to think of me as a little girl. But I'm not. I'm capable, I have a mind, and I'm strong.'

'I don't dispute any of that, darling. I'm sorry if I baby you. I'll try to stop it.' Isabella stood up and walked towards her daughter, reaching out to pick up the hair-brush. She'd been counting the strokes; fifty Honour had reached, there were another fifty still to go. 'Anyway, I've been showing how capable I think you are. After all, you've taken over a great many of the jobs that I did until recently. I couldn't do – '

'Don't say it.' Honour turned round quickly on her chair. She had to face her mother, to see her reaction. 'Please don't say you couldn't manage without me. It's not true. I know it and you know it. It doesn't matter what anyone else thinks. I'm sure most of the village believe I'm really useful to you, quite indispensable, but that's only because you want them to think that. I know you've been trying to make me feel needed. And some of

15

the times I have. But I have to go away now. It's my time. You heard what Eli said this afternoon: Uncle Timmy's daughter, Jill, is coming to England. She's going to become a nurse. Heavens, she's no older than me, and she's sailing halfway round the world to do her bit for King and country. And there's Margaret, nobody even considered stopping her going to London, or Neil or Nigel joining up, and they're all my generation. I'm the only one still cosily tucked away at home. I have to go, Mummy. Anyway, I've already set things in motion.' Her face flushed pink, suddenly she really looked the child she was trying so hard not to be.

'What are you going to do?'

'I've enlisted in the RAF. I'll be off in a couple of days to do some square-bashing at Cirencester, then on to do a driver training course. I'll end up based in London, and I'm going to share Margaret's flat. It's brilliantly positioned because it's just round the corner from Herbrand Street, where the garage is. That's it in a nutshell, I'm going to be a driver for the RAF – I've already had quite a bit of practice on the estate, haven't I?' she laughed. Her eyes were very bright, full of tears. Her mother was so very dear to her and it was hard to bear the thought of leaving her alone, with a chronic invalid to care for, and the great, beautiful house of Pencombe being transformed around them into the sanatorium that it was only right and proper it should become.

'You'll look very pretty in uniform.' Isabella was coping very well. Her voice was quite steady, her throat had become painfully tight, but that was all. All, except for an aching emptiness that threatened to engulf her. 'It isn't necessary, you know, for you to go away to "do your bit" as you put it,' she said. 'You are being very useful here,

16

you could be even more useful when the men arrive. There will be a lot of work, convalescents need – '

'It is necessary, Mummy. It's necessary for me.'

Isabella knew all the words she could say, all the arguments she could lay out in front of her daughter, to make her see she couldn't leave. But the girl was right, it was her time to go. 'This isn't because of James, is it?' It was the only question she knew she had to ask.

'No, it's nothing to do with him.' Honour didn't want to say his name, to conjure up the picture of his face.

'We won't tell your father until the morning.' It would be kinder to let him sleep another night secure in the belief that at least one of his children, his beloved Honour, was safe beneath his own roof, Isabella thought. She left the room, smiling gently. Only when she reached the safety of her own bedroom did she allow her face to crumple and the tears to fall.

Honour picked up the brush and turned back to face her reflection in the mirror. 'Fifty-one, fifty-two . . .' The blue stone flashed at her neck, trembling with the pulse that beat beneath it. She still had the letter to write. She believed she owed James that much, and a girl named Honour had to pay her debts.

She had to compose herself, to remember James with kindness, rather than the sickening shame that would steal up on her in the early hours of the morning. It was Lucinda's son, Tom Cade, who'd brought him into her life and he would never have hurt her willingly. Tom lived at Reason Hill, the red-brick farmhouse that had been the home of Lucinda and her husband Thomas before a tragic accident left the Cade children fatherless. Nearly twelve miles from Pencombe, the property was the hub of the farming empire founded by Tom's father – over two thousand acres of Kentish orchards and fine grain land.

Since Thomas's death the Pencombe estate had been added to the Cade acreage, and when James's father asked Tom to show his son the modern methods of agriculture, he had been more than happy at the prospect of another pair of capable hands.

'And this is James.' Tom beckoned the tall, red-haired young man standing awkwardly in the doorway to come further into Isabella's drawing room. 'Your aunt Isabella; Michael; Honour.' The farmer performed the introduction perfunctorily. The 'aunt' was a courtesy title, he had too much on his mind to be bothered with working out the actual relationships. He was farming over two thousand acres, and a high percentage of his land was down to grass. It was time he grew more grain, he had a feeling it would be a sensible move. 'I'd like a word in private with you, Michael, if you don't mind. I don't mean to be rude, Isabella, but my time is limited today, and besides, our absence will give you and Honour a chance to get to know your Irish cousin.'

The older men left the room to go to Michael's sanctum – the chill, austere study that hadn't changed since his father's day. Isabella walked towards her visitor, who had still not advanced very far into the room. 'Come and sit by the fire, James. You must tell us all about your family. I haven't seen your mother in goodness knows how long. Are they all well? You have quite a number of brothers and sisters now, don't you?'

James Sullivan nodded his head, cleared his throat ready to speak, and then, apparently not able to think of anything to say, sat down on the gold damask-covered armchair Isabella indicated. Up until this moment he had thought of Isabella simply as a distant relative, a cousin several times removed. Coming over on the boat he had

18

formed a mental picture of the house at Pencombe. He knew it was the seat of the family that his mother was part of, but he had never imagined grandeur. He had thought in terms of his own home. That was big enough, comprising large airy rooms full of the generous-sized, elderly furniture that was as much a part of the fabric of the Sullivan family as the house itself. There were six children, three girls, three boys, their ages ranging from James, who had just turned twenty-one, down to Erin, who at eight years old was the baby. The splendour of Pencombe made him feel awkward, clumsy-footed, as he made his way through the minefield of genteel, piecrust-topped wine tables and ladies' footstools placed just so as to trip a young man trying to make a good impression.

'I have to say you look very like your mother, James. I remember her quite well, even though we last met when we were both children. We've exchanged Christmas cards over the years, of course, but not much more. She wrote a letter when she married and moved to Ireland. And then Tom did some agricultural business with your father and we were all properly in touch again. It's a small world when it comes down to it.' Isabella leaned encouragingly towards him from her own chair. The poor boy was nervous, she thought. The healthy glow of the farming life he led did not cover the fact that his skin was pale, and his eyes flicked around the room. He would undoubtedly have been happier in the open air. 'I gather from Tom that you're going to spend some months staying with him at Reason Hill. That will be nice. We'll be able to see a lot of you, get to know you properly. Honour will show you around and introduce you to her friends.'

Honour's eyes widened at the thought of the gauche young man perched on the very edge of his chair meeting her friends. It was the thing to be elegant and poised. 'I think James might find we're much too shallow,' she said, carefully not looking at her mother. 'You're involved with the land, aren't you? I'm afraid we're all awfully townie. Despite my living down here, town's the place for me.' She laughed lightly, knowing her mother would be furious. But her mother would have to agree that this distant relative was being wet.

'I like towns right enough.' James leaned forward. Now that he was sitting down, the room didn't look so daunting. 'I have to follow an interest in the land, for the family. But my own ambitions lie in a different area altogether.'

It seemed there was more to James than had first appeared. Honour kept her eyes averted from her mother, so that she wouldn't see the look that said 'I told you so.' Now that James was speaking they could hear his accent. It was soft, warm and somehow charming. And he was very positive, quite different from a moment ago.

'Perhaps you'd like some tea?' Isabella lifted a little bell, tipping it sideways so as not to set it ringing before her guest accepted the offer. 'Then we'd love to hear all about your ambitions, wouldn't we, Honour?'

Honour nodded her head energetically, to hide the fact that she wanted to giggle. It was all so funny, so stilted, and James looked so serious, staring at her earnestly with his light blue eyes.

'I want to own a chain of shops,' he said. 'Department stores, like they have in America.'

Isabella was surprised enough to put the bell down unrung. 'Department stores – do you mean like Harrods?' she asked.

'In a manner of speaking, only mine wouldn't be just for the rich. I want to sell to everyone, to reach the

20

ordinary people. One shop where they can buy clothes, furniture – a shop they can trust.'

'That sounds a very interesting idea. But do the ordinary people have enough money? And what about the cooperative societies, surely they would be difficult for you to sell against?'

'Why, Aunt Isabella.' James smiled for the first time, and his face became quite different, full of life and amusement. 'How clever you are,' and he laughed out loud.

Honour smiled too. She was beginning to regret having been such a prig. 'But how would having shops fit in with your farming?' she asked.

'They don't fit in at all. But I've reached an agreement with my father. I'll spend the next five years setting our estate in order and getting it running profitably under a manager. Then I can use the freehold of the estate itself to borrow against, and I'll have my business in no time, no time at all.' He sat back in his chair. He seemed much bigger now, almost dominating the room.

'To use the freehold of your father's estate is a tremendous risk.' Isabella's face showed her disapproval. In the past she'd known the difficulties of having an estate encumbered with onerous mortgages.

'A risk it is, but a calculated one, Aunt Isabella.' James stood abruptly. 'If I may, I'd like to take you up on your offer of a tour of the place. I don't have much time and it would be good to feel that I know my way about.'

'I'll take you.' Honour, too, stood up quickly. She wanted to know more of the strange young man who talked about 'calculated risks'.

They hardly talked as they walked through the state rooms. The house was closed to the public on Mondays and so they were alone. Crossing the great hall their steps echoed in a silence made oppressive by the thick stone walls that denied sounds and air from the outside. When they reached the state apartments the heavy wall hangings absorbed even the noise of their footsteps. The final part of the tour led past the entrance to the buttery. Honour pushed the door open to show the giant white sink, the double wooden draining boards that were scrubbed to a pale blonde. She paused for a moment as James stopped, and then nodded to himself. He was like a dog familiarizing himself with alien territory. A setter, she thought, an Irish setter. Ahead of them the great Gothic door was open wide in an effort to let the mild spring breeze into the house. 'Come and see the gardens,' Honour said, and turned to look at James in surprise as he took her hand.

'You don't mind, do you?' he asked. 'After all, you're a pretty girl and it's a lovely day.' He slowed when they reached the open air, and the sun shone on the redness of his hair as he tipped his freckled face back to feel its warmth. 'You know, I haven't felt at home since I came to your accursed isle, but now . . .' He swung her arm and laughed out loud.

'Accursed?' Honour was taken by surprise and she looked up at him, trying vainly to read the expression on his face.

'But of course. You English, you're the oppressors. Has no one taught you history, then, Honour me darlin'?' He laughed again at the artificiality of his thick Irish brogue. 'Come on and I'll race you to the grand fountain I can see yonder, spittin' up at God in His Heaven. And when we get there I'll tell you a few home truths that I'll bet you never heard from your daddy's knee, or your clever mother's either, come to that.'

* * *

22

They became friends, but it was a strange friendship. The more James told Honour of the history of his persecuted land, the more she became proud of her own ancestry. She never tried to justify the past to him, but it seemed that she understood the strength of her own forefathers. Wrong although they may at times have been, they had created the beautiful land she saw around her every day. 'How can you expect me not to be proud?' she'd once asked, as with a sweep of her arm she encompassed the glory around her. 'Montfords have lived in this valley for centuries, all their memories are in the soil, the river, even the stone of the walls.' She sounded very passionate, with a catch in her voice that made James put his arm around her thin shoulders.

'Why, you're a poet,' he said. 'Perhaps you're one of us, after all.' The 'us' he meant was the Irish, and Honour struggled from his grip, furious as always at the divide he put between them. She wanted him to feel how she felt about England. She didn't want him going back to Ireland to farm acres that he didn't love, to lavish his care on land that was only a stepping stone to his true ambition. She wanted him to stay and build his empire close to her.

They had their first argument when she told him she thought he should give up his plans to mortgage his father's estate. Isabella brought the subject up at every opportunity, filling his head with facts and figures of the early problems of the Montford estate, family secrets that he had no wish to know. When Honour added her weight to the argument, he lost his temper and told her it was none of her business. It was inevitable, but it didn't make Honour any less furious. She ran out of the house, away from the drawing room and its overheated atmosphere, out into the garden, where the wet summer had made the trees hang heavily.

She hurried down the gravelled paths, her cotton frock billowing out behind her. She relished the feel of the air on her body, the tears of anger cooling on her face. The heavy, damp air had been pressing down on her. The gate in the boundary wall ahead was shut and she tugged at the rusted metal ring, twisting it, feeling the pitted surface under her sweating fingers. The latch lifted suddenly and she was free. She paused for a moment. The carriage drive that bordered the river in front of her led left to the fields and the Home Farm, right to the village. James would follow her – she was sure of it. He would come after her and he would search in the country, convinced that she would not go to the village with tears on her face. She sniffed loudly and rubbed the back of her hand across her cheeks. She had no handkerchief, and she didn't want to be seen . . . Then she had an idea that made her smile. She would pay James back for being such a stubborn ass. She knew him well enough now to know how important it would be for him to apologize. He enjoyed an excuse for a moment of tenderness, holding her gently, with his broad hands on her shoulders. Well, she would deprive him of his consolation.

Honour turned towards the village, walking quickly but not running, as she didn't want to call attention to herself. The air was full of the scent of roses, red and yellow they festooned the wall beside her. She kept looking back over her shoulder, but there was no sign of James behind her yet. If she was lucky her mother would be having a few well-chosen words with 'young James', as she called him. It would give Honour the time she needed.

The village was ahead of her, a cluster of red-brick cottages with tiled roofs, a jumble against the heavy, thundery sky. A car was pulled up outside the shop, and there were two girls on bicycles going away from her.

Apart from that the street was lifeless. She turned left quickly, taking the road that led over the bridge, and began to run. Soon she would reach the copse that came close to the water and then she would be hidden.

James walked determinedly down the path, and the gravel crunched under his shoes. He pushed up the sleeves of his white shirt. It was his best one, worn for the ritual of tea with Isabella – he felt easier with her once he'd discarded the 'aunty'. He was finding his feet away from home, learning a few of the social graces. They would be helpful to him in the future. His plans had changed somewhat since coming to Pencombe. He now saw that to succeed he should carry out his business in an atmosphere of moneyed refinement. Even his plans for the stores had changed – he saw that it was the middle classes he must woo, and they would expect Mr Sullivan of *the* Sullivan's stores to be a gentleman, the type of gentleman they could understand. So be it. But that was all in the future.

He glanced down at his watch and quickened his pace. Half past four, and he wanted to be back at Reason Hill for dinner. He had a lot of talking to do to young Honour. She should take his side with her mother, generation against generation, that was how it was meant to be. After all, she loved him – he'd known that ever since her birthday party, when she'd had a glass of champagne and kissed him on the lips for the first time.

He went through the boundary gate, closing it behind him and smiling. Honour had left it open so that he would know where she'd gone. The drive led through the outlying buildings of the Home Farm and he whistled as he walked, reckoning she would let him know if that was where she wanted to be discovered, but all he found was a few chickens scratching in the dirt. He stopped to loosen

25

his collar. He was growing hot and irritable, and felt that Honour was taunting him. The hop gardens were ahead. They stretched down the valley side to the edge of the drive and then, as the road swept up the hill towards the farmhouse, the avenues of green led down to the river. He knew now where she must be and he left the drive, walking between the high green walls, the bitter perfume of the hops making his eyes itch. Ahead of him, as yet unseen, there was a bend in the river where the swallows darted. Honour had taken him there one evening. The place was somewhere special, she said, cool and secretive, yet open to the sky.

Honour was there, waiting for him. She smiled a greeting, her mouth curving up, taunting. She was on the far side of the river. James stood, hands aggressively on hips, dressed in his Sunday best, and Honour's smile deepened. She had scored a victory over him. The river was wide here, fast-moving close to her bank. She put her fingers to her lips and blew a kiss. She would go in a moment, run back and let him apologize as he walked her through the garden.

James put his hand up to his shirt front and slowly, methodically, all the while looking at her, he began unbuttoning his shirt.

'James!' she called out to him in alarm. 'James, don't. The river, it's dangerous here, please . . .'

He pulled his shirt off, dropping it beside him on the grass, and his pale skin glowed like pearl in the reflection from the water.

'Please . . . I'll run back, honestly, I'll – ' She took a few steps along the bank, back towards the village, but then she stopped. He was paying no attention to her at all. His face was expressionless as he took off his shoes, his socks, and then he moved forward, clambering down

26

the bank. She put her hands up to her face and her cheeks were flaming.

The yellow mud of the river was cool under his feet. The sharp leaves of a wild iris caught at his ankles, but he didn't feel the weals they made. The water was soft – he stared down at the swirling surface, feeling the tug of the current round his legs. But it wouldn't stop him, nothing would. He took a step, and the bank shelved steeply down, the water was suddenly up to his waist. He flung himself forward, arms outstretched, and the water came up to him, slapping his chest, stinging his eyes. He was a strong swimmer and he kept his face down in the water, not taking breath, but beating the river by his strength and his determination.

She stood still, waiting for him.

He came out of the water, pulling at the reed stalks to climb the crumbling bank in front of her, and still she stood, her hands at her cheeks. He towered over her, and as she bent her head back to look up at his face it seemed that he cut out the light. He put his hands on her shoulders and pulled her to him. Their lips met. His were cold for an instant, and then they were hot. She leaned towards him, her thin dress clinging to her with the wet from his body. She put her arms around his neck. His tongue flicked between her teeth and a shiver ran down between her breasts. He pulled at her skirt, pushing it up to her waist, his hand slipped between her thighs and she opened them for him. She was quivering under his touch, straining against his hand.

They lay in the uncut grass and there was no sky, no earth, nothing except their touching bodies. He watched her face, the flickering eyelids, the faint blue veins beneath the whiteness. She was drawing him into her – her mouth, her hands were pulling him down on top of her, he fumbled with her clothes, his hands still chilled from the water, and then there was nothing between them. As he entered her she seemed to stop breathing, and then her hands were in his hair and she was moaning, a soft, low sound from deep in her throat. It was a rhythm that he moved to. 'Honour, Honour,' he whispered. He had his face pressed into her hair, breathing in the smell of it. 'Honour.' He was shaking, trembling as she clutched him. 'Mother of God.' He threw himself from her, shuddering face down on the bone-hard ground. 'I'll not make you pregnant.'

She cried out as he left her, curling into herself, like a child she lay there sobbing.

On the first of September Hitler invaded Poland. A week before that James had left suddenly for Ireland. The family thought Honour's breakdown was a result of his leaving her beloved country, abandoning it in a time of need. In a manner of speaking it was.

'No, I mean a real thrash.' Nigel ran his finger through the pool of beer on the bar. 'I'm fed up swilling this muck.'

'Now, now, Nigie, listen to your elders, there's no more cash . . .'

'Do me a favour and bugger off.' Nigel's bright shining smile had for once deserted him, and even his twin brother Neil had to take him seriously.

'You shouldn't let them get at you. You were an idiot to admit it. I expect most of them are in the same boat, anyway.'

The activity in the Black Lion was beginning to pick up. It wouldn't be long before the bar was crowded, soon someone would start thumping on the piano, and then the evening would be off on what had become a ritual. Pints

of local brew, a sing-song and all the stories of conquest –
conquest in the air, and conquest on the ground. It was in
the latter category that Nigel had yet to score. 'At least
you've broken your duck.' He looked balefully at his
brother, then his good nature broke through. 'Mind you,
it was a bit dangerous, considering the position of the
gear stick in that car . . .'

'Didn't notice it, didn't notice a bloody thing.'

'Look, we're pretty nearly identical. How about, the
next time I take your place?'

'Don't be disgusting.' Neil laughed down into his glass
as he gulped at his drink. Thinking about the heights of
passion he had scaled in the Bugatti made him thirsty.

'I bet Margaret's got some friends who might.'

'Margaret's got some friends who do,' Neil leered. 'In
fact, Margaret does.'

'Good God, you're having me on.'

'No I'm not. She told me herself, she reckons it's her
patriotic duty to spread as much happiness about as
possible. Her war effort, she calls it.'

'Good Lord.' Nigel looked shocked. He hadn't thought
of his cousin in that light before. 'But that's awful. What
on earth would Uncle Albert say, or Aunty Maggy, come
to that – she's so strait-laced it's not true.'

'She wasn't always, she had to get married, you
know . . .'

'Had to get married?' A familiar loud voice behind
them made them start. They hadn't seen Percy come into
the pub. 'Who had to get married? Not one of our poor
boys being dragged off to the altar?'

Percy the persecutor, Neil nicknamed him, in a vain
attempt to amuse his brother after Percy had wheedled
out of Nigel that he was the group's only remaining virgin.
Percy announced that it made the boy precious to them.

At twenty-three, Percy acted like a man of the world. He was the one whose conquests had reached double figures, the one whose handlebar moustache spanned a good six inches. He was tall and wide, with fair ginger hair, pale blue eyes and a voice like a fog horn. The war had saved him from studying at medical school, and he loved it for rescuing him from a fate that, in retrospect, seemed worse than death. He had launched himself into the business of fighting the Hun with all the enthusiasm with which his father wished he would pursue a career in medicine. The Harley Street address that had been in the family for forty-odd years could have been Percy's one day, still could be if he lived long enough. Only no one was thinking much about after the war. Soon they would be alone in their battle; France was going to fall, it was inevitable. Percy spoke for them all when he said it would be a good thing and clear the decks for action.

'You're not drinking bitter, are you, my dear Nigel? It'll stunt your growth. Barman! A pint of your finest stout, if you please. My friend here needs building up, preparing for the – Now that's what I call a real corker . . .' Percy's loud voice trailed off in open admiration. The girl who had just entered the bar was straight out of his dreams. Blonde curly hair fluffed out under her hat, a tailored dress that enhanced a curvaceous figure; she had the smile, he thought, of an angel, except for the sparkle in her eyes that promised . . .

'Nigel!' she cried. 'Darling!' And then she was throwing herself at him, wrapping her arms around his neck, kissing his cheek, tousling his hair. 'You absolute sweetie pops, I've missed you awfully, awfully. Neil!' Her voice was high and musical, and it set them all smiling. 'Kissie, kissie. Well, aren't you surprised to see me, then? Go on, say something, say, "Margaret, you gorgeous, adorable thing, how have you appeared like a vision out of the blue." Go on, dumbos. Only first,' she manoeuvred herself up on to a bar stool, showing an interesting amount of leg, 'I'm desperate for a drink, and second I'm desperate.' She looked slowly around the bar, smiling at the faces turned towards her in open admiration. 'I want to meet your friends, especially this one. My goodness, is that real or is it stuck on?' She reached forward as if to pull at Percival's moustache, and then she laughed.

'Margaret, meet Percival,' Nigel said, admitting the inevitable to himself: here came Percival's fifteenth, and it was their cousin. The whole thing was damned unfair. 'Percival, meet Margaret.'

'Fair lady,' Percival said, dropping his voice that requisite half-octave for adoration of the fair sex, 'allow me to rescue you from the babes of the squadron, Nigel and Neil, known to us all as Tweedledum and Tweedledee.'

'Oh, but you mustn't be like that, they're my cousins.'

'My dear, we all have our cross to bear in life.' He reached out, taking her elbow gently but forcibly so that he could escort her to the table in the corner that had become fortuitously vacant.

'Jesus Christ!' Nigel's hand shot out towards his father's bed. The thunder of bombers overhead shook the house, the sound of their engines made the jug in the basin on the washstand rattle.

'Would you like to go down to the cellar, Master Nigel?' the night nurse smiled. She would stay with her patient, no matter what. It was funny to see the young airman so upset by the noise of the enemy planes.

Nigel shook his head. He was closer to the bombs at the top of the house, but in the cellar there would be the whole weight of the house to fall on top of him. He couldn't bear the thought of being buried alive.

'We've had no bombs drop near here yet, there's nothing for them to bother about in Cadogan Gardens, and anyway, you'd hear them whistle before they hit. You don't need to worry until then.'

'Does my father never wake up?' The planes passed over, flying on to another target, and suddenly he found himself shouting ludicrously loudly.

'At first, when the sirens went off he would panic and try to leave the bed. But nothing disturbs him now, poor soul.' She always thought of the dying as poor souls. It was a blessing when they were rid of their decaying bodies and winging their way to a better place.

'Did you tell him I was coming?' Nigel asked. His father had been asleep ever since he arrived and it seemed a shame now to force the pathetic white-haired creature into the trance-like state that meant he was conscious. Luke Jones had aged pitifully over the last five years. The age gap between him and his wife – some thirty years – would soon separate them irrevocably. Senility had overtaken his once fit body and there were times when he didn't even recognize her.

'I said you would visit sometime, but I didn't promise it would be today. I talk to him all the time. One can't tell if he understands, of course, but I always think it would be dreadful to be trapped inside your head and have no one say anything to you. So just in case, I tell him about the little things of the day. Not about the war, I don't think that's right, not for a man in his condition. Of course, he'd be proud of you if he understood. Anyone would be proud to have a child of theirs playing their part.'

'How about you, Nessie?' Nigel hoped her name was

Nessie, he was fairly sure that's what his mother had said. 'Do you have any children?'

The nurse stood up, her uniform rustling with starch as she moved towards the bed and straightened the already immaculate coverlet. 'I have not.' She stared down at the old man lying there. These youngsters, they never bothered to look at a woman's ring finger before asking such silly, hurtful questions. She was fifty-one. There was a good few years' work left in her gaunt frame, but then what? She had no home, no family to fall back on. She had always 'lived in'. When there was no longer anyone willing to employ her she would be destitute, penniless. She had nothing put by. Out of the pittance she earned she had to buy her own small luxuries that made life bearable. Chocolates for the night shift – but she couldn't treat herself the way she'd like to any more, not with the rationing. Then there were the embroidery threads; it was astonishing how the cost of a nice tray cloth mounted up. She only really liked to work on the best Irish linen but perhaps she wouldn't be able to get that now.

The wail of the all-clear cut across her thoughts.

'I'll go down now.' Nigel squeezed his father's hand briefly. It embarrassed him, paying attention to a body that seemed so unfeeling, more in the land of the dead than the living.

Eli was letting himself in the front door as Nigel came down the stairs. 'Looks as if we're in luck tonight,' he said, 'but there's a red glow towards the north. Some other poor devils have copped it.'

Nigel checked his watch. 'Eleven o'clock and all's well, or I suppose if you live where the bombs dropped, not well at all. Is this you coming back from work or play, Eli?'

'Work, my child. Everything I do these days is some

33

kind of graft. Mind you,' he laughed as he took a bottle from his overcoat pocket, 'there are perks that go with the job.'

They sat in front of a small fire in the study. The coals were little more than dust, but the glow was cheerful and the inner heating of the whisky helped provide an illusion of warmth. Eli eased his feet out of his shoes. The soles were thin with all the walking he was doing, and there were so few staff in the house that it seemed he'd have to do something about getting them mended himself. 'Do you know any good cobblers?' he asked, staring down contemplatively at his socks. There was a suspicion of a hole at the heel; economies could be taken too far.

'That sounds like the beginning of a music-hall joke.'

'Wish it were. God! I could do with an evening on the town. A good show, pretty girl on your arm, cosy dinner, then back to her place. Sheer heaven. Come on, drink up and I'll tell you all about what's going on.'

Eli helped himself to another generous measure of spirit. 'The only way I'm going to stop our black market escalating out of all control is to be part of it. And it's not the odd bottle of Scotch that worries anybody. At the moment the big panic is the misappropriation of medical goods. Quantities of drugs that should be in the system and being shared out fairly are finding their way to those who can afford to pay way, way over the odds. Wouldn't do if the only lot left alive at the end were the stinking rich, because they could get hold of medicines. No, you can take it from me, the fact that we're drinking a drop of smuggled hooch does not endanger the nation.'

Nigel was silent as he slowly and contemplatively finished his drink, then he asked, 'Do you know any good brothels, Eli?' He stammered over the 'b'.

'Good Lord, I had a feeling you had something on your

mind, I knew you weren't really listening to me. What the heck do you want me to recommend a brothel to you for? No, no, don't answer me, that was a silly question. I'll rephrase it.' Eli concentrated for a minute. He was a different generation from the boy airman, his tastes were different. Nigel should be the one recommending a good place for an interesting hour, or three. 'Where have you been up until now?' he asked.

'Never mind.' Nigel wished passionately that he hadn't asked the question. 'Look, I've got to go. Just forget what I said, OK?'

'Anything you say, old chap.' Eli saw Nigel to the door. He was careful that they didn't show a light as he let his visitor out into the dark street. He remembered suddenly seeing Victoria standing there, it must have been twenty years ago, framed in that same doorway before she ran off to be with some nightclub owner she'd thought she'd fallen madly in love with. Now it was her son looking for a physical replacement for the real thing. He went back alone into the study. Nigel had a problem. He needed a steady girlfriend, regular access to a lithe, twining body – he was at that age.

It was the first time Honour had been home since joining the RAF and suddenly the house seemed enormous to her. She was more than happy to give up trying to be pleasant to Lucinda in the drawing room and go out into the fields with her uncle. 'Oh, Eli,' she said as she sat down abruptly on the grass, 'sometimes I think you're the only one of the family I can talk to.'

'Don't be too hard on them. They're only concerned about you.' Eli looked down at his pale cream Oxford bags. He was very fond of them and didn't want to risk a green stain, however dry the ground looked, and then of course there was always the risk of a bird dropping – that would be fatal. 'Let's walk on a bit,' he said.

'Walk, walk, walk. For Heaven's sake, I'm not a dog, I don't need exercise that badly, you know. It's the universal cure, isn't it? That or a cup of tea.' She got stiffly to her feet. She had sat around the house for hours, 'seizing up' Nigel called it. But they didn't know how much she deserved a rest. After Cirencester she had been sent to Morecambe for driver training. It was nothing like she'd imagined and the theory of car maintenance threatened to flummox her completely. The 4v8 cars they drove to Kendal and back were quite different from any of the vehicles at home, but at last she mastered them. She had a tendency to ride the clutch and that was cured by her instructor kicking the ankle of her offending foot. The fact that she eventually passed her test driving a lorry pleased her enormously. She was tired but proud of what she'd achieved. The last thing she needed was to return to a vitriolic letter from James.

'You'll go through a lot more love affairs.' Eli began to stride out, making Honour almost run to keep pace with him. 'And each one will hurt when it's over. Even those that end on your own terms. Take it from an expert.'

'I've never seen you upset by a girl.'

'That's because I'm good at hiding my pain.' Eli laughed as he held a hand to his heart. He didn't suffer that much; when something was over it was best just to let it go. Occasionally he had a patch of pitying himself – wondering why he'd never met the right girl, the one he'd want to devote the rest of his life to. Then he'd come across someone new, a bright, bouncy creature just aching to be taken to the bright lights, and his fit of self-pity would fade.

'Daddy said that if there wasn't a war he'd have sent

36

me on a tour to recover – the Continent, Paris, the artists' quarter . . .' Honour let her voice drift away. She wasn't going to cry in front of Eli; it seemed that the only thing to do was to be trite and cynical, as he was.

'Your papa would never have meant the artists' quarter. You'd have been chaperoned by a dry old spinster, or worse.' With a flourish Eli stopped beside a rustic bench strategically placed to catch the view down the river. He pulled out a handkerchief and dusted it before sitting down. 'Yes, it could have been a lot worse. You could have ended up with Lucinda.'

'You're heartless. You know that, don't you? I wrote to James saying I'd forgiven him and when I saw his second letter waiting for me, I thought he was going to admit that I was right. I didn't for one minute expect him to be so selfish, he was horrid. You should know what he called me.' But Eli wouldn't know, no one would ever know. She breathed in the fresh air. It was lightly scented with pine from the plantation that stretched away behind them. There was a faint blue haze over the tree tops, and a distant breeze carried high white clouds majestically across a blue sky.

'It's funny to think, looking up at this, that there are people suffering.' Eli gestured above him. 'And I don't just mean our boys. Think about the Poles, for example. Imagine being overrun, Honour. Not able to walk out as we have and sit down where you want. The very thought makes your skin crawl.'

'He should have stayed.'

'Your beloved James? Why should he? It's not his war, or that's what the Irish seem to want to think. And they hate us – not without some cause, you might say.'

'But he'd become part of us. He knows Neil and Nigel, wouldn't you think he'd want to be alongside them?'

37

Honour's voice was rising. She wanted Eli to agree with her, it was important that she was right.

'Anyway, it wasn't as simple as that, was it? You were carrying much too flaming a torch. It was no good imagining lots of little Sullivans around your skirts. A man won't settle down unless he's ready. You should count yourself lucky. You've got a lot of fun years ahead of you; you're not ready to be lumbered with a couple of squalling brats. Come on.' He stood up. 'I'll race you to the Browns'.'

They ran over the rough pasture, flattening cowslips and daisies and startling a flock of starlings searching for grubs. Ahead of them a red-roofed huddle of farm buildings nestled in a hollow on the hillside. It was time for the evening milking, and the warm smell of cows carried towards them on the dry air. Honour felt tears on her cheeks. It was the first time she'd cried since James left. She'd been frozen at first, that was what the family called her 'breakdown' and then it had seemed too much to let her grief show. So it had eaten at her, making her pale and withdrawn. Suddenly the sight of the homely farm, with Eli running towards it in his incongruously elegant outfit, made her realize how doomed her love of James had been from the start. He didn't belong here, but she did – it would always be her home.

The milk they drank was sweet, hardly cooled in the churn. Mrs Brown smiled approvingly at Honour, whose cheeks were pink from her running and whose eyes were sparkling now that the crying had passed. She was such a nice girl, the whole village thought so. And such a help to her mother, especially now that his Lordship was confined to bed. Eli was a different matter, he was known to be a bit wild. If Mrs Brown had had daughters instead of three fine, strapping sons, she would not have welcomed him.

As it was, he was harmless and always charming, making her laugh in spite of herself. He treated her as if she were a pampered lady expecting entertainment in her drawing room instead of a large-boned, apron-wearing woman whose main pleasure in life was watching her menfolk eat the good, wholesome fare that she cooked them.

'Race you back to the house?' Honour asked.

'No thank you, my dear.' Eli dusted specks of dust from his trousers. 'I've had quite enough exercise for one day. A gentle stroll will be quite sufficient.' He tucked her hand into the crook of his elbow. 'Evening is falling, and the poet in me wishes to savour the moment,' he sighed theatrically.

Honour laughed and squeezed his arm. He was such good company. She felt better than she had in weeks.

'Well then, Michael.' Eli walked quickly into the bed-room, shutting the door firmly behind him. He had the feeling that if he gave himself time to think, he would find an excuse not to visit Isabella's husband. That was how he thought of Michael now, as Isabella's ailing husband, not as his one time well-meaning if introspective friend. Their relationship had had its ups and downs. In the early years Eli had been wild – Young Eli he'd been known as then, to differentiate him from his father – and Michael had been an authoritarian, always laying down the law, reading the riot act. Then, after the Montfords came back from Australia, Eli found Michael changed, more willing and able to relax. Relaxing was Eli's forte – at least, it had been until the war.

'Eli.' Michael whispered the name. He had been dozing, daydreaming of being on the river, and Eli had appeared. 'I was just thinking about you.'

39

Eli's face lit up with genuine pleasure. 'The good old days, eh?' he asked. 'Two men in a boat.'

'And the crew.' One half of Michael's face twisted up. It was an expression that Eli took for a smile.

'All aboard the *Bunty*. You wouldn't recognize the old girl today, she's decked out with rope fenders, looks like an aged tart with her drawers round her ankles. Pity really.' He sat down on a chair by the bed.

'At least she's got a job. And so have you. Got to say,' Michael shifted slowly under the covers, 'we're proud of you.'

'Surprised at me, you mean. I think your old pal Sandy Maclean caught me at just the right time. With all the boys going off to fight, I was all gee'd up and ready to go. Of course he pulled me in gently, spouted a lot of stuff about the river, said my knowledge of the waterways would be useful to the war effort. Then zap, gaffed me good and proper and I'm in for the duration.'

'In what, exactly?' Michael asked. 'You never have told me the name of your set-up.'

Eli tapped the side of his nose with a bony forefinger. 'No names, no packdrill.'

'Sandy always was a devious chap,' Michael smiled. 'At one stage I thought he might pack up the sea and take up politics, but he never could give up the Navy. What's he now, a rear admiral isn't it? I find it hard to keep track.'

'Right now he answers to a plain "Mr". But he still hangs out at the Admiralty, except for when he meets up with me in seedy bars.' Eli leered theatrically and started searching through the pockets of his blazer. 'God, I'm desperate for a pipe. Issy won't stand for it down there.'

'I can still take a hint. I won't press you any more, Eli. But don't forget, if you do need a sympathetic ear, I'm no security risk. Though God only knows, even if I was, I

40

wouldn't have anyone to pass my information on to. I can't do a damned thing from here. I still haven't heard anything about my letter, you know.'

Eli made a performance of filling his pipe, tamping in the tobacco carefully. He wanted to choose his words deliberately, and he had no intention of setting Michael off on his monologue. 'Actually, there is something I wanted to talk over with you,' he said. 'I'm getting involved in something new. New and nasty.' He sucked hard on his pipe, drawing the air through the smouldering tobacco. The perfumed smoke settled like a blue haze over the bedclothes.

'My God, I'd give anything for a smoke.' Michael closed his eyes and breathed in carefully, savouring the forbidden smell. He didn't want to cough.

'What have you heard about the black market?' Eli asked. He tried not to look at Michael's face. It wasn't a good colour, not just pale but yellowish, and the hollows under his eyes were a dull brown.

'No one's been offering me any beluga caviare, if that's what you mean. Come to that,' Michael opened his eyes, turning his head jerkily as he wanted to watch Eli's face, 'if I'd wanted any, I'd have asked you.'

Eli laughed. This was the best visit to Michael he'd had in a long time. 'Naughty, naughty,' he said. 'I'm a reformed character, old bean, and I get a monthly salary to prove it. No, it's not me who's doing any profiteering, and the small fry really don't bother anyone too much. There's always going to be a bit of something being flogged on the side. Organized crime is different. It looks as if there's a scheme to shift tons of stuff through the docks. That's why I've got involved.'

'You want to take care . . .' Michael's words began slurring. 'Bad types . . .'

Eli couldn't bear to watch the struggle. If this was growing old, he didn't want any part of it. He sat quietly, giving Michael time. He'd visited Luke a week or so ago. Poor Victoria's husband was totally senile now and when Eli'd got back on board dear old *Bunty* he'd just wanted to open the throttles up and head out into the open sea, not that he'd have got far. Bloody war. 'I heard from Timmy,' he started, changing the subject. He knew it would be impossible to carry on a conversation with Michael as he was today; better to perform a monologue of his own. 'His daughter, Jill, is coming to England,' he continued.

The constriction in Michael's throat was easing. He kept his eyes open as he forced his muscles to relax. Try and overdo things and they'd go into spasm, that was what the damn fool doctor said. He half-listened to Eli. He would have liked to know more about the black market but he wasn't really interested in Timmy's girl. One nurse more or less wasn't going to make much difference. It was the shore defences that really mattered. He began going through his well-reasoned arguments again, the ones he'd struggled to get on paper, and so far no answer.

Eli had a feeling he was talking to himself, that Michael had drifted off somewhere. He'd finish his pipe and go down to the others, then make his way back to London. There was a Gaiety girl, a real smasher – he'd take her on for a meal after the show. A fellow had to live it up. He stood up abruptly. A fellow had to live it up while there was still time.

'You can have no idea, Bella, how dreadful it is having to travel up to town by train.' Lucinda leaned heavily on her

42

stick as she walked along the gravel path leading to the rose garden.

Bella Montford found the slow pace aggravating. Whenever she visited Pencombe, she left almost bursting with nervous energy. She was the daughter of Michael's dead brother Johnnie and his wife, Adele, an American who now lived in London with her brother Bill. Bella was a creature of the town, as her elegant day dress of red and white silk showed. Before the war she had delighted in having so little free time that a trip to the country was almost unheard of. She had been creating quite a name for herself, the society magazines had written delightful articles about the daughter of the American side of the Montford family, highlighting how successful she was, while still only in her early thirties. The war had brought a sudden end to her glittering career. Her collections had always been modern, not at all in the taste of the few remaining buyers, and the gallery was scarcely functioning at all. That was why she had found herself gratefully accepting her aunt Isabella's invitation to spend a few days 'cheering them all up'.

'All those ghastly people crammed in like cattle,' Lucinda continued. 'Why, even in first class – ' She stopped suddenly. 'What on earth . . . ?' The gate in the wall ahead of her was open, and through it they could see Isabella. She was facing away from them, her hands on her hips, and there was thick smoke rising from the ground in front of her. 'Isabella, what in God's name is happening?'

Isabella turned round quickly. She was smiling, looking happier than she had in a long time. There was a streak of mud on her cheek. Sensing her sister's scrutiny, she rubbed at it with a chamois-gloved hand. Behind her the fire burst suddenly into life, and with a roar and a crackle orange flames shot up and the smell of burning defiled the morning air. 'Too late, you're too late, Lucinda. But I've saved you the climbers.'

Lucinda stepped through the gate and looked around her in fury. The rose garden had been vandalized, the flower-beds were empty. There was bare earth where just yesterday there had been an abundance of rose bushes, and even the edging pansies were gone. Lucinda's eyes flashed with new fury as she saw a wheelbarrow overflowing with uprooted purple and yellow flowers. 'You've killed them, you wanton!' She raised her stick as if she would hit her sister.

'No, Lucinda.' Isabella's smile died as she realized that beneath Lucinda's anger was sadness. 'It's only the really old bushes, the ones that were on their last legs that I'm burning. I've sent the others down to the village.'

'The village? You're letting *them* have my beautiful, beautiful flowers.' Lucinda put all the scorn she felt for the villagers into the 'them'. 'You have no soul, Isabella, no sense of propriety.'

'On the contrary, Lucinda. I have a great sense of soul and I also have a great sense of what is required to keep body and soul together. There is no way we could justify the work it would need to keep this garden in good heart. But we can justify using this fine soil,' she stooped quickly picking up a handful of the rich brown loam, 'to grow food. We must be realistic, there's all of us who live here to feed, and the day may come when there are several more – Bella, for one. I know you're intent on staying in London for the moment, my dear, but Pencombe is home for you, whenever you want it.'

'You're too kind, Aunt Isabella, but I think I'd be a bit like your roses out here. I don't think I'd justify my existence.' Bella smiled tightly, her perfect white teeth gleaming against her reddened lips. 'And I'd hate to end up on the bonfire. Come on, Aunty, I think you'd be better off not watching this.' The two women left, Bella having linked her arm through her aunt's. She thought Isabella was a philistine, and to dress like that! The brown roughspun skirt was splattered with mud, the blouse looked like something a servant would wear. Bella could feel close to Lucinda, but never to her other aunt, she was too, too . . . Bella searched for a word then seized upon one she thought eminently suitable: Aunt Isabella was *rural*, and if she didn't take care, then before long she would be positively rustic.

'Was that true, what you said to Aunt Lucinda?' Bella had taken Lucinda into the house and then come back to the rose garden. A thought had struck her, and it was something that should be acted on instantly.

'What, about giving the roses to the villagers?' Isabella was paying her niece scant attention. She wanted to get on, she didn't want any roots left in the soil; when they rotted they could spread disease.

'The whole thing, about clearing out these beds to grow vegetables.'

'Well, of course it was true, what earthly other reason could there be? If you really want to know, I loved this garden, I've spent many happy – ' She pulled her thoughts together sharply, there was no point in wasting time on memories. 'You obviously have your own thoughts about the war, Bella. After all, by not going back to America your family has made a statement of its own. Personally I think we could be in for a long, long struggle. It makes sense to be self-sufficient. To a cottager, that might mean digging up a much loved flower-bed and growing a few more cabbages. To me, well, to me it means clearing out this garden and growing food to feed us, and perhaps a few more. It is only right that we too should give up some things we love. Good God, child, it's nothing to sacrifice, nothing at all.' Isabella wanted to shake the girl in front of her, ruffle the smooth surface. There were young men and women laying down their lives every day, every hour, and here they were squabbling about a measly patch of earth.

'What I meant, Aunt Isabella, was, are you doing this because you can't afford the upkeep? What I want to know is, are you hard up? Because if you are, there are some rather nice little paintings about the house that I could sell for you. I don't mean any of the big, grandiose portraits, I can understand you wouldn't want to part with them, but, as I said, some of the little ones, ones from the bedrooms. There's quite a market . . .' Her voice tailed off. She had never seen her aunt look so intimidating.

'Go away.' Isabella's breathing was too loud, she could hear it herself, and she could hear the scrunch of the wheelbarrow on the gravel path as one of the men returned. 'Go away at once.' There was a tightness in her chest, her sight was hazy and she was so cross that she wanted to shout. More than that, she wanted to slap the silly girl's face. 'Go . . .' But she was talking to empty space. Bella had turned and walked away, rather than run, as she had wanted to.

Victoria tipped the cup towards her. 'There's a single tea leaf floating in the bottom. Now I think that means I should look out for a tall, dark, handsome stranger.' She laughed. It was a high, tinkling sound, like the teaspoon that rattled as she put the cup down on the silver gallery-rimmed tray.

'Now, Victoria, please don't get involved with cup

46

reading or palmistry or any other of the tea-time vices. I have quite enough middle-aged lady parishioners regaling me with that kind of thing,' the Reverend Colin Barnes smiled. He so enjoyed being with Victoria.

'Middle-aged? Thank you very much, Colin. I suppose at thirty-eight I might just be considered one of that genre, but I don't like to be reminded of it.'

Colin laughed comfortably. He knew he wasn't misunderstood – that was the thing about Victoria, she was so understanding, considerate, that was why . . . He pulled his thoughts together hastily. 'How's Luke?' he asked.

'Miserable.' Victoria smoothed the skirt of her beige shantung dress. Against the rose-red velvet of her chair it seemed so pale as to be cream. 'I really don't think we should persevere with Dr Crowther any longer, and he did seem so hopeful when he started.'

'Has he come up with any diagnosis?' Colin stared thoughtfully at the crumbly shortbread biscuit he was holding carefully over a plate. Victoria would have to face up to the truth one day but he couldn't make up his mind if it was his duty to tell her that there was no hope for poor Luke. Age was having its way; the man was close to seventy, and there was nothing Victoria could do, however much money she spent, to arrest its course.

'Oh, he comes up with bits and pieces. One day he says the problem is high blood pressure, and he gives us pills for that, then the next time he comes he says it's something to do with the kidneys. It's all so upsetting for Luke. He's becoming more and more irritable, and no one can blame him.' She put a hand up to her throat. She was so tense, at times she wanted to scream, to stamp her feet on the floor at the sheer injustice of it all. 'People keep saying we should move out of town, and with all this,' she gestured at the blackout screens, incongruous against the

Georgian perfection of pale yellow panelling, the multitude of gilt-framed watercolours, 'I wouldn't mind at all. It would be lovely to get down to the coast.' In her mind she saw the sloping pebble beach at Deal, where they'd often gone when Luke was able to drive. It was a civilized spin out from town.

Colin knew what the beaches were like, he'd seen the barbed wire reality that Victoria fortunately couldn't imagine. 'It'll be easier when the war's over,' he said.

'When the war's over,' Victoria echoed the words. She was frightened of the future, even she was beginning to understand that Luke would not be there to share it with her. 'He was so handsome,' she whispered. 'So strong and successful. We had wonderful times together.' She sat silent. Colin was used to silences, he was adept at coping with grief, more used to that than joy.

'I have something to tell you.' He put his own tea cup down, admiring the perfection of its shape, the round open bowl, the deep blue colour patterned with gold. It was beautiful, chosen with exquisite taste, as was everything in the room, in the house. It was good for him. He could feel his face changing. He must be humble, must know his place.

Victoria watched her man of the cloth and a surge of irritation swept her thoughts of Luke aside. Colin was such an ass, he was about to be pious, she could see it. It annoyed her immensely. He was a talented man, he could do more with himself than minister to a few souls who could quite adequately find God on their own. Even if he did insist on remaining in his 'calling', he didn't have to look like the proverbial paschal lamb.

'I'm going to the front.' He held a hand up, stopping Victoria's exclamation of shock. 'I should have gone earlier, as there's so little for me to do here and I'm needed where the men are, where they are dying, suffering.' His voice lifted. Now that his declaration was made he felt so much better.

'Colin, you can't possibly.' Victoria's thoughts of how small a congregation he ministered to vanished. 'Think of everyone here. We need you. We're being bombed, for Heaven's sake.' Her voice rose. 'You can't leave us alone, not with those dreadful Germans trying to kill us all.'

'You won't be alone, my dear. I will be replaced. There's a very able man . . .'

'Send him to the front, send him.' Victoria jumped to her feet. In her agitation she looked very young. 'Don't leave, please, Colin.' She stretched her hands out. Three dull thuds shook the ceiling above them. 'It's Luke.' Victoria looked up desperately. He would want a drink, or his pillows smoothing, something the nurse could do perfectly well, but Luke would want her to do it, so he banged his stick on the bedroom floor. 'Please, please . . .' There were tears in her eyes. She crossed the room quickly, the rustle of her dress a cool, intimate sound. She stopped for a moment at the door, and when she turned it was silently to beseech him, to give him a look that made him instantly aware of the pounding vein in his temple. He stood quite still after she left the room. He should have gone before, he knew. He was called to service, but she wanted him to stay. To stay. The words were revolving in his head. He had loved her, adored her, from the first moment he saw her, but he'd never dared to hope she would feel something in return.

It didn't take long to settle Luke. It never did. Victoria smoothed his pillows, poured him a glass of barley water and held it to his dry lips. She laid a hand on his brow. The skin was like paper, dry and lifeless.

49

'Would you like me to read to you?' she asked.

Luke shook his head irritably. The sheets felt rough as he plucked at them with his fingers, and it hurt his eyes to try and focus clearly. He could see nothing more than a white blur. Victoria's face swam in and out of his vision, and it too was white. 'I want to sleep.' His voice was thin, like a cross child's.

'Here you are, darling.' Victoria put the tablet into his hand, then held his wrist. She could feel the compulsive trembling as Luke slowly put the pill to his mouth. 'Have a sip more of this.' She held the glass once again to his lips, then carefully wiped the trickle of liquid that ran down his chin. She was aware of the tightness of the muscles across her stomach. It required a conscious effort not to feel revulsion for her husband. Her throat was tight and she wanted to cry. It was all so pitiful.

The tea tray had been cleared from the drawing room. Colin had gone and the afternoon stretched endlessly empty ahead of her. Victoria walked slowly to the mirror. Her reflection framed in gilt, she stood quite still, her image a waist-length portrait. The mirror had shared so many of their happy times together. She put a hand up to touch the two strands of pearls she wore around her neck. She could remember standing there, with Luke behind her, fastening them. That had been five years ago, her thirty-fourth birthday. In her imagination she watched her husband – his hands at her neck. His dark hair was streaked with silver, his face shining with health. They'd just come home from Deauville – such a lovely weekend, Roly Manners had flown them there and back – such fun. Roly was dead now, crashed on one of his madcap jaunts. Roly was dead, and Luke might as well be. Her eyes widened, startled at the horror of the thought. She stretched a hand forwards, sightlessly gazing at the mirror.

She had never meant to think that about Luke. Her hand was sweating but thankfully it closed on something smooth and cool. It was the paperweight of Caithness glass that Isabella had given them. Her sight cleared and she could see her own face with a sudden clarity. Strain had etched lines around her eyes, her mouth turned down – it was a stranger who stared back at her. A stranger who had wicked, evil thoughts. She hurled the glass ball, smashing the stranger's face to a thousand jagged fragments.

The crash was very loud. The silence that followed it was broken by three slow thuds on the ceiling above her. Victoria stood quite still, glass around her feet, then slowly she lifted her hands to cover her face and began to cry.

The man in the collarless blue shirt slowly rolled up his sleeves and adjusted the elderly corduroy trousers that were tied around his waist with string. He half-heartedly began sharpening his spade, spitting close to the metal-grey edge and wielding the whetstone with a casual dexterity. 'John Biddle,' he muttered to himself, 'you're a disgrace.' Around him the early-morning light was clear, touching the green of the broad-bean plants with an almost continental blue and the yellow of the marrow flowers with apricot.

John was nearing sixty. He'd worked at the Place all his life, and it had been his whole existence; he'd had no wife or child to dilute his application, he was a part of the garden. To find himself thinking seriously of marriage had shaken something deep inside and for the first time in his life he wanted to be somewhere other than at his work. It was no longer a matter of pride to him that there was an abundance of young fruit on the espalier apples and that

51

the redcurrant bushes were festooned with jewel-like sprigs. Lady Montford had told him she didn't intend to make any jelly this year. He was to offer the fruit to anyone from the village who cared to pick it. But no one else had the heart to make anything as frivolous as a condiment to go with a haunch of venison – there wasn't the sugar, for one thing. Daisy said if he'd like to bring her some of the fruit she'd make a pudding, but she wouldn't come up to the Place, she was too shy for that.

Daisy – he let his eyes rest on the fruit-laden bushes. He'd hardly known her until she came and asked him if there was any chance of him helping her with the rabbits. The plump, middle-aged spinster that he'd known no more than to exchange a 'good morning' with, walked up to him after church, her round cheeks pink and quivering with embarrassment. Her sister, Fanny, and she lived off their garden, she explained to him – off the vegetables and herbs it produced. But so many of the men of the village were off at war that there was a plague of rabbits stealing in under the wire, nipping off flower buds and eating the grass on the little patch they kept their goat on. No one who was left seemed to have the knack, and she'd heard that he snared the little pests up at the Place. So . . . Then her sister joined them, standing silently, small and timid, her head tipped to one side like a mouse, straggly grey whiskers trembling on her chin. In another age she would have been called a witch.

That was the beginning. It was natural, as his snare-setting visits were at dusk, that he should go into their cosy cottage for a glass of home-made wine. He tried the damson, the parsnip, even sipped at the elderflower that he found too genteel, too ladylike, and when he said that they laughed, Fanny and her mouse-like tittering, and Daisy, who at first had always lifted her hand to shield

52

her mouth, while her dark eyes sparkled, then as John became a regular visitor so Daisy relaxed in his company. When John had the toothache there was nothing more natural than her going to the corner cupboard and taking out their own special mixture, made from the seeds of the poppies that tossed pink and red tissue-paper heads in their garden. From then on John found going back to his own tiny dwelling like going into the dark after having been in the light. He noticed, for the first time, the smell of damp that greeted him as he opened the sun-bleached wooden door. His needs had been simple, his material comforts few, and that had suited him – until he discovered the siren song of a woman's comfort.

John sighed heavily. He had to get going. Plant out the leek seedlings that had grown so well. His Lordship was partial to a nice leek in cream sauce – only of course he wasn't eating anything too rich any more, those days were over. John placed his boot firmly on his spade and pushed it down into the moist earth. He would turn over the soil of the bed that he'd just cleared of the last of the spring cabbages, and then he'd get down to the leeks. He was to have his supper with Daisy, and the inevitable Fanny. He just wished that the older Brown sister would find an interest to take her out sometimes, but she was an unmoveable object. He had to have a chance to talk to Daisy on her own. The only thing he could think of was that Daisy would have to come out of the cottage on her own, perhaps – he smiled as he had the idea. His weather-beaten face crinkled and his lips parted, showing the strong even teeth that Daisy so admired. He had a meeting later on. He was to take his shotgun, his by right as vermin controller in the Place gardens, and his symbol of authority now in the defence of his village. He would ask Daisy to walk down to the village hall with him.

Fanny had been complaining of a bunion – she was always seeking sympathy – and this was one occasion when John would be more than happy to oblige. He would butter her up over supper, telling her how she should rest her foot, and then afterwards he and Daisy could have a little time on their own.

Victoria watched the gardener from the library window. He kept stopping and standing still, staring about him. He obviously wasn't working at anything like his normal rate. The war must be getting to him as well. She glanced up at the sky. It had become a habit since coming down to Pencombe. She'd been there four days of the seven that the doctor had insisted on. It was odd, but out in the country she was much more aware that the empty blue space above her was ready at any moment to be filled with the enemy than she was in town. She felt so guilty about leaving Luke. It was impossible to tell if he'd understood. She'd cried and held his hand, dropping her forehead to rest on his ice-cold fingers as the doctor told him how essential he thought it was that Victoria should get away. But none of them knew if Luke understood or, even if he did, if he cared. It was chilly in the house and she hugged herself; the cardigan made little difference. She supposed it was the weight she'd lost that made her feel the cold so much.

There – John was leaning on his shovel again. It was incredible, he was a different man these days. Perhaps he too was struggling to find a meaning for it all, a justification for the wasted years. What a relief it would be if there was someone else, like her, who wasn't carried away by the patriotism. Perhaps, after all, that was only the emotion of the small circle of friends she had in town; surely a countryman would have more sense. She would go and talk to him, she decided, and turned gratefully away from the window. It was good to have an excuse to do something. Poor John. So much in the garden had been changed. The rose garden was now full of potatoes, there were no longer melons in the cold frames, and the lemon tree in the greenhouse had died during the winter – it would have been unpatriotic to waste fuel heating it. Yes – she paused at the door of the flower room, slipping into her garden shoes – John must be finding it all very difficult.

She stepped out into the sunshine and suddenly felt much better. She breathed in, savouring the heady smell of delphiniums and the scent of orange blossom.

An overpowering scent of marigolds clung to Victoria's gardening gloves and she was glad to take them off and put them down on the wooden shelf by the white glazed sink. The back of her neck was stiff and she rubbed at it, rolling her head back, trying to loosen the tension. A dull ache spread across her shoulders. She was so tired; she was sleeping dreamlessly, but never seemed to wake refreshed.

There was something in her right eye and she blinked rapidly trying to clear a smear that blurred her vision. It was unpleasant and she put her hand over the eye, cutting out the light. She felt oddly disoriented and leaned forwards against the chill edge of the sink for support.

'Viccy, are you all right?' Isabella had come in through the garden door. She was instantly concerned – it wasn't like her niece to stand with her head in her hands.

'I'm fine. It's nothing. I've got something in my eye, that's all.' Victoria turned away from the sink. 'Will you have a look?' She put her hand down and opened her eyes wide.

55

'I can't see anything – except perhaps it's a little bloodshot.'

'Oh, my God!' Victoria seemed to be staring at some space over Isabella's head. 'Oh, it's horrid, Issy, I can't see. I can't see anything out of that eye! No, wait . . .' She put her hand up, covering her good eye. 'It's a silvery sheet, nothing at all, just a bright light except for a ragged patch in the middle, and through that I can see perfectly – just a tiny scrap that's normal. Oh, how horrid.' She turned away from Isabella and clutched at the sink.

'Darling.' Isabella was alarmed. 'You must sit down. Wait just a minute.' She hurried out into the hall and carried back a gilt-framed side chair. 'Here, sit on this.'

Victoria sat very still, her eyes wide open. Only a few minutes passed before she spoke, but it seemed much longer to both women. 'It's getting better.' Her voice was quite controlled. 'I'm sorry to have made such a fuss, but it was very strange and not at all pleasant.' She smiled nervously.

'Has it happened before?' Isabella asked.

'No – well, actually, that's not true. It did happen a while ago, only not as badly. I mean, it didn't really get much worse than a sort of bleariness. As if I had grease in my eye, something like that. I'm quite all right now, but I'd love a cup of tea. I think I must have been overdoing it out in the garden just now. It's quite hot even though it's overcast.'

'You'll have to see about it, Viccy, you can't ignore something like that.'

'Maybe you're right. I've been thinking I should have a thorough check-up. I still don't feel quite myself.' She laughed, feeling a lot better. 'Not that I'm sure who I do feel. Everything is so confused – I expect it's just the war. Yes, let's put it all down to the war. Everyone else does.'

* * *

56

The rest of the day seemed to stretch endlessly away ahead of Victoria. She couldn't settle to read a book and didn't feel like taking a walk. Isabella sat sewing a new sampler for the church. The design was the RAF insignia and the rector had raised his eyebrows when she told him what she was doing. He thought it a warlike symbol, not suited to his House of God, but then Lady Montford had always been a law unto herself.

'Have you ever thought of writing, Viccy?' Isabella laid down the tapestry square.

'What, writing short stories for genteel magazines? I don't think I'm like that. I think I'd probably write something that would shock their readers too much.' Victoria stretched in her chair. She was so stiff and uncomfortable, a swim would have been lovely. 'It's such a pity you've never put a swimming pool in here. Just one of the paintings tucked away in the attics would more than pay for it.'

'Don't tempt me. One of the things I loved about Australia was the fact that I could swim every day. There you are, you didn't know that I was so sporty, did you? I know you think I'm an old fossil, but I'm sure I would still enjoy a dip.'

'You're not the old fossil around here, Issy.'

'Victoria!' Viccy and her mother had done nothing but bicker, and Lucinda did treat herself as if she were precociously aged, when she was really no age at all.

'A pool would be good for the convalescents when they arrive.'

'"When" is the operative word there. Do you seriously think it would be a good idea?'

'But of course.' Victoria stood up, stretching her arms above her head, suddenly looking much better. 'Let's go and choose a spot for it.'

'Now wait a minute, I haven't actually agreed.'

'Oh, but you have. And just think, you'll be doing so much good all at once. You know that Bill is concerned about Bella – you can ask her to arrange the sale of the painting for you. It will give her something to do and her commission will come in very useful now Bill's cut off her allowance.'

Isabella frowned, irritated. 'He did that to stop her gadding about. He wouldn't be very pleased to have me subsidizing her socializing.'

'You're quite wrong there. He actually asked me to offer to lend Bella some cash – money that he would secretly give me himself. He doesn't want her unhappy, he just wants her to understand that she mustn't go against him and carry on with that ridiculous German art business. Whatever you decided to sell would be so English nobody could object. Yes, it's perfect. Now come on, let's go and find a good position. It has to get as much sun as possible through the day, and I think it's awfully important to have the evening sun, don't you? I mean, the best pool parties go on into the evening and it's hateful if it suddenly feels chilly.'

'Pool parties? Now how about those convalescents you were persuading me would benefit? I'm not sure about this.' But Isabella was smiling as she and Viccy walked out of the room. 'It's too frivolous by half.'

'Just think that you're planning for posterity, Aunty. And there won't be any problem about getting materials because a swimming pool is really just a hole in the ground, isn't it? And there's all sorts of building stuff around the estate and you could have it built – is that the right word, built? Or is it dug? Anyway, *made* by some of the old duffers hanging about in the village. This is great 'fun, isn't it? It makes me feel there is a future to look forward to, after all.'

'Well, if we can justify it being built then we will go ahead, but if not you will just have to wait and, in the meantime, I didn't mean writing short stories, I meant writing a book.' They stepped together out into the glorious sunshine. 'There's so much here, all around us, and I'm sure you'd make a very good job of it. There you are, I set you a challenge to write about us all.'

The girl straightened up slowly. Her head was swimming and she could hardly focus on the greeny brown field swirling around her in the heat haze. She pressed her hand hard into the small of her back. 'Damn!' she said. It made her feel much better. 'If anyone had ever told me that Lizzy Bokes would end up diggin' in the mud for a livin' I would have told them they were barmy,' she laughed. It was a loud, happy sound and the other two girls working alongside her joined in. The sun was beating down on them where they were, mercilessly exposed high on the sloping Wealden field.

'It's hot, isn't it?' Sally Jenkins spoke so softly that they had to strain to listen. She looked as shy as she was. Tendrils of fluffy fair hair curled around her freckly cheeks and she screwed up her eyes to peer through her wispy fringe at Lizzy, whom she adored.

'Hot? No, it's not just hot, it's sizzling.' Lizzy laughed again and lifted the hoe in her hands high up into the air before crashing it down on to the bone-dry earth.

'Hey!' The man's shout made them all turn. They hadn't known anyone had been watching them.

'It's the boss.' Anne Miller began furiously wielding her hoe, her generous bosom shaking like a blancmange.

59

'He's going to give us a rollicking. Oh, I love him when he's angry.'

They all giggled, and they were still giggling when Tom reached them.

'You bang a hoe down on to the earth like that and the handle will sheer off,' he said.

The three girlish faces looked earnestly at him. Each of them had a scarf wound round her head in a vain attempt to stop her hair from blowing about. At least, that was what Tom thought the scarves were for. In reality the girls thought they brightened up the awful dinginess of the land girls' uniform.

He didn't have the heart to tell them off. They didn't belong on the land, but they were doing their best. 'Are you all right, then, out here in the heat?' he asked. Three heads nodded at him.

'It's a lovely view,' Lizzy volunteered. She turned away from the farmer, shading her eyes with her hand to look out over the plain spread far below them. 'I've never seen anything like it. I could almost get to like the country.' Her voice was oddly wistful.

'Do you miss your family?' The question came involuntarily. He hadn't intended to stay talking to the girls, but he was lonely, feeling the loss of the other young men of his family, who were all away at the war now.

'Family, and friends. All the boys . . . still,' she laughed suddenly, the free, joyful sound making him smile, 'I've got new friends now. I'm happy enough, and I'm not like some of my mates – at least I'm not in munitions. I know when I'm lucky.' She began poking at the dry earth with her hoe, loosening a patch of stunted weeds topped with little yellow flowers.

'You can break at twelve,' Tom called back over his shoulder as he walked away. They knew well enough what time they could stop work to enjoy a packed lunch and a cool drink in the shade of the orchard, but it was good just exchanging a few words with a fellow human being.

'I think he fancies you, Lizzy,' Anne murmured. She didn't want the farmer to hear her, and in the wide open spaces she thought a voice would carry for miles.

'What, me? I should cocoa. No, if he fancies anybody it'll be our Sally – all that blonde hair. Bet it drives the boys mad, doesn't it, Sal?'

Sally smiled happily. Their boss didn't fancy her, she could see that, but it was fun to think he might. Some lucky girl might capture the bachelor farmer's heart and end up married to him, living in the lovely big house at the top of the hill. Never have to go back to the smoke of the town again. 'I wouldn't mind never goin' back,' she said, and then they were all silent with their thoughts, the only sound the scratching of their hoes and the cawing of crows winging high above them.

Tom made his way back to the farm buildings. He couldn't stop thinking about the piles of paperwork he had somehow to get through. Rising at six and not stopping work on the fields until well past nine in the evenings, he was striving his utmost to produce every last ounce of produce that could be coaxed from the land. If the powers that be saw his best war effort in growing food, then so be it. He and his land would do their bit. He was in the prime of his strength, and the acres he farmed were in good heart. They'd been in the family for most of his lifetime; the Home Farm of Reason Hill had been farmed by his father long before Tom was born.

The warm sweet smell of cow hung heavy around the wooden buildings as he walked between them. The animals had been herded in and penned up earlier for the men from the ministry. Tom slapped at a sudden prick in his arm but he was too late, a horsefly flew off leisurely. It had come in with the cattle and now would return to the fields, leaving its victim to swear under his breath and rub at the tiny puncture.

Lizzy scuffed her heavy shoes in the dust of the drive. She was happy to collect the milk from the house on this beautiful evening. The sun was setting way down on the far horizon and birds were singing all around her in the orchards that bordered the farm drive. She'd watched the planes go over earlier, their friendly red, blue and white roundels gleaming in the slanting sun's rays. They'd flown so low above her head that she'd reached up towards them, laughing at herself for acting like a kid. Then they'd swooped down towards the plain and straight towards the golden ball. She'd stood to watch them until staring at the light had made her eyes ache. She wasn't frightened of the planes, not bothered by their noise, like some of the girls. She thought they were romantic. She kicked at a loose stone, sending it skidding away from her into the orchard. The pilots were romantic too, she'd seen them in the newsreel in the cinema. Cuddled up to Bob she'd been, or was it Sid? She couldn't remember. She liked going to the Odeon, liked the dusty smell of the velvet-covered seats and the rustle of the paper bags full of sweets. It was fun in the back row, a kiss and a cuddle, and a bit of a scuffle when the boy got carried away.

There were apples hanging from the trees, green, fat ones. She looked round, but there was no one about. They'd been told not to eat them, that they weren't ripe, but she didn't think they could be that bad. The fruit felt heavy in her hand even before she twisted it, making the stalk snap and the branch quiver. She rubbed the apple on her sleeve. Her mum wouldn't like her to eat it without a wash – she missed her mum, but the little kids were better off with her and not boarded out with a family of strangers, or worse still split up. Out of the seven Bokes children, the two eldest boys had gone off to sea, merchant seamen they were. Then came Lizzy. She was quite proud of being a land girl – it was a pity her dad wasn't alive to see it, he never would have believed his little Lizzy could work on a farm. She stared hard at the apple. Thinking of her dad always made her a bit sniffly. She bit down into the inviting green. 'Bloody hell!' she spat the words out, and along with it the forbidden bite. 'Bloody hell,' she said again, and threw the apple far away up one of the cool green alleys between the trees.

The farmhouse rose up in front of her – soft red-brick walls tile-hung with russet, cream-framed windows glowed pink from the sunset. There were yellow roses climbing up the walls and blue hydrangeas blooming in front of an old wattle fence. A great yew tree spread a wide shade over a flat cut lawn. Beneath the yew tree was a bench and on the bench sat Tom, papers spread out on the seat beside him and on the grass in front.

'Hallo,' she said.

Tom hadn't heard Lizzy coming. He couldn't work out half the form-filling, and his temper was rising. When he turned towards her she was standing in front of the sunset. She'd taken off the headscarf she'd been wearing when he last saw her and her dark hair was thick and long, hanging down to her shoulders. The pink flowery dress that she wore seemed like a part of the evening, the colours of the flowers in the gathering dusk, the purple-streaked sky. 'You look pretty,' he said, and blushed. He wasn't used to talking to girls.

'Thanks very much. That's the nicest thing you've said to me since I arrived. You good at paperwork, then?'

'No,' Tom smiled. It didn't seem so bad now he had some company. 'I'm no good at all it. I'm a farmer pure and simple, but for some reason I'm meant to be able to fathom this lot out as well.'

'My dad used to have a lot of paperwork, he was a commercial traveller, see. In paint brushes he was. He couldn't stand all the forms he had to fill in. So I used to do it for him.' She smiled, remembering that the girls had thought the farmer fancied her. A little bit of fun would help pass the time, and he was good-looking, even if he was a bit old for her. 'How old are you?' she asked.

Tom said, 'Thirty-nine.' It didn't seem odd to him that the girl had asked him his age. He had a strange feeling about her, as if he'd known her for a long time, and yet he'd never met anybody like her before.

'Well, how about it? Would you like me to help?' she asked.

He picked up the papers from the bench, moving up to give her room to sit down beside him.

'I'll do this lot for you,' she said as she flicked efficiently through the pile he'd passed her, 'and you can take me into Maidstone to the cinema come Saturday. How's that for a bargain?' She held her hand out for him to shake on the deal. He really was a looker, she decided, and his hand when it clasped hers was warm, big and comforting. She settled down to the task in hand with a smile on her face that was caught by the last rays of the sun, and Tom felt something inside him turn over. He'd never felt like that before.

Lucinda prodded irritably at the lamb chop on her plate. 'This meat is fatty, and it's cold. I cannot abide lamb fat, it congeals in my mouth. No, it's no good.' She pushed the plate away. 'I really shall have to have something else to eat.'

'Lucinda, you can't waste food like this. Every evening this week you've turned your nose up at what I've cooked.' Isabella was struggling to control her temper. 'We're lucky to have this lamb at all.'

'For goodness sake, you don't seriously think anyone else is suffering this kind of rubbish, do you? You don't imagine for one moment that Eli's eating miserably up in town, do you? He was telling me this afternoon, he's dining out every evening and very nicely thank you. I want to go to London, I want to go to Cadogan Gardens,' Lucinda pouted. It made her eyes sink deep into their puffy sockets and her double chin seem formidable.

'I'm sure Victoria would welcome you,' Isabella lied, with her eyes fixed on her plate. 'She could do with some help looking after Luke. With you there she could have some free time, and perhaps Eli would take her out for one of his dinners.'

'I'm not an invalid-minding service, you know.' Lucinda began crumbling the bread roll on her side plate in her annoyance, and flakes of crust fell to litter the floor beneath her. 'I want to have some time to myself. If Victoria wasn't so selfish she'd put that man in a home and leave the house free for us to use.'

'Don't include me in your "us", Lucinda. I don't want to use it. And the amount of money that Luke has spent both on Cadogan Gardens and the house here, over the years, certainly entitles him to see his time out on home ground.'

'She should never have married him, I always said so.'

'You did not always say so. You were as happy as anyone at Victoria's catch. Luke was, or I should say, is,

65

a wealthy man. Victoria has had a good, happy marriage and I'm sure she wouldn't have missed any of their years together for anything, even though it is so difficult for her now.'

Lucinda shut her mouth firmly. She knew that she herself had been the pick of the bunch. She'd been courted by any man worth mentioning – Luke himself had wanted her, come to that. Her fingers worked ever more furiously with the bread roll. Michael should have been hers, and the title. Michael and Luke, they were both dying now; men seemed destined to leave their women. But Lucinda should have been a Lady. Marriage to Michael would have meant that, and if only her own dear Thomas had lived, he had vowed to work for a knighthood. He'd known what his Lucinda was worth.

'I really wish you would stop making that mess, Lucinda.' Isabella couldn't help herself. She knew that it would tip Lucinda's temper over the edge, but there was so much to do, so little time, and Lucinda did nothing but make work for others.

Lucinda rose ponderously to her feet. She opened her mouth to speak, her eyes flashing righteous indignation, but the sound of planes silenced her. They were low above the house, and the lead-framed panes rattled ominously. The sound of anti-aircraft guns came suddenly, joined by the far-off wail of a siren. Isabella stood up swiftly, to go to Michael. She left the room in front of Lucinda, who was making her stately progress to the cellar. 'If they hit us this time, at least you won't have to worry about my crumbs, Isabella,' Lucinda laughed mirthlessly.

'Go to hell,' Isabella muttered under her breath as she hurried up the stairs to Michael. 'Go to hell, Lucinda.'

* * *

The Honourable William Montford pushed a small leather-bound diary firmly down into his battledress pocket. He watched as a new wave of enemy bombers swooped low in the direction of the oil tanks behind the harbour, then the earth shook and fresh billows of blackened smoke and scarlet flames shot up to stain the azure morning sky. All around him there were soldiers waiting on the sandy shore. The scene was chaos. The beach was a litter of bomb craters and the tired men clung together in clumps, but there was an underlying organization that faltered only temporarily as the German shells fell, creating new pits in the sand, killing and maiming, making more work for the desperately overworked medical teams.

It was the second day of the evacuation. William kept looking up at the sky. The men he marshalled into line might have thought he was keeping an eye on the enemy, but in reality it was the weather he was checking. He had been warned that there was something nasty building up over the Channel and he kept praying that it would hold off so that they could get some more of the boys away. They were all hungry. William hadn't eaten a decent meal for days – or perhaps it was weeks – and his mind kept playing odd tricks on him. Like the time he'd thought he saw Eli balanced precariously on the prow of one of the pleasure boats pulled up close to the beach. He'd watched a giant waterspout envelop whoever the poor devil was as a shell dropped close by. Just as well there was no likelihood of it being his uncle – he'd be safe at home, reading about their exploits in his copy of *The Times* over his breakfast.

'William!' Eddy shouted at the top of his lungs to his brother. He had to bellow to be heard over the din of the bombardment. 'I'm being sent up on to the mole.' He held his hand out briefly. The sea wall – or mole, as they called it – was very narrow and jutted some three-quarters of a mile out into the sea. It could take the men out to the bigger boats, those who couldn't get close enough to the shore. The Dunkirk beach was flat and the tide went out for miles.

William squeezed his brother's hand tightly, then he did an unprecedented thing, he pulled Eddy close to him, holding him for a moment. In the din Eddy couldn't be sure if he'd heard William correctly, but a long time afterwards he thought he'd said, 'God bless you, and give my love to Mother.' After Eddy had gone William felt a new surge of energy. He'd been worried having him on the beach, feeling that he had to keep an eye on his brother, to be there if he got hurt. The mole was too far away for him to be of any help, whatever happened, and despite the pounding it was taking hc had a feeling Eddy would be all right. He'd always landed right way up, even when he'd been little more than a baby and had a habit of throwing himself out of his high chair.

The docks were still burning like Dante's inferno, but as William kept up his relentless organizing of the men filing slowly towards the sea, he was only vaguely aware of the roar of the flames, the awful noise of destruction. The German bombers were wreaking a fearful havoc.

The storm came on the third day, turning the sky into a vast cauldron of smoke and swirling black cloud as the sea crashed on to the flat shore. Small boats overturned, men drowned, and still the air attack fell ceaselessly on them. Where were their own planes? On the mole, Eddy swore endlessly at the lack of their own fighters. He understood that their destroyers were bombarding the German shore guns and helping drive off the air attacks – when he listened to his commanding officer he appreciated for a moment that their planes could only stay for a precious half an hour over the beaches, then they had to fly back to refuel. And they were outnumbered by forty to one. They were doing sterling work, he was told. But when he was on his own with the men, desperately loading them like cattle into the already dangerously full vessels that lurched and heaved on the wild sea alongside the wall, then Eddy joined with the men in his thoughts, and he too wanted to know where the bloody fliers were.

Just as William had decided that they could never get the great bulk of the men away, dawn broke on the fifth day and the storm abated. The sky was still black and smoke-laden, which gave them a sense of relief because it hid them from the Germans. As the sea calmed, they began building a giant causeway out of lorries and wreckage. It meant the men could get much further out towards the waiting flotilla. Many of the small boats that were fortunate enough not to be blown out of the water by the continual shelling made several return trips, even though their owners had never made the crossing to France before.

Eli's boat, the *Bunty*, kept on going, despite the fact that he had had to be taken off on the first return trip. He'd been pulled back on board, half drowned off Dunkirk beach. The bruise made by the boat hook as it caught in his belt had hurt him more than the injury that his rescuers worried he might bleed to death from. In the calm coolness of Margate Hospital, just after lunchtime on the second day of the evacuation, Eli's left arm was neatly removed just above the elbow. Beds were scarce, and he came out of shock quickly – even before the whole news of the rescue at Dunkirk reached England, he had discharged himself and was back amongst his family.

By the evening of the fifth day over forty-five thousand

men had been rescued. They were men whose families' prayers for safe deliverance had been answered, but most importantly for those responsible for the long-term destiny of Britain, they were men who could fight again.

William was working on reserves of energy that he'd never even guessed he had. He changed under the constant barrage – the starchiness that had made the men wary of him disappeared and he became a great back-slapper. 'Well on your way back to Blighty now,' became his catchphrase. 'What a way to jump the queue, eh?' he'd say to the newly wounded, even to those who were dying in his arms, and it always seemed to work, to summon a final smile. In every minute of this new life, he lived more than he had done before. His shyness no longer tied his tongue and he didn't feel constrained to remember his position. He was the future Lord Montford – so what? All that mattered was getting the lads off the beach, sending them back home to catch their breath before packing them off to have another crack at the bloody enemy who were chewing up the beach with their bombing, rendering the once quiet Dunkerque – dune-church it translated as – into a name that history would link forever with blood and courage.

On the seventh day the Germans hurled all their might at the remaining forces on the beach. The embarkation slowed during the daylight hours. The men hid amongst the dunes and burrowed into the sand, fooling themselves that it offered some protection against the flesh-ripping bombardment. William took his diary out of his pocket. He wanted to update what had been happening. What day was it? He had to struggle to work out how long it was since he'd started the endless task of getting the chaps off. He ticked the days off on his fingers – it must be the first of June. He smiled as he put the point of his pencil down on the empty space.

William was the only one to be killed outright by the shell. His was the best option. A soldier to the right of him had half his face blown away and suffered an agony that only ended when the boat his friends had struggled so hard to get him into was sunk by a shell. It was one from a salvo that fell short, fired by one of their own destroyers moored offshore.

The last Allied ships to leave Dunkirk at midnight on the second of June were full of French soldiers. Eddy Montford was with them, having been one of the last English officers taken off the mole. The French garrison surrendered to the Germans shortly afterwards. Over 345,000 men rescued from Dunkirk reached England, while 4,700 members of the British Expeditionary Force were killed at Dunkirk and had no known grave.

William's family were luckier than most; they were informed of his fate early in June. His diary and other personal effects had been hastily collected from his body by a fellow officer. In less than a week these were sent back to them, along with the information that he had lost his life serving his King and country.

Eddy climbed the stairs to the nursery. He could only move slowly. There was a heaviness in his legs and it was an effort to breathe. He felt like an old man. He paused, looking out through the narrow stone-framed window at the turn of the stair, and through the curtain of cobwebs he could see the fields. The scene was a rural idyll, fertile acres of rich green parkland populated with fat white sheep. They were the fields they had played in as boys. William and he, William always ahead of him, taller, stronger, those magic two years older. They'd had a falcon – what had the bird been called? Eddy leaned forward, resting his forehead against the cool stone wall. He couldn't remember the bird's name and for a moment it seemed so important. But he had to get on, keep moving, to stand still was to think, to remember. And yet, what was his visit to the nursery for, but for memories?

His shoes echoed loudly on the brown checked lino-covered floor, so he slipped them off and began walking in his socks. A chill spread through him and he shivered. He felt fevered and it would be good to be cold. The yellow-painted walls of the corridor were peeling, patches of an alien eau de nil showing through. He didn't remember the walls ever having been green. He paused outside Nanny's room. Slowly he pushed open the door beside him, and it creaked, as it had always done, to warn them of her appearance, give them time to tidy their beds, their thoughts. The tiny room was empty; it contained nothing, not even the vaguely remembered smell of lavender.

He walked on silently, breathing shallowly so as not to disturb the past. He stopped as he reached the day nursery. Shock made his head tip back and he drew in great gulps of chalk-flavoured air. Nothing had changed. Nothing at all. The black painted screen in front of the fireplace waited to air their small clothes, the diamond holes through which he'd poked his fingers still challenged him to count them. On the mantelpiece the nursery clock was ready, its beaming round face eager to count the hours again, the slow-moving lessons, the fast-passing afternoons of play. He moved his head jerkily, taking in the shabby overstuffed armchair, the blue-lidded ottoman he was walking slowly towards. Under the lid there would be the toys. He reached out towards it, but he couldn't bring himself to touch. He swivelled on the balls of his feet, turning to meet Dobbin, his old friend who had waited so patiently, his wooden neck bent, his carved ears pricked in welcome. A sharp light filtered through the barred window behind the rocking horse, and it wasn't until Eddy laid his hand on the yellow string mane that he saw the dust. The feel of it was warm, soft, under the damp of his palm.

'Hallo, old chap,' he whispered. He ran his hand down the neck, over the muscled shoulders. The red leather saddle was smooth, polished by little boys' shorts, by hours of riding, hours of fantastic journeys, shared dreams. He pushed gently, forward and back, forward and back, the remembered rhythm, the familiar creaking. He felt soothed, his mind easing.

'Eddy?' The call made him start. 'Eddy, are you up here?' It was his mother's voice.

But he didn't want company, not now, not –

'Eddy.' Isabella stood in the doorway. Her son was facing her. As if it were yesterday, she could see him as a child standing there, worried at something he'd done, the set of his shoulders suggesting defiance. The picture faded; this wasn't the same Eddy. This boy was hurt, more hurt than he'd ever been in his life, and alone. There was a vulnerability, a desperation. 'Father's awake.' Isabella spoke softly, as if she were indeed speaking to a child. 'I thought, since your time is limited . . .' She let the words trail off. She didn't know if Eddy really had to leave that night, she knew that most of the others who'd got back had seven days' leave. She had the feeling Eddy didn't want to stay at Pencombe, it wasn't that he couldn't.

'Where did Nanny's furniture go?' His voice was high, strained.

'I sent it up to Cadogan Gardens, when Viccy's boys were small.'

'The twins?'

'Yes, darling. Do you remember they had that Irish woman to look after them? She let them run wild, really. Victoria was so rarely there. But it doesn't seem to have done them any harm.'

'Bloody fliers.' Eddy pushed down hard on the rocking horse, sending it cavorting into noisy motion. 'Where were they when we needed them, eh? Running wild, all right, the whole bloody lot of them.' He turned abruptly, staring sightlessly out of the window. There were grey-slated roofs and lead-lined gulleys ahead of him; it was the view that had set him dreaming as a child. But he was no longer a child. In his mind's eye he saw no glorious knights – war wasn't glorious now he knew the reality.

'You will be careful not to upset your father? He's weaker than when you last visited him. Every day takes a toll.' Isabella wanted to hold her son, to clutch him to her, but there had been too many years of the perfunctory kiss on the cheek. They weren't a demonstrative family. Where Lucinda had cried over her children, Isabella had worked to teach them dignity, self-reliance. But where did it all end? William was dead, nothing would bring him back. She wished now that she'd shown him how much she loved him, she wished that she had been more like her sister.

'I'll be down in a minute.' Eddy's voice was calmer. 'I just want . . .' He cleared his throat, stood up straighter. The strength that Isabella had taught him was being tested. 'I just need to lay a few ghosts. You understand, don't you, Mother?'

Isabella nodded. She couldn't have spoken; to have

74

begun to speak would have been to let the words spill over.

'Eddy.' Michael held out his hand to his son. 'So good to see you.' The voice was so weak, so faint, that Eddy, against his will, came closer to the bed. He had to steel himself. Sickrooms terrified him, and the gaunt-faced old man in the bed was scarcely recognizable as his own father. He didn't want to think of him this way, he wanted to remember him as upright, commanding. 'On leave?' Michael whispered.

Eddy nodded his head abruptly and shuffled closer to the bed. His father's hand was still outstretched towards him.

'Good of you to spare the time, son.'

And then Eddy was on his knees, clutching the thin fingers, burying his face in the covers. 'Oh, Dad,' he sobbed. 'Oh, Dad.'

Michael closed his eyes. His own tears were all shed, he was dried up, withered by emotion. 'My son, my son,' he whispered. It was an incantation.

'Go on then, tell us what he was like.' Anne wriggled out energetically from under the bedclothes and turned to plump the pillows up behind her. She wanted to be comfortable to hear all the details. Sally had quietly followed Lizzy into the little bedroom her two friends shared and sat down on the edge of Lizzy's empty bed. She'd wrapped herself up in a thin grey Forces-issue blanket, to help keep the night air from her pale skin. The pink flannelette pyjamas she was wearing had a pattern of tiny red rosebuds on them and Lizzy thought she looked about twelve years old.

'Look at you, Sal, all bundled up like a Christmas puddin',' Lizzy said. 'Aren't you too hot?'

Sally shook her head. 'I feel the cold, but I can see you don't,' she said. 'You look as if you're cooking.'

'It's not the weather that's got her all red in the face,' Anne laughed, 'it's her lover boy. What's he like, then? Go on, tell us. Is it true what they say about farmers?'

Lizzy smiled at her reflection in the scrap of silvered glass that their landlady liked to refer to as the 'dressing-table mirror'. 'What do they say about farmers, then?' she asked, her head tipped on one side. She was egging Anne on because she was in a good mood, such a good mood. She didn't care if she didn't sleep a wink all night.

'Did you sit in the back row?' Sally asked what they'd been wondering all evening.

'Of course not. He's a gentleman. Front row of the circle. Up there in state like a duke and his duchess we were. And a box of chocolates – a big box, mind. And an ice in the interval.'

'Hold your hand, did he?' Anne held her hand out towards Sally. 'May I,' she lowered her voice, sounding like a music-hall comedian, 'hold your tiny hand – why, it is frozen!' They all laughed.

'He didn't hold my hand at all. And he didn't give me a kiss goodnight either. Like I said, he's a real gentleman.'

'Oh, poor Lizzy,' Sally said, her face creased in concern. 'Do you think he'll ask you out again, or do you think it was just a one-off? I mean, if he didn't kiss – '

'You forward little hussy, Miss Sally Jenkins.' This time Anne put on her schoolmistress voice. She was good at impersonations, and it did make Lizzy laugh. It was really nice, her two friends staying up to see her come back, and such a lovely evening she'd had. Still, it was a shame he hadn't given her a kiss, just a little one. She'd felt really special having him as an escort, and so many people had recognized him in the town – he was quite a celebrity.

'I'm going to help him pick blackcurrants tomorrow,' she said, and blushed furiously at the look of disbelief on Anne's face.

'You're not giving up a day off, he's not getting you to do more farm work – on a Sunday?' Sally was shocked out of her normal reticence.

'Not farm work. He'll be picking as well – just a bit of fruit from the garden. And then he said we'd drive over to visit some relatives of his. They've got a lovely house, he said. Pencombe, I think it's called. Anyway, it's his aunty's and his mum stays with her. I think they must be goin' to make jam with the blackcurrants.'

'He's taking you to meet his mum – already?' Anne's eyes were wide with astonishment.

'No, no, it's not like that. I mean – ' Lizzy paused. She was a bit confused herself, after all. 'Well, since he hasn't even kissed me yet, it can't be like it would be for us, at home, I mean. If a boy took me back to meet his mum then I'd think there was something in it. It must just be different in the country. Oh look, come on, I'm tired. I need my beauty sleep. I wonder what she's like, his mum. I should think she's a real old dear. After all, he's so sweet and kind. I bet I'll like her. It'll be like seeing my gran. Yes, just like my old gran.' She started pulling her dress off in a hurry. She wanted to get to bed and go to sleep to be ready for the excitements of tomorrow.

'Honour, be a dear and fetch me that footstool, will you?' Lucinda smiled at her niece – the girl was so much sweeter than her mother, it was hard to believe that Isabella had had a hand in bringing the child up.

Honour carried the tapestry-topped stool to her aunt,

77

then tactfully looked away as Lucinda arranged her legs. 'You know, I'm really worried about Mummy,' she said.

'Worried about your mother?' Lucinda let out a sigh of contentment at having her legs comfortably supported. 'What on earth are you worried about her for? Now if you said your father, I could understand. I really do not like his colour, and that doctor . . .'

'I don't think that there's very much the doctor can do.' Honour's face was very pale and set. Lucinda thought yet again how much the girl reminded her of dear Michael when he had been young. The same high brow, clear well-spaced eyes. 'But Mummy is run off her feet. She will try and do everything herself. I thought, when I left, that she would take things easy. I mean, I always thought that she got so involved in the village just to make me feel I was being useful. Everything makes work for her. Even Tom coming over this afternoon means that he'll bring the blackcurrants from Reason Hill and Mummy will want to pot them or make them into pies or something.'

'Nobody can tell your mother what to do, Honour. Nobody ever could. But you can take it from me that she's in her element. Nothing makes her happier than being indispensable.'

Honour's face relaxed as she heard a car pull up on the gravel outside; it would be Tom. At least he would agree with her. Aunt Lucinda did nothing at all these days, and she was getting steadily fatter. Tom should have a word with her – she could help, even a little.

Tom reached into the back of the car and pulled out the boxes piled high with currants. He and Lizzy had worked hard. He reckoned there must be nigh on twenty pounds of fruit, and that took a lot of picking.

'Do they live round the back, then?' Lizzy looked apprehensively at the great house stretching away on either side of them. She didn't think they should have parked right in front of it, it didn't feel right.

'Round the back, round the front and in the middle,' Tom laughed. 'No, actually they don't live in all the rooms any more. The house is going to be used as a convalescent home pretty soon, and that's a good idea really because it hasn't been opened to the public since the war began.'

'Live in all the rooms? You mean,' Lizzy swallowed, more to stop her words running away with her than anything else; her mouth was quite dry enough, 'your family own all this?'

'Yes. Good, isn't it?' Tom felt in his element. Lizzy was a pretty girl, pretty as a picture in her pink dress. It struck him suddenly that it might be the only dress she had; it was certainly the only one he'd ever seen her in. 'My mother lives here, along with my aunt Isabella and her husband Michael. He's Lord Montford, and his family have been here for generations.'

'A lord?' Annoyance suddenly flashed across Lizzy's face. 'Oh, you should have warned me.'

'Why?' Tom looked puzzled.

Why? Why indeed, Lizzy thought. Because she would have taken even more care getting dressed. She looked frantically at her fingernails; the blackcurrant juice had stained them. What should she say to a lord? Hallo, my Lord, Hallo your Lordship? She suddenly wanted to be back at the poky little lodgings, back with her friends. 'Oh, Tom,' she wailed, and there was more intimacy between them in her distress than there had been before.

'It's all right,' he said, and stepped towards her, the boxes of fruit firmly held under one arm. He took her gently by the elbow, leading her towards the house.

'You've got nothing to worry about, you look as pretty as a picture.'

She leaned closer towards him as they passed through the chill stone portico and into the heart of the house.

The red-brick terraced cottage was cheerless even in the sunlight. The blue-painted window frames were peeling and the curtains clumsily drawn back. It had the desolate air of a house unloved. Lizzy pushed the creaking wicket gate open ahead of her with the toe of her boot. The rotting wood had given her a splinter yesterday. She was in no hurry to go indoors and stood looking down at the struggling vegetable plants in the tiny front garden. She wondered why everything seemed unwilling to grow. It was odd, because the farm was only a little way away and there everything grew like mad. Mind you – Lizzy felt warm at the thought – the land at Reason Hill belonged to Tom, and anything would grow for him, he was so gentle and kind. The miserable lettuces edging the path at her feet had been planted by Bert, so it wasn't really surprising that they weren't doing their best.

'Thought I 'eard you.' Thinking of Bert had made him materialize. He was on the far side of the privet hedge that separated his own garden from the one next door. 'I was givin' Doreen a bit of a hand,' he leered, showing his brown cracked teeth and wrinkling the flaking skin around his grey cat eyes. Doreen's husband was away at the war. She was in her late twenties, a colourless straggly woman who always seemed to be wrapped up in a pinny and wielding a grey-tinged feather duster. Lizzy forced herself to say a polite hallo. He made her feel sticky, as if she wanted a good wash. He was in his sixties, but he was a like a dirty old dog, sniffing around. She'd heard an expression once, about a man undressing a woman with his eyes, and that's what Bert did. It was odd that his wife put up with it. Phyllis was a big woman, and there was twice as much of her as there was of her husband. She had great arms, like the country hams that used to hang up in Sainsbury's, which always seemed to be folded, as if they had to be because they were too heavy to hang loose like other people's. Lizzy pushed back the hair that she could feel clinging to her forehead. She couldn't remember whose turn it was to have the first bath. But she was so looking forward to a good soak that she didn't really care if she was first or last. It was Friday night and the tin tub would come down off its nail on the back of the scullery door. A succession of pans heated on the stove would fill it with six inches of precious hot water that they'd use one after the other, her and Sal and Anne. The other two should be home soon.

'Hey!'

She'd forgotten about Bert.

'I want you to give me a hand later. I got a job needs doin'. I'll give you a call, later like.'

She opened the front door with her key and stepped straight into the sitting room. Her own home had a corridor – somewhere to stand the bike and hang up the coats. But Bert and Phyllis's house was so small that there was no hallway at all, only the sitting room, and through to the kitchen with a tumbledown scullery stuck on the back. There were two bedrooms up the narrow stairs, one that Lizzy and Anne shared and the other that was almost filled with Bert and Phyllis's creaking marital bed. There was a tiny room tucked in the attic and Sal had that. It was just as well that she was short.

It was after nine when Bert called up the stairs. Lizzy was sleepy. She'd had her bath – she'd been last, so she'd be first next week – then she'd washed her hair and wrapped it up in a towel. Afterwards she'd sprinkled herself with the carnation-perfumed talc that her mum had bought her to come away with. It was lovely to feel so fresh and clean. She had a strip wash every evening after work, but it wasn't the same as a bath.

Bert led the way down the back garden. It was a narrow plot, just as wide as the house, with a crumbling brick path that ran down one side and a washing line, empty now except for a sprinkling of abandoned pegs, that hung low and swung gently in the evening breeze. There was a smell of cats mixed with the decaying green of the compost heap that steamed beside the chicken run ahead of them. Lizzy's brow wrinkled. She didn't want to stink of chickens. It was a nasty sour smell that made her feel sick and would have put her off eggs, if there had ever been any chance of having one, but her ration was always disposed of by Phyllis, as were those of the other girls. 'Gone into the cookin',' their landlady would say. With the monotonous diet of a series of meatless puddings and gritty vegetables, the whereabouts of the egg itself was a mystery.

'You stay there.' Bert held a hand up, as if he was directing the traffic. He was quick on his feet, nimble like a ferret. He was inside the ramshackle netting enclosure, banging shut the trap door and stepping into the dark interior of the henhouse before the newly roosting birds had time to protest. It was as he came out again into the dusk that Lizzy understood what he was up to. He carried a hen upside down, grasping it tightly around the butter-yellow legs, holding the wildly flapping creature up and cackling like an old cockerel himself. 'Treat for Sunday lunch,' he crowed. 'It's the old girl's birthday, see? This one ain't been layin' much recently.' He poked with his finger as he peered at the moist pink opening under the

82

tail feathers. 'At least, I think I've got the right one. Still, it don't matter really. Christ, how long is it since I had a good bit of chicken? Like a bit of breast, I do.' He came close to Lizzy, breathing over her as he slowly stroked his hand down the front of the bird. His eyes seemed to bulge from their sockets as he peered at the buttons fastening her blouse.

'I won't touch it.' She took a step backwards down the path. 'I couldn't.' The hen was still for a moment, hanging limp in his hands, and then suddenly, manically, it was beating at the air again, its beak straining open, the pink tongue forced out.

'What, frighten yer, does it?' He held the bird towards her, then seeing that she was ready to run indoors, he pulled it back towards his own body. 'No, no, I don't want yer to touch it. I just need you to help. Come on.' He jerked his head to her to follow as he clambered up on the edges of the compost heap that made a convenient step over the broken-down fencing bordering Doreen's garden. 'Quick, quick.' He darted ahead of Lizzy and she followed, absorbing his tense, furtive mood.

There was a brick-built garden shed in solitary splendour in the centre of the garden ahead of them. It was almost dark and Bert fumbled for a moment with the padlock on the door, then he stepped inside. Lizzy could hear him swearing and then suddenly there was light, the soft yellow of a hurricane lamp that showed rows of tools neatly hanging on the walls above a small workbench. The inside of the shed was so tidy, so organized, that it made Lizzy wonder if it was where Doreen wielded her feather duster. The silliness of the thought cheered her up a bit, as did the shining, cared-for tools. Doreen's husband must be a nice man.

'Come on, quick.' Bert had his back to her as he stooped in front of the bench. 'Here, give us a hand.'

Lizzy went up to him. He was holding the hen the right way up now. The glass-bead eyes swivelled and seemed to stare into hers.

'Come on, turn the bloody thing.'

The stretched scrawny neck was in the jaws of a vice, and the metal machine gleamed with grease.

'Turn the bar, will you. Turn the bloody bar.'

The slim piece of metal drew her eyes. 'I can't,' she whispered.

'You bloody will. Come on, I ain't got all night. You're a land girl, ain't you?' His voice rose. 'You've got to do it. It's farmin'.'

She felt herself growing hot. She couldn't do it, she knew she couldn't.

'If you won't do the bloody handle, then you'll have to hold the bird.' He turned suddenly, thrusting the creature at her. She put her hands out to ward it off, feeling the warm dry feathers, the sharp scratch of claws.

'No, oh no.'

'Then turn the handle!' He was shouting now. All pretence at stealth gone, he was roaring at her. 'I can't wring its neck, me wrists won't let me. Come on, for Christ's sake, me back's bloody killin' me. Turn the handle.'

She reached forward. She could hear his breathing and it seemed to fill the shed. The metal was cold between her fingers. She had thought it would be stiff to turn, but the grease made it easy. She stared at the screw turning, willing her eyes away from the bird. The living thing that –

'Turn the bloody thing.' He was shouting again, his voice thickening. She felt the moment the jaws gripped the bird, then she had to turn harder. She closed her eyes. The man's breathing was a roaring in her ears as she turned and turned.

'Stop! You'll have the fuckin' head off.'

She stopped instantly, her hand leaving the vice as if the metal had been red hot instead of ice cold. Her eyes were still closed.

'Hold your hands out.' The words were slurred, as if he had been drinking. Silently she held her hands forwards, the palms turned up, the supplicant in church. 'Blood,' he said. 'Blood and a woman.'

She opened her eyes at the warm sensation. He was holding the dead bird over her hands, and a red stream poured down from the open beak. She stared for a moment at the brimming cupful and then she ran out into the dark. She pushed sightlessly past Doreen standing in the doorway, putting out a bloody hand as if to fend her off.

''ere!' Doreen's cry didn't stop her as she ran wildly. She had to get away. But she was trapped. The high end fence shut her in. There was no way out except through the cottage, past Phyllis, who would be sitting in the sagging moquette-covered armchair with her great arms folded. She cowered in the corner of the garden, tight against the chicken run. Her hands . . . She held them away from her, gripping her fingers through the wire. She could hear the birds moving on their perch, a gentle rustling, then the musty smell of the chickens reached out to envelop her. She lurched away, and was sick.

'Percy,' Nigel said, 'something makes me think that this time you're serious.'

Percy lifted the pint mug in his hand in salute. 'Seriously

pissed.' He slurred his words with the expertise of long practice.

'No, old boy, seriously in love,' Nigel beamed. Percy acting the lovelorn swain was just what he needed. It took everyone's attention off the one remaining virgin of their group.

'Let me give you a bit of advice, a word from the expert. Just make sure you never fall in love, old son.' Percy stared balefully into his pint. The edges of his moustache were touched with beery foam and they drooped. 'It's a miserable state. Truly miserable.' He tipped his head back and howled softly at the smoky ceiling, like a dog in pain. A chorus of catcalls quickly drowned the noise he was making. The pub was crammed, with blue uniforms shoulder to shoulder along the wall behind the piano. 'Sing us a song, Perce,' someone shouted. 'A good old-fashioned love song.' And they all roared with laughter.

'No one understands me,' Percy muttered as he manoeuvred his way off the bar stool.

'What, not even the object of your desires?' Nigel took a generous mouthful of the watery bitter in his personal pewter tankard to hide his grin.

'Least of all her. She won't take a word I say seriously.' He stood swaying gently as if blown by the wind, the tip of the middle finger of his left hand held precariously to the edge of the oak-topped bar. 'Someone told her all about me, she says. Told her my score, all the intimate little details of my love life right down to how I tick 'em off on the end of my bed.' He shook his head, trying to clear the fog that engulfed it. 'Who would do such a wicked thing, eh? I ask you, I mean, it's time I settled down. A fellow needs a bit of stability in life.' He'd found the word 'stability' a bit of an effort, but he managed it in

86

the end. 'My little angel, that's what I call her. Angel, with her big blue eyes and her beautiful golden hair. Just like a halo it is, just like a ruddy halo. A man should marry a girl like that. I'd even give up my motor bike for her if she asked – that's how serious it is.'

Nigel put his drink down slowly on the bar. The penny had dropped. He stared for what felt a long time at the slowly retreating back of Percy, the one-time libertine, his one-time persecutor, and now, he realized, his would-be relative. It was Margaret. The object of Percy's totally given affections was Nigel's cousin. Of course Margaret wouldn't take Percy seriously, they'd told her everything about him and his pursuit of the female, plus a whole lot more that it had been fun to make up.

'Neil!' he shouted as he looked vainly around the crowded bar. Where the hell had his brother got to? 'Neil!' He bellowed this time. They had to do something, only as yet he hadn't got any idea what.

Bella drummed her fingers on the Bauhaus desk. She was humming tunelessly under her breath. Beneath her breastbone there was a painful constriction and across the back of her neck a tautness that would not go away. She was furious, absolutely livid.

'You'll break your nails doing that.' Her mother Adele's words cut across her thoughts. The voice was still heavily accented, although she hadn't lived in America for nearly twenty years.

'Let her alone.' Bella's uncle Bill's voice was softer, less transatlantic, but then he wanted to belong in England. 'Everybody, sometime, has to grow up, and it's a painful process. Especially if it's left till late. Like in Bella's case.'

'Sarcasm I don't need.' Bella stood up abruptly.

'No, my girl, perhaps you don't. What you do need is a good spanking on the behind. Only your mother never saw fit to give it to you, and I've always been too soft. Now you're thirty it's too late for that and I apologize for my leniency. It would have saved you a great deal of embarrassment.'

'I'm not embarrassed.' Bella flushed deep red, belying her words. 'I'm upset, that's all.'

'Well, I am embarrassed even if you're not.' Bill closed the newspaper he had given up trying to read and began trying to calm himself, folding it slowly and carefully. 'And I'm sure that your mother is too. What you did was insulting to a great many people. What am I saying? What you did was an insult to the entire British nation. We're foreigners here, however much we're allies. We're at the whim of toleration at a time when suspicion is a very natural emotion. How could you, Bella?' Bill's usual air of sophistication abandoned him. He was seriously worried about possible repercussions following his niece's stupidity.

'Art is above politics.' Bella stood up and walked quickly across the room to face her uncle. Her slim figure was accentuated by the bias cut skirt of her French-blue dress and the white piping at the collar made her look fresh, ingenuous. 'I had planned an exhibition of Fritz's work long before this silly war. His work is meaningful, in context for the present time, the contradictions one can see –'

'Shut up.' Bill too got to his feet. 'Don't say another word of that drivel. If you can't think about the reality of the boys dying out there then at least you can shut up – think about the death of your own cousin William. They may have contained their grief at Pencombe, but it's eating into them – Isabella looks ten years older. And there are the other young men of our own family facing death, having to come to terms with it although they're little more than children. If none of that touches you, then you must at least shut up just because what you're saying is dangerous. You go on this way and you'll end up being interned. Do you understand that, Bella? Your smart dresses wouldn't be much use to you then; you wouldn't be able to wear your frivolous hats in a camp. I forbid you to talk about that any longer. His name is forbidden in the house.' He was trembling in rage and in his desperation to evoke some response from the perfectly made-up face regarding him. He felt he had to break through a lacquered shell.

'I shall go to my room,' Bella said. 'When you've calmed down you might like to remember that I was insulted at my show yesterday evening. I would have thought that would be more important to you than the wailing of a few philistines.'

Bill gripped the rolled-up paper in his hand like a club, and deep blue veins stood up on the back of his hand. 'We've ruined that girl.' He had to force the words out, his jaw was clamped tight with his emotion. 'God knows, I think she's beyond redemption.'

Adele sat very still. Slowly she stabbed her needle down into the tapestry. Should she continue with the rose pink, or perhaps a cerise? She forced her mind away from the scene that had threatened the serenity of her drawing room. There had been too much emotion in her past; she couldn't cope with strain any more. 'I should like a sherry, please, Bill.' After a few minutes' silence she coughed gently to remind her brother of her request. She watched as he struggled to pull himself together. He should never have got involved in the American Embassy, he didn't need to work. His sense of duty was changing him and it was a nuisance not having him always available as an escort. She sighed softly and laid her tapestry down. Poor Bella. It was a difficult time to be young.

'I'm sorry, Viccy.' Margaret rushed out into the hall after Victoria. 'I really am sorry. I thought you were still on the phone, otherwise we'd have been more careful. After all, it is your house.' Her aunt turned to face her, standing very erect, her hand at her neck, her cheeks pink.

'Margaret.' Victoria had to cough to clear her throat before she could speak. 'What on earth were you thinking of? It could have been anybody who'd come into the drawing room just now, one of the servants . . . anybody.'

'I'm sorry that you were embarrassed, honestly I am. But I'm not going to apologize for what we were doing.' Margaret's face still carried the marks of passion, the soft mouth, the reddened lips, but her sincerity gave her dignity. 'I'm not apologizing for the fact that Percy and I are lovers. Time's too short to waste.'

Victoria couldn't think what to say. She couldn't get the picture of the two of them together on the sofa out of her mind: Percy's hand under Margaret's skirt, her arms round his neck, pulling him down on top of her. They had been kissing, locked together in an embrace that seemed to last for ever as Viccy stood there, her heart beating too fast and a dreadful sense of emptiness washing over her.

'If you'd like to wait in the study, Viccy, we'll leave. I don't think it would be quite the thing to stay for tea just now, do you?' Margaret smiled. It was a bright, managing smile. If Viccy wanted to fall to pieces then that was her affair. All Margaret and Percy had done was take advantage of some time together. There was precious little of that.

'Are you going to get engaged?' Victoria clung to the

90

conventions. War or no war, reputations had to be safeguarded.

'Absolutely not. Dear Perce thinks he's in love, but I know all about him. The boys have set me right.'

'The boys? You mean Nigel and Neil – my boys?'

'Yes, that's right. They're all pals together and all Perce's little secrets have been laid out before me. It's a pity, really.' She looked wistful. 'Because he's rather a dear. Be an angel and do a disappearing act, Viccy. Perce will have straightened himself up and all that and now he'll be desperate to do a bunk. See you.' Margaret leaned forward and kissed her aunt on the cheek. They usually had such a good relationship, more like two girls together than aunt and niece, and Margaret was surprised at the fuss Victoria was making. After all, she couldn't possibly have thought she was still a virgin – or could she?

Victoria almost stumbled into the study. She felt so confused. She sat down on the edge of the desk. What should she do? Should she phone Margaret's father, Albert? His wife, Maggy, would have a fit. They were so much holier than thou, which was inevitable, she thought, considering the scandal they themselves caused when they'd had to get married. She would have to talk to Margaret herself. The girl couldn't possibly carry on like that, she'd get herself pregnant. And saying that she had no intention of getting engaged – what a hussy! Victoria stood up, feeling restless.

The sound of the door to the drawing room opening across the hallway was loud in the hush of the book-lined room. Victoria could imagine the two of them, hand in hand, sneaking out of the house. She needed a cigarette. There was a green onyx box on the desk and she reached out to it quickly, not allowing herself time to change her mind. She smoked very seldom now. The smell seemed

91

to cling to her clothes and Luke was irritated by it. The lighter was sterling silver, a Dunhill that Luke had bought years ago, and she picked it up, feeling the cool solidity of it filling her hand. She bent her head to meet the flame, breathing in to draw the smoke deep into her lungs. The act was sensual, tipping the balance of the feelings that had been aroused inside her.

'My God,' she whispered as she ran a trembling hand through her hair. How she needed to be loved – she needed a man to make love to her, to hold her, possess her. She had never felt like this. She inhaled deeply on the cigarette again, making her head swim. She needed – The front door slammed. Margaret was right. There was no time, they could all die tonight, tomorrow. Dear God, she was still young, she wasn't a withered old woman – and she needed a man. Luke was gone from her. The strange old man in the room upstairs wasn't her Luke, wasn't the man who had made her body quiver with desire. What in God's name could she do?

The telephone rang out in the hall and she spun round, running towards it, desperate for something to occupy her mind. 'Hallo,' she cried, 'hallo.'

'Hello, Viccy? It's Tim here.' Tim Gribben from Biggin Hill – dear Tim.

'Oh, how lovely, I just needed a friend . . .'

'Viccy, look, is there anyone there with you? You see the thing is . . .' He paused, wishing now he'd left it to official channels. 'Prepare yourself for a bit of a shock, old girl. I've got some bad news. It's Nigel. He's gone down in the sea; not been picked up yet, I'm afraid.'

John's arm fitted snugly around Daisy's waist. There was no one to see them as they walked the footpath through Bowen's Wood and he was free to act like the young lover he felt. Daisy's waiting for him outside the village hall in the evening had become a habit. It gave him an added reason to look forward to his regular Land Defence Volunteer meetings.

'It makes me feel so safe – you in the Volunteers, with your shotgun and everything.' Daisy leaned her head against his broad shoulder. 'It's such an important position you've got, John. I keep saying so to Fanny. Only she doesn't understand the same as I do. Between you and I, she's not quite right in the head, like.'

John bestowed a kiss on the top of Daisy's head. Fanny was potty, not just 'not quite right'. 'I reckon that when they were handing out the brains, you got her share as well, my dear. But it suits well enough, it wouldn't do if you were both the same. You'd fall out quick enough then.'

'Tell me more about what they think those awful Germans are planning.' Daisy shivered deliciously. It wasn't real, it couldn't be, with John's strong arm around her. It was like a good story, a frightening one that it was fun to read curled up in front of the fire. There was no way that the Germans could come into Daisy's world; it was too orderly, too secure.

'The real danger's the parachutists.' John lifted his head, breathing in the scents of the wood. He knew every lane and byway, and he'd know if there was an enemy lurking on his ground. 'And they could come in disguise. Like the gentry, some of them's been dressed, or even done up like nuns. Nothing's too clever for them. You've got to catch them as they're landing, before they get amongst us, that's the thing. Only there's danger there as well, we were told tonight . . .'

'You will be careful, John.' Daisy suddenly stood still. They were nearing the edge of the wood, getting close to

93

her cottage, and soon they'd have to part, to walk decorously side by side.

'Silly little thing.' John tugged playfully at her grey curls. 'Nothing's going to hurt me and nothing's going to hurt my little Daisy. The war won't last long, and when it's over we'll . . .' He paused. He thought she knew what he meant right enough, but he couldn't pluck up the courage to say the words.

'Yes, John?' Daisy looked up at him. It was a miracle that had brought him into her life, to bring such a new, trembling emotion to her more than ample bosom.

'Well, we'll talk about things when it's over. It'll be our own little victory celebration, like.'

Daisy's face fell. She so wanted him to propose to her. All the books she'd ever read had had as their climax the hero falling on his knees to beg for the hand of his heroine. They hadn't got that much time to spare, they weren't that young, however they felt.

'It might take years, John. Lady Montford said, at the church meeting, that we should plan for a long siege. That's what she called it, a siege. She said we were lucky being country born, we have a tradition of living off the land, and however bad it gets, we'll still have our vegetable gardens. She said she's turned the rose garden . . .' Then she laughed. She'd forgotten for a minute that John would know more than she did about the gardens at the Place. 'Well, she said how we should be frugal, that it was our duty, and I don't mind that. We've never needed much. But waiting till the war's over. You and I, I mean. I'm not sure about that, it could be a long time.' She was silent, waiting for him to speak, but then she saw her sister running into the wood, her skirts flying and her face contorting as she struggled for air. 'Oh, it's Fanny! Fanny, whatever's the matter?'

'Germans,' Fanny cried, throwing herself to the ground at their feet. 'The Germans are coming . . .'

They put Fanny to bed. She didn't need a doctor, Daisy decided, just peace and quiet, and a good long sleep. She gave her sister a dessertspoonful of the poppy syrup. She blamed herself – she should have forbidden Fanny to listen to the radio on her own. She always got things wrong. Not that it wasn't frightening enough, all this talk about invasion, but poor Fanny thought they'd meant here and now . . .

John left Daisy to prepare a quick supper and went out to potter in the garden. He filled a watering can from the rain butt and made his way to the peas. They were coming on nicely and he ran his thumb along a soft green pod. He could feel the pearl-like bumps that would soon swell to fill it to bursting. He watered the plants generously – he was a great believer in watering. He thought of it as giving God a helping hand, and usually it pleased him, but his mind was only half on what he was doing. He hadn't told Daisy what they'd been told that evening about the German parachutists. It was bothering him, preying on his mind, but their instructions had been clear enough. And after all, there was a war on. But to shoot a man as he hung there, strung up in the air, would be a hard thing to do. Still, those Jerries were devils. They'd raise their arms in the air as they fell towards the earth, giving the sign of surrender, but they'd be holding grenades, ready to hurl them at their English enemies the moment they landed. He would remember what he was told. He nodded his head grimly as he walked back up the path to the rain butt again. If he saw one of them coming down like that then he'd give them the works. Both barrels, no messing about. After all, he had his Daisy to protect now.

Daisy got her proposal that evening. Over a good, wholesome bowl of vegetable soup John admitted his desire to be wed. If Daisy felt cheated of her romance, then she didn't show it, and after supper, as they sat cuddled up close together on the old leather settee, she felt in his kiss more than she'd ever understood from all her reading. Later they talked about Fanny, whispering in case she should hear them, although Daisy was sure she would sleep after her medicine. There were two bedrooms in the cottage, and Fanny had the room that their parents had used, complete with the mahogany-framed double bed. If she would move into Daisy's room, then everything would work out beautifully. The trouble was, as Daisy said, you could never tell with Fanny; she saw things differently from most folk.

Fanny strained to hear what her sister was saying. If only they wouldn't whisper. They wanted her room, they wanted her bed. She clutched at the covers, twisting her fingers into the multicoloured patchwork coverlet that had been her mother's pride. She had been closer to her mother than Daisy had been – that was only natural, because she was the elder by four years. She stretched her neck, pressing her head back against the goose-feather pillows. She always thought of herself as taller than Daisy – she had been, she remembered. Only now Daisy was so big, and Fanny had grown bent with age.

They couldn't have her bed. She could hear them going out into the garden. She wished now that she'd warned Daisy, when there had been time, before that man had stolen her away. They were going down the path, their feet sounding loud on the gravel. Fanny sat up gingerly. Her head felt funny and her tongue was swollen in her mouth. It wasn't right, any of it. She'd lie awake and worry all night while Daisy dreamed her silly dreams. She felt for her slippers. The boards were cold under her feet that were still cosy from her warm bed. That reminded her again; they shouldn't have it, they shouldn't. The door opened silently and she stepped out on to the landing, listening – she didn't want to see them. The stairs creaked as she went down, but it didn't matter, she knew she was alone in the house. Just another spoonful, that was what she needed to help her drop off. She had her hand on the cupboard door when she heard Daisy coming back up the path. Her sister was singing to herself, making a display of how pleased she was. The bottle was cold in Fanny's hand as she hurried up the stairs. She had picked the fat poppy heads herself and spread them on the window sill to dry. In the late autumn she had ground them to a dust and then mixed them with wine and a little precious sugar. She unscrewed the cap as she closed the bedroom door silently behind her. The bed was still warm, waiting to gather her into its softness.

Daisy made quite a noise of washing. Fanny was still asleep and she wanted to get it over with, she wanted to tell her that John and she would be getting married, and it was only right they should have the big double bed. She looked down at her shell-pink corsets as she rubbed her neck with the soapy flannel. She'd get a new set. There was enough put by in the tea caddy. It was their emergency money, but what was an emergency if it wasn't being seen in your corsets for the first time by a man? She reddened at the thought, but she wasn't ashamed of it. It was natural, a man and a woman, and she felt such a warm glow when John held her that she wasn't frightened, not a bit. She'd told him she was a virgin and then she'd had to laugh because he'd said he was one too. They'd have a bit of fun finding out what it was all about, she reckoned.

The goat began bleating outside. It was late for her milking and her udder would be swollen, milk dribbling from the teats on to the straw of her bedding. Daisy put her hands on her hips in exasperation. How could Fanny take today of all days to sleep in? She went up the stairs slowly. Climbing them made her breathless and she tried not to go up more than she had to. Trust Fanny. Daisy was trying hard to work up a righteous indignation because deep inside she felt guilty at what she was going to ask.

'Fanny!' She banged her knuckles on the door. 'Fanny!'

It was quiet and the curtains were still pulled tight. She walked noisily across the room to pull them back, blinking as the light flooded in. 'Fanny, it's well gone eight . . .'

She was no bigger than a child, her slight body outlined by the bedclothes. Death had taken the lines from her face; her hand was like ivory.

Daisy bit her lip. This was her doing. Fanny had been in the way, and for the first time in their lives, Daisy had wanted to be alone so that she could have the love of a man. She sank moaning to her knees, biting her knuckles, her throat on fire. God had done this. It was hard to see through the red-hot tears – Fanny's still face, the claw-like hand. The bottle. She breathed in sharply. The bottle of poppy syrup lay on its side on the pillow. She hadn't left it, she knew she hadn't. She got stiffly up off the floor. Last night seemed a blur, but she was sure she had taken it downstairs – she remembered putting it back in the cupboard. The bed seemed to draw her closer and she stretched out her hand. What should she do? Her mind was so muddled, frantically she tried to think what it all meant. They would say she had murdered her sister.

There would be enough gossips in the village ready to tell the Law about her and John. Fanny made it difficult, they'd see that, for Fanny to die was most convenient. 'Most convenient.' She whispered the words; they were from some book – she couldn't remember which.

The bottle was empty, the last sticky drops of liquid had spilt on the pillowcase close beside Fanny's face. Daisy stood staring at the brown stain. The doctor would have to come in. That was what had happened when their father died, she remembered that. She had to change the pillow. It was so hard to lift Fanny's head, she would never have believed the weight of it, and her breath would only come in short gasps. A tight band pressed round her ribs. What if she should die too? She suddenly felt agonizingly vulnerable. A summer breeze rattled the window in its frame and she spun round, open-mouthed. If she should be found out before she was ready . . . Then she heard the goat again, bleating in its distress. What if someone passing came to see what the matter was? She felt sweat on her brow as she tugged frantically at the pillowcase, and nearly fell backwards when it came off in her hands. She was talking to herself, muttering soothing words to help her.

The doctor was most understanding. It took only a moment of his time. There was a young woman in labour in one of the outlying cottages, and he was worried about her – she was very small and it was her first child. Poor Fanny had done very well, he said, all things considered. He called the words back over his shoulder to Daisy as he hurried down the stairs ahead of her. She'd enjoyed a few more years than he'd ever have put her down for, and that was no doubt due to Daisy's care. He turned to give her a warm smile, he wasn't an unkind man, if he hadn't been in such a hurry he would have lingered. Daisy would find it hard being on her own, at first.

John went down to the village in the early afternoon to collect some papers for Lady Montford. That was when he heard the news. Fanny, with her odd ways, had been a local character. The postmistress volunteered the information; there weren't so many eccentrics left that you didn't notice one of them going. John struggled to hide his elation. His one fear had been that Fanny would become a bedridden invalid, tying Daisy hand and foot to the house, hanging on for useless years. It must have been her fright. He thought of her running out to them in the wood. She'd looked mad enough then. He had the sobering thought that it was as well that he and Daisy were past child-rearing. It would have been worrying having a strain of madness in the family. John paused at the bridge. It was only a short walk through the wood to the cottage, but he should get back to work in the gardens. No, he would have to wait until later. He began to walk along the carriage road, but his steps were slow. If he explained to Lady Montford . . . He turned quickly and set off, almost running. He had to see Daisy.

It was quiet in the cottage. Fanny was laid out upstairs; Mrs Beams had been in and helped with the rites of death. Daisy was sitting very still. She had a book in her hands, but she wasn't reading, her heart was beating too fast and she listened to every creak of wood, every rustle of the climbing rose on the wall outside. She would not feel safe until Fanny was buried, hidden away. Even then, she knew, she would not feel really safe ever again. She heard John's steps, recognizing his gait for all his hurry. She moved swiftly from the chair, running to bolt the door. He must not come in, must not.

John pushed at the door. It was always open, and he stared at it in surprise as it resisted him. 'Daisy! Daisy!' He banged on the door as he shouted. He was worried now that perhaps the village had it wrong – but it had to be Fanny. 'Daisy!' The door was shaking under his fist, then suddenly it opened, and she stood there before him, his beloved Daisy. He went to step forward to take her in his arms, but she held out her hands, fending him off.

'Who are you?' She whispered the words, her voice thin and weak, uncannily like Fanny's.

'Daisy.' Again he went to step towards her, but she was ready, pushing the door to, leaving only a narrow gap through which she whispered.

'Go away. Go away and don't ever come back. You hear me?' Her voice rose, and cracked. 'I don't ever want to see you again, not ever.' Then she closed the door finally. She leaned against it, safe now. No one could say that she'd wanted Fanny dead; she'd be safe and secure. There was the garden, that would feed her, and the goat. She was talking to herself as she made her way back to the chair. When Fanny had gone she would move into the big bed. She'd be closer to them all then, to her mother, her father and now dear Fanny up in Heaven. She gathered their memories about her, blocking out John as if he'd never been.

Bella stroked the thin camel-hair brush unenthusiastically over a block of watercolour. It was raining outside, a thin grey drizzle coating the London streets. She sighed heavily with boredom. The painting in front of her was grey too. Desperate for something to occupy her mind, she had decided to make a sketch book of the settings that she existed in, the rooms that surrounded her as she waited for the war to end and Fritz to come back to her.

She had begun with her mother's drawing room, which was a composition of orange and brown. The colour scheme was avant garde and surprisingly different from Adele's usual conformity, but it was her statement of independence. She was an American, and as such she was free to flout accepted taste as and when she wanted. The quality of the furnishings, however, was totally traditional British upper middle class. The Heal's delivery van was regularly parked outside the black-painted front door that was flanked by two mopheaded bay trees.

It was Bella's mood that had influenced her painting. There were too many shadows in it, and the furniture was insubstantial – the chairs were not for sitting in, the cushions were too rounded, unused.

Adele was, as usual, sitting on the beige and apricot striped sofa, her tiny feet supported by an embroidered footstool. She did not exist in the painting. Earlier, when Bill looked over Bella's shoulder he was annoyed, thinking that Bella had deliberately left her mother out of her work because they were in a continual argument. That wasn't so. Bella had not painted her mother because she found it very hard to portray people. She was an artists' agent and gallery owner because her own abilities were less than she had once hoped. She had told herself so often that it was because she did not have the time to practise; now, faced with nothing but time, she had decided to paint only those things at which she was proficient.

Fritz would have been so confident – she looked at her own, watery effort and in her imagination she could see the bold strokes of colour that he would have laid down. Then the few masterful touches of black. His style was unique. That was why his paintings had still sold well, even after the war began. It was ridiculous of a few uneducated critics to claim that it was unpatriotic to buy, or indeed to sell, his works. Bill should have supported her, and the fuss would soon have died down.

She had learned the lesson not to be so public in her business. There was a large circle of cognoscenti that she could still cater for. Peter Savage had promised to set something up; after all, his friends were just the sort to invest in an area that was bound to do well. And if Germany won . . .

She laid down her paint brush and sat very still, her hands folded in her lap. It was what no one was saying, but she was sure an awful lot of people were thinking. The Germans were an orderly race, as Fritz had told her time and time again. They would follow their leaders, never querying, never even thinking of disobeying. Compared to the British – the common men who were so rough, so argumentative – she could only see them as the victors. After such a conquest it would be good for her if she had carried on with her art sales. It would be a proof of her loyalty. That was something else Fritz had told her – his family were so close, so loyal to each other, and it was a national trait. Bill wasn't loyal to her; he had abandoned her reputation to the jackals, adding his own hurtful comments. She would never forgive him for that. Even her own mother had sided against her, agreeing that her allowance should be stopped. Together with the gallery closing, it had been a death knell for her business and for her independence. She stood up. It might be wet outside, but anything was preferable to sitting in this mausoleum.

'I'm going out,' she said, as she gathered up her paints and picked up her sketch book. She would leave it in her room, she didn't want the others discussing it in her absence.

'You will be back for tea?' Adele's soft voice held more than a question – Bella heard in it a command. After all, she was even dependent on them for her food now.

'Yes, yes, of course. I'm always back for tea, aren't I? Breakfast, lunch, tea, dinner. Only now it's not dinner any more, is it? Now it's supper – so economical.' She sneered the word.

Adele bent her head over her embroidery. She didn't have the energy to cope with another of Bella's tantrums. Bill had been right. All those years he had told her she spoilt her daughter, and he had been right. Only now, as he'd said yesterday evening, he would be much happier to have been wrong.

Was it too late? Adele sincerely hoped not, but Bella didn't seem to be changing, she wasn't repenting her stupidity. If anything, she was more difficult than ever. Of course it was hard on the girl . . . Adele stared briefly at an empty space a few feet in front of her: Fritz had been a nice young man. Nicer than the others Bella had gathered up, her 'waifs and strays', as she and Bill had laughingly called them at first. Then it had stopped being funny and every new young man had seemed a threat, because as Bella got older they got younger and Bella's infatuation for them became quite embarrassing.

Until Fritz. He had been young enough. What was he now? Only twenty-four, possibly twenty-five, but he at least had talent. Real talent that marked him as different from his predecessors, as did his impeccable manners and his obvious fondness for Bella. That had been genuine. The war, for Bella, had been a personal tragedy. Without it, in all probability she would have been married, possibly even started a family.

Adele sighed and went back to her work. Bella's moods

104

were understandable, but it didn't make them any easier to live with.

Fritz rubbed the palm of his hand over the coarse-textured drawing paper that he had fixed firmly into his clipboard. He pursed his lips, whistling soundlessly. He was able to shut out the noise of the aircraft engines and cut himself off from the sheer insanity of flying over a most unappealing sea, but he could not divorce himself from the stupidity of the inferior quality of paper that he had been supplied with. It was impossible to draw a straight line on the rippled surface. He made a few exploratory strokes with his pencil – that, at least, he had been allowed to supply for himself, and it was of an artist's quality. He was convinced that only his own direct superior was so bigoted as to insist he could not provide all his own materials. But then the man was a philistine and he clearly thought artists effeminate and a disgrace to the fatherland.

Before the war, a small canvas with the signature 'Fritz Helmer' would have sold for several hundred pounds, and it would have been hung in a room of taste – to be appreciated and savoured. Now he was expected to produce dozens of what were no less works of art for the fleeting use of mindless bomb-aimers. Fritz did not approve of the war, but he did not think it politic to make his views known. He had his mother and father to consider, and his two brothers, who, unlike him, saw the war as their chance for glory. He pressed down too hard on the fragile tip of lead and it snapped.

'Bloody hell!' he muttered, and smiled wryly. It was as well that the din made normal dialogue impossible – it would not endear him to his fellow voyagers if they found out that their eccentric war artist swore in English.

105

There was something different this time, something personal in the way the shells burst above and beside the plane. Until now Fritz had known no fear and he had found that surprising. As an artist, and possessed of an overdeveloped sense of imagination, he had supposed his sensitivities would provide a likely route to panic. But he had discovered to his pleasure that he was, after all, as placid as his mother, as phlegmatic as his father.

Until now.

He scratched at his kneecap. It itched as if he had been bitten by an insect. There was nothing for him to do until they reached the River Medway, so he had to think of something, to lose himself in a few precious memories. He scratched his knee again. He had been bitten by insects the first time he made love to Bella. He smiled. Even in his nervousness he could remember how embarrassed he'd been to discover that his buttocks were covered in red itchy bumps inflicted by the riverside gnats. He deliberately did not make love to Bella again until they had faded – he had been little more than a child then.

The aircraft lurched suddenly and he clutched at his clipboard as it slid madly towards the floor.

Yes, they had made love . . . He closed his eyes, removing himself from the chaos, the jumble of noise. There was a sudden smell of fabric burning and a flicker of fear unsettled his stomach. He breathed in deeply, counting to ten. It was a trick to reduce nausea, according to an experienced airman. Fritz had never been airsick and he did not intend to begin now. The memories returned . . . Which had been the best time? Bella was more experienced than him. She had taught him to take his time, to please her, and in the end he had learned that it pleased him as well. Afterwards he would feel wonderful, ready to face anything. It would have been good if she had been German, so much easier. He could have visited her on his leaves, and then afterwards he would have felt regenerated, ready to face the unpleasant reality, able to cope with the changing note of the engines. Amateur flier though he was, he understood that they were dependent on the machines to take them home – more important even than that, to keep them up in the sky and then bring them safely down to the ground. There was something different this time, a clatter that grated on his nerves.

The plane tipped sideways again and he nodded abruptly to acknowledge a sudden grip on his arm, grateful for human contact however brief. He opened his eyes. It was time for him to work – there was the valley. Dark green trees and hedges made a chequerboard pattern of the pastures, a black and white timber-framed cottage like a doll's house marked the position of the road. He felt a surge of optimism as he recognized the shape of the river. He forgot about the inferior quality of the paper, he forgave his superior every small persecution for the warm glow of recognition that flooded through him. They were close to Pencombe – he had walked these banks himself.

He began drawing, his firm swift strokes marking the pillboxes. In his imagination he could see them as they were, built of smart red brick, despite their camouflage. The beauty of it was that he knew the fields, the river bank. He saw where they had been preparing their defences. White puffs of smoke appeared beneath him. They were firing at him – how unreal it was, he thought. He wondered if it was the Army, or perhaps someone he knew, the woodman, the gamekeeper. He had met many of the country people of Pencombe.

His job on this stretch of the river was nearly finished. There – there was the house, he grinned widely. The yellowed stone welcomed him. It was four o'clock, he checked on his watch. They would be having afternoon tea – would they still have their usual crumpets when they were governed by Germany?

Suddenly it was as if the floor fell away beneath him.

The green baize-covered door leading off the hall was wedged permanently open with a wicker basket piled high with wooden bowling balls. There were no longer any living-in staff at Pencombe, so there was never enough noise coming from the kitchen to justify keeping the heavy swing door closed. When Cook had given in her notice so that she could go and stay with her daughter and family in Wales, Isabella had decided that she would make do with a skeleton staff until things sorted themselves out and the sanatorium became established.

Until things sorted themselves out . . . There would be a lot to do. They were to move into the west wing. The rooms there were of a more manageable size and it made a lot of sense in terms of heating and maintenance. Then she would have to empty William's room. Isabella hadn't been able to bring herself to touch anything in it, since Dunkirk. She began putting the tea things together with an unnecessary clatter. William had died a hero's death, one he would have chosen for himself if that were the way of things. She had no right to weep, that was a kind of selfishness.

Michael would enjoy a ginger nut – he always dunked them. She looked into the glass biscuit barrel as she struggled to think of William with gladness. That was how the rector had explained their duty – to be grateful for the joyous times they'd shared together. But William had not always been a happy child. She believed that he had found the prospect of inheriting Pencombe daunting, especially in those early days when they had always seemed to be selling parts of his potential inheritance. Isabella stood still, the teapot unwarmed in her hands. She could still remember the awful scene when William had found his father bundling up the sporting guns for sale. Today there was enough capital in the bank to go out and buy back everything they'd ever sold. But she would never do that. After having been in such a position, Isabella was very careful of her money. She wondered if William would have been the same, or would he, once the glory of taking over had palled, have set to spending his way through it all? Who could tell?

Isabella shivered suddenly. It was chilly in the kitchen and she walked quickly to open the windows – it was warmer outside than in. The catch stuck for a moment, the casement hadn't been used in a while, and a spider scurried away as she forced it open. The view that the window afforded wasn't very beautiful: a small square of sparse grass encompassed by a beech hedge, several washing lines criss-crossed the space, and an untidy cluster of washing poles leaned against an outhouse wall. Isabella could remember when all the lines would have been covered with white linen sheets; that was in the days when the house was full of people, when Lucinda and her children lived in the west wing, and Isabella and Michael entertained a regular stream of guests in the main house. There had been days when there were fifteen or more beds to change. Now there were only hers and Michael's. Lucinda used every possible excuse to get away, and most guests stayed only for the day.

There was someone shooting down the valley and she listened to the noise. If there hadn't been a war on, she would have thought it was a shooting party, there was such a clatter. Then she heard the plane – it was an intermittent noise, coughing and spluttering, and then at last firing into life, as Eli's pleasure boats had sometimes done. Only this engine wasn't starting, it was stopping – and it was horribly close to them. She was still holding the teapot as she began running. The corridors had never seemed so long and she was gasping for breath before she reached the stairs. She was halfway up, her hair coming infuriatingly undone, her heel catching on the corner of the carpet, when there was the most terrible crash. She clutched at the banister for support. The stairs beneath her feet were shaking, a fine white dust fell around her and she began coughing, choking. 'Michael!' she shouted. 'Michael!'

John heard the failing engine as he was weeding between the broad beans. He laid his hoe down carefully on the newly turned earth and walked purposefully towards the potting shed. The routine that had been worked out for him at the evening meetings of the LDV fell into place. His shotgun stood, oiled and ready, in the corner. He lifted his jacket from the nail on the wall. In his bulging inner pocket there were ten cartridges. As he pulled the door of the shed closed behind him, he was loading the gun – both barrels, as he had been instructed. The spluttering engine was coming closer and he hurried his steps to get out into the open. The plane was almost above him. It was so low he felt he could touch it, and he could smell the foul black smoke that poured out from its belly. He began to run – it was going to fall on him. He hadn't felt any panic until now, but the sudden silence as the engine failed entirely unnerved him, then there was a sound like a gale rushing through the trees. He was running flat out now, still gripping his gun. He had to hold it carefully, keep it broken open – it wouldn't do to fall, not with two shots in it.

The white of the parachute floated high above the park oaks. John ran towards it – it gave him a reason to run away from the house. He heard the crash behind him and would have stumbled if it weren't for the fact that his fear gave him back the agility he'd had twenty years ago.

'Bloody Hun,' he began shouting as he waved his gun in the air, shaking it up at the clear blue sky now defiled by the enemy. The land had never looked greener to him and he felt an overwhelming urge to protect it. He looked back quickly. Flames were shooting high from the Place behind him and the crackle of burning sounded loud on the clear air. 'Bastards,' he screamed. 'Murderers.' It was the main part of the house that the plane had dived into. Lord and Lady Montford – John choked on his emotion. He slowed his mad, headlong dash. There was justice to be done. He planted his feet wide apart, taking a firm stance on his beloved British soil.

The parachute swayed in the breeze. Fritz alone had escaped from the burning plane. He felt an inevitability about it all as he saw the land rushing up to meet him. He'd seen the figure with the gun – his reception committee. He hadn't seen exactly where the plane had gone down, but it must have been close to the house. He hoped it hadn't caused too much damage. He wondered, as the last few yards of air between him and the ground rapidly diminished, if he would be able to get a letter to Bella – he didn't know what the form was in a prisoner-of-war camp.

John sighted the gun carefully. The man in the air had

111

his hands up, but he wouldn't be tricked, he remembered what they'd told him. He took careful aim and fired the first barrel, and the figure jumped convulsively. It smashed to earth as John took one slow step forwards and fired the second shot.

Fierce warrs and faithfull loves
shall moralise my song.

Edmund Spenser, 1552–1599

Eli leaned back against the deep leather upholstery of the rear seat in the Daimler and closed his eyes in appreciation of his cigar – this was the life, all right. He was just about to fall asleep as a thought struck him and he leaned forward to tap on the glass partition separating him from the chauffeur.

'I say, Miles, you do know the way to this place, don't you? I'd like to arrive by eight. Just in time for a drinkie before dinner.'

The chauffeur nodded and his peaked cap tipped forward with the gesture, so that he had to reach up and straighten it.

'That wouldn't happen to a real driver, you know.' Eli laughed.

Miles Hawthorn grinned at Eli in the driving mirror and touched his temple in a mock salute. He wasn't doing too badly, considering that he normally got ferried around by a chauffeur himself. And yes, Eli was right, chauffeurs' caps did not tip forward unbidden, and it wouldn't happen again. He wouldn't forget the cough either, the harsh, painful sound that hinted at lung problems and explained why a six-foot thirty-year-old was not doing his bit for King and country.

The Essex countryside stretched away on either side. There were more weeds in the roadside verges than in his part of Kent, Eli decided, and the fields were different, the grass dock-infested, the hedgerows somehow thinner. The house, when they reached it, was set well back, approached by a gravelled drive flanked by wide, well-tended flower-beds. The Georgian façade shone red in the setting sun, long shadows stretched from the base of a dozen or more clipped yew trees and made stripes on the immaculate lawn. It was remarkable, Eli thought, as his car slowed to a halt, that the house hadn't been taken over by some ministry or other. It was quite large enough and the position seemed ideal. Perhaps the fact that it was still owner-occupied, and obviously well maintained despite the labour shortages, was proof of the influence of the man who lived in it.

Miles opened the car door with just the required amount of obsequiousness. Eli realized he had to hand it to his boss Sandy. The small team of erstwhile men-about-town was showing flexibility and compatibility. It was bringing out the best in all of them, and as this evening would show, he hoped, they could function, as had been the intention, in areas where a more orthodox approach would never have worked.

'A white dinner jacket – how charming.' Babs Coombes, who had introduced herself as the hostess for the evening, couldn't take her eyes off the empty sleeve that was pinned across Eli's chest. 'I always say a man looks his best in one, it's really Oscar Wilde.' Her voice was high and only just coping with the overdone upper-class accent that she affected.

'I'm not sure about the Oscar Wilde bit.' Eli looked at her over the rim of his champagne glass and raised his own voice to be heard above the social babble around him. 'He had some very funny habits.'

'Oh, we're all quite broad-minded here. After all, down in the country anything goes.' She raised her thin plucked

116

eyebrows, her eyes widening with such an obvious come-on that Eli was surprised by the red glow that suddenly spread up her neck. She actually was aroused – it was the arm, of course. He drank deeply. It made him feel sick – it was just as someone had told him in the hospital, a certain type of woman found a disability sexually stimulating. 'What a lovely room,' he said, looking around, taking in the white panelling, the multitude of oil paintings. He changed his empty glass for a full one. He had to put up with the woman; the reason for his being there at all was to find out what was going on. 'And so many people. I haven't been at a party like this since the war started. How about introducing me around?'

'No, don't go yet.' She put a hand out, hesitantly running a finger down the empty sleeve. 'How did it happen? How did you . . . ?'

'It was a car accident. I was drunk – just as well,' he forced a laugh, 'because it didn't hurt a bit.'

She laughed then too, but uncertainly. Even after three gins she could tell she was on tricky ground. 'I get up to town a bit,' she said. 'I'm not needed here all the time, and I have a little flat. I could give you the address.'

Eli put his empty glass down on a side table. 'I . . .' He'd been ready with the brush-off, but then he realized she was a link, and that was what he was there to establish. 'Make sure you do,' he smiled. 'And now, how about circulating a bit? After all, we don't want tongues to start wagging, or you might not get up to town as much as we'd both like.'

There was a great deal of money in the room. The women wore expensive jewellery and couture perfume; the men flashed gold watches and heavy cufflinks. Before the war, Eli would have identified the gathering as a horsy set – the new-moneyed owners, the camel-coat brigade.

117

Now, the common ground was the pursuit of pleasures that the rest of the country had long abandoned. There were canapés in abundance – pâté de foie gras piled on minuscule slivers of toast, quails' eggs coated in aspic in tiny tartlets garnished with smoked salmon. The champagne was flowing as if France was still just a few hours away – a pleasant sail. The thought almost made Eli's concentration slip. For a moment he was back in the boat, the sea slapping at the clinker-built hull, the tang of salt, the noise of the guns. He felt the sweat break out on his brow. He was holding a glass, and the absurdity of it struck him. He would have to put down the glass to get his handkerchief. He'd been refusing the canapés, convincing himself that he declined to enjoy the food of profiteers, but in reality he had been embarrassed by the physical limitations of the loss of an arm.

'Here, let me.' A woman's hand, beautifully manicured, took the glass from his hand. As he fumbled for a handkerchief to wipe his brow, he turned to look at her. She was in her mid-twenties, tall and slim in an off-the-shoulder tightly fitting plum-red dress. Her dark hair was piled high on her head, and long diamond earrings hung almost to her shoulders. She was like a mannequin, but when she smiled as she spoke, her face came to life. 'I should think it's a bugger, isn't it?'

He laughed, surprised by her profanity.

'You don't look as if you're happy here. Don't you know how lucky we all are – don't you know there's a war on?' The cynicism didn't hide the pleasant resonance in her voice.

'Hard to tell, isn't it?' Eli pushed the handkerchief back into his pocket and reached out for his glass. 'Thanks for the rescue act.'

'Don't mention it. It's about the only useful thing I've

118

done this week.' She turned away from him, surveying the room slowly, clearly looking for someone. 'So what have you done to get included *ce soir*? Sold Peter the key to Granny's wine cellar, or magically pulled a few tons of bacon from your magician's hat? I know,' she turned to face him again; it seemed she hadn't found whoever she'd been looking for, 'you smuggled in the pâté de foie – in a boat. You look like a sailor.' She stood very still, just looking into his eyes for a moment, and then she said, 'You must let me introduce you to my husband. He'll be with Peter, he always is.'

The clamour in the room died suddenly as a red-jacketed flunkey hit a great brass gong. 'Ladies and gentlemen,' he shouted into the expectant silence, 'a few words from your host.' A space cleared at the far end of the room and into it stepped Peter Savage. He matched to perfection the description Eli had been given: the slicked-back black hair, the aquiline nose beneath eyes set slightly too close together. It was a face that could have been seen in any of the gambling halls of Europe – the anonymous gentleman of pleasure. And then he spoke, in a soft, surprisingly warm voice that carried to the furthest corners of the room, and Eli saw the twist of the lip and heard the almost lisp that was the only legacy of the beatings he'd taken as a youngster on the streets of the East End of London. He'd come a long way, all things considered.

Peter Savage welcomed his guests and said he hoped they would enjoy the food and the wine; as they knew, his sole purpose in life was to make the war a little less onerous for his friends. They laughed amicably at that. 'In the time-honoured phrase,' he finished, 'my house is your house.'

All through the speech of welcome a giant of a man

119

stood beside the host. He was white-haired, with great florid cheeks and a nose so small for such a gross face that it was almost a joke. But he didn't seem a laughing matter as he ceaselessly surveyed the gathering, his hard blue eyes probing the corners of the room. They paused on reaching Eli's companion, until she raised her glass in a silent salute, and then they passed on.

There was a general move towards the doors that had been opened to the dining room. 'Are you coming?' She turned to him. 'Simon will want to know who you are before you meet Peter. Simon and Peter, they're quite biblically close, don't you think?' And she made her way ahead of him, through the crowd.

'Wait,' Eli said. 'I don't know your name.'

'You don't?' She turned right round to stare at him, amusement making little lines at the corner of her mouth. 'I must have changed more than I thought. I'm Sylvia.'

'Sylvia Vartan!' Eli hadn't recognized her at first. She was the girl whose face had smiled at him from a hundred glossy magazines.

'Ah, now, who have we here?' Sylvia's husband turned ponderously to look at Eli. 'But of course – it's our new contact from the docks.'

Peter Savage stepped quickly towards them. He didn't always like the way Simon chose to blazen their business about, even if they were among friends. 'Mr Bradbury.' He held out his hand in greeting. 'I hope Sylvia has been looking after you.'

Eli nodded as they shook hands. 'One of the requisites for a good party, isn't it – a famous fashion model. What are the others? A film star, a writer, a couple of politicians.'

'And a sprinkling of whores,' Simon Vartan added.

120

'We have them all here and in our empire. And now, of course, we have a sailor – a wanderer of the dark and dangerous seas.'

'Only an amateur, please,' Eli smiled self-deprecatingly. He had a great urge to smash his fist into the fat face smiling so smugly. 'I don't do anything very dangerous. Just a bit of pottering about.'

'Your pottering, as you put it, gets you into some very interesting places. Interesting for us, that is,' Peter Savage said. He was studying Eli intently. 'You must come across facts that would be very useful, and it seems by your being here with us this evening that you are willing to share that information. So, all we need is your price.'

'I think a few cases of your champagne.' Eli raised the glass in his hand. 'And perhaps the odd tin of foie gras . . .'

'Oh no. Always money. I always pay my informants in money, never in kind, Mr Bradbury. What you choose to do with it is, of course, your business. If you wish to buy my champagne, then all well and good. But I like to deal primarily in cash. It is important to know a man's price.'

The words conveyed evil. Peter Savage worked on the figures a man was prepared to sell his country for – and his soul. Eli realized then that Savage was as clearly an enemy of Britain as the Germans. He was manipulating people on a grand scale; it was no simple case of a spiv who'd hit the jackpot.

Miles had done well. The chauffeurs had gathered at the back of the house and chatted amongst themselves, as they always did. They'd accepted his story of having had TB as a youngster, and laughed with him at how safe he was, like them, in a 'cushy' number until the war was

121

over. He had picked up the name of a top-flight industrialist who had been, up until now, beyond suspicion, and of several lesser figures who could all be pulled in when the time came.

Eli sat back. It was dark and Miles had to concentrate to see his way, with the headlights so covered up as to be almost non-existent. Sylvia Vartan. She'd been the toast of the town. How many years ago? Three, four? Vartan, that was her married name – she must have been married to the odious Simon when she was very young. She could only be twenty-five or so now, and he must be in his fifties. What could have made her choose a creature like that? Even less understandable, what on earth made her stay with him? Eli was tired, but he couldn't sleep. He kept seeing her face, remembering how she'd been the only one who'd known how to handle his disability. What had she said? He smiled as he remembered: 'It must be a bugger.' He reached into his pocket for a cigar, and jammed it between his teeth while he awkwardly lit a match. She was right – it was.

'Eli's asked me to go with him to watch the Free French parade at the Cenotaph next week,' Honour said. She put a mug of tea down on the dressing table for herself and passed the other to Margaret. 'Would you like to come too?'

Margaret sat up and took a tentative sip of the tea – it was too hot to drink. Then she began to try and rub the sleep out of her eyes. She was exhausted. Percy hadn't brought her home until two in the morning, and she had to be at the hospital by eight. 'What day's it on?' She was yawning as she spoke.

'The fourteenth, Bastille Day. He thought it would be nice to turn out. I mean, it must be dreadful for them,

122

not knowing what's happening to their families. That General de Gaulle will be there. Apparently he's terribly impressive. Eli's seen him.'

'I don't know.' Margaret pushed the bedclothes away from her – if she didn't get up right away she'd be late. 'I'll try and fix it. But I'm always swopping duties. That reminds me, are you in tonight?'

'Yes. Sorry.' Honour laughed as she saw the disappointment on Margaret's face.

'That's all right. It's just that I felt like cooking for Perce. Silly, isn't it, how gaga I've gone about him.' Margaret laughed self-consciously. 'But he's much nicer than I ever thought he'd be. On his own he's so kind, and he isn't loud at all.'

'You don't have to justify yourself to me. And you don't have to go without your breakfast, even though you've slept in. There's a roll for you in the kitchen. I've been down to the baker's – even though it was your turn – so don't forget you owe me. I bought a pot of marmalade as we'd finished the last one.' Honour finished fastening the clip at the back of her hair. She had started to wear it pulled away from her face, which she thought made her look older. She checked her uniform in the mirror. She would be driving out of Lord's Cricket Ground, so she could wear her battledress. All her buttons were polished, as were her flat black shoes. She had on a new pair of lisle stockings, and her blue shirt was immaculately ironed. It was a pity she looked so tired, she thought as she looked hard at the mirror. There were black rings under her eyes. 'God, I could do with a lie-in,' she said. She picked her handbag up off the bed and hurried through to the sitting room to get her coat. She shouted goodbye as she closed the door behind her.

As she ran down the stairs for the second time that morning, she thought of Pencombe. Life there was so orderly, so leisurely, and she'd thought that she was busy then. What a sheltered life she'd led.

Honour had to stand on tip-toe to see over the shoulder of the man in front of her. He was standing stiffly to attention; he must be old, because his hair was thin and white, yet he'd stood like a ramrod for half an hour. She knew Margaret would be sorry that she'd missed the sight parading along Whitehall. The Free French forces had brought foreign colours to the grey buildings. Honour made herself as tall as she could; she wanted to see the men from the Foreign Legion. Their hawk-sharp faces were expressionless under steel helmets and they clearly saw nothing unusual in the eccentric addition of a knitted white scarf to their uniforms. There were sailors with red pompoms on their caps; airmen in blue; French tank crews; and a corps of women in khaki tunics and neat forage caps.

Eli's face was drawn and pale and it wasn't just from the pain from his arm. He felt deeply for the French. He had spent so much time in Paris in the years before the war that he suffered with them. He knew he must have lost some of his old friends, men he would never see again – women he would never love. He watched the French girls marching past. They were chic in a way that British women soldiers would never be – but that wasn't him being disloyal. He edged closer to Honour, thinking how beautiful she was in her uniform. He was proud of her. She had been brought up to be a lady of leisure, to marry a man who would support her in style. In volunteering, she had proved herself to be made of so much more than anyone had the right to expect.

Eli felt suddenly that he wanted to cry. He was being maudlin, and he knew it was a wasteful emotion. He fixed his eyes on the General, who was so tall that he was head and shoulders above the troops greeting him with cheer upon cheer. Eli joined in. They all did. When the trumpet call rang out clearly over the noisy crowd, an impressive silence fell. The General placed a laurel wreath at the foot of the Cenotaph, tied with a tricolour ribbon that fluttered gently on the warm breeze. Then he straightened slowly and called out, '*Salut aux morts*!' The tribute to the fallen. When he made his salute, so did the entire gathering, soldiers and sailors, airmen and civilians alike. The troops shouted out, '*Vive la France, vive Général de Gaulle*,' then began marching off.

'We won't be going with them,' Eli whispered in Honour's ear. 'There's someone I want you to meet.'

Honour looked at her uncle in surprise. She had assumed they would follow the procession. It was to march to Grosvenor Gardens, where the General was to place another wreath at the foot of the statue to Marshal Foch. Already a crowd of civilians were pushing their way through the cordon, joining the marchers. They were eager to show their solidarity with the French. It was like a great gesture for freedom.

'Come on.' Eli began to make his way out of the crowd.

They were silent as they walked. All the colour and pomp seemed to Eli to underline the recent pain and suffering. He wondered how many of the men who marched past would live to see Christmas and how many would greet it disabled, as he was.

Honour had changed shifts to have the day off. She wanted to follow the parade, to become a part of it. She was trying to convince herself that Eli wasn't simply planning to take her for a slap-up lunch, the way he used to. If he did, she knew that she was going to be very angry with him.

'Eli!' A man's voice rang out above the noise of the traffic. Honour turned her head. She was red in the face; they were close to the Café Royal, which was obviously their destination, and her temper was about to give way. How could Eli be so trivial?

'Carl.' Eli's face lit with a smile. 'I thought we were going to meet inside.'

'I was watching the Froggies,' the man smiled, showing even white teeth that made his brown face seem even darker. He was dressed in the uniform of the Polish air force, but his English was very good, his accent light with just a foreign intonation. He wasn't very tall, about five foot nine, and he was probably about thirty years old, Honour decided. The brown eyes that appraised her were very continental, and somehow they managed to be both happy and sad at the same time. Honour smiled shyly. He was looking at her with open approval, and to her surprise she found that for once she didn't mind such obvious appreciation.

'Meet your first live Pole,' Eli said. 'At least, I assume it's your first. I've no idea who you've been picking up at those dreadful dances you go to.'

Honour held out her hand. She had a sudden thought that Carl might be going to kiss it, and she blushed. But she was quite safe, he shook it gently, tenderly, and the corners of his lips lifted charmingly. She felt flustered. She had been studying him far too intently, but then he had such funny ears, like a faun's, and his skin was soft, like a girl's. She pulled her hand too quickly from his grip, to cover her embarrassment.

* * *

126

It was dark, and in the light of the dimmed headlights Eli could see the rain falling in torrents. It was impossible for his driver to stop the car outside the Café Royal for more than an instant, so Eli opened the door for himself and hurried across the streaming pavement into the welcoming dryness. The marble-lined foyer was crowded with men and a sprinkling of women – there were a lot of uniforms in evidence. He made his way through the crush, catching sight of an old friend and subconsciously turning his back; he hadn't seen the chap since before the accident. He made his way to the reception booth, to check that there were no messages before going on up. He was looking forward to the evening. The rain meant that Nigel and Neil would probably make it after all – with luck, there shouldn't be any action on such an appalling night.

'Mr Bradbury.' The warm, feminine voice beside him made him turn in surprise. 'Sylvia Vartan, do you remember?'

Of course he remembered. She'd been in his mind ever since they'd met.

'Are you like us? Did you come in to get out of the rain?' She was smiling, her flawless face more beautiful than he had remembered. There was a man with her, in his early thirties, an Army officer with an unpleasant air of superiority. Eli supposed it was because his charming companion had deigned to talk to a civilian.

'I'm involved in a function upstairs.' He couldn't stop looking at her escort. He'd thought about trying to contact her but had convinced himself she'd be the faithful wife. His sleepless nights had been a waste of time – she clearly wasn't the paragon he'd invented.

'I would have suggested you joined us for a drink.' She looked disappointed and Eli smiled cynically. She didn't have to pretend for his benefit. 'I mean, my brother and

127

I . . .' she laughed. 'But how rude of me, I haven't introduced you. This is Bertie, short for Bertram – dreadful for him to be saddled with such an old-fashioned name, isn't it?' She was giggling, hanging on to her brother's arm, obviously adoring him.

Bertram held out a hand. 'Bertie Samuels,' he said and as his face came to life the superiority faded. 'Nice to meet a chum of Sylvie's. She's prattled on about you – gather you're a bit of a sailor?'

He talked on, keeping up the amiable chat of a socially aware new acquaintance as Eli's head was spinning. She'd talked about him!

'She dragged me in here just because it's one of your haunts. Never use it myself, more of a club man.' He looked around. 'I say, I see a chap over there I'm desperate to have a word with. You wouldn't mind if I popped off for a minute?' And he left them, Sylvia flustered like a schoolgirl and Eli with a pounding in his chest that made it hard to speak.

'How did you know . . . ?' He smiled at her, looking at her eyes, her lips, wanting to hold her to him, to breathe in the perfume that was so faint but alluring.

'Peter said you were often here. Oh, please don't let's talk about him. I couldn't bear it.' Her smile had faded and she looked lost, frightened.

'Let's try and get a drink.' Eli reached out, taking her by the elbow, ready to propel her through the crush.

'No, let's not waste the time we have. It's so short . . . Simon has me followed. I think I'm all right just now – because I'm with Bertie they'll leave me alone. Please, please be careful.' She put her hand on his arm.

'How can I see you again?' A crowd was gathering around them. There were several functions on in the rooms above and more guests were arriving; now evening dress outnumbered the uniforms.

'I don't know, I couldn't think how. I hoped you would have a way.'

They were pressed together and he could feel the warmth of her body. She had to tip her head back to look up into his eyes. 'I couldn't meet you anywhere public. I mean, if they knew . . .'

She seemed so pure, in her worldly way so innocent, and yet he was wondering – was this part of their ploy, to ensnare him with the beautiful Sylvia? Was it all just a trick?

'Give me a phone number,' he said. 'I'll think of something.'

'No, no, there's nowhere you could phone. Oh dear.' They could hear Bertie's voice. He was making his way back to them. 'There's no time . . .'

'Here.' He thrust his card at her. 'The Cadogan Gardens address. It's my sister's. Ring tomorrow morning, and leave a time in the afternoon when you can make it.'

She couldn't read the expression on his face. 'I'll have to have Bertie with me,' she said. 'There's no other way I can get out without one of them.'

'Doesn't he have any work to do?' Eli felt the cynicism returning. His lip was curling up. Any minute now he'd see her in her true colours, he thought. She'd kiss him goodbye, give him the 'come-on' and flutter her eyelashes. Perhaps she was nothing more than the tawdry Babs Coombes, whom he hadn't been able to bring himself to follow up.

'He's on leave until Friday. When he's gone, I don't know . . .' She looked down at the card in her hand. 'I'll try, I promise I'll try to come. We have to talk, I have to warn you.' The worry on her face changed quickly to a smile as she turned to greet her brother. 'Bertie, darling, I thought I'd lost you for ever.'

Eli began to climb the stairs and then stopped, using his vantage point to watch her leave. She made her way through the throng with practised ease. They had to talk, she'd said. She had to warn him.

Victoria answered the door herself. She wanted to see Eli's mysterious young woman. She recognized Sylvia instantly, and then she looked at the man with her. Victoria's perfunctory smile of welcome wavered uncertainly. She held her hand out to Sylvia, making herself concentrate on the accepted phrases of welcome. She had never seen such a good-looking young man. He had Sylvia's high cheekbones, the same straight nose, but his hair was fair where hers was dark, he was lightly tanned, and his eyes were such a deep blue. She stepped back into the hallway, ushering them in. For the first time in ages she felt proud of her home, and she hoped he would take in its opulence, the fresh sweet scent of the roses in the silver bowl that were reflected in the hall mirror.

'Do come this way.' She ushered them into the drawing room, eager that he should admire the beauty, the symmetry of the elegant furniture she herself had arranged, the pink slub silk curtains she'd had made just before the war.

Eli was standing by the fireplace. He was waiting for them, his face inscrutable. Victoria could see that he was in a quandary over the girl, and that wasn't like Eli. Neither was it like him to say so directly to Victoria that it would be a good idea if she showed Bertie the library. She turned silently to leave the room, and Bertie followed. In the library they faced each other.

* * *

The moment Carl set eyes on Neil's red Bugatti, he asked if he could drive it. When they told him that Nigel had the same model in green, he laughed. The English were amazing. The fact that the cars had been in the family for twenty years made the whole thing seem funnier than ever to him. Eli sat beside him in the front passenger seat and Neil squeezed in the back beside Honour. Carl glanced up at her in the rear-view mirror. As their eyes met, he shouted, 'Any more for the *Skylark*?' and they were off, heading west towards Bagshot.

Carl kept up an unending stream of talk as he drove uncomfortably fast on the town roads. He began by saying how suitable he thought the name Bagshot was for their day. In the boot of the car were shotguns, travel rugs and a hamper packed with sandwiches and a thermos flask of coffee. It was Eli who'd invited Honour; Carl hadn't mentioned the trip, even though he'd taken her out to the cinema a few evenings before. He'd held her hand during the cinenews. He'd kissed her goodnight outside the flat, a tender, lingering kiss that had made her want to cling to him, but he seemed to be putting on an act, as if he didn't want to reveal his true self, and she was frightened of trusting herself to someone she felt she couldn't understand.

When Carl ran out of talk he began to sing and the other men joined in, singing, 'Run, Rabbit, Run' and roaring with laughter at how apt the song of the moment was. Honour began to wish she'd never said she could come. It was a men's outing – they were going to have a day's fun shooting rabbits and then the glory of bringing back their trophies. She could have spent her day off lying in bed and reading a good book; that was what would have done her the most good. She tried to hide a yawn; she had the beginnings of a cold and wasn't sleeping well.

However hard she tried not to, she kept dreaming about William. Sometimes, the dreams became nightmares and then there were flames eating at Pencombe, devouring everything and everyone she loved.

'Been burning the old midnight oil?' Neil playfully jabbed his elbow into her ribs as he grinned at her. 'Who's the lucky fellow?'

'Neil, darling.' Honour knew she had to play up to her cousin, that the only way to stop him teasing her was to join in with his games. She put on an artificially high voice, squeaking her words. 'Who could I ever love but you?' He roared with laughter, but she caught Carl's eye again in the mirror. She couldn't bring herself to look away. It was as if he was sharing some private joke with her, but she couldn't understand what it was.

Rough pasture dotted with clumps of flowering gorse spread away as far as she could see. They'd parked the car inside a farm gate, on a clear patch of green where they could have the picnic later. Each of the men had their shotgun and a pocketful of cartridges. Eli said the guns had to be returned to his supplier first thing next morning at the latest. Honour felt awkward. The group was clearly splitting up, each of the men going off on his own. Eli saw her unhappy expression and was turning to suggest she should come with him, when Carl spoke. 'I think that, as the driver, I should have Honour's company. Agreed?' He walked off without waiting for anyone's answer. Honour kept her eyes averted from Eli as she followed Carl's slim figure.

At first they walked in silence, then Carl began pointing things out – a patch of rabbit's fur on a gorse bush, a jay that darted from a small stand of birch trees ahead of them. A family of magpies fluttered up from the grass, then hopped to what they considered a safe distance before they began stabbing their beaks down into the sparse grass again. 'One for sorrow, two for joy,' Honour counted them out loud, 'three for a girl, four for a boy, five for silver, six for gold.' She paused in surprise – it was the most she'd ever seen together. 'Seven for a secret never to be told,' she finished.

'So, what is your secret, Honour?' Carl was walking slowly and he kept glancing at her, watching her face.

'A secret wouldn't be a secret if I told you what it was,' she smiled.

Suddenly he took hold of her hand and they walked a little way. He was swinging her arm, almost as if he felt self-conscious. 'You know, you make me feel awkward, Honour,' he said. 'You're so proper, so reserved. Do you ever relax and say what you really feel?'

'No, I suppose I don't. At least, I don't think I've felt relaxed in a long time. There's so much going on, isn't there? I feel that I have to be on my guard. Not against being hurt myself – after all, if a bomb fell on me then I wouldn't know any more about it, would I? But if a bomb fell on my mother, or if one of the boys was shot down and killed – if Nigel doesn't come back – then I'll have to cope with it. I was brought up not to show my feelings; it's an English trait. When my brother died, I was expected to go on as if nothing dreadfully devastating had happened, to carry on with my job, to be the same old Honour. And then there was Daddy – however much everyone said that it was a blessed release . . . I don't know if I'm capable of coping like that ever again. So I can't relax, just in case I'm put to the test.'

'Poor Honour.' Carl put his arm around her shoulder. 'You can rely on me, you know. If you ever need someone to lean on, I'll be around.'

'But that's just it.' Honour stopped suddenly. She was

133

so angry that she forgot to think about what she was saying. 'I have to be on guard for you as well. You're a flier too. I don't know if I'll see you again. The other evening, when we said goodnight, it could have been goodbye.'

'And would it matter to you?'

There was a plover somewhere, crying plaintively, but the humans were too involved in each other to notice the bird.

'Yes.' Honour felt her face was burning. He'd compromised her into being the first to make a commitment. 'Yes, it would matter,' she was almost shouting.

'Then I will take great care of myself.' He took her hand to his lips. His eyes were sparkling and she thought it was with amusement. 'I should never like to hurt a lady.'

'You bastard,' she cried, as she slapped him open-handed across his cheek. How dared he make fun of her.

'Oh, Honour.' He caught her wrist before she could hit him again. 'My beautiful, darling Honour.' He held her close to him and his lips were soft and warm against hers. They parted for a moment, and he said, 'I have loved you from the first moment I saw you,' then he kissed her with all the passion that had been building in him. She put her arms around his neck, pressing herself against his body that she could feel hardening with desire. The sudden crash of a shot, dangerously close, forced thcm apart. Honour was trembling. She felt glowing, every part of her body aware that the man she loved felt the same way about her. Without taking his eyes from hers, Carl raised his own gun into the air and fired twice in quick succession. A loud curse from close by showed that Neil had been much too near to them to fire with safety. 'I love you,' Carl whispered, and then turned and shouted to where Neil's voice had come from.

'This is so nice.' Isabella sat back and let Honour pour the tea. 'It's very good of you two girls to spend some of your precious free time cheering up a silly old lady. Your father must be proud of you, Jill. After all, you're following his tradition – he went off and did his bit in the First World War. Of course, he was the only one of the boys who was old enough. He's been a credit to the family; the best day's work Lucinda's Thomas ever did was to adopt him. Yes, Timmy must be a proud father. I'm sorry, I can see I'm embarrassing you. Rambling on is one of the perils of old age, I'm afraid.'

Jill smiled. There was something about Aunt Isabella that made it impossible to think of her as old, even though she'd changed so much after her husband's death. Her face was gaunt, and the way her clothes hung so loosely on her, it was as if her body was only made up of bones. Jill had written to her parents to tell them all about the aeroplane crashing into the house. It had been a bad time for her to arrive in England, to a family still recovering from the loss of William, and then the accident. 'I can't think of anywhere I'd rather be,' she said. 'I'm still struggling to find my feet over here. The nursing regime is terribly strict and it's difficult to fit in. Life's more than a bit complicated for me at the moment.' Her accent seemed more pronounced in the total Englishness of the setting. Isabella was surprised how like her father Jill was. She was tall and slim, with his reddish hair. Somehow she'd always imagined Jill would be petite like her mother.

They were sitting on deck chairs, the tea tray on a small folding table beside them, and ahead the green lawns sloped towards the river. Above them the high blue sky was patterned with dark swifts darting after insects.

'I have to tell you, Mummy.' Honour stood up to hand round the cups of tea. 'Our visit wasn't simply to cheer you up. There's something else as well. Jill has an idea that we think you could help with.' It was so much easier having Jill's company to visit her mother. Alone, they would have had to talk of her father, and she found even mentioning his name started up the pain again.

'You know quite a bit about first aid, don't you, Aunt Isabella, from your work in the Red Cross, and all that?'

'Yes, I do. Well, at least enough to care for the children when they were young, and everyday medicine in the home. That sort of thing. If you tripped up the garden steps and broke your arm, I expect I could cope with that too – I'd bundle you into the car and drive you straight down to the cottage hospital.' They all laughed.

'I don't mean quite like that.' Jill paused. It was one of the young doctors at the hospital who'd given her the idea. They'd gone out for dinner, and part of his charming attempt to get her into his bed had been to expound his theory on the possible problems for his profession over the next few years. 'I mean, about the old-fashioned remedies. Honour says she remembers you used to give her a cough mixture you got from some old ladies in the village. Something made from poppies, she said.'

'Yes, that's right, but I can't get it any more. One of the sisters died, and the other went off her head. It was a sad little story.' Isabella stared out over the rural idyll that the war hadn't changed one bit. Only behind them, where green tarpaulins covered the worst of the damage, did the reality show. 'John was involved in it . . . I think he was going to marry one of them.'

136

Jill carried on briskly. She didn't want her aunt day-dreaming. 'And my mother said you sent her the recipe for pansy tea when I had eczema as a child.'

'Did it help? I expect it did. However much Michael used to tease me – he would say I was a witch sometimes – the remedies worked more often than not. The old cures can still be the best.'

'It might be that we'll have to rely on them.' Honour put her teacup down. She was eager for something to occupy her mother's mind, for her to feel needed, and this she thought could well be it. 'A doctor friend of Jill's says that anyone with a knowledge of folk medicines is going to be in great demand.'

Jill joined in. 'It's obvious, when you think of it, isn't it? Either we just do without, and let simple aches and pains cure themselves – which they will, nine times out of ten – or we really get involved with things like the tea for the itches, and compresses made from leaves and bark. All that sort of thing. What he wondered was' – this part was a fantasy, but Jill was convinced that whatever work Isabella could do on her project would ultimately come in useful – 'could you write everything you know down? In an organized fashion – the complaint followed by the cure. And with ingredients that are easily available; obviously you can't use lemons or other fruits that can only be imported. But things that grow in the garden and the hedgerows would be fine.'

'I'm not the best person to do this for you girls. There are plenty of others I can introduce you to who know far more than I do. Come to that, I'm sure some of the women's associations are doing this kind of thing already, and even that doctor on the radio is starting to talk about the old cures.'

'But we know that you know what works. That's the

137

important thing.' Honour spoke quickly. 'You can gather up all the things that other people know, and sort out the wheat from the chaff. It's not like an exam,' she smiled. 'It doesn't have to be all your own work.'

'The longer the war goes on,' Jill said, 'the more important this kind of thing is going to be.'

Isabella thought for a moment, and then she said, 'If this is serious, there are some plants that it would be worth growing in bulk. I could set John to splitting up the comfrey, for example.'

'Poor John,' Honour smiled. 'Everything seems to end up being handed on to him.'

'He loves it.' Isabella's voice was firm. 'He's like me, he thrives on work. Idle hands make idle minds. My mother used to say that.'

'You never talk about your mother to me.' Honour had grown to envy Jill her maternal grandmother, who seemed to be a never-ending source of small but exciting food parcels and long, chatty letters.

'Well, I was so young when she died. Just a child. I used to follow her about like a little dog. Lucinda was more independent, but I was younger and she was my whole life. I remember going with her to the infirmary.' Isabella's eyelids drooped. She could hear the tram bell. The rides that had begun by being so exciting ended by being terrifying. Her mother had been fading, each time more tired than the last. 'We were poor then,' she said. 'Not poor in the sense of not having enough to eat – I never remember being hungry – but we always had to go by the tram, when a carriage would have been so much more comfortable, and private. Your grandmother was tremendously brave, Honour. Each time that she went to the hospital she would come away in pain. The examinations distressed her dreadfully, and yet she'd smile at the conductor as she bought our tickets and point out the things that she thought I'd enjoy seeing. She never gave in, until the very end.'

'Did you miss her very much?' Jill asked.

'Yes, and I still do. I suppose I always will. It's strange when someone dies young. They never grow any older, you see, and now I'm much older than she is in my memory. But I still think of her as my mother, someone who would protect and care for me. It's very odd.' Isabella gave her head a shake, trying to clear her thoughts. 'But feelings aren't always rational; that's one fact I'm learning to live with. As time goes on, God willing, I shall become older than Michael ever was, and that will be the same, I expect.' She didn't want to put her hand up to her eyes, but she could feel tears stinging them.

'Do you have any cures for nausea?' Jill asked her question briskly. She hadn't wanted to upset Isabella. 'I don't dare ask anyone at the hospital or they'll decide I'm pregnant – which I'm not,' she laughed. 'But we get up so early in the morning, and often I can't bear to leave my bed in time for breakfast, so I start work on an empty stomach and then by the time I get a chance to grab a bite I'm feeling sick with hunger.'

'Peppermint tea.' Isabella felt revived by the girl's brusque good humour. 'A few dried peppermint leaves in a mug of boiling water. Let it brew for a minute or two, and take it quite strong, otherwise you'll just feel worse. It makes you smell nice too – which is important, with all those handsome young doctors around.'

'Then I shall take some as well.' Honour began gathering the empty cups together on the tray. 'After all, I have all these handsome young officers to consider.'

'Perhaps you should have asked me about love potions,

then.' Isabella didn't think either girl needed to resort to that, but it was fun to be frivolous, once in a while.

'And the opposite. Sometimes it would be more than useful to calm a little ardour,' Honour giggled. She felt that she had made a start in bringing her mother back to life. Now she could look forward to the rest of her leave at Pencombe.

Lizzy's hands were ingrained with mud from the fields and she looked down at them despairingly. They would give Tom's mother something else to turn her nose up at when they met at tea that afternoon. It wasn't much fun now that Tom was always over at Pencombe. Since the accident which killed Lord Montford he seemed to be spending most of his time over there. He was so busy that Lady Montford's daughter, Honour, was driving over to collect her for the afternoon, but at least Tom had said he would manage to take her for a walk later.

Honour took her time driving the well-remembered route. She paused to let a horse-drawn cart across the Yalding bridge. The woman driving it raised her hand in acknowledgement and Honour waved back. It was wonderful to feel that life was going on as usual in the country. Recently living in London had been like being in the front line. There was a raid almost every night and the following morning there was the aftermath. There were crumpled buildings that blocked roads, ruptured water pipes, leaking gas – it was a struggle to keep up a pretence of normal life. The silver barrage balloons that had first seemed such a joke were becoming a symbol of the Londoners' ability to survive.

The little car struggled to climb the hill up out of the village. Honour was driving her mother's old Ford, which didn't use as much petrol as the bigger cars in the garage.

She had the hood folded down and her hair was blowing about her face. She breathed in deeply. There was a scent of woodsmoke from the gardens and the fruit hung heavy in the orchards. She passed a cluster of tents, probably for some of the land girls, and she wondered suddenly if Carl would like the country – her country, the land she loved. He was a strange man, not like any of the other Poles she'd met. But he'd explained that by telling her that his mother was a Norwegian and he spoke such good English because she had been a teacher.

She wondered how she would feel if he didn't ask her out again. Perhaps it had been politeness that had prompted his first invitations; after all, Eli had introduced them, and Carl seemed to like him a lot. That could explain the trips to the cinema, and the couple of dances he'd taken her to. He hadn't talked of love again since their outing to the country. A dispatch rider on a motor bike roared past her and she watched him disappear at speed. Everyone seemed to expect love affairs to be fast like that, because of the war. Carl wasn't pressing her, he hadn't 'tried anything on', as some of the girls put it. Was that because he didn't really care for her? The other evening he'd told her how his parents had met and for a moment she thought he was equating it with their meeting, that perhaps he was trying to say he was serious about her. She twisted her hands on the steering wheel, refusing to admit to herself how important he was becoming to her.

She concentrated on what she could remember of the story of his parents' meeting – it sounded like a Norse legend. A handsome young Polish sea captain sailed his boat on to the still, mirrored waters of a Norwegian fiord. The majestic mountains that loomed up on either side of him were like the setting for a play, and the air was cold and still. Years later, he told his son that he'd felt as if he was dreaming. He managed to reach his destination with the boat sailing silently, as there had been enough air to fill the sails and let him dispense with the engine that he so despised. In the stillness a ramshackle jetty ahead of him floated on its own reflection, a low bow wave ran back from his craft, leaving a silver wake on the water. At the end of the jetty, apparently waiting for him, stood a girl from his dreams – a blonde goddess with hair like gold that cascaded down to her waist. With her were two small children whom she held by the hand – the three of them stood quite still.

The woman was waiting for him. She was the widow of the trader he had expected to meet; her husband had drowned in one of the sudden squalls that could strike the fiord. Carl's father stayed three days loading his boat. On the fourth he sailed, and the woman and the children went with him. The two boys, Olaf and Leopold, were too small to remember their Norwegian beginnings. Carl was born a year later, dark-haired where they were fair. At the outbreak of war, the three boys had been staying in Sweden and they had come to England together. Only Carl was a flier; his brothers had gone to sea with the Merchant Navy.

Honour took the right-hand turn towards the farm cottages. When Carl told her the story, she had been able to picture the mountains and almost feel the chill of the water. She couldn't understand a woman who would leave the land she had been born in so easily. She slowed to a stop. Laburnum Cottage – this was where Lizzy was staying. What if the war was to end tomorrow and Poland was free again? What would she do if Carl asked her to go there with him?

She slammed the car door unnecessarily hard. He didn't

feel that way about her, she was just a bit of fun for him. She walked up the front path to the cottage and rapped her knuckles on the door, thinking that Lizzy didn't know how lucky she was.

'All the family will be there this afternoon?' Lizzy's voice rose in panic. 'I thought it was just an ordinary Sunday.'

'I'm afraid we don't seem to have ordinary Sundays any more.' Honour kept her eyes on the road ahead of her.

Lizzy stared again at her hands. Honour's were white and smooth as they gripped the steering wheel. 'What kind of handcream do you use?' she asked.

'Handcream?' They had reached the outskirts of Pencombe and Honour slowed for an old black dog lying in the middle of the road. She waited as it got slowly to its feet and limped towards the verge. 'I use Nivea usually, or sometimes, if I'm feeling extravagant, there's a beautiful rose-scented one that comes from a chemist in Tunbridge Wells – I can't remember what it's called. Why do you want to know?' She turned to look at Lizzy. They had never relaxed together and talked as friends. Honour didn't know what Lizzy was like, what made Tom so mad about her.

'Because my hands are in a dreadful state.' Lizzy held them out in front of her. 'The mud's got under my nails and sunk right into my skin. Look, they're like a navvy's. And your aunt.' She paused. It wasn't right to run down Honour's family. Fortunately Honour understood what she meant.

'Aunt Lucinda is a tartar,' she said. 'It's quite all right, everyone thinks that. You're very polite not to say it. Are you really worried about how your hands look?'

Lizzy nodded.

143

'Then we'll go in the back way. We'll sort them out before you meet anyone.'

Lizzy was worried about steeping her hands in the lemon juice, but Honour convinced her that it would be all right, and it only stung on a scratch on her thumb. Honour hoped her mother would appreciate the necessity for using several tablespoons of the precious bottled lemon juice that Bill had brought them as a present. Lizzy held her hands under the running tap until the sharp smell had washed off and her hands were ice-cold. There was a jar of soft goose fat in the larder, and Honour told her to rub a little of that into her skin, which was now white but very dry. The fat disappeared quickly, leaving a smell like roasting potatoes. 'Final touch,' Honour said as she produced an almost empty bottle of orange-flower water. 'Makes brilliant cakes, and sweet-smelling ladies,' she laughed. The hours that she'd spent in the kitchen with Cook hadn't been entirely wasted.

Lizzy was so amazed at her rescuer's ingenuity that she forgot to keep up her exhausting act of over-refinement. As Honour put the bottles back in the larder, she decided to tell Tom to get a move on and declare his intentions; Lizzy was a naturally nice girl.

'Thank you.' Lizzy held one of her newly restored hands out to Honour. 'That was really kind of you. I shan't feel half so bad at meeting them now.'

'You mustn't feel bad at all. Tom is having the time of his life showing you off. He's never had a steady girl-friend before – has he told you that?'

Lizzy shook her head.

'Well, I think the world of him, so I consider you jolly lucky. I'd love to have someone wonderful who got a thrill out of introducing me to his family.'

'Don't you have a boyfriend, then?' Lizzy asked. She'd

have thought a girl as pretty as Honour would have the pick of the bunch.

'There is someone.' Honour started to walk towards the drawing room. She didn't want to have time to investigate her feelings about Carl. 'But I don't know if I'm all that special to him.'

As they walked through the hall the telephone rang and Honour picked it up. Almost before she'd finished saying the number, Carl was telling her how he'd been confined to his base for some minor misdemeanour. He wanted to know how she was, what she'd been doing and, most of all, if she'd missed him. He loved her, he said, more with every day.

'You know, it's only when I manage to spend a few days down here that I realize how cooped up we all are in town.' Honour flung her arms out wide and breathed in the cool, calm air of the great hall. 'It's decadent, isn't it, for one family to be able to enjoy all this. Decadently delightful,' she laughed with pleasure. She was wearing a short white tennis dress and it felt so fresh, so summery compared to her uniform. There was no trace of the damage in this part of the house, and for a little while it was as if nothing unpleasant had ever happened there.

'First up against the wall after the war, that'll be the fate for all you aristos, then the brave new world will be divided in equal shares all round.' Eli turned the tennis racket over, pointing the handle at Honour like a gun.

'I surrender, I surrender,' she giggled. 'And anyway, the tourists will be back with a vengeance then, and we'll all be squashed into a couple of rooms making up sandwiches for the tea rooms.' It was wonderful to feel so free. She was safe in Carl's love, secure in her dreams for the future.

The tennis court was screened by a high yew hedge. They approached it arm in arm, Honour carrying both rackets – as Eli had said, his status as a one-armed hero gave him some privileges.

'So, are you going to bring your mysterious ladylove to the tennis party next weekend?' Honour asked.

'Mysterious ladylove? I don't know what you're talking about. I'll be bringing the Pimm's, at great personal sacrifice to myself, but nothing else. I shall expect you to provide me with a suitably luscious partner for the mixed doubles.'

'Viccy's told me all about her.'

'Well, if there was a such a thing as a mysterious lady in my life, I would say that Viccy was definitely out of line for telling tales out of school. But as there isn't . . .'

'Oh, go on, Eli. You know I won't tell another soul. You can tell me about her. What's her name, where's she from? Is she someone you've met through your work . . . ?'

'Quite the little detective, aren't we? Come on, last one on the court's a cissy.' He started to run, grinning back over his shoulder at her. He had no intention of talking about Sylvia.

He rounded the corner of the hedge and stopped still. 'My God,' he said. And then he began to laugh, great howls that had him struggling for breath. There were geese inside the tennis netting, dozens of them. There were piles of dried droppings in the corners, fresh steaming green lumps obliterating the white lines.

'What on earth . . .' Honour couldn't believe it. The smell was horrid. She put her hands up to the wire as she

146

stared in disbelief. Half a dozen birds ran towards her, flapping their wings wildly. 'Go away!' she shouted, waving the rackets at them as they burst into a raucous chorus of abuse. 'Mummy must know about this . . . how could she have let it happen?' She was upset. Upset and cross at the same time. She loved tennis, it was the one game she was good at and she'd played a lot before the war. The court would never recover and it would be impossible to have the party next week. The whole place was going to rack and ruin now that her mother seemed too tired to cope.

'You can take this as your extra bit of war effort, old thing.' Eli was still bent double with laughter. Honour's dismay had been funny in itself. And after all, what was a game of tennis against a goose dinner? 'Rest assured, my sweet, after Christmas these fellows will be just a memory and you'll be able to play as much as you want.'

'God, you're soulless, Eli. When we get back to the house I shall insist that these putrid birds are taken out of here.'

'Insist – you're going to insist to your mother? I think you're on a sticky wicket there. Of course . . .' He paused. He too had been looking forward to the tennis party. Isabella could be getting carried away with all this sacrifice-for-the-good-of-the-country bit. She was listening too much to the rector. Once she'd told him what to do, but since Michael's death she seemed to think that his was the voice of her conscience. 'If the birds were to sort of wander off, on their own accord . . .'

'Wander off? I don't think we should let them out. I mean, for a start they'd create absolute havoc in the garden.'

'No, not just let them out to go where they want. You can herd geese, you know. What we need is somewhere

147

convenient to put them, somewhere . . .' Eli's eyes brightened with inspiration.

Isabella wasn't at the house when they returned. Instead there was a note saying that she would be home after tea. She had taken the train to London. It had been bothering her that she should write a new will and now, while Eli and Honour were at the house, it seemed an ideal time to attend to it. Her solicitor was very kind, an old friend. They met at his house, and over a light lunch drafted the new will taking into account the fact that Isabella had inherited all Michael had to leave. She got back in the early evening. The train journey had been overcrowded and slow, but she'd talked to a very nice man who was some kind of journalist and had a fascinating theory about the mental attitude of the German people. He was convinced that, unlike the British, they did not want to know as much as possible about the progress of the war. They enjoyed, he said, only being given a limited, strictly edited view of events. It made Isabella feel that every British man, woman and child avid for news was fighting for freedom, whereas only a handful of the enemy was truly committed and the others were just following them like sheep. She found that very reassuring.

They were having supper when the rector arrived. Eli was tentatively biting into a remarkably untasty mock sausage as he contemplated another verbal attack on Isabella's self-inflicted purgatory.

'Your Ladyship!' The Reverend Arnold Smith burst into the dining room unannounced. His entry was so unexpected that Isabella had no time to consider her new relationship with the man of God.

She laid her fork slowly down on her plate. In an icy calm she lifted her napkin to her lips and then turned in

148

her seat to survey her visitor. 'Calm yourself, rector,' she said icily. 'Are you aware of the state you are in? There is a mess – that seems to me to consist of feathers – all over your trouser legs, and there is,' she breathed in, sniffing the air loudly, 'there is something extremely unpleasant on the soles of your shoes. Please take them off and put them outside the door, at once.'

'The geese, the geese, your Ladyship . . .' the rector croaked. He had run all the way from the church.

Eli wiped his eyes with his napkin. He was close to choking on his laughter – he hadn't felt so good in ages.

Isabella looked slowly at each of them in turn. Her daughter was sitting so upright, her eyes so bright, her cheeks so pink, that she obviously knew exactly what was going on. Eli was looking better than he had since Dunkirk and had quite recovered his old devilment.

'Where are they?' she asked, and then, before the rector could answer, a discomforting thought struck her. 'They're not in the church, are they?' She would like, very much, to believe that Honour had not gone that far.

'In the vestry. They are, they are . . .' But he couldn't bring himself to say what the geese were doing all over his beautiful black and white tiled vestry floor.

'I have no idea how they got there.' Isabella stood slowly, majestically. 'But you will remember that I asked you to have the birds removed from the tennis court. When I said that you could keep them on the estate if you found a suitable place, I did not mean in there. For one thing, it is much too close to the house, and if they escaped they would wreak utter chaos in the vegetable garden. Come to that, I hope for everyone's sake that they have not touched so much as one spring onion.'

Honour bent her head towards her plate. If she even

149

smiled she was lost. It was hysterical, the funniest thing that had happened in ages.

'You can have no idea how near I was to laughing myself.' Isabella held her glass out towards Eli for a small brandy. She thought she deserved it after calming the odiferous rector. 'Mind you, if you'd put them in the church itself . . .'

'Oh no, we would never have done that, Mummy.' Honour didn't even glance at Eli. She'd had to argue at length to prevent him getting his way over that.

Isabella leaned back comfortably in her chair. It was so nice being home. Now that she had dealt with the solicitor, she felt it was time to begin living again. 'It was quite a good idea of his, really. The villagers are plagued by foxes. Putting all their geese together in one safe place makes sense. Mind you, I gather there was the most frightful rumpus when they first mixed them up. Apparently they were fighting and squabbling, hissing and spitting.'

'Just like people,' Eli said.

'Yes.' Isabella put her glass down beside her on a leather-topped wine table. 'The human race is no better than those geese, fighting because it can't bear to share its territory.'

'You don't mean that countries like Poland should have sat back and let themselves be invaded, that it shouldn't fight now for its freedom?' Honour looked at her mother in disbelief.

'No, no I don't mean it like that, darling. But if you look at this world of ours, it's a finite thing, isn't it? There is a fixed amount of land, a regulated amount of sea. There's more than enough space and food for everyone but it's human nature not to want to share. Everyone wants their own territory, and then there are the evil people who want even more.'

Eli topped up his glass. 'Careful, Isabella,' he said. 'You'll be turning communist next.'

'I shan't be doing anything of the sort. But I am beginning to look at things rather differently. I don't think anyone has struck the proper balance yet. It's a tremendous challenge for the future, and perhaps, when the war is over Churchill will be just the man to face up to it.'

'Daddy believed it was possible to wipe out poverty, by giving the poor people more of an opportunity in life.'

It was the first time Honour had talked of her father without stiffening, and Isabella felt that time was indeed beginning to heal them all. She smiled as she spoke. 'He also believed that it was the duty of the able to support those who couldn't support themselves. Opportunity isn't always enough, sometimes it has to be straightforward help – clothing, housing, food.'

'All right, Isabella.' Eli smiled fondly at his half-sister. 'You've put the world to rights, now can we get down to planning our tennis party?'

'Oh, I'm so sorry, I forgot to tell you I've had to postpone it. I can't tell you how many have had to drop out. There's Albert and Maggy and Tom and lots more. I've arranged to go up to Cadogan Gardens with Lucinda for that weekend. I have some papers to sign, and it would be nice to give Victoria some company.'

'We might as well have left the damn geese where they were.' Honour stood up quickly. She had invited Carl to be her doubles partner for the weekend. It would have been an ideal time for him to meet the family. 'I'm going up to bed and please don't wake me in the morning. I could do with a lie-in.' She slammed the door as she left and Eli settled down to tell Isabella all about Carl.

* * *

'I'm so sorry, Victoria.' Isabella held her niece close to her. She couldn't think what to say to lessen the impact of Lucinda's words.

'How could she?' Victoria sobbed. 'How could my mother bring herself to say such things? She must hate me. I never knew, I never understood . . .'

'You mustn't believe what your mother said, Viccy. She's distraught. It's not you she hates, it's herself. She feels trapped. She thought coming here to London would be an escape for her, but it's not, it's only forced the reality of the war on her. Think of all the travelling she used to do – Paris, Rome – she had friends all over the continent. I think she was happier with them than she ever was at home.'

Victoria stepped away from her aunt and turned to face the gilt-framed overmantel mirror. Her reflection made her grimace; her tears had played havoc with her make-up. 'You mean she's worried about those friends? Scared about what might have happened to them? Oh God, this bloody, bloody war.' She dabbed at her eyes, which were smudged with black, then despairingly she turned back to Isabella. 'I thought coming to stay with me would help Mummy.'

'She's scared, Victoria. She's frightened of the bombings, frightened of dying, or worse still, possibly, she's terrified of being injured, being left a cripple. And your mother has hated growing older. It isn't only the war that's trapping her, it's her own body.'

'Well, if only she'd lose some weight. I've tried . . .'

'No, it's not her size that's slowing her, Viccy, it's just time. I feel it too. I'm a couple of years younger than your mother and I've always been active, but recently everything's been so much more of an effort, and then, after Michael . . .' Isabella's voice drifted away and she

152

looked suddenly lost and alone. Victoria felt herself stiffen. She found grief such an awful, embarrassing emotion. Then Isabella smiled as she remembered Michael young again. They'd had so many years, so much precious time together. 'I'm not frightened of death any more, Viccy,' she said. 'I was for a while – I kept worrying about what might happen to Michael if he was left alone. But now he's safe.'

'Safe in the arms of God.' Victoria said the words softly. It was what Colin would have said, if he'd been with them.

'I don't know – it would be nice to believe that, wouldn't it? I used to find it all so comforting, but I don't believe in God any more. I think death will be just like sleeping. An endless dark, no noise, no sensation, nothing. Sometimes I should just like to slip into it, into the silent dark. I'm sorry, Viccy, it's all this business with my will – it makes death a natural subject. I won't talk about it any more.'

Victoria shivered. She folded her arms, holding them tightly against her body as she walked slowly to the window. The thick net curtains shone a bright cream from the sun. It would be warm outside but the drawing room was chill. Did Colin really believe in God? She thought of him more now that he had gone away than she had ever done when he was close at hand. The newsreels showed the troops in action; there was a great rushing, a clamour, and then inevitably death. Would Colin find strength in his God? 'Do you think Luke ever really loved Mummy, the way she said?' she asked.

'It was all so long ago.' Isabella had to struggle to pull her thoughts together. It was so much easier to let them drift and start reliving times that she and Michael had shared. 'But Luke scarcely knew your mother when she

153

was young. I suppose he may have admired her from afar. She wasn't like other girls, she was wilful and reckless. To someone who didn't know her it must have been very attractive. But your mother went to – ' Isabella stopped. She didn't know how much of the past Victoria had been told. Lucinda had gone to live with Thomas, and before they married they had been as man and wife. Their first child had been conceived out of wedlock. Luke had met her when she already belonged to another man, and that was when, according to Lucinda's hysterical outburst, he had fallen in love with her.

'Mummy said Luke adored her, and always has. That he would never have married me if she had been free. Is that true?' Victoria's voice had risen.

'No, I don't think that's true.'

Isabella's vagueness made Victoria want to grab her by the shoulders, to shake her. 'But what is the truth? Did they have an affair? Oh, my God.' She slumped down suddenly into a chair. 'Is that the truth? After Luke and I were married they had an affair, and now she thinks he's going to let it all out. Now that he can't control what he says she's terrified he'll expose their nasty, sordid secret.' She buried her head in her hands.

'No, no, there was never anything like that, my dear.' Isabella's mind was clear at last. 'Your mother was a pretty girl, beautiful, I suppose you would say, and full of fire. She was always the centre of attention. She expected men to fall at her feet and they did. Luke will have been just like the others, captivated for an instant, but it didn't last. The sad thing about her was that she always wanted the impossible. Michael wouldn't bend to her will, and there were other young men before that who courted her, flirted with her, you would say today, but in the end they all drifted away. She always had a fine temper.' Isabella laughed suddenly.

154

'You can have no idea what a temper she had. No, don't look at me like that, Viccy, I can promise you that anything you've seen, even this morning's outburst, is nothing, nothing at all compared to how she used to be – until she met your father. There, you see, that proves me wrong in saying they all left her. One man did love her enough to tame her. And that's just what he did; he stopped her tantrums and changed her so that for a long time she seemed placid, at peace with her world. It's only old age that has stirred up the last dregs of her temper, and I can promise you she is nothing like as effective as she used to be.'

Victoria stared in disbelief.

'But, my poor Viccy, she said silly, hurtful things to you. Can't you see that they were all a fabrication? Your mother hates being old and withered, and I expect she imagined London would bring her youth back to her. Instead, it's been frightening and possibly even more than that, it's been an awful disappointment for her. You'll have to be magnanimous and forgive her. She'll feel embarrassed, and so she should, because she made a fool of herself. You have Luke, you always had. She should have remarried. Having a man about would have taken her mind off herself. In fact, I think that's what we should do – look for a suitable match for your mother. Come on, Viccy, there's a challenge. There must be someone, somewhere, willing to take her on.' Isabella was laughing as she spoke, determined to cheer her niece up. What Lucinda had said was unforgivable, and there had been enough of the truth in her words to undermine Victoria at the very time she needed all the help she could get just to cope with everyday life.

Eli spun the wheel and the boat responded instantly, bucking through the churning wake of the frigate. The

155

Bunty was in her element, handling the waves like a thoroughbred. There wasn't far to go. The journey had been uneventful but not uninteresting. The traffic on the river had told a dozen different stories. There were small boats still boasting the damage they had received at Dunkirk. It made him proud of how quickly he'd managed to have his own vessel put to rights. There were naval vessels, like the one whose wake he was still steering into, which was making at speed for the open waters of the Channel. God only knew if it would return.

It was good to be alone on the water. It was a grey day but beautiful. The water's steely glint reflected a painter's sky that was coloured with all the shades of a pigeon's wing. Eli tipped his cap back on his head in a subconscious gesture of pleasure. The engines throbbed beneath his feet, the deep throaty voice of the twin diesels reassuring him of their dependability. His boss was delighted at how things were going; Eli wasn't the only one in their group who had managed to penetrate one of the circles of crime that were feeding off London's society. He felt he was on an adventure. The seediness of the backstreet deals irritated him, however essential he knew they were as part of Savage's plan for his indoctrination. But this, hurrying through the choppy river water, making for a destination where there could well be danger, gave him a thrill of pure pleasure. It was almost better than being with Sylvia.

He spun the wheel again, taking himself back on to a course parallel with the shore. The riverside development was growing sparse, and now there were only a few dilapidated jetties and a sprinkling of wooden huts. He wondered what would happen to the area after the war. He had a chum whose great ambition was to buy up as much river frontage as he could. He was convinced that the returning warriors would want to spend their leisure hours messing about on the water. Mile after mile of veranda-fronted weekend cottages spread along the banks in his imagination. Eli put his head out of the open hatch beside him. He breathed in the oily smell of the working river and scanned the grey mud banks revealed by the waning tide. He doubted his pal's vision of an extended Henley; somehow he thought that those who'd been to war would have other priorities.

This must be his rendezvous point. He checked the chart again, following the bend of the river, the huddle of buildings. A jumble of pylons stuck up out of the water and a small launch was tied up to one of them. He slowed the engines and the sound of them dropped as they idled.

'Ahoy!' he shouted.

A large man in black oilskins appeared instantly, gave a brief wave and then stood waiting, motionless, as Eli manoeuvred alongside.

'Simon!' Eli recognized the man as soon as he took off his sou'wester.

'You sound surprised to see me.'

'I wouldn't have thought that you involved yourself at this end of the business.'

'I'm involved in everything, Eli. That's my speciality, what makes me irreplaceable. I see and know everything.' His blue eyes were disconcertingly devoid of emotion.

'Then you'll know where you want me to put these.' He gestured to the stacked-up boxes behind him. They contained an assortment of canned meats.

'Don't unload. There's been a change of plan.'

'Don't unload? But I have to. I told Peter I couldn't hang on to this stuff for long.'

'You don't tell Peter anything, nobody does. Not even me. You're to take that stuff back. You'll be contacted.'

157

Eli leaned on the transom. He could feel that there was danger. Not just the risk of being found out, and the consequent blowing of his cover, but danger from the man Simon. How much did he know about Sylvia?

'We'll leave a message for you at Cadogan Gardens. You use that address, don't you?'

Eli nodded. All Sylvia's fears must have been true and she had been followed. God help her, her husband would be a bad man to cross.

Lucinda laid her cup down. She accomplished the action in an icy silence; not even the chink of china was to be allowed to lessen the awesome hush. Lizzy chewed nervously at the corner of her lip. She was perched on the edge of her chair. The house at Reason Hill had never seemed daunting before, but suddenly, with Lucinda's presence, it was forbidding. The low windows had frowned at her as she walked up the drive, the creak of the oaken front door as it opened had been one of disapproval.

Even Tom seemed changed. There were just the three of them in the house, and he was sitting stiffly, obviously ill at ease. He was wearing grey trousers and a blazer. His shirt was very white and the dark-coloured tie he wore had some kind of crest on it. It was a cricket club tie, he'd said in answer to her query. She understood from his awkwardness that it had been too personal a question for her to ask in front of his mother. If she didn't stop biting at her lip it would bleed. The old woman was horrid; she was white and swollen and she moved slowly, like a slug. Lizzy almost found herself looking for a silvery trail, like the ones the silent invaders of her bedroom left on the wallpaper every night.

Tom offered his mother a jam tart. They were beautifully made, the pastry short and light, and they were generously filled with raspberry jam. He knew she must be desperate to eat one, but she held her hand up – an immaculate white manicured creation – to fend off the offending treat. It had been a mistake to say that Lizzy had made them, and a bigger mistake to remind his mother that the jam had been made at Pencombe, from fruit that he and Lizzy had picked together earlier in the year. He could imagine how his mother would have heard it, and how she would have put it together with the fact that Tom was living on his own at Reason Hill, while Lizzy lodged a few hundred yards away. He knew it was up to him to break the silence, as neither of the women would.

'I've found Aunt Isabella a very useful housekeeper,' he said.

'A housekeeper? For Pencombe?' Lucinda's voice was very sharp, her accent acute. It made her lips purse and a hundred tiny lines radiate outwards from their artificially pink source. 'I wouldn't have thought she'd want any more staff – you know what a show she's making of giving up everything for the war.'

'Well, perhaps she sees taking this woman on as a kind of war effort. It's a relative of Jenny's – you remember her, don't you, Mother? Luke's sister. She still lives in one of the tied cottages.' He smiled at Lizzy, trying to cheer her up. She looked nervous, a mouse in the den of the cat. His mother was being a scratchy old moggy today. It didn't lessen his love for her, or change it; he understood her moods, probably better than she did herself.

'Jenny?' Lizzy forced herself to speak. She wasn't going to let herself be shut up for ever. 'Do you mean Jenny

Jones? She lives just along from us. She's really nice, tells all sorts of stories of the old days.'

Lucinda stiffened. 'Of the old days.' Her voice was tremulous. 'And just what kind of stories does she tell?'

'Oh, about how the farming was here, when the traction engines were new. How old Thomas – I'm sorry, I mean how Mr Cade upset all the locals to start with, and then how he took over all the small farms about. He must have been a very clever man.' She tried a tentative smile at Lucinda.

'He was.' Lucinda's eyes narrowed; she wasn't going to be taken in by a chit of a girl pretending to admire her dear Thomas's memory. 'But I doubt if Jenny Jones could ever appreciate *how* clever. After all . . .' She wanted to say that the woman was a nobody, but of course her brother had married Lucinda's only daughter. In a very distant way she was family. 'She's very old now.'

'She's about an age with you, Mother.' Tom relaxed a little. His mother was not at her best, she was allowing him to score the occasional point.

'Won't you have a tart?' Lizzy stood up, smoothing down her skirt before holding the plate out once again. 'It's such a treat to have jam these days. Actually,' she blushed a little, 'it's a treat for me to have jam at any time. What with all my little brothers and sisters.'

Tom felt himself swell with pride. Lizzy wouldn't be bested by his mother. She was a rare woman and it was fate that had brought them together.

'You come from a large family, do you?' Lucinda's fingers closed around a jam tart as with a great surge of relief she felt she might have discovered a valid reason for disliking the interloper. 'Roman Catholics, are you?'

'No, we're Church of England. Why, are you a Catholic, then?' Lizzy looked guilelessly at her inquisitor.

160

'Have some more tea, Mother.' Tom stood up to cover his amusement. Lizzy was doing well.

Lucinda licked a morsel of jam that had strayed to the corner of her mouth. Tom and the girl were both standing up and moving around to serve her, but she wasn't taken in by them. They were having an affair – it was as plain as could be. The girl was a gold-digger. The lure of such a beautiful house – she looked around her, admiring the solid, well-polished furniture, the mellow chintz covers that she had never allowed to be changed since Thomas was killed. That was twenty years ago. Her eyes shone with unshed tears. She had been a faithful widow – there were a few memories that she hastily submerged, of stolen hours of pleasure in the arms of an Italian count, a sophisticated dalliance with a French gentleman of great distinction, the owner of a famous vineyard. And yet, Lucinda sighed, the men who had loved her had never been free. Her life had been one continual tragedy, and now this. 'I shall be coming back to live here,' she said.

'What on earth for?' The question burst from Tom before he had time to stop it, but he knew very well why his mother was coming back to Reason Hill.

'Because it is my home.' And not yours, she added in her head as she glared challengingly at Lizzy.

Tom stayed silent. There were so many things he wanted to say. His mother had not lived with him for years – she had preferred Pencombe. At first she had lived in a wing of the big house, self-contained from the main apartments. Then, when Michael had taken to bed, she had moved in with Isabella. Her return to Reason Hill would not be permanent – she would stay for long enough to see Lizzy off, and then she would go again. Leaving Tom on his own, more alone than he had ever been now that he had discovered what love was.

161

'It would be useful if you did, Mother,' Tom said slowly. He wanted his mother to understand, very clearly, what he was saying.

'Useful? But that's a strange word, Tom. I would have thought you might say how pleased you would be to have me share the danger with you.'

'I am certainly impressed that you are prepared to come back, although I'm not so sure myself that I agree that it's dangerous here. I know we're exposed, but there's no reason why we should be seen as a target. No, I said that it would be useful because I have been considering how convenient it would be for me to be based permanently at Pencombe.' He didn't look at Lizzy, not wanting to see the hurt he hoped would be in her eyes. But she was quick, she would grasp what he was up to soon enough. 'Now that you are coming back, it has removed the only obstacle that prevented me. I didn't want to leave the house unoccupied.'

'To Pencombe? You would be going to Pencombe? But you couldn't expect me to stay here on my own. How callous that would be to leave me, how unfeeling.'

'But I wouldn't leave you on your own, Mother. Lizzy could move in, along with her two friends. Obviously it wouldn't have been right for them to stay in the house with me, but four women on their own, there's nothing unusual in that these days. Yes, you've taken a big weight off my shoulders, Mother. I'll phone the factor at Pencombe right away.'

'Wait!' Lucinda's voice was close to a scream.

'Yes?' Tom stood, towering above her. He was sorry to have upset her. Her cheeks were quivering, her lips working furiously as she talked soundlessly to herself.

'I wanted us to be together,' she whispered.

It would have lasted less than a day before she was

162

shouting at him, trying to change his ways, finding fault with everything he did. 'I know you did, Mother,' he lied kindly. 'But everything's difficult at the moment and we can't always have what we want.'

Lizzy held out the plate of tarts again and absent-mindedly Lucinda took one. 'I prefer strawberry jam,' she said, her temper flaring petulantly.

'If I'm here next year at strawberry time, and I can get hold of enough sugar, I'll make you some specially,' Lizzy said. She didn't feel nervous any more; she was so happy inside that she wanted to jump and shout. Tom was wonderful – he was strong and kind and he was managing his silly old mother beautifully. For a few moments she had thought that he meant it, that he was going to Pencombe for good, away from her. But she understood now, and she had never been happier.

Lucinda woke late. It was very quiet in Honour's flat. She sat up slowly. Her eyes were misty with sleep and she reached out blindly to the bedside table to feel for her glasses. Once she had put them on, the room came into focus. Her watch was on the dressing table, which was against the far wall, and there was no bedside clock. Honour must have taken it through to put beside the settee, where she had slept. Lucinda wriggled irritably. She would have to get up to find out the time. She yawned, pulling the thin blankets closer to her chin. What a miserable room, she thought. The slope of the roof made it feel horribly cramped, and there was only space for the narrowest of wardrobes, so Lucinda knew her dresses would be creased, however much room Honour had made for her. She yawned again. Last night she had almost regretted her impulse to invite herself to stay with Honour. But now that Margaret had moved out of the flat

163

there was no reason why Lucinda shouldn't use it as often as she liked. It was a pity in a way that the girl had taken her bed with her, but at least it meant that she had a bedroom to herself. There was an empty day stretching ahead of her. Victoria was at Pencombe for a few days' quiet and she didn't like going to Cadogan Gardens when her daughter wasn't there. Luke's slow, protracted dying seemed to chill the house and it was already like a morgue.

There was nobody worth considering left in London, only Johnnie's widow and her daughter, Bella. Adele was most boringly involved in good works but the girl had more possibilities. She would no doubt be involved with her own, younger interests – or would she? Lucinda carefully peeled off the soft white cotton gloves that she had worn to bed; the handcream would be quite absorbed by now. Perhaps she would try to contact Bella.

There were two eggs in the food cupboard. Lucinda smiled. She would show that she could be domesticated when she tried. Honour had said she would be back just after five and Bella was coming at four. She would prepare a really special tea for four-thirty, so that Honour could join in on the end of it. She opened the cream and green tin labelled 'flour'. There was a small bag inside, and tucked down beside it a thin recipe book. That was quite a relief. She was almost sure she could remember a recipe for cake but it would be better to be safe than sorry. '"McDougall's Cookery Book",' she read out loud, '"price sixpence". Jolly good. Now, what can I find?' She started to turn the pages. There was a recipe for madeleines – she adored them, but it was essential to be able to decorate them correctly. They needed coconut, cherries, angelica and, of course, some apricot jam. She

164

didn't think Honour's store cupboard would stretch that far. Lucinda kept turning the pages. Raisin cake, marmalade cake – wasn't there anything she could make other than a victoria sponge? She put the book down irritably. There was a loaf of bread and a small tin of salmon; she would make sandwiches, using only a smear of the small piece of butter she'd found. She wanted to add the rest to the lump of margarine – whatever she baked would taste better that way. But she did want to bake something memorable. She remembered suddenly that she had some chocolate in her handbag. It was one of the bars that Eli had brought down. She'd been going to eat it square by square in the privacy of her bedroom, when the strain of the bed-sitter existence got too much. She sighed loudly. She would give it up in a good cause.

The chocolate sandwich recipe took two eggs weighed in their shells, with equal amounts of the butter and margarine mixture, sugar and self-raising flour. Lucinda broke the four-ounce bar of chocolate into pieces. Fortunately the recipe only needed three ounces. She hummed happily as she worked, chewing the remaining ounce. A few drops of vanilla essence and two tablespoonfuls of milk were the only other things she used. She had put on a small flowered apron that she'd found hanging on a hook beside the miniature stove. She was actually enjoying herself, she realized. It was like playing at being a housewife. The sink was tiny and the chipped enamel bowl in it diminutive. There were so few dishes in the sideboard that it was a challenge working out how she could lay a pretty tea tray.

She dissolved the chocolate in the milk. The gas pressure was very erratic and she had to concentrate quite hard. One minute it was trying to boil over and the next there was hardly any heat at all. There was no greaseproof paper, so as the chocolate mixture cooled she smeared the last of the margarine around an oval-shaped pie dish – there was no cake tin. Her arm began to ache very quickly as she started creaming the fat and sugar together, but she persevered, still humming to herself. It took quite a while as she had to keep resting, but eventually the mixture was white and fluffy, just as it said in the book.

She looked at her watch. It was half past twelve, lunchtime. She had worked out that if she had half the tin of salmon for herself, then the other half would do quite enough sandwiches. After all, young girls were always dieting. She laid up a small tray and carried it through to the sitting room. Sun was streaming through the dormer window, and there was a faint film of dust on the sideboard. Lucinda clicked her tongue in irritation. She would have to dust before Bella arrived. Honour had no pride, she thought. Fancy leaving the flat in such a state.

After her lunch Lucinda put the kettle on to boil while she carefully mixed the eggs, flour and chocolate cream into the fat and sugar. She gave it all a final stir. In the book it said to beat it again, but her arm was quite sore enough. The kettle began to sing merrily as she quickly scooped the cake mixture into the dish and put it into the oven. 'Damn!' she cried, it was cold, she'd forgotten to turn it on to warm it.

Bella arrived exactly on time. She was dressed very smartly in a full-skirted navy-blue dress with a collar like a man's shirt. She was wearing red shoes and carrying a matching handbag, and a wide white belt complemented her white stud earrings.

'Red, white and blue,' Lucinda said, as she kissed her guest on the cheek. 'How very patriotic you look, my dear.'

'What a wonderful smell.' Bella breathed in the

166

deliciously rich chocolatey odour that filled the small flat.
'Has Honour been cooking?'

'Not Honour, she's much too busy for that kind of
thing.' Lucinda showed how she felt about Honour's
bustling war effort by a quick downward droop of her
lips. She bent forward to whisper conspiratorially at Bella,
'I had to clean the whole place, you know. I dread to
think what Isabella would say if she saw the state of things
here. Still, I've done my best.'

Bella had visited Honour before, and she'd been surprised to find the attic rooms so comfortable. Despite its
smallness, or perhaps because of it, there was a solid feel
about the two rooms. It was reassuring, like visiting an
old nanny. The furniture might not have been Honour's
but the home-like atmosphere was.

They sat down on the two armless chairs either side of
the gas fire. Lucinda poured the tea, almost quivering
with anticipation. She nibbled her salmon sandwich. The
cake looked delicious. It was a pity, she decided, that she
hadn't saved the final ounce of chocolate to melt over the
top, but the shiny brown gently rippled crust looked good
as it was.

'I must say, you've done us proud, Lucinda. Did you
bring all the goodies with you?' Bella asked.

'No, I just had a look in Honour's cupboard. It's
surprising what was hidden away in there. She had two
fresh eggs. Two. I mean, that's almost hoarding, isn't it?'
Lucinda laughed happily.

'Did you use them both?' Bella knew how rigidly
Honour stuck to her rations. She might not do that
herself, but something inside her admired the act of
conscience.

'Yes.' Lucinda picked up the knife – it was time to cut
her handiwork. 'And there was some butter. I used that,

and the margarine. Such fun.' She cut down into the cake. It was a little more difficult than she'd expected and she had to push quite hard.

They ate in silence. It was difficult to talk around the dryness of the cake. Bella knew that Honour would be back soon and she felt uncomfortable. There would be a scene. Fancy Lucinda having eaten everything in the cupboard. She swallowed hastily and reached for her tea – she would have to wash the awful, clagging goo down somehow. They heard the key turn in the lock and Lucinda turned expectantly. She felt that Honour was paying her a visit, coming into her room, and suddenly she was quite possessive of the little changes that she'd made. The subtle difference of the ornaments she'd moved around.

'Bella – what a nice surprise.' Honour was tired. She'd started work early and all she wanted to do was crawl into bed and sleep. But Lucinda was staying and she knew she'd have to make polite conversation and cook supper. Thank heavens she'd saved last week's egg. They could have them boiled, with fingers. It would be something to laugh about, a kind of nursery supper. She looked in surprise at the tea tray. There was a small sandwich curling at the edges on her one pretty plate; crumbs showed that it was obviously the remains of a pile. And there was a chocolate cake. She looked at it in surprise. It was a strange shape, like an upside-down bath, and it looked very dry. 'Where on earth did you get that?' she laughed. 'Don't tell me you smuggled it in here in your suitcase last night, Lucinda. Is that why it looks so odd?' She was still laughing as she took off her coat, turning her back to the others to hang it on the hook behind the door.

'Lucinda made it,' Bella said. She suddenly saw the funny side of the whole situation. It was pointless being sorry for Honour, she decided. After all, the girl was suffering unnecessarily – with Eli around she didn't have to go without. 'She said she found a couple of eggs and was inspired. The chocolate was her own. Wasn't that sweet of her to share it with us? Oh heavens, the fire's gone out.'

Honour turned in disbelief. She'd filled the meter that morning, so it should have lasted for ages. Lucinda couldn't possibly have used that much gas. 'Have you any change?' she asked her two guests. She reached for her coat as they both shook their heads. The baker's would be shut by now – she'd have to walk as far as the newsagent's. As she stepped into the street it began to rain.

The heat made shimmering silvery columns of the clear blue air above the rocks. Great tilted slabs shone mustard yellow above the tide-line then paled to white where barnacles clung to every surface that could be reached by the sea. The dark stripes of navy-blue mussel beds accentuated the deep horizontal clefts formed in an age before man was even imagined.

Nigel breathed in deeply and the crystal air filled his lungs. In his pleasure he clutched convulsively at the tweed jacket he carried. The first sight of the rolling, majestic sea always brought a catch to his throat, and he swallowed – it was painful, tart with salt.

The others were somewhere ahead of him, careering down the cliff path on their bicycles. Neil would be in the lead, his feet flung out wide so that the pedals would spin madly as their cries of joy mingled with the raucous gulls. The scent of seathrift tantalized him; it was the smell of summer. They were too late for the primroses that smothered the hillside in spring, too late even for gulls' eggs. There was a stone in his shoe, and he sat down on the red mud verge, his feet swinging out over the crumbling edge that fell to the rock shelves leading to the sea. If he had only one day left of his life he would want to spend it here, at Cockburn's path. The pure air of Scotland seemed to reach a zenith of perfection where the wide green rollers hurled themselves to pieces on the elemental shore.

It was dark in the cave, and the way through the hillside, from the cliff road to the harbour, was eerie. There was a point in the centre where no daylight penetrated, where as a child Nigel had trembled in delicious fear. Was there a way out? Or had Ali Baba's boulder rolled to seal the entrance behind him? Then, if the grown-up with him was brave – his father or mother, or even Uncle Michael, but never Nanny – they would take the narrow opening that led to the smugglers' chambers. The lantern would make giant shadows as they stumbled over the uneven floor, the children holding their breath for fear of . . . but they never knew what they were frightened of, except that there were all the terrors of the nursery lurking in the two chambers that opened silently, almost airlessly, ahead of them. The choking sensation he so remembered caught at his throat, a frantic secret struggle for air; he mustn't let the grown-ups see, or they'd never take him there again.

The air of the cave was soft on his face, gentle and soothing after the cliffs. The tiny harbour opened out beneath him. There was a short granite breakwater curving in protection and within its shelter a calm circle of water. A small fishing boat was drawn up on the beach and behind it was the house, welcoming and square, bright green and white paint proclaiming its holiday status. Whoever had rented the property this year had the usual paraphernalia – the stripy deck chairs, the jumble of fishing tackle by the door. They'd stayed there themselves one blissful summer and it had been the best holiday the twins remembered. But it hadn't really suited their parents. The rooms weren't quite big enough, the access was too narrow and difficult. From then on they'd taken a house further inland, one equipped with bicycles, and a neighbouring farmer who provided milk and eggs, and an admirable daily help. Most important, it had a telephone, so that their father could carry on his business – he wasn't really happy unless he could do that, and Luke had to be happy for Victoria to enjoy herself.

Nigel could feel the barnacles crunching beneath his plimsolls, but the sound that they made was lost in the roar of the rollers. He made his way forward towards the sea, and a fine wind-blown spray stung his eyes. The backs of his legs ached and his knees were stiff with the effort of clambering on the rocks. He slipped and put a hand out to steady himself, and there was a sudden lurch in his stomach that was surprisingly like fear.

'Damn!' He sucked at his knuckles, which were raw and bleeding, stripped by a myriad tiny razor-sharp shells. He sat for a moment, feeling the damp through his shorts but not minding. This close to the sea the noise was a physical assault. There was the crash of the wave, the sucking, devouring backwash, then yet another all-embracing roar as a new monster hurled itself up from the deeps. He saw the diamonds and emeralds thrown up from the foam, to hang in the air for countless seconds before they disappeared into the ocean.

Time stood still.

* * *

It was cold. Clouds had gathered on the horizon, building block upon block of threatening darkness so that eventually the sun succumbed. He stood up stiffly. He had no idea of the hour. He wondered for a moment why the others hadn't come for him. It must be late. Mother would be worried. He thought of her waiting, looking out of the window. Oddly, he'd imagined her waiting at home – it was Cadogan Gardens that he'd thought of.

The sea had come much closer, washing the rocks before and beside him. The slab on which he was sitting was above the others. He turned back towards the cliffs and saw then that the sea had come behind him. Slow billows of water had spread, turning the white to grey, and fronds of green floated, hair-like, in the eddies. He would have to jump, from knife-sharp edge to edge. He wasn't frightened; after all, he was fit, an athlete, and this was just another race, like the hurdles at school. A trick of the failing light, and he saw the rocky crags as white-painted barriers and the roar of the sea came from the throat of the crowd. He and Neil were racing together, lungs bursting, pride in every pounding step. It was as if his brother was beside him as he gathered his strength, poised to launch himself above the bottle-green water that swirled between him and his goal. He took a deep, shuddering breath that was like fire in his lungs, and then he was flying, soaring above the chasm. He flung himself forward, gripping the rock, burying his fingers in the crumbling shells. His legs were ripped and he could feel the pain, but it was at a distance. The cold sea rushed over the searing flesh and his mind accepted the salt as balm.

He must leap again. He gathered himself up, aware of every sensation – his toes pressing through the thin rubber soles, the stinging in the palms of his hands. There were

172

fragments of shell embedded under his skin. This time he shouted as he jumped, a cry to rival the thunder as a vast new wave swept over and around the towering edifice ahead of him. He leapt as the wave leapt and together they embraced the rock, clutching, holding it close to his chest, and then the wave retreated, falling, dragging itself away. Taking him with it, pulling him down, and turning him. All the time the shells ripped at his clothes, his flesh. He was shouting, screaming with joy as the pain ate into him, because now at last he was one with the sea. He would go with it, close his eyes and become part of the vast deep greenness. Then he heard a voice, a woman's voice. It must be his mother calling. She had come, after all, to find him, only it was too late.

Too late . . . He tried to say the words but the salt had sealed his lips and the pain now was sweeping over him in waves. The rhythm was the sea's but the pain was his own. Too late . . . He had to tell her, and then he was lifted up. He would be dashed to pieces on the rocks, smashed to a million tiny fragments and abandoned on the land – but he wanted to stay with the sea. He screamed. There was his mother's voice, her arms that were holding him while he struggled for breath, fighting the dreadful burning that was inside him, everywhere around him. The sea was gone, and he was on fire.

The dream faded – there was no more sea, no fire. Only the chill calm of the hospital ward, the sour smell of the bandages, and the pain that threatened his sanity.

Bella folded the letter carefully and laid it down slowly on her dressing table. All the time she gazed sightlessly at her reflection in the mirror. She had known that her account was overdrawn, but she hadn't worked out by how much. It had seemed like tempting fate to put a

173

definite figure on it, and now it was too late to think that fate might be kind. A cheque she had written had not been met. It was the money for the quarterly payment on the lease of her gallery in Cork Street. There had been no reduction in what she had to pay, despite the fact that she'd had to close; there was no sale for her kind of art, thanks to the war.

'Damn the bloody war!' She spat the words out, standing up too quickly and sending her spindle-legged stool tumbling. How dared the bank! She remembered when the manager had been obsequious enough. She'd even invited him and his insignificant little wife to a preview – it just showed what a wasted effort that had been. But how mortifying. She had sent the cheque to the solicitors acting for the trustees who were her landlords – their practice was in Lincoln's Inn. How often would they come across such financial embarrassments? A voice inside her head answered her unspoken question – they had no doubt come across them often enough, before and during the war.

The voice was something she often relied on, the part of herself that was enabling her to cope with her present greatly reduced circumstances. Damn Bill for cutting off her allowance. She walked quickly to the wardrobe and flung open the mirrored door. What on earth could she wear? There would be new people at the party that evening, new opportunities. She pulled out the cerise cocktail dress that was always a success, but no, everyone had seen it. It was pushed hastily back amongst the others. It was impossible. She needed a new dress – half a dozen, to tell the truth, if she was to find herself a new beau, one with money. There was only one thing in the wardrobe that she had never worn before. She took out the cream silk reverently. It was a creation she had bought in

174

Vienna, intending it to inspire Fritz to propose. Thick scalloped lace hung from the hem and from the tiny cap sleeves. In style it was almost old-fashioned, reminiscent of the thirties, but the cut was exquisite, moulding to every curve of her body. It was just the thing to stand out amongst the present austere fashions.

The wardrobe door swung closed and she held the dress up against her. Her cheeks were still flushed from her earlier irritation, but now all she could think about was how she would look. Her hair was long enough to pile on top of her head, and then she would roll it forward into a 'bang' to show off her smooth forehead, her almond-shaped eyes. She knew her attributes well, and also her failings. It was a pity that nature had not blessed her with a bigger mouth, but where nature had failed, artifice would succeed. The length of the dress was tricky; it ended at mid-calf. To look its best it would need her highest-heeled shoes. She bent to look under her bed, where at least thirty assorted pairs of shoes awaited her choice. The beige kid were perfect. They were unworn – she had bought them a few months ago, tempted by them in a Bond Street window.

'Madam has such exquisite taste,' the assistant had murmured. The price had been equally exquisite, but then Bill had been doing the right thing and paying her allowance into the bank and all had been well. She pirouetted in front of the mirror, admiring the way her ankles looked so slender. She would have to do something about money. She thought fleetingly of a personal appeal to the manager, Mr Jones, who had once been so eager to woo her custom, but she dismissed the thought as too awful – he wasn't her type. She would borrow from Victoria. At least part of the family was approachable.

* * *

There was a sudden hush. The pyramid of champagne glasses sparkled, emulating the magnificent chandelier hanging above them. Peter Savage stepped forward, holding a magnum of Moët up high for them all to see.

'Ladies and gentlemen,' he laughed, 'friends. We are here this evening to celebrate the birthday of the most beautiful girl in London.'

Bella felt her jaw tighten. She couldn't even force herself to forgive the wealthiest man in the room for such a tasteless remark.

'For Sylvia.' Their host was still laughing as he stepped up on the chair dexterously provided for him by a green-jacketed butler. 'Long may she reign!' He began pouring steadily into the top glass. It rested on three others, which in turn rested on eight, and so on, increasing downward. As he poured into the top glass it overflowed, filling the ones beneath, which in their turn spilled over.

'Quick, quick.' He held his spare hand out behind him for a full bottle.

Bella watched the scene with distaste. Sylvia Vartan had been a model – so what? It meant that she was a paid clothes horse, nothing more, and yet the way she was fêted was ridiculous.

'Bella!'

She turned quickly at the accusing whisper and to her surprise found Eli, a look of annoyance fading from his face and being quickly covered by his usual fatuous grin. She put her finger to her lips; it would be impolite to talk while their host was doing his party trick, and in any case, she needed time to think.

'Olé!' The trick was over and a bevy of waiters stepped forward to begin passing out the champagne. Applause burst out, followed at once by chatter, the high-pitched social babble that usually made Bella feel so much at home.

'What are you doing here?' She asked the question first, giving herself a few more precious seconds to work out how to prevent Eli telling Bill about the crowd she mixed with.

'Oh, you know me, Bella – always where there's a party. I haven't changed that much, you know.'

She glanced down at the arm of his jacket pinned across his chest, and to her delight he noticed her look and it bothered him. 'I'm so sorry, Eli, I thought that gallant heroes gave up the little luxuries of life when all around are . . .' She gave a brittle laugh. 'Well, you know what I mean.'

'Who are you here with?' Eli proffered his cigarette case. He had worked out a system whereby he could oblige with at least one of the civilized functions and not feel awkward.

'With myself. I am my own best company.' Bella accepted the slender eau-de-nil-coloured cigarette, and a faint smile turned up the corners of her lips as she waited for the lighter. 'And it's not really a question of who you come with on an evening like this, is it, Eli?' She bent towards the flame, and then straightened to look him straight in the eyes. 'It's more a question of who you leave with.' She saw the anger then, the fury and disgust in his face. He wasn't the same as the rest of them in the room, he was covering up his new-found sense of honour. It would give her a lever to use on him.

'Does Bill know you're here?' It was a foolish question to ask, but Eli had to do something – he couldn't act as if she wasn't family and didn't need protecting. But protecting from what? He watched her preparing her answer.

177

There was the faintest hint of lines running from the corners of her eyes and her mouth was pursed too tightly. She was an attractive woman – in the dress she was wearing she was close to sensational – but if she wasn't careful the slenderness that so appealed would become her enemy. If she became gaunt, she would age ten years overnight.

'I made my decision earlier.' Bella clasped her hands firmly in her lap. She refused to be compromised into having a row with her uncle. The figure-hugging scarlet dress that she wore was bare at the shoulders and she wanted to remain cool and calm, so that her skin looked at its creamiest best. 'I shall not go back to America. Anyway, it's ridiculous to say "go back". I've spent most of my life in England, certainly the part I can remember. It doesn't count that I was born in America and was a small child there. You're a real American, Uncle Bill, and so's my mother. Why don't you both go?' That would solve all Bella's problems. They'd have to leave her with an allowance, and without them she could entertain at the flat and enjoy herself as she knew she could with her new set of friends.

'I forbid you to see that man again.' Bill stood up. He wanted to impress on Bella how important his instruction was. 'He is evil. Before long . . .' He paused. He couldn't say what Eli had told him. He had no idea if Bella would warn Peter Savage or not, and the realization of his distrust made him feel physically sick. 'If you've ever cared for me, or for your mother, come to that, you'll listen to what I'm saying.'

'You know, melodrama really doesn't suit you, you don't have the right temperament to carry it off.' Bella also stood. They made an elegant picture in the lamp-lit room. Bill was about to go out to a gathering of his peers at the American Embassy. His svelte black suit contrasted well with his iron-grey hair and he appeared a man in control of his body and his emotions. Bella looked beautiful. She had her hair pulled up and back from her face and there was a glow about her. It was excitement – she intended to capture Peter, totally and for ever. She could see her way ahead so clearly and nothing that Bill could say would alter it.

'Cigarette?' Peter Savage leaned towards the lighter set in the walnut of the car interior. He had made a show of closing the glass partition that gave them privacy from the chauffeur; he understood that Bella was the type of woman who enjoyed the small details of courtship.

'No, thank you.' Bella smiled into his face. She didn't intend to taste of tobacco when he kissed her, and she was quite sure that he would.

'You know, there's something about you that fascinates me.' Peter sat back in his corner of the wide seat in the Daimler limousine. They were intimate because they were alone, but not because of their proximity. It was an exciting feeling.

'Well, it's up to you to tell me, Peter – do you enjoy being fascinated?'

'Oh yes, I enjoy new sensations. I always have.'

Bella filed the information away. She would have to be careful – he would continually be seeking something new and different, and she would have to work to keep him. 'I think we're rather alike.' She turned on her seat to face him.

'Like to like, is that what you mean?' He reached out. His hand paused, very close to her face. 'Tell me, Bella, is it danger that excites you?'

179

She didn't say anything, she didn't move to acknowledge his words. He ran the tip of his finger slowly down the soft smoothness of her cheek.

'As lovely as you are, I would have you destroyed if you crossed me.' His voice was low – a caress that chilled. 'I could have your face ruined, and with it your life – it would be nothing to the people I employ – if you ever crossed me.' His words rang in her head, stirring a fear that mixed with the soaring excitement inside her.

'If you didn't trust me, would I be here now?' she asked.

'Yes.' He laughed abruptly, taking his hand away from her face. 'Because I want you, and I intend to have you. I'm not usually considerate enough to give a woman warning of the kind of man I am.'

'Then I should thank you. I'll have that cigarette now, if you don't mind.' She was trembling, and the nicotine would calm her. He was a dangerous man, she accepted that, but then these were dangerous times. 'Where are we going?' she asked.

'We're going to have a meeting with a traitor. A man who pretends to love his country, to be a patriot, and who sells facilities to me. You'll learn, my dear, that there are degrees of badness, and the worst type is the man who has two faces because he is never to be trusted.'

'What's his name?' She asked the question for something to say, as she wasn't yet in complete control of herself.

'Eli Bradbury. He's involved in the docks. Quite a charmer, lost an arm at Dunkirk, but just remember, he's taking my money. Don't be fooled.'

Bella stared out into the inky blackness. There was a sane world out there, people about their humdrum lives. She was so muddled. Eli had been the black sheep of the

180

family, the one who drank the most, womanized the most, but in the end he'd come through a hero, and it had seemed so natural, so right. She'd thought, when she saw him at Peter's house, that he had just been a part of the crowd, simply enjoying the good wine and food, but after all, he was bad, rotten all through.

'I know him,' she said, knowing she had no choice. 'He's kind of a relative.'

'Yes.' Peter stubbed out his cigarette in the ashtray in the door beside him. 'I know all about that. It's my business to know everything.' He moved towards her, sliding his arm along the back of the seat until he held her.

'Peter?' She didn't know what to say, she thought fleetingly of Fritz, of the other young men who had made love to her. This was different – she realized suddenly that she was in the arms of a stranger. She stiffened and he laughed, pulling her towards him.

'If we're alike then this is what excites you – that sudden flare in the stomach.' He cupped her breast in his hand. She made herself relax, put her arms around his neck, looking all the time into his eyes, waiting for him to kiss her.

'It would be a shame to spoil how you look.' He bent his head, kissing her softly on the neck. 'And it will wait; *à bientôt*, my pretty.' He sat back, away from her.

'I – ' she wanted to speak, to calm herself. She put her hand up to her chest. She was flushed and red, she could feel it.

'Here.' Peter leaned forward, opening the window a fraction. 'Fresh air will cool you down. Quite the *amoureuse*, aren't you, my Bella? Your eyes were devouring me. Let's just hope you live up to what they promise. Now . . .' Abruptly his mood changed and he was no

181

longer the lover. 'I want you to say very little to this Bradbury chap. Let him do the talking. Do your family know about me?'

'Yes.'

'And disapprove, I expect.' He laughed mirthlessly. 'And yet they themselves produced a turncoat. The world's gone mad all right, and the strangest thing of all is that the oldest families produce the biggest villains.'

Honour felt her temper rising. An afternoon off work was precious; to spend it arguing with Bella was a waste. 'I shouldn't have come, I could have sent you a cheque in the post,' she said.

'I'm sorry.' Bella was standing behind the sofa. She couldn't sit down and stay still. She was so highly strung, it only took the slightest thing to make her irritable. Victoria had been at Pencombe, so she'd had to ask Honour for a loan, and it had to be in cash. The bank didn't want her using her account at all – it was all such a mess. 'Look, it was sweet of you to bring the money round, and it won't be too long before I can let you have it back, I promise. I know I'm in a rotten mood, I'm so strung up I could cry. At the least provocation I could sit down and burst into tears.'

'Well, I certainly wish you would sit down, but watching you howling your eyes out wouldn't be my idea of a good time.'

'You're too forthright, do you know that, Honour? You've been brought up to tell the truth and shame the devil, but it's not always for the best.' Bella perched on the back of the sofa. 'If my mother found me sitting on here there'd be hell to pay. It's only because she's at some meeting that this place is bearable. She's having the time of her life, doing tremendously good works. It's amazing

182

the energy she has to spend on the welfare of perfect strangers – it's a pity she never acted like that over me.'

'Any more of this, and I think I'll cry with you. Look,' Honour stood up, 'I'll go. This isn't doing either of us any good.'

'No, please don't go. I'll try to be better company. Heaven knows, I could do with a woman to talk to. What am I saying? You're just a girl, it's just that ghastly uniform makes you look grown up.'

'Do you really think I look ghastly? Most of the girls prefer the battledress but I thought this wasn't too bad.' Honour smoothed the skirt of her suit. She had laid her cap on the table alongside her gauntlet driving gloves and navy shoulder bag. 'We have to wear this for driving the staff cars – that's when we're ferrying officers about. Anyway, I'm just as grown up as you are. Neither of us are married, we've both had boyfriends, but we're still mummy's little girls at heart. I don't think age matters after a while, and anyway, being in uniform does make you grow up quickly. I know things now that . . .' She paused. 'Well, let's just say that I understand now that I should never have shown I cared so much about James.'

'James? Who's James? Don't look at me like that, Honour. I haven't ever heard about a James and you – why did you think I would have?'

'I thought the whole world knew. Certainly the family.' Honour found to her surprise that she could think about James without pain. It was amazing how recently she'd suffered agonies if anyone mentioned him. There had been a mixture of shame, embarrassment and a dreadful feeling of loneliness that she'd thought would never end.

'Well don't leave me like this. Tell all, spill the beans. There – my uncle would have me packed off to America faster than you could say stars and stripes if he'd heard me say that – too American for words, darling,' she finished off, enunciating her vowels even more roundly than usual.

'His name is James Sullivan, and he's a kind of cousin. He came over from Ireland to stay with Tom at Reason Hill.' The words came haltingly. Honour was finding it hard to begin. 'The very first time I met him, I began by laughing at him and ended up admiring him, then I progressed very quickly from liking to loving. He's that sort of person.'

'All the charm of the Irish,' Bella interrupted.

'Yes, it might be that, I don't know. I haven't met anyone else from there. And now . . .'

'Now you're not likely to, not till this boring war's over. But don't stop, tell me all the gory details.' Bella was laughing. She felt good – Honour was struggling to put her innocent little story into words and Bella could feel superior, the woman of the world.

'I'd never had a real boyfriend before, I mean, I'd been kissed – you know the sort of thing, at parties, and there was one of the tenants' sons at Christmas.' It seemed unbelievable to remember the days when one kiss was excitement enough to colour weeks of cold dismal winter. 'But with James it was different, right from the start. We talked about such serious things. He had great plans for his future, and he talked for hours about his country. He kept trying to make me agree with him. He wanted me to despise our values and to understand how we'd persecuted his countrymen. Perhaps he was right, but I was never totally under his spell. His words seemed like that, some kind of magic that worked inside my head until it was hard to think straight. He opened up a whole new world for me. I realized how narrow my life was at Pencombe,

184

and he had so many plans, even though he wasn't much older than me, I felt I'd wasted so many years.'

'And then he made love to you.' Bella's face was twisted in cynical amusement. All Honour's high thinking was let down by the flush on her cheeks. James, whatever had happened to him, been Honour's first lover.

'Yes,' Honour whispered. 'It was my fault, I teased him – ran away and tormented him. I led him on.'

'Don't you believe it – men don't need leading on. And all that rubbish about you and me being the same, if that's how you feel about a man who made love to you, then it just proves that we're so far apart that . . . Well, it doesn't matter, but just don't ever believe you led a man on. They take what they want, all of them, and it's only ever one thing.'

'You sound so awfully hard. Is everything that bad for you, Bella?'

'Is what bad? Is losing my business, my independence, and then discovering that I'm in love with some bastard who cares less for me than he cares for his precious best friend's wife – is that bad? Yes, yes it is.' She looked so bleak, so sad, that Honour went over and put her arm around Bella's narrow shoulders.

'You have to understand, it wasn't that he took me, it was that he left me.' Honour hid her face behind Bella's back. 'None of the others know. How on earth could I tell them? They thought I was upset because he went away when it was so close to the war and all the boys were talking about going to do their bit. I was so desperate for him to stay. They saw it as him running back to escape from danger. I think they probably suspected that we had been lovers, even though there was no proof. But it wasn't his running away, it was that I was ashamed.

185

He . . . he didn't make love to me. At least, he took my virginity, but then, well, he didn't . . .'

'You mean he couldn't come?'

'No, he could come.' Her voice was calm now. 'But not inside me. He said he didn't want me to have a baby.'

'Dear God, I should think not. You can't hold that against him, Honour. That's the only thing I've heard in his favour, so far.'

'It was so calculated, that's what I felt. When it all began that afternoon I was lost inside my head, in some strange place. Everything I'd believed in seemed to have vanished, and all I wanted was for him to hold me and make me his own. If he had made me pregnant, I didn't think it would have mattered. After all, I'd assumed we would get married, I'd imagined our future, everything, together. And then, at that moment, when I was so desperate to take, and he should have been so determined to give, he was in control of himself enough to know that he didn't want a commitment. Everything else, the fact that he left and went back to Ireland when he might have stayed and played a part, all that was nothing to me.'

Bella took the girl in her arms. 'You poor, silly child. You're a dreamer. Life's for those who see a straight route; it's not romantic, paved with a primrose path or whatever. Romance doesn't exist, and I should know. After all, I was in the art world, a seller of pretty pictures. Milud wants a genteel painting for his lady's boudoir? But certainly, I'd say. And while he was handing his wife the work of art, he'd be thinking about giving me something quite different. If that sounds crude it's because it is. And don't you bother what anyone thinks about you – my mother never made a fuss about me in those days. She was delighted that I was mixing with the "right sort", as she saw them. She didn't complain about my coming

186

home at four in the morning as long as it was with someone whose mama she knew, or a chap who'd come down from Cambridge with one of the "boys". Now, of course, everything is very different, and I'm the scarlet woman who goes out with a racketeer. Eli's done his best to convince them I should break up with the only man who can get me out of the hole I'm in. I'm a disgrace to the family. Only, I could tell you something about Eli that makes him far, far worse than me. But it doesn't matter. None of it does, because I'm in love. For the first time in my life, someone else means more to me than I do. Oh, I've thought I was in love before, with Fritz, who I planned to marry – who I may well still end up with when the war is over, come to that, because I'm still not sure of my ground. However much I give to Peter, he always wants more. He said the other night that we don't make love, we make electricity, and I think perhaps he's right. It's so powerful, so unbelievably overwhelming that I can't leave him alone. When I'm not with him I think about him all the time. Even when you were talking about your James, I was thinking about Peter, wondering how it will be the next time, remembering how it was the last.'

'Does he feel the same? Do you know how he feels about you, Bella?'

'I think I must be useful to him. I'm an asset, I'm charming to the people he wants to cultivate, I'm able to talk about art with the new rich, the ones who are making fortunes out of supplying the strangest things.' She laughed, and it was a hard sound. 'You'd be amazed at the things some people make money from, Honour.'

'I know it's a wicked thing to say, but I'm glad there's a war.' Honour clutched her hands tightly round her knees.

187

The grassy bank beneath her crumbled abruptly a few feet ahead of them. She couldn't see the river where she sat, but she could hear it, and the liquid notes accentuated the stillness of the fields behind them. 'What I mean is, without a war we never would have met, and I can't bear that thought. I just can't stand the idea of never having found you.'

'We would have met. There would have been other ways.' Carl smiled. He was watching Honour's face, the intensity of her expression, her eyes screwed up against the light, her mouth set and determined. 'It was fated that we should be together, written somewhere up in the stars.' And he laughed to lessen the words, for he was embarrassed by too much sentiment.

'When I look at the stars at night, I think of you. Flying up there, in the sky.' She tilted her head back, staring into the endless blue. 'What's it like, to fly?'

'One day I'll take you up, when the war is over. We'll fly over here, over these very fields, and you'll be able to look down and see the trees, the river. It's important to us, you know, a river. Easy to follow, can't be disguised from the air. When I was a boy I used to love a river like this. My river, I thought of it as my property. Now,' he lowered his voice, his chin sank to his chest and it was hard for Honour to hear his words. 'Now it is mine no longer. But one day, one day, my little Honour – ' He reached out for her hand, gripping it fiercely.

There were birds singing, all around them, the songs of summer. A small breeze rustled the corn, sending the warm green scent towards them. They were sitting very still, feeling more than thinking, absorbing the heat, hoarding its energy. A brown mouse scurried from a tangle of brambles beside them. It paused, sniffing the air, its whiskers vibrating and glinting in the sunlight.

Tiny black eyes, pin-head beads, seemed to stare at them, the great humans, the interlopers. Honour held her breath. It seemed so precious, seeing a private world they were privileged to share, and she was very conscious of Carl's strong hand holding hers. She could smell him, a soapy smell, fresh like the fields. There was a wildness about him, and she felt he, like the mouse, could leave her at any moment, yet she felt safe when he was with her – happy and secure. She wanted to speak, to say, 'I wish this moment could last for ever', but that was silly; he'd be cross and think she was being too emotional, and speaking would make the little animal run away. She turned her head to look at him, and the mouse fled for safety.

'You were a long time. I thought you'd be late for lunch.' Lucinda studied her niece intently and Honour blushed. She could feel the warmth spreading up her neck, and the annoyance at betraying her embarrassment made her blush even more.

'It's so nice to be down here, so green, so quiet. So different from London, Mummy, you've no idea.' She turned her head towards her mother. She wouldn't let Lucinda's insinuations ruin their day.

'You should have taken a picnic, darling.' Isabella paused, putting her forkful of potato down carefully. 'You've got colour in your cheeks from your walk – you need more fresh air. Next time you manage to come down I'll remember to have a nice packed lunch ready for you.' She put her hands on to the table, almost as if to push the plate away from her. She had so little appetite, but it was a sin to waste food. She stared down. They'd made an effort for the visitors. There was some home-pressed tongue, tiny new potatoes from the garden, a salad with

189

lettuce and radishes – more home produce. Soon there would be tomatoes. Carl was eating heartily, spooning chutney over the meat on his plate. He was a nice young man, good-looking and well-mannered, but he was a pilot. Isabella felt an ache inside every time she met one of the brave, bright young fliers, with their charm and their excitement. Her nephews were just the same. Somehow they seemed the most exposed of all the men who went to war, and they appeared the most brittle, because of their banter, their jokes – 'nonsense' it would have been called before the war. This young man was different, Isabella could see that. He was more serious than most of them, more intent. Of course, his country had already been taken over, already invaded. Isabella found it so hard to imagine. If it happened here, she wondered, what would it be like? Not the awful early days of invasion, the bloodshed and pain, but the future – what on earth would it be like? She wanted to ask Honour's young man, but she couldn't, he wouldn't understand that her wanting to know was almost academic. She picked her knife and fork up suddenly, rattling them and making Lucinda sigh with exasperation. She must eat something, she was quite light-headed.

'Did you get any sleep at all last night, Mummy?' Honour asked.

'Yes, yes I slept, thank you. I had quite a good night.' She had tossed and turned, trapped in her bed by memories that were so bad at night she was frightened to close her eyes. She had eventually slept, to wake up sweating after some tangled dream that she had struggled vainly to interpret.

There were still a couple of hours before they had to leave, Honour to get back to town, Carl to Biggin Hill. It was hot and humid, and it seemed natural to seek out the coolness of the stable yard.

'I remember when most of these boxes were full.' Honour leaned over the half door. The dark blue paint was peeling and it smelt of linseed. 'When my father came back from Australia he became quite the horseman. They used to breed steeplechasers. It was sort of a hobby that made money. This was all so alive then.' The stable was empty, swept of even a wisp of straw. There were thick dusty cobwebs in the corners. 'Will I get to see your home one day?' She turned to face Carl suddenly, taking him by surprise. What did her question mean? He could get no clue from her clear blue eyes. She could mean the obvious; would there come a time when she could go to Poland, be free to travel there. Or she could mean did he want her to come to his home, to visit his family, be shown off – as what? As his intended?

'Would you like to?' he asked.

'Yes,' she said. 'More than anything else in the world.'

He took her in his arms, holding her gently at first, his fingers feeling how soft her arms were, how smooth and cool her skin. He pulled her closer to him. She moulded herself against his body, and then she was kissing him, her arms around his neck, pulling him closer, arching against him. Her lips parted, and a great aching void inside her cried out for him.

'Honour, Honour.' He buried his face in her neck, breathing in the sweetness. He was desperate for her, but not here, not now. He knew it couldn't be.

'Come back with me to London tonight,' she whispered.

'I can't, you know I can't.' His voice was muffled against her neck. 'And before we do – before I ever make love to you – there is a truth that I have to tell you.

Something that may change the way you feel about me, although nothing could change how I feel about you. Remember that, whatever else happens.'

Isabella's voice, calling them, seemed far away. It was time to leave. Honour felt sick. There was something he had to tell her – but she didn't want to know anything that might alter their relationship, she wanted to give herself to him, to love him totally. Was it always to be like this? Men worried about what might happen to her; she seemed to strike some protective chord. She realized suddenly what the problem was – it was her name. 'Honour, honour,' she was whispering as they walked out to the car.

'I'm going to take the bus down to Hyde Park,' Honour said. 'Would you like to come with me, Aunt Lucinda?'

Lucinda shook her head. The thought of going anywhere on a bus was dreadful. The thought of milling about with a lot of aimless young people intent on nothing other than meeting members of the opposite sex made the trip impossible.

'You'd better have tea without me, then. There's someone I'm going to meet, and I won't be back till later.'

'Then may I ask what you would have done if I had said I'd come?' Lucinda was very annoyed. 'You took it for granted I wouldn't go with you. Your invitation was nothing but a sham. I think that's very low, very low indeed, Honour.'

'It wasn't a sham at all. I would have been delighted if you'd wanted to come. We could all have had tea together.'

'All? Who exactly is this person you're meeting?'

'It's Carl . . . the Polish airman you met at home. Did

192

I tell you his mother was Norwegian, and his father was a sea captain who – '

'Enough.' Lucinda stood up. 'I shall come, after all. It would be most unsuitable for you to meet this young man on your own.'

Honour laughed. 'I'm sorry to enlighten you, but the age of the chaperon is quite dead, Aunty. I'm not committing any dreadful impropriety. But do come, I'm sure you'll get on very well with Carl when you know him better. He's quite cosmopolitan.'

Lucinda gathered together the things she needed for her trip. She took quite a long time looking for her umbrella, and Honour became more and more impatient. The sky outside was clear and there wasn't the slightest threat of rain.

Honour was almost running as she saw the bench they had chosen as their rendezvous. She scanned the crowd as she passed. There were soldiers and airmen in uniform, civilians with their shirt sleeves pushed up. It was blissfully warm, and there were splashes of colour from the flowers in the park, and from the pretty, summery dresses of girls walking arm in arm. She didn't appreciate any of it, because he wasn't there. She stood still suddenly and Lucinda caught her up, clutching at her arm furiously. 'I nearly lost you back there,' she said. 'I would never have found you again in all this crowd.' She looked around, her anger directing itself against the cheerful faces.

'We're too late.' Honour was close to tears. She thought of Carl waiting, thinking she wasn't coming, and then going off on his own. How would she ever find him? She looked around her, but there were so many people.

'Eli.' Lucinda's voice was high with surprise. 'What on earth are you doing here?'

193

Eli kissed his sister hello and she pulled back from him, showing her annoyance at his intimacy in front of strangers.

'Slumming,' he said, 'the same as you.' But he grinned as he said it and Lucinda was crosser than ever. He stood in front of Honour and held the bunch of carnations he carried towards her. 'I'm Carl's messenger. He sent you these. He's sorry he couldn't make it, but he's flying tonight.'

Honour took the flowers and held them tightly. 'I thought . . .' there was a catch in her voice. She'd been so looking forward to seeing him, and now he would be flying, in danger before she could talk to him again. 'I thought we were too late.'

'He said that he'll be in touch. "Give her my love" – that was the message to go with the flowers.' Eli felt very sorry for Honour. She looked like a very miserable little girl; it made him think of the time she'd lost her toy – Dinah, she'd called it – a tired-looking fair-haired doll that she'd found in the nursery. Nobody remembered where it had come from. But it was lonely, in need of a friend, and so to Honour it had been more precious than any of the well-dressed, well-cared-for porcelain creatures she had been given. They had turned the house upside down looking for it because she had cried so badly. Was that why she loved Carl, he wondered, because he was lost, out of his own environment?

'Can you reach him?' she asked urgently. 'Can you get a message to him?'

Eli shook his head. He wanted to stop her committing herself in front of Lucinda, and he still wasn't sure about the love affair that was blossoming so quickly.

'But you must be able to.' Honour gripped his arm fiercely. She wouldn't be thwarted; this was so important.

'You've to tell him I love him too. Please.' There were tears in her eyes. Eli felt his resolution softening. The only thing that stopped him saying he would try to help was the memory of how badly she'd been hurt when James Sullivan left her. Carl might not walk out on her, he seemed a good chap, but there were other ways of leaving. Eli knew his reputation, and he was a maniac. A delightful, charming maniac, but as a flier he broke all the rules. He was dashing, a pirate of the air. Percy had talked about the first time Carl showed off his own special brand of aerial acrobatics over the airfield. It was a fine day and there was a crowd of fliers out on the grass in front of the mess, so a good few glasses were raised in salute to the lone plane that came out of the sky. They knew who it was and his perfectly executed loop was greeted by a cheer. He got bollocked for it, of course, but then he was a foreigner. They got off lightly – the first time. Then he came back for another pass and he was flying lower, and then another. In the end they all hit the deck in self-defence, glasses went flying, tempers were lost. Maniac was the politest thing they called him.

No, Eli convinced himself, he would not get the message through. 'You'll be able to tell him yourself before long,' he said.

They went for tea at Lyons Corner House. Honour was distant, her mind clearly far away. Lucinda, however, for some inexplicable reason, was happier than she had been in a long time. She even decided to enjoy watching the couples so intent on each other that their excellent afternoon tea was hardly noticed. 'Such a shame the boys can't be here,' she said. That was what she always called them now, 'the boys'. She never referred to her grandsons by their names. And while it was Viccy to her daughter's face, it had become Victoria behind her back. She didn't refer to Luke at all. Eli wondered what she called *him* when he wasn't around.

'I'll get you back home in time for this evening's fireworks,' Eli said as he reached for his wallet to pay their waitress. 'The bombing's becoming a bit of a habit – night after night. Still, at least they left us alone today.'

'Honour wouldn't come down into the shelter yesterday.' Lucinda's voice was sharp. 'I told her it was quite irresponsible.'

'If we all went down into the shelters all the time, Aunty, then there probably wouldn't be enough room for you. Anyway, I can't sleep down there. I've always hated to be cooped up. It was noisy last night, but not so bad that I didn't drop off eventually.'

Eli backed his niece up. 'You're missing a lot of the fun if you go underground every time they put on a show, Lucinda. There's all sorts of excitement to be had. Have you ever spent the whole night in a dance hall, for example? Because that's what happened to the little girl who types my letters. She and her girlfriend take themselves off to the Locarno in Streatham. She's described it to me, and apparently it's beautiful, like fairyland – whatever that's meant to look like. Anyway, they had the time of their lives the other evening. They couldn't get home because there was a raid on and so they stayed all night. Came home with the dawn. She was over the moon about it.'

'My goodness, Eli,' Lucinda said loudly, 'I do wish you wouldn't mix with the common people.'

The waitress handed Eli his change. Her mouth had almost dropped open. Where had they dragged that old bat out from? she thought. Eli winked at her as he handed over a tip. At the same time Honour vowed silently never to go anywhere public with her aunt again.

* * *

196

'Would you like a sherry?' Bella gestured towards the decanter. She was playing the hostess, enjoying being in command of the scene she had worked so hard to contrive.

'No, thank you.' Sylvia smiled to cover her refusal of hospitality. 'You have a beautiful home, Bella.'

'Yes, I do, don't I.' Bella had brought in extra flowers; tall salmon-pink gladioli and a low arrangement of roses augmented the pot plants in her mother's drawing room. She was wearing a fuchsia and white silk dress and had a white cardigan draped loosely around her shoulders. Her stockings were deliciously fine – a present from Peter. It had made her feel quite kittenish to be given such a traditional gift from a lover.

'Bertie will be picking me up in a few minutes . . .' Sylvia trailed off. If Bella had something important to say, then she would have to hurry up.

'No he won't, my dear. Peter asked him to perform a little errand, and he'll be a lot longer than you thought. In fact, you might have to take a taxi home.'

'I don't understand.'

'Of course you don't. Why should you?' Bella slowly and studiedly lit herself a cigarette. She hadn't offered one to Sylvia. 'You don't smoke, do you?' she asked eventually.

'Only among friends.' Sylvia had disliked the woman with the brittle cut-glass accent from the first time they met. It had been a mutual feeling. But now that Bella had Peter, Sylvia couldn't work out why she was bothering to escalate the friction between them. They would make an inevitable foursome; after all, Simon and Peter were inseparable.

'I think we should clear up a few things.' Bella touched the tip of her cigarette into an enamelled ashtray. 'We should establish a pecking order, so to speak. You see, I know all about you and Eli.'

Sylvia glanced quickly at the sherry decanter. She needed something in her hand, something to hold on to to help her concentrate. 'I think I'll have that drink now, if you don't mind.'

'You don't need a drink, Sylvia. You just need to listen to me. Simon understands his place. He puts everything he has into working for Peter, and he gets treated accordingly. They have an excellent relationship, one that no two women could enjoy because there is no jealousy in it.'

'You needn't be jealous of me, Bella.' Sylvia was breathing quickly, concentrating her whole being on keeping one step ahead of her antagonist.

Bella's eyes narrowed and it made her look older. 'Don't be silly. The whole point of my having you here was to explain to you that I don't want there to be difficulties through your inevitable jealousy of me.' Bella tipped her head back. She felt aggressive. 'You've been used to having them both doting on you. Simon clearly adores you, and it has suited Peter having you around. After all, even though you stopped modelling years ago, yours is still a face that people remember.'

'Two years.' Sylvia's voice was low and Bella had to lean forward to hear it. 'It's not that long a time.'

'Let's not be petty about this. I know it must be hard on you. You've had it all your own way.' Bella paused. She had worked out what would suit her. 'Simon was talking to me the other evening. He said how eager he was to have children.'

'Oh no.' Sylvia clutched at the arm of her chair. 'That's not true, he never said that . . .'

'But of course he did. It's only natural, after all. And

198

you wouldn't suffer because of the shortages. You could have the best of everything – good food, expert medical care. Why, you owe it to your husband. He works so hard to provide you with all the luxuries.'

Sylvia stood up, her eyes fixed on Bella. 'If you've put it into his mind I'll kill you,' she whispered.

'Don't be ridiculous.' Bella was taken aback by the intensity of venom in the girl's words. 'Marriage, a family. It's the most natural thing in the world.'

'If it's true, if you've really made him want a child . . .' Sylvia clutched at her stomach. Her hands were splayed, her shoulders hunched forward like a theatrical parody of despair. 'I'd kill you, and then I'd kill myself.'

'Stop it! Stop it at once. Here.' Bella walked quickly to the decanters and poured a large cognac into a brandy balloon. 'You're being hysterical.'

Sylvia wouldn't take the glass. She would take nothing from the woman who might have ruined her life. After so long, after all the degradation that she had suffered, at last she had a glimpse of happiness. If that was to fade then she would want to die. 'Have you honestly said anything to him?' she asked.

'No.' Bella smiled as she saw her victory. 'But I shall if you don't do everything I want. I have the two options now, don't I? I could talk to him about the baby, or I could oh so accidentally let slip about Eli.'

'What is it? What on earth could be so precious to you that you'd be so heartless?'

'I told you, I simply want you to understand that from now on, I am in the premier position. You are married to my lover's employee, and that is all.'

'You're mad.'

Bella smiled as the door bell rang. Bertie was on time – there had been no errand – and her little lies had worked

199

excellently. 'Tell me,' she said as she handed Sylvia her jacket, 'why would having a child be so very awful? You'd get your figure back afterwards. Your sort always do.'

'It doesn't matter.' Sylvia wouldn't allow Bella to know anything more about her, anything at all. 'I understand what you want. You needn't worry about me.'

Bella went back to her cigarette. It had almost got out of hand. It was ridiculous – all she'd wanted was for the silly girl to get pregnant. After all, they'd been married for quite long enough, and what she'd said was right – Sylvia and the child would want for nothing that money could buy. Having gradually seen Sylvia transformed to motherhood, Peter could lavish his care and attention on the baby, and it would make him want a family of his own. And for that, Bella would be more than willing to give up her freedom. Sylvia was a silly girl. She stubbed out the last of her cigarette. If there was any justice in life she'd get pregnant by Eli and then she'd have to inveigle Simon on top of her to credit the child as his. Bella assumed that was what it was all about. Simon was a big man, but there was a certain softness about him. It wouldn't be hard to imagine him wanting Sylvia simply as a possession, something to put on a shelf and admire. The telephone rang shrilly. With luck it would be Peter. Bella smoothed her hair as she walked towards it.

Sylvia clutched her brother's hand tightly. 'Is it still so impossible?' The tone of her voice was pleading, her eyes frantic. 'There must be something you can do, please.'

The enforced intimacy of the taxi felt suddenly claustrophobic. Bertie was far too hot in his uniform. He ran a finger around the inside of his collar and his neck above the tight band turned a deep red. 'You promised, you said you'd keep up your part of the bargain. What the hell do you expect me to do?' His voice was thick, choked with emotion. He felt trapped and he wanted to escape.

'I can't stay with Simon. I thought I could once, but I can't, not any more. I've been trying to fool myself, to pretend that to be protected from the harsh realities, not to be on my own now, makes it all worth while. But the truth is I only married him to save you. I hate him – I have from the beginning.'

'There's no need to rub it in. I know the sacrifice you made.' Bertie's voice became a sneer. 'But you've done pretty well out of it – all the pretty clothes you wanted, good jewellery, furs. You don't want for anything.'

'But I do. I want my freedom.'

'Freedom, is it?' He pulled his fingers from her grip. 'You don't want your freedom, you just want to change horses in mid-course. You've found someone you prefer, or at least you think you do. When you get to know your Bradbury fellow a bit better you'll be crying to come back. Whatever you say about Simon, he's never cheated on you, and I wouldn't trust the saturnine Eli on that front. He's promised to call on Babs – you didn't know that, did you? He phoned her the other day. He's not a one-woman man, Sylvie. Don't chuck it all up for him.'

'I do know he's going to see her, and I know why. We don't have secrets from each other any more.'

'You mean, he knows all about me?' Bertie's voice rose.

'Yes.'

'Christ Almighty!' He felt winded, as if he'd been punched in the solar plexus. 'What did he say?'

'He said a gentleman pays his own debts. So I had to explain that it was too big a debt and you couldn't.' She was quite calm now. Speaking the truth was a relief after living a lie for so long. 'And I explained that your gambling only went wrong after Mother died. I told him how she died too. He's the first man I've ever told. Simon just thinks I don't want to have children because it would spoil my figure. He's more than happy to accept that. It's such a selfish motive that it's one he understands.'

'He'll throw me to the wolves if you leave. That money's still owing, and it's only him that's stopping them coming for me.'

'There must be something we can do. It felt such a fortune then that you'd lost, twenty thousand pounds, but now – seeing the kind of money Peter moves about. There must be something . . .'

'Don't do anything yet. Promise me. Go on, promise. Stay with him for a bit longer, I'll try and work it out.'

'Bella said that Simon wanted me to have a baby. It was a lie, of course, but I didn't know that right away. You can have no idea of the fear I felt. It never goes away.' She shuddered and Bertie put his arm around her.

'I think of it too sometimes. But she was too old, you know. It wasn't that there was anything wrong with her. There's no reason you would have problems. Honestly, it was just that she was too old. It was her heart that gave out.'

'I shall never have a baby, never.' Sylvia was whispering and he had to lean close to hear her. 'I would rather kill myself quickly and cleanly at the beginning, I swear it. Mother was trapped. She knew it all along and she couldn't escape. Being pregnant killed her. It made her haggard and ugly. All her life went into making the baby, and then they died together.'

'Poor Sylvie.' Bertie cradled her head on his shoulder. 'Poor, sweet Sylvie.' She'd got this way before and he knew how to calm her. She would stay with Simon and he would be safe. That was the bargain that had been struck.

202

The perfect creature that was Sylvia Vartan had been sold, and she had fetched twenty thousand pounds.

'Here, take this.' Victoria reached under the tablecloth. She held fifty pounds in notes crumpled in her hand. 'Please, it's nothing. Just take it.'

Bertie glared at her, his cheeks flushed. He kept his hands very obviously on the table top. 'Put it away. For God's sake, put it away, Victoria.'

Victoria bit her lip. He was being so silly. She was sure he didn't have enough to pay for the meal. They had been extravagant over their dinner in the Grill Room and had a very special claret from the head waiter's store. She hadn't wanted to argue, to spoil his moment of pleasure, but now she was determined to pay.

'I think I'll have another cognac. How about you?' He disdained to look at the folded piece of paper the waiter had placed beside him. 'Victoria?'

'No, I won't have anything more to drink, thank you.'

'Waiter!' Bertie took his time about ordering his drink; he was only having it to make a point. He'd had a bit too much already, and he knew it. The bottle of champagne that some unknown benefactor sent them with their dessert had been too much for them, but it wouldn't have been polite to leave it half-finished so he'd persevered. He wasn't a praying man, but if he had believed in any kind of deity he would have prayed just then that what was in his wallet would cover what he owed the Café Royal. Victoria was too managing by half. She wanted to baby him – well, she wasn't going to get away with it.

The lights were dim in the Cadogan Square drawing room. Victoria let her head rest against Bertie's shoulder as they sat together on the sofa. She tucked her legs up beside her and took his hand in hers. 'I can't tell you how at peace I feel,' she said.

He squeezed her hand briefly. He was still irritated with her behaviour at the restaurant.

'Would you like some music?' she asked, twining her fingers through his, moving to fit into the curve of his arm. Her perfume was warm, intimate, but his temper was still rising.

'Come here.' He spoke abruptly, pulling her head round, forcing her lips hard against his mouth. His kiss was hot. He'd had too much to eat and drink and he felt queasy, but forced himself to want her. 'Come on, come on.' He spoke more to himself than to her. He put his hand down inside the front of her dress, cupping her breast, squeezing his fingers hard on her nipple. She jerked away from him at the sudden pain.

'Bertie!' She stood up, rearranging her dress, smoothing it down, and the satin folds fell creaseless. She realized then that he was quite drunk.

'Come back here, come on, Viccy.' He patted the seat beside him. He was smiling at her now, his voice wheedling.

'Oh, Bertie, don't spoil it. I know I was silly earlier on. I'm sorry, only I thought . . . Look, let's not talk about it now. Why don't you go home, get to bed? I'll get you a taxi.'

'No need to go home to go to bed.' The warmth of the room was making him feel worse. His words were slurring; he could hear it and it made him angry. He stood up abruptly. 'Perfectly good bed here. Better than a damn sofa any day. Here.' He reached out, pulling her towards him.

'You're hurting. For goodness sake, Bertie, stop it. You're drunk – go home.'

204

'I'm drunk, am I?' His breath was heavy on her face, and the sickly sweet smell of brandy made her turn her head away.

'Please, please Bertie, you'll feel dreadful in the morning.' She tugged, trying to get away, but his grip on her arms was vice-like. 'I'll get you a seltzer. And some coffee – yes, have a coffee. That'll make you feel better.'

'Never felt better in my life.' He pressed his body up against her. Despite the drink, and the fog in his brain, he was ready for her, but he felt her recoil. 'Too much for you, is it? Too much of a man.' He dropped his head, kissing her breasts, feeling her repugnance.

'Please.' She pushed hard at his chest and suddenly she was free, falling back across the room. She banged her ankle sharply on the coffee table and then steadied herself against an armchair. 'God,' she laughed uncertainly, pushing a stray lock of hair from her forehead, 'I know it's hackneyed, but you're going to hate yourself in the morning.' From a distance he wasn't frightening any more; he was dishevelled, red in the face, and he looked about twelve years old.

The telephone bell surprised them both. As she picked it up Victoria was checking her watch. It was two o'clock in the morning. Who on earth could be calling? She had a sudden awful thought that they must have found Nigel. He must, after all, be dead. Her voice was trembling as she spoke. 'Hello. Who is it?'

'Mrs Luke Jones?'

She didn't recognize the man's voice. It was low, cultured, and somehow she didn't think it was from someone in the services, or even a doctor.

'I have a message for Eli Bradbury. One that he is expecting. Tell him that he is to complete the rendezvous tomorrow. Same time, same place.'

205

'Have you any idea what time it is?' Her voice was quivering with anger. Her fear for Nigel had turned to fury.

'Now, you weren't asleep, were you, Mrs Jones. If I interrupted anything then I apologize, but all things considered I very much doubt it. I do hope you enjoyed your champagne, although I suspect that Bertie had the lion's share. Goodnight.'

Victoria stared at the receiver in her hand. 'Who the hell was that?' she asked. She looked up at Bertie. 'He called you by name. This man I don't know left a message for Eli, and called you Bertie, and,' her voice rose as she saw that Bertie knew who she was talking about, 'he was the one who sent the champagne. What the hell's this all about?'

Bertie's earlier bravado disappeared. He felt sick again, quite ill, as he sat down heavily on the sofa. He'd acted like a pig, but things had been getting on top of him. He'd been sure that Simon knew what he was doing, and he'd been equally sure that he wouldn't be allowed to slip quietly out of the Simon–Peter net. 'I'm sorry, Viccy, I'm sorry.' He sat forward, covering his face with his hands. 'Can I take you up on that coffee? I think I need some.'

'And then you'll tell me what the hell is going on.' She sounded as furious as she felt. How dared he treat her like that, acting like a drunken lout. And yet she loved him. The crosser she felt the more she wanted to put her arms round him, to hold him close while she scolded him.

'I'll tell you everything.' He looked up and there was such anguish in his face that all her anger faded. 'God knows, I've kept it bottled up for far too long.'

'Don't you understand!' Victoria pushed Bertie away from her. 'I'm telling you it's over, finished.' She stood

206

by the window, her figure outlined by the light. She was trembling, insubstantial, her face so pale and drawn that she looked like a ghost of her former self.

'You don't mean it, Viccy.' Bertie checked an impulse to step forward and take her in his arms again. 'You'll see things differently in a few days. It was only because you thought there was news about Nigel . . .'

'Don't.' She put her hand up to cover her mouth, blurring her words. 'Don't tempt fate.'

Bertie realized then, for the first time, how serious her threat to break with him was. 'You think that it's some divine judgement on us, don't you? You believe that our relationship is to blame for his going down in the sea. Viccy, oh my poor Viccy, how could you be so silly?'

It was very quiet in the house. Luke was sleeping and the nurse reading in her room. The routine jobs for the day had been accomplished; only Cook was busy, baking a fatless sponge. A friend of hers who had been visiting relatives in the country had brought back a few extra eggs – duck eggs – and the cake was rising a treat.

'Let's sit down and talk things over.' Bertie held his hand out. He wanted to comfort Victoria, but he couldn't help unless she let him.

'What we're doing is a sin,' she whispered.

'Viccy, I love you, and I thought – no, that's not right. I *know* you love me. Luke is dying. No, please don't stop me, don't say anything yet. He is dying – we both know that. He doesn't know where he is or who you are, and he's been like that for months. Eli told me how difficult it's been for you. He admires you, you know, and he thinks you've been a real brick. The fact that we're in love is not a sin. My God, with life so damn fragile it would be a sin to waste what we feel for each other. Come here, Viccy. Come and sit beside me.'

But she couldn't take comfort, she had to be strong, to cope within herself, and she shook her head abruptly. 'No,' she said, 'you won't convince me. I shan't make love to you again – it would be like asking God to do something awful. I'm sure he's been picked up. He must have been captured by the Germans. Sometimes relatives don't hear for months. Neil's convinced he's alive, and they've always known about each other, ever since they were small.'

Bertie was close to shouting at her. He was strung like a violin, taut to breaking point. He only had to start talking and he would be saying things he'd regret for ever. The night that Simon had telephoned, he'd told her his failing, told her everything about his gambling and how Sylvia had only married Simon to get him out of the most terrible trouble. He had revealed his innermost soul to her, and all she had done was to go on and on about her son. He stood for a moment, a vein beating wildly in his temple, and then he turned quickly, his heel leaving an imprint in the Chinese carpet as he walked quickly from the room.

'Morning, Miss Honour.' John touched his cap in greeting.

'Hallo, John. I suppose you do know it's only half past seven. Don't tell me my mother has you working from first light.' Honour laughed at John's embarrassment. He was like a boy caught stealing cherries, but all he was doing was hoeing around the runner-bean plants.

'These fine mornings it's a shame to lie abed.'

'I know, I couldn't stay indoors myself. It's heavenly, isn't it?' She looked up. The dawn clouds were breaking up, their remnants stretched thinly to make a mackerel pattern on the last pink wash over the high blue sky.

' "You are nearer to God's heart in a garden . . ." ' John smiled. Miss Honour had always liked the rhyme that was engraved on the sundial. It didn't matter that she had her hair up and was wearing a straight skirt, he found it impossible to think of her as a woman; she was still a child to him.

'John, do you find things difficult sometimes? I mean, do you feel that nobody else has problems, only you?'

'Everyone has problems, Miss Honour.' John stared down at the mud clinging to his boots. 'Some big, some small, but inside your head, they're all problems, all have to be sorted.' He was a quiet man, not given to philosophy, but it had seemed natural for Honour to seek help from him. After all, her problem was a simple one; it was just the answer that was difficult.

'Do you remember when I was born, John?' she asked.

'I remember when it was, all right. The squire – Mr Luke, that is – told us he'd had news from Australia, and he stood us all a drink down at the pub. Came in with us. "Drinks all round," he said. Very generous man I always found him to be.' His tone implied that others had found differently.

'What did you think when he told you my name?'

'Your name – what, you mean Honour?'

She nodded, watching him carefully. His answer was important to her.

'I thought it was a nice name. Very suitable, very Victorian, a little lady. That's what I thought right away – you'd grow up to be a real lady with a name like that.'

'It's very difficult being called Honour, you know.' She was frowning, her brow wrinkling as it had when she was a child puzzled by something in a grown-ups' world. 'I feel I have to live up to it. And now, when everything is so difficult, I feel I can't talk to anybody, in case I let something slip. I get to know quite a lot of secrets, you see, from the conversations I hear when I'm driving – we all do. But no one else seems to worry about it. And my name seems to affect other people as well; they seem to think they have to treat me differently, to look after me, when all I want to do is make my own decisions.' She couldn't tell him that she thought her name was stopping Carl making love to her.

'You don't have to worry talking to old John,' John smiled. Miss Honour had always been his favourite, and it was just like her to get into such a state about nothing. 'I've got sawdust between my ears, just like the scarecrow that's down in the nursery garden. There's nothing you can tell me that's going to cause any bother. And I don't reckon you'll let anything slip. You always were a clever little thing, and secretive. Do you remember that hare?'

Honour remembered the hare well enough. She'd hidden it while the beagles and their followers were scouring the ground. It was the first time she had told a deliberate lie. It had seemed necessary to save the animal's life, and thinking back, she hadn't worried over that subterfuge. It was pleasant being with John, out in the fresh air, and perhaps she was overreacting about her name. But it had been the final straw when Margaret laughed at her – better the name Honour than Chastity, had been her cousin's contribution. 'I suppose I'd better go in for breakfast,' she said. 'Thanks, John.'

'Nothing to thank me for.' He was smiling as he went back to his hoeing. It was good to know that in the changing world some things never altered. One of them was Miss Honour. She was just the same little girl she'd always been.

* * *

210

Bertie was gone, finally and for ever. How could she bear it?

Victoria tried vainly to concentrate on the task she had set herself. Last night she had lain awake for hours planning what she would write, how she would begin her family's saga. It had been a way of stopping herself worrying about Nigel. She felt that for him to have any chance at all, she had to believe that he was alive and well. In the bright light of morning, faced with a blank sheet of paper and an endless expanse of time stretching ahead of her, the first words of the book that Isabella had suggested she should write were an insurmountable hurdle.

She placed her left hand on the white paper, spreading the fingers wide. The diamonds in her eternity ring sparkled, the ruby centre of her engagement ring gleamed like rich blood, and the wedding band was overpowered by their opulence. Her fingers were long and tapering, her hand smooth and white. She clenched it to make a fist.

Bertie would never come again. The house seemed emptier because of that, the silence of the cool rooms deeper. She could see him in her mind. His fine wavy hair, the jaunty moustache, his smile when he was happy, how he looked like a little boy lost when he was sad. She believed he was the type of man who would age well, and yet people said it was character that showed in an old man's face. If that was so, would Bertie show the weakness she had found was in him? Was that why she loved him so much, because she knew that he needed her? She had always fallen in love with weak men. So long ago that it seemed in a different life she had thought she loved a man who was strong – and hard. But that hadn't been love, and through that man she had discovered that, for

211

her, passion was not always linked with love. Luke had been weak, doubting her for so long. Their life together had been a succession of tests. She had been happy through those years, playing a game of showing her husband how indispensable he was for her, pretending not to notice his ageing body, his declining abilities.

Victoria crumpled the paper under her hand, despoiling its virgin whiteness. She stood slowly and then took a cigarette from the box on her desk. The time was past when Luke noticed the smell, so there was no reason why she should deprive herself any longer. How many more years would he live? It was possible for her to consider the question dispassionately now that he was nothing more than a vegetable, his bodily needs provided for by the nurse. If there was no medical crisis, he could go on for years, surviving in his cocoon. If there had been no war she would have gone abroad, far away, and spent some of the seemingly limitless funds that lay, hardly touched, in the bank. Marooned as she was, it would be logical to have a lover. There was a cynical streak in her make-up that smiled at how detached she was able to be. But then it was only possible to review the situation so unfeelingly because she had already ruined whatever chance she had of happiness. Bertie was gone.

She sat down again at the desk. It was easier to think with a cigarette. She reached forward to pick up her pen, relishing the cool slimness of it between her fingers. She was at a crossroads in her life, just as her country was, and possibly the whole world. But what had been the beginning of her journey, where had her own, personal history begun? Not with her birth, but long before that. What had moulded her, formed her strengths, her weaknesses? What were the traits in her mother and father that had descended to her, and would be part of Nigel

212

and Neil? She had to begin with her parents' beginning, when her mother had thrown over Michael and run to Thomas. Without that, Victoria would never have been, and Luke would never have entered their lives at all.

She wrote her name on the top right-hand corner of the page, and on the left she put the number, one. Then there was the title – it must go in the centre. What would show what she meant, how everything that happened then, in the summer of 1901, made her what she was today? The past was her . . . She smiled, writing the word in a clear, flowing script. It was perfect. The past was her 'Heritage'.

All actual heroes are essential men,
And all men possible heroes.

Elizabeth Browning, 1809–1861

Lucinda drew her breath in sharply. 'Just look at that, Issy. That's a bad omen, if ever I've seen one. I said they shouldn't have held the reception here.'

Ahead of them, marring the splendour of the stone-walled hall, a painting lay drunkenly on the stone-flagged floor, its ornate frame splintered beyond repair.

'For Heaven's sake, Lucinda.' Isabella hurried past her sister, bending to pick up the pieces. She had to struggle to turn the canvas over; it was large enough to be awkward. 'Look, the string's broken, that's all. It's nothing to do with omens, good or bad, and please don't say anything to the others about it. It's a happy day, a wonderful chance to bring some joy back into the house. Goodness knows, it could do with it.' She stood up, holding the painting of the cavalier away from her clothes; she didn't want to get messy. It was the first time that she had changed out of mourning and she was wearing a well-cut dress and jacket in a subdued blue floral print. Pencombe was her home, and despite all that had happened there, she intended to show that she and the house still had a role to play.

Lucinda shrugged her shoulders theatrically. Isabella had never had an ounce of imagination, whereas she herself was a martyr to her intuition. 'Well, I'm going into the drawing room to wait,' she said. 'We should have done all this at Reason Hill. It would have made so much more sense. That is, if we really had to make such an effort at celebrating what is, as Margaret so blatantly

217

admits, already a fact.' Lucinda's voice faded as she walked heavily away.

Isabella was alone and now she had no excuse not to face up to the nameless fears that had made sleep so difficult over the past weeks. It was all so familiar – there was nothing at all strange in the hall. At first she had had no problem coming to terms with the damage to the house, but it had unsettled something deep inside her. For the first time ever, she was uneasy whenever she was on her own, imagining that she heard noises, sensing a stranger's presence. She knew it was all nonsense and the happiness of the wedding would lay all the imaginary ghosts to rest. She looked slowly around. The painting would have fallen from the wall because of the shock of the blast. It had been insensitive of Lucinda to make a fuss about it, but then sensitivity had never been her strong point. Everywhere was clean and dusted – Maggy had seen to that. When Margaret had been so adamant that she wanted to be married from Pencombe, Albert's wife had moved in to supervise a major spring clean. Only for the last night before the wedding had she moved back to the farm, so that she could be with her daughter for her final evening as Margaret Elizabeth, spinster of this parish, who was so eagerly preparing to give up her freedom.

There was a honeyed smell of polish, and bowls brimful of garden flowers graced every possible surface. Margaret had been quite right, it was a beautiful house to begin her married life in, and she and Percy would stay for the three days' leave that would be their honeymoon. It would all be perfect – as long as no one went to the west wing. Involuntarily Isabella's eyes strayed towards the stairs. There was a rope stretched across, as there had been before the war when the day trippers came on the guided tours. Then it had been to prevent them wandering into the private apartments; now it was to shut off the wreckage of the rooms that had once been the centre of her life. She could remember it all so clearly. That beautiful afternoon, when Michael had seemed so much brighter than he had been for a long time. She had been sitting reading a book, with the windows wide open. A bee had flown into the room, its legs yellow with pollen from the roses as it drunkenly searched for more. The droning had made her drowsy and so she'd stood up to go downstairs and make some tea. She remembered Michael sitting there, propped against the plump white pillows, sitting up in the bed that they'd bought from Maples on their return from Australia. They'd had money then, their own money, and for the first time they had been able to indulge in some luxuries to impress their own taste on the house. Michael had raised his hand as she'd left the room and smiled sleepily at her over the rim of his glasses.

Isabella stepped forward uncertainly. She wanted to see how the room was now – the visions, the ones that woke her in the night, were of the awful chaos, the taste of smoke, Michael lying as if asleep, while fire ate at the curtains . . .

'Isabella!' Eli's voice made her turn sharply, guiltily. She didn't want anyone to know how fresh the suffering still was.

'Hallo, Eli.' She waited for him to come to her and kiss her cheek. 'You're earlier than I thought. Do you think the others – '

'They're here. Come on, buck up. Give me that.' He took the painting from her, leaning it against the wall and kicking the broken frame behind it. He began to sing raucously, 'Here comes the bride, here comes the bride,' and put his arm around Isabella, making her dance a few steps with him down the hallway. She looked so awful that he felt sick with sympathy. It was going to be hard on her – a wedding always revived old memories – but it would be a good thing in the long run to start the house living again.

John Biddle waited in the church porch. The music of the organ told him that they were signing the register. Not long now before young Miss Margaret would come out into the daylight as Mrs . . . Mrs what? He couldn't remember the young officer's name, even if his life had depended on it he couldn't remember what he must have heard a dozen times. He reckoned that it was his age. He had felt suddenly older after that nonsense with Daisy. He stared down at his boots – they still weren't shining as much as he'd like – and he lifted his feet slowly, one after the other, and rubbed the toes on the backs of his trousers. He'd seen young Eli do that often enough, and he'd disapproved. He wouldn't have done it himself, if the trousers he was wearing had belonged to him.

He felt a bit of a fool, dressed up in the chauffeur's uniform. The jacket fastened right up to his neck and a double row of brass buttons down the front glinted in the odd rays of sunshine that penetrated the sanctified gloom of the porch. He tugged at the grey serge jacket. All morning he'd been pulling it down, but it had been made for a smaller man, and it kept riding up, wrinkling around his waist. As long as the buttons held, he was all right, but he was afraid that they might give up under the strain and burst open to reveal his elderly, long-sleeved vest and the braces he was wearing to keep up the trousers that, in contrast to the jacket, were a good size too big.

* * *

220

'My God, Viccy, that cough sounds dreadful.' Eli studied Victoria over the edge of his glass. She looked pinched, her shoulders were hunched and her elegant blue wrapped dress looked a good size too big. It was crumpled from where she had been huddled in her chair. She was still dressed as she had been at the wedding. After coughing all the way back in the car, she hadn't had the energy to change.

The pain across Victoria's back was so bad that she couldn't answer. It was hard for her to breathe and she swallowed convulsively, desperate to stop the coughing. She had to get some air.

'Christ, I'm phoning for a doctor.' Eli stood up quickly.

'No, no, don't . . .' She forced the words out. 'It'll pass. I'll see the doctor when he comes to visit Luke tomorrow.'

'You can't go on like this, Viccy.' Eli was still on his feet, undecided whether or not to go against her wishes. 'You look appalling.'

'Please.' The cough was subsiding and she leaned back in her chair, breathing in gratefully. 'You see – I told you it would pass. Pour me a drink, will you?'

Eli poured a generous measure of Scotch into a cut-glass tumbler. Despite the opulence of Victoria's drawing room, the atmosphere was chilly, unwelcoming. 'I know it would be an unpatriotic waste of manpower, but I wish you'd change this room. It's never felt quite right since you had it done. Nothing insulting, you understand.' He turned to hand her the glass, feeling his way carefully with his words. 'But it's not a happy room.'

'It was a compromise.' Victoria sipped her drink cautiously. There was a burning in her throat that threatened to get far, far worse. 'Everything was, in those last few years. Luke wanted his way and I should just have let him

221

go ahead. I'll change it all some day. It won't matter now that he won't ever come downstairs again.'

'Bloody cheerful talk, I must say.' Eli forced a laugh. 'I fancied a jolly evening after the wedding, and this is how it ends up. Come on, drink up. They might be closing the theatres and depriving us of the spice of life, but at least I can still come up with the hooch. I'm not all that reformed, thank Christ.'

'You still swear too much,' Victoria smiled. The alcohol had taken the edge off the pain in her chest.

'And you're still drinking and smoking too much. It's just as well we enjoy each other's company – we're just two middle-aged reprobates.'

'How's Sylvia?'

'That's below the belt.'

'I'm not asking about the position of your feelings for her, Eli, just her state of health.'

'Now that's reassuring,' Eli laughed. 'You're not half as ill as I thought. You're being vulgar, and that's a good sign.'

'I'm not ill.' She stood up carefully. She didn't want to start coughing again. 'And as for being vulgar, I'm just jealous. I don't have any lovelife, so I'm going to torment you about yours.' She took a cigarette from the inlaid ebony box on the hexagonal coffee table.

'There, that's a good example of what's wrong with this room. That table – it's in the worst possible taste. Chuck it away.'

'Not yet. I'm not ready to go that far yet. My God, this cigarette tastes foul.' She stubbed it out angrily. 'You can't depend on anything these days.'

'You can depend on me, Viccy, if things get bad.'

'Maudlin, ducky. You're being too sweet by half. You should know I can't bear sugar. Now come on, tell me a decent bit of gossip.' She curled up in her chair and tucked her legs under her, then she picked up her glass and took a sip.

Victoria slept fitfully till dawn. She woke to the sound of birds outside her window and to the most awful pain she had ever known. There were red-hot skewers forcing their way up, in between her ribs. There was no air in the room despite the billowing muslin curtains. She had to sit up. She pushed her arms down on to the deep, soft pillows that gave no support at all. More pain. There were knives stabbing into her lungs – she could feel the inside of her chest; she was aware of every innermost part and it burned, it seared. She had to breathe, but there was no air. Then she cried out.

'Victoria!'

The voice came from far away. It was her mother calling.

'Here, drink this.'

Cool, delicious water trickled on her face, through her lips. She wanted to take great mouthfuls, to immerse herself in it entirely, then at last she would be cool. Suddenly there was no air and she began gasping, choking on the liquid, drowning. Now she was burning inside again, with that awful searing pain, and then it was dark.

'But I insist on knowing, doctor.' Lucinda barred the elderly practitioner from leaving the bedroom. Behind him two nurses worked quietly and efficiently. They wiped Victoria's face and lifted her up on to the pillows, and all the time she lolled, like a doll, in their capable arms.

'Madam.' The doctor was a man of patience, but even he was on the verge of being tried too far. 'Even God

223

might not be able to provide you with an answer at this stage. Indeed, if He could, it might well be an answer you would not want.'

'And what on earth is that supposed to mean?' Lucinda's habit of sloth had disappeared over the days that her daughter had been so ill, and she was once again a creature of fiery passions. 'You're paid to speak to me in plain English, and paid more than well to look after my daughter. So far I have noticed no improvement in her condition – none at all.'

'I don't find that surprising, Mrs Cade, because there has been none. We are doing everything we can, but the patient is very weak. She was obviously run down before she developed this illness. The pleurisy itself would have been sufficient to make her most unwell. The pneumonia – ' he paused. He was concerned about the girl he had left lying unconscious. He thought of her as a girl, despite the fact that she was nearly forty and had two grown-up sons. He himself was fast approaching seventy, and he wouldn't be doctoring at all if it wasn't for the war. At least in one way it had been a blessing, inspiring him to get up from his armchair and into the real world again. 'And it is unfortunate that it has affected both lungs. Perhaps that was as a result of your having her brought down here from London. Yes, as I said, we are doing everything we can. Now, if you will excuse me, I have other patients to visit. I shall be back later, in the evening.' He thought the crisis might well come that night.

Lucinda wavered. She wanted to create more fuss, to force the man to stay and lavish all his time and attention on her daughter, but she had a miserable, niggling suspicion he might be right that everything possible was being done. In that case – terror was set to take possession of her. It went against the natural order of things. As a mother, she could not accept that her child might be approaching death. She put her fingers to her lips. They were dry and withered – she was old, it should be her they were nursing, and she felt a pang of guilt that it wasn't.

'Hallo, little girl, and who are you?' Doctor Groak smiled at the child who had quietly come into the room behind Lucinda. She was small, about eight or nine years old, he supposed, and she wasn't startlingly pretty but she was appealing. Her dark hair was curled tightly close to her head and she had bright, periwinkle-blue eyes that looked as if they smiled easily. Her features were undistinguished, but then not all beauty develops early.

Lucinda turned round quickly. 'You,' she hissed. The girl was an irritant, always appearing at the door of the sickroom, where she had no business to be. 'Go back to your mother, right now. Do as I say.' She pointed away from her, out towards the cool dark corridors. Somewhere the girl's mother would be busy, dusting or ironing, or even arranging the flowers. Jenny Jones' relative, that Tom had discovered, was a regular paragon of virtue. A pillar of strength, Isabella called her, but she had no idea of her proper, subservient position and it infuriated Lucinda beyond measure.

'My mum wanted to know how Miss Victoria was.' The child spoke with the accent of Kent. She gazed steadily at Lucinda, quite clearly unimpressed by her.

'Mrs Jones, you should call her. Mrs Jones is extremely ill and your mother doesn't have to be told that. But clearly she does have to be told to stop you wandering about the house.'

'I wonder . . .' The doctor ran the fingers of his left hand over his dry chin. It was a habit he had when he was

225

deliberating. 'Would you do a job for me, missie?' He smiled at the child and she smiled back. 'Will you sit beside the bed and talk to Mrs Jones? Just tell her about your day, what you're doing, the things that are going on. Chat away as I'm sure you do to your mother. I'm right, aren't I? You look like a little chatterbox to me.' He turned to Lucinda, drawing himself up to his full five foot eight, expanding his chest to dominate the woman he saw as meddlesome and unconstructive. 'We have to call your daughter back to the land of the living, Mrs Cade, to spur her into fighting for her life – and I don't seem to be able to achieve that medically. The problem, I believe, is that she is wandering in her mind. Obviously, some of the medications we are using will lead to hallucinations, and her temperature is fluctuating widely. When it is high, there is little we can do except to strip her off and sponge her down.'

Lucinda shuddered at the thought of Victoria's body being subjected to the indignities of medicine.

'However, there will be moments when she is close to the surface. If she has something to hold on to, something other than the pain and discomfort, then I believe it will help. Now, are you going to assist me, missie?'

'Yes,' the child nodded firmly. She liked Miss Victoria and so did her mother. 'And my name's not missie, it's Bobby. That's short for Roberta. My daddy's name is Robert.' She was quite self-possessed, fearless in front of the impressive grown-ups, and not overawed by the atmosphere of the sickroom. But then her much loved father was away at some dreadful place that her mother called 'the war'. She had been to the cinema with her mother and seen the noise and the hundreds and thousands of men. She'd looked for her daddy, but in their uniforms all the men seemed the same – until, suddenly,

226

there he was! She'd squeezed her mother's hand frantically, but then, she'd realized, it wasn't him at all, only someone else's daddy. That was when her mother had started crying into her handkerchief, the one with the border of clowns that Bobby had given her for Christmas.

It was Nigel Victoria kept seeing, his face floating towards her. He was a little boy, and she could hear his voice, talking, chattering on. He was always wanting to know something. If he asked her a question, she would answer him, but then his face changed. It faded, grew faint, and she was in the heat again, that awful, painful heat.

'And there's a secret place in the garden, somewhere only I know. Would you like me to tell you about it?' the little voice went on.

Victoria struggled to concentrate. Was it Nigel talking to her? No, it was a girl's voice. A girl. She and Luke had longed so much for another baby after the twins. A daughter would have put the seal on their happiness. She sighed, which hurt her in her chest. But she and Luke had been so sad when they were told Victoria could not conceive again. It had been such a blow – she sighed again.

'You can eat the petals, and they're golden-orangey – they taste spicy. John's my friend. I never had a friend like him before. He's telling me all about the flowers. That's about the weeds as well. He says the weeds are ever so interesting. Shall I tell you what they can do?' Bobby paused. She wished the pretty lady would answer her. It was tiring talking to herself, and the nurses' faces never changed. They moved round her as if she was part of the furniture – another bed, or a chair. 'The baby hawthorn buds, the tiny little green ones, you can eat them in sandwiches. I bet you didn't know that, did you?

Goodness, I wish you'd wake up. I'm bored. Bored and hot. Yes, it's hot in here. Everywhere else in the house is cold. But in here it's boiling. I wish they'd open the window.'

'Open the windows,' Victoria whispered. She knew now why she had been burning. How silly of Luke not to open the window.

'I've never known a real home,' Carl said. 'Except the sea – that's been the only constant thing in my life.'

Honour looked out over the fields of Kent that stretched away as far as she could see. This was her land, her country. 'But your mother must have lived some-where.' She remembered the story Carl told her of how his parents had met. 'After all, she had two other children as well as you, didn't she?'

'We went with my father. Wherever he had a job, then we would all go. That was how I learned to speak English, and French, come to that, as well as German.' He laughed, and it sounded bitter. 'That might come in handy if I'm shot down.'

'It must have been exciting. My brothers would have loved to have been able to be on a boat all the time.'

'No they wouldn't. It was cramped and smelly, and sometimes it was dirty as well. We would have given anything to have a proper home. But it was easier for my parents the way it was.'

'Easier?' Honour turned to face Carl. They were sitting on the bench that she and Eli had sat on, all those months ago when she had been still in love with James. In love? She now realized that she hadn't understood the meaning of the word until she met Carl.

'They were never married.' He stared down at his hands that were clasped together on his lap. He wouldn't

228

touch Honour until he'd told her everything. Then she would have to decide her feelings for him. 'It wasn't true, what I told you about them meeting. At least, the part about my father thinking she was a creature out of his dreams was true enough. But she was another man's wife and her husband was a wealthy man, much older than she was. I think he must have spoilt her, because she always believed she should have anything she wanted. That was why, when she fell in love with my father, she was prepared to run off with him. She lived in a dream world, always reading her fairy stories – we had to be quiet for hours. Life was so . . .' He couldn't think of the words to explain how it had been, how he'd always felt cramped, too close to his brothers – even though he loved them. His parents were engrossed in each other, and Carl was little more to them than a living proof of their love. His two brothers – the other man's sons – were tolerated, nothing more. The three boys were fed and clothed and grew to be strong, healthy young men, but the only emotional support they had was from each other. 'I'm illegitimate, Honour, and I've never known what it's like to have a real home, to stay in one place. Now – now I want to marry a girl whose family are a part of the history of England. Your life has been so different from mine; we have no common ground.' He stood up suddenly. He saw how great the gulf was between them and it frightened him.

'We love each other.' Honour spoke softly. Carl's words still seemed like some tale – a story that she'd read in a book. It was him she wanted, not his past. Why couldn't he understand that?

'After the war, I always thought, I would go back to working with my brothers. We had a tugboat and we were becoming very successful, because we had no fear, because we knew the sea so well . . . But it is no place for a woman, or for children. I don't know what else I could do.'

'Neil has no idea what he'll do when it's all over, either. He was saying just the other day that the only thing he enjoys, apart from flying, is driving his car. He thought he might go into racing. Apparently he and Nigel had made some plans . . .' Honour's voice trailed off. It was hard to keep believing that Nigel would turn up safe.

'When I first met your cousin I thought he was crazy, and those beautiful cars – to have one each.' He smiled, and it was the first time he'd looked happy since they arrived at Pencombe. 'But now I know the whole world's gone mad.'

'Because?'

'Because I'm so in love that I want to give up the sea. I don't want to face a future fighting the elements. I want to come home every evening to my beautiful wife and children. I want a fire burning in the grate, and a meal cooking in the kitchen. I want to go to the theatre, and to eat out in wonderful restaurants. I want to enjoy the life that Eli has shown me exists for the privileged few. I would work so hard for you, my darling.' He took her hand in his. 'If you give me a chance, I will put everything I have into giving you the life you deserve.'

'If I have you, that will be enough for me to be happy for ever.' Honour could feel her heart beating – it was so fast that her voice was trembling.

Carl got to his knees. He was looking into the eyes of the woman he adored, willing her with all his being to accept his proposal. 'Will you marry me, Honour? Will you make me the happiest man in the whole world?'

'Yes, oh my darling, yes.' Honour leaned towards him and they kissed, so softly, so gently, until Carl jumped to his feet, holding her to him. He began to waltz, and round and round they spun as he sang in his light, musical voice. He began the tune of 'The Blue Danube'. Louder and louder he sang. Then he stopped suddenly. 'There will be peace,' he said, 'and when there is, I shall take you to see the Danube and the Rhine and all the great waterways of Europe. No longer shall they be for my business, they shall be for my pleasure.'

They walked back to the house hand in hand. Carl would have to ask Isabella for her blessing on their proposed marriage. He would do that when Honour went upstairs to visit Victoria – that, after all had been the purpose of their visit. He felt a guilty sense of relief that there was no Lord Montford to ask permission of. Honour's brother Eddy wasn't likely to be back in England for some time. And in any case, as she'd said herself, he wasn't the type to bother with ceremony.

'How thoughtful of you to give Honour this little party for her engagement, Adele.' Lucinda accented the 'little' heavily. She thought there was an air of stinginess about the canapés, and the hired waiters were very slow in serving the champagne.

Adele smiled falsely. She hadn't talked intimately to Lucinda in a long time. Years ago they had been what passed for close friends, but that was before the abdication. 'It was the least I could do,' she said. 'After all, now that your Viccy is out of circulation I'm sure you'd find it too much to cope with by yourself at Cadogan Gardens. It must be years since you gave a party. In fact – ' Adele paused. She'd had two very dry martinis before her guests started to arrive. 'Dutch courage' she'd called them, but they'd made her feel argumentative. It was time Lucinda

231

had her come-uppance. 'It must have been the time you celebrated *the* engagement.'

Lucinda's eyes narrowed. No one had mentioned her social gaffe for so many years that she had learned to live with it. She no longer blushed at the mention of the royal family, no longer felt constrained to remain silent in conversations that featured the Windsors.

'Do you ever hear from her?' Adele continued. 'From that woman Simpson, I mean.'

'Wallis – you used to call her Wallis, I seem to remember.' Lucinda held her glass out to a white-jacketed youth proffering a half-full bottle of Moët.

'I was never really friendly with her. Not like you, Lucinda. And of course, the moment I realized things were becoming so serious between her and the King, I stopped seeing her at once, as did Bill. He'd been quite a pal of her husband's – I think they saw a bit of each other after she divorced him.'

'I wasn't to know.' Lucinda gripped the stem of her glass tightly. She hated remembering how badly it had all ended. She'd been ostracized, cut out of the supreme social set that she'd worked so hard to get into. And it was all so unfair. 'You sent me those American press cuttings, the ones that said she'd end up queen. Without them I . . .'

'They were to warn you, more than anything. You interpreted them to suit yourself, Lucinda. What they said depended on how you read them.' Adele was becoming bored. She turned away from Lucinda and looked around her room. She wanted to circulate; she didn't want to stand still, being monopolized by Lucinda and her very old scandal. 'Bella, my dear.' She reached out and touched her daughter on the arm. 'Let's get the party going – why don't we swop partners?' she laughed, and in the sound there was a rare echo of her old, gay youth. She stepped quickly towards Bella's guest. It was Peter Savage. This would be the third time she'd met the man, but the first that they would have a chance to talk properly. Bill disliked him, and Eli was dead set against him – Adele looked again, reappraising the handsome, aquiline nose and the forceful dark eyes. She couldn't see what the men were so excited about. He looked ideal for Bella.

'What on earth's the matter, Lucinda?' Bella was quite cross at her mother for getting her stuck in a corner with her aunt. 'You look absolutely furious. This is meant to be a party, you know.'

'Your mother is the matter, that's what.' Lucinda's voice was very high. She felt strangled by her anger. 'Some while ago she got me into a most unpleasant situation. Most unpleasant indeed. She never admitted it was her fault. All the stigma was attached to my name and she escaped scotfree. It wasn't fair, not at all. She was as eager to be friends with the woman as I was. After all, what an entrée . . .'

'What woman?' Bella twirled her glass between her long, tapering fingers. She was always happy to hear about any little sin her mother might have committed; there seemed to be so few of them.

'Wallis Simpson.' Lucinda almost spat the name.

'Good Lord.' Bella's surprise was genuine. It was the first she'd heard of any family connection with the royal scandal. 'When did you know her?'

'Years ago.' Lucinda struggled to remember exactly when it had all started. 'In the thirties – thirty-one, or was it two? No, I think it was later than that; it must have been in thirty-four. Of course, everyone knew that the Prince of Wales was fond of married women. There was

Mrs Dudley Ward, the MP's wife – Isabella knew her vaguely – and then there was Thelma, Lady Furness. There was nothing very wrong in it; after all, the royal men have always needed their – ' Lucinda paused. She couldn't quite think how to put it. 'Let's say, their lady friends. It must be very lonely, to be royal. So then Wallis came on the scene. She was so elegant – very, very slim and she always wore the most beautiful clothes. The Prince was quite besotted and his other two ladies were utterly abandoned. I'd met her a few times, and your mother knew her quite well. That was through the American connection, of course. Then, after a couple of years, when it had been rather fun meeting her off and on, and the Prince became King, one felt quite close to the throne. Your mother paid a visit to New York, and she sent me back all the newspapers. There was a great pile of them. I remember quite clearly. Some of them contained nasty little jokes, others absolute filth.' Lucinda looked disgusted. She couldn't remember exactly what had been said, but it had been smutty and she had considered that as *lèse majesté*. 'But the *New York Journal* – I remember that quite clearly – it said that the King would marry Wallis. I was astonished. She had never talked about another divorce, at least not in front of me. Perhaps I didn't know her well enough. You have to understand that there was nothing in our newspapers about the possibility of marriage. I asked Michael why there wasn't and he was quite rude. He said that I should mind my own business, and that if I knew what was good for me, I wouldn't see so much of her.'

'And I never knew.' Bella turned so that she could watch her mother. Peter was being his most charming and her mother was responding like a girl. With a start of surprise, Bella realized that she was still surprisingly pretty.

'Well, she wouldn't tell you, would she? I mean, it was me that suffered most but your mother was certainly implicated.'

'Suffered? You mean because Mrs Simpson didn't become queen, you were upset for her – is that what you mean?'

'No, no. It was the most awful time – I mean, for the King to abdicate. Nobody thought, least of all I – ' Lucinda paused. She had been emotionally shattered; she had never thought the romance would lead to that. 'There was the most tremendous upsurge of hate. Wallis was reviled – she was talked about as the scarlet woman. And I'd been close to her, even though it wasn't as close as people said. But it destroyed me socially. I went abroad for a while, and when I came back it was a little easier, the initial fury had died away. Perhaps in the long run . . . Well, our King and Queen have been so good, haven't they? And their little girls are so brave. The royal family are sharing everything with their people, the danger and the suffering. I don't know if he would have done that.' Lucinda's voice drifted away. She was remembering the Edward whom his family had called David. His pro-Hitler sympathies had sparked off yet another furore. Perhaps he had never been meant to be King. She was tired and she needed another drink. She looked around for a waiter and realized that Bella had left her.

Honour held Carl's arm tightly. Her cheeks ached from smiling as she accepted the best wishes of her family and friends. Isabella was making sure that the young couple met everyone; even Bella's boyfriend, Peter Savage – who, Eli had told her, was a thoroughly bad lot – but it would have been bad manners to miss him out.

'Mummy.' Honour let go of Carl's arm to whisper to her mother. 'We really ought to go. Carl has to get back this evening, and I'd like to see him to the train.'

'You can't leave now.' Isabella's expression didn't change as she squeezed her daughter's hand briefly. She was sympathetic with the young lovers, but Adele had arranged a supper for close family. 'I'm sorry, my dear, but you'll have to stay. Adele's been very kind and it would be impossibly rude for both the guests of honour to abandon her. Besides, she's had a special cake made, and you'll have to cut it later.'

Carl leaned across his fiancée. She was always so desperate to spend every possible minute with him, it was as if she doubted he would come back to her. 'I'll let you keep Honour for now, Lady Montford,' he said. 'But after the wedding it will be different. Then I shall keep her for life.' He smiled as he spoke. He liked the woman who would become his mother-in-law, even though he was sure they would have some difficult times until he established that her daughter would owe him first allegiance when she was his wife. But he was prepared, and he was already being teased by his friends in the traditional English way – to them a 'mother-in-law' was some kind of joke.

'I'll come with you to the door.' Honour walked ahead of Carl and picked up his raincoat from a pile on the stand in the small hall. She smiled into the mirror as Carl stood behind her, looking over her shoulder. 'This would be a nice engagement photograph,' she said. The topaz necklace sparkled at her throat, echoing the blue of her dress and heightening the colour of her eyes.

'Don't be too upset.' Carl knew her moods so well; she was putting on a brave face for his benefit. 'When you cut the cake, you can make a wish. I wonder what it will be?'

He ran the tip of his finger down the nape of her neck and she reached up to hold his hand and trap him close to her for a moment.

'It's bad luck to tell a wish,' she smiled.

'You English, I've never come across so much superstition! I thought my mother, with all her trolls, was funny enough.' He no longer felt any awkwardness talking about his mother. A new sense of his love for Honour made him squeeze her fingers gently. How lucky he had been to find her. He was very close to her, only having to whisper, 'But some of the other things . . . Do you know Percy throws salt over his shoulder if he spills some on the table? And he won't walk under ladders, or wear green on a Friday. I wonder if Margaret knows what she's getting herself into.' He laughed, putting his arms around the girl he loved and holding her against him. 'I have a leave coming up soon. If we were married we could have gone away, to Scotland – that's where I'd like to go.'

'We could go anyway.' Honour kept looking into his eyes. 'You mean so much to me, that in a way it's as if we were married already.'

They stood very still.

'Honour!' Lucinda came through the drawing-room door towards them. 'You must get me home. I can't stay here another minute.' There were tears on her face and she looked distraught.

Isabella came quickly behind her. 'Don't leave, please don't go, Lucinda. Come and talk to me, come on, there's someone I especially want you to meet.' She looked at Carl over Lucinda's head, and silently mouthed, 'Good luck.'

'Piece of cake.' Carl raised a hand in farewell, and touched the tip of his thumb with the tip of his forefinger.

'Piece of cake,' he repeated and grinned. He was becoming more English than even the inimitable Percy. He gave Honour a quick kiss on the cheek. He felt lightheaded as he ran down the stairs. She would come away with him. They would go to some little hotel, out in the wilds. He wanted to see the moors, the wild expanses that Neil had talked about so lovingly. They would fish in bubbling rivers, lie on purple heather and watch the eagles fly. There would be no planes, nothing but the true masters of the air above them. Then at night, as the chill of evening made them hold together for warmth, they would make real love for the first time. He stood still as he stepped on to the pavement. He wanted to shout, to leap in the air, he was singing inside. He glanced down at his watch. If he hurried he had just time. He had to fly for himself, to use the freedom of the air to express his feelings. He began to run along the pavement towards the station.

'Bobby?' Victoria stretched her hand out tentatively. She couldn't open her eyes, because if she did the pain in her head would begin again. 'Is that you, Bobby?'

'I'm here. It's all right, she isn't up yet.' Bobby knew that Victoria's mother would send her away when she paid her ritual morning visit to the sickroom, but until then they could talk in peace. 'Do you have a story for me, then?' Bobby had woken up that morning thinking about Victoria's promise. She had said she would make up a story, a very special one.

'Yes, I have your story. It kept me awake last night, thinking about it. It's all about a beautiful young girl.'

'Oh.' There was disappointment in Bobby's voice. She'd hoped it might be about her and she knew she wasn't beautiful.

Victoria guessed her thoughts, and said, 'It's not about the kind of girl that you will grow up into, Bobby. You'll be strong and clever and very, very pretty. But Jasmine was quiet and delicate.'

'Jasmine? That's a funny name.'

'Yes, it's foreign – the girl was Japanese. She had a tiny, oval face, with eyes as dark as sloes, and skin as pale and smooth as a petal from a damask rose. Her hair was dark and thick and quite straight. She didn't have any curls; they wouldn't have been quite the thing in Japan.'

'Did she go to school?'

'No, she stayed at home, in the house of her mother and father. She learned her lessons from a very old man. He was bent and wrinkled. In fact, he looked just like a bonsai tree. I don't suppose you know what that is, do you, Bobby? It's a plant that is quite small – only about the size of a geranium – even though it is very old. It grows in a pot and it could be a hundred or more years old. It's very gnarled and wrinkled – a cousin of mine has one, and she has to prune its roots.'

'I don't think I'd like to be taught by someone who looked like that,' Bobby said.

'Perhaps you wouldn't, but Jasmine loved the old man. He was very wise, and he taught her the beauty of the things around her – the flowers and the birds, the little creatures. They were her only friends because her parents were too frightened to let her play with other children in case she should change and become less perfect. She didn't see her parents very much, but they watched her through a screen that was made of sandalwood. It was carved into the most fantastic design of two dragons fighting. Their eyes were pierced in the wood and through them her mother and father could watch the girl, each day noting how she grew more beautiful.'

'They were spying on her and that's horrid. My mummy and daddy wouldn't do that to me.' Bobby's voice was high with annoyance. She was a very fair child, and she liked other children. Jasmine was in need of her friendship.

'One day the teacher didn't come to the house. Instead there was another man. He too was old, but he was fat – round like a butterball, and just as yellow and oily. He was very gentle with Jasmine, and very polite. She was frightened of him at first, but soon she went back to her studies, sitting quietly in the garden, reading a book that her teacher had given her. It was the story of a young girl who had come to the age to be married. As she read she became cold. The sun shone down on her but she didn't feel its heat. Suddenly she jumped up and cried out. The fat man came quickly to her side and took her icy hands in his. He told her how much he loved her, and said that he had watched her through the screen, and had fallen in love with her when she was very small. Now he and her parents were agreed that it was time she should become his wife.'

'But that's dreadful, if I was her . . .' Bobby's imagination began to work feverishly, 'I should run away, I should . . .'

'You must remember that Jasmine had never been anywhere except in her parents' home. She had no idea of the world outside, other than the things she had read in books, and those had been stories so grand, so full of warriors and strange, mystical animals, that it was a terrifying place. No, she had to accept what her parents had planned for her. But the fat man, whose name was Ahwoh, really was in love with her and wanted her to be happy. So he told her about the palace he had built for her to live in. It had thirty rooms, like the days of the month, and twelve courtyards, like the months of the year. The most precious month of all was May, when she was born. In that courtyard there was a stream, and the sound of it was music and the water shone like diamonds. He promised that every morning she would see her perfect reflection in a golden bowl that received the stream, before it spilled over to descend into a field of blue and white irises.'

'Did that make her happy?'

'Oh yes, then she was very happy, and that night she dreamed about the golden bowl. In the morning Ahwoh bound her eyes with a silken scarf and very gently, taking her by the hand, led her to a carriage that took her on a journey to her new home. Only when Jasmine was in the May garden did he take off the blindfold.'

'And was it beautiful?' Bobby could see it in her mind. She thought of the garden of Pencombe, the grey stone fountain that had been empty of water since she'd arrived; now she could picture it overflowing with water, and a field of irises spread all around.

'It was more beautiful than anything she had ever imagined. Day after day she came to gaze down into the golden bowl. Ahwoh was a busy man and he was away for a long time, so she became lonely. One day she dipped her fingers into the cool waters and wished. She wished for someone to talk to. The next morning a small green frog sat on the edge of the bowl. He was very clever and charming and all day long they talked of the universe, the stars and the moon. Jasmine had never been happier. But Ahwoh was a jealous man, and he had spies watching his wife. The next day the frog was gone, killed by the servants. But there was something magic in Jasmine's life, and under the water, painted on the gold, appeared the picture of a small green frog. This was the work of a

241

secret admirer. Then Jasmine became lonely again, and wished – '

'Victoria!' Lucinda swept into the room. She had lost weight worrying about her daughter and her face was formidably lined and imperious. 'You are straining yourself talking to that child.'

Bobby jumped up off her chair. She wasn't going to stay when the old dragon came into the room. Dragon – the word reminded her of the story. She must go and look in the stone fountain. Perhaps there would be a frog. She escaped with a quick squeeze of Victoria's hand.

'Good morning, Mother.' Victoria opened her eyes. The pain came back instantly. It was beneath the brow bone of her right eye and it throbbed, deep-seated and unmoving.

'What kind of night did you have?'

'I slept well, thank you.' I was in Japan, she thought, staring down into a golden bowl.

Lucinda breathed in sharply in irritation as Isabella came into the room. Her sister was dressed smartly in a cream silk blouse and a fitted beige skirt. Lucinda wished that she herself had been wearing something other than a loose-fitting house dress. Isabella was regaining all her old strengths, she thought. It was unseemly how quickly she had recovered from Michael's death.

'Good morning, everybody.' Isabella's quick smile of greeting included the nurse, who had begun the morning ministrations. 'Now, Victoria, I have a plan. But you will have to promise me to be better next week. Don't look so scandalized, Lucinda. I've talked this over with the doctor and he's in total agreement. Victoria will have to take things easy for quite a while, but there's no reason she shouldn't be up and doing a little walking about at the fête next week.'

242

'The fête?'

'Yes – sideshows, a play on the lawns, cream teas, everything just as it should be. The only reason it was cancelled last year was because Michael was ill. When you think of it, we were selfish to do that; the villagers have always enjoyed it, and it's always been such fun for the children and the grown-ups too, come to that. It would be wrong for the village to remember that Michael was the reason for it being stopped for good. This is something we can do in his memory.' She smiled brightly. Every time she spoke of Michael her throat tightened unbearably, but that was her own private emotion. Publicly she was going to act stoically, as he would have wanted.

'It's not patriotic,' Lucinda pouted.

'But of course it's patriotic. It makes sense to keep things going on normally. If it's really hot I thought I'd see if Tom could get the fountain going. Then the children could splash about in it. You were quite right, Viccy, I should have had a swimming pool put in. Perhaps we'll have one by next year.'

'Oh, my goodness.' Lucinda stood up with a great show of dignity. 'I think you're off your head. Here we are with these ghastly raids every day, and you're talking about swimming pools.'

'They're not raids, Lucinda, just air-raid warnings. They've been like a lot of little pinpricks. Very useful for getting everyone into the routine. That's what the doctor said yesterday, he said every time we go down to the shelter or check the blackout screens, it's an inoculation, preparing us for the disease, if it ever comes.'

'Well I'm glad you've got time to talk such rubbish, Isabella. Victoria, you are to rest quietly. I am going to write some letters. Though heaven only knows if they'll ever get there.' Lucinda's final words drifted back along the corridor as she made her majestic way to the morning room.

'Dear Mummy, she doesn't ever change, does she?' Victoria let her eyes close. It was so much easier with only Isabella in the room.

'She loves you very much, Viccy. She's eaten hardly anything since you became ill. But you're right, her temperament is set in its mould. Mine is too, and yours. We're a formidable set of females.'

'Especially if you include Honour.'

'Honour? Do you think she's formidable too? I find it difficult to be objective about her. She was such a sweet child, but not a paragon, thank heavens. There were quite a few things that I had to keep hidden from Michael. He liked his children's behaviour to be exemplary, poor dear.' She laughed, and it was a warm, affectionate sound. 'He set such high standards for all of us that we were bound to fall short of them sooner or later.'

'I don't expect you ever did.'

'You'd be surprised. I know it's the way of things,' Isabella laid her cool dry hand on Victoria's, 'for a younger generation to think their elders never got up to anything, but we've all had our moments.'

'Seriously?' Victoria turned towards her aunt. Headache or not, she had to look at Isabella. What an amazing thing, to think of her having 'had her moments'. 'What are you talking about, Aunt Issy? What were you, mistress to some vastly rich Australian sheep baron? Is that where all the Montford wealth came from?'

Isabella smiled. 'I was right to say you should be a novelist, Viccy, you have a splendid imagination. No, I never really considered the Australian ranchers as suitable for a lady of my standing. Don't look like that – I am

244

joking, you know. Actually, there were some very attractive men out in Australia, but no, I never had any lasting liaisons.'

'Not there, or not anywhere?'

The nurse came back into the room and Isabella stood up. 'I don't think this conversation is doing as the doctor said and keeping you calm.'

'Will you tell me, afterwards? When I'm up and about, will you tell me about your past?'

'I'll tell you some things, perhaps, some mistakes I made that I wouldn't like you to make. Forty is a dangerous age. I was lucky I conceived Honour, and some of those years were used up. But a woman's a strange creature and she has to feel loved.' She put her hand up to her necklace. It was a simple strand of pearls, one that Michael had given her. She had doubted him, once before Honour was even thought of, and then . . . She stood quite still. It was wrong to think of that time, so close now to his dying. But it was possible – no, probable – that Victor was still alive. After all, he had been so strong and healthy. Would she really tell Victoria?

'If you see Bobby, send her back in here, will you?' Victoria surrendered herself to the nurse. It was time for her blanket bath, and whereas she hated the indignity of it, she loved to feel cool and fresh again afterwards.

The grey stone griffin stared impassively over Bobby's head. There was dry green lichen on his toes and a chip off one ear, but in spite of his defects he was quite in command of the garden. At his feet a wide stone trough waited vainly to be filled with water, but it was at least damp. It had rained overnight and the stone was cool. Suddenly a tiny brown figure darted out from under the griffin's claws. Bobby held her breath. It was so small, so alert – a miniature dragon. The creature paused, its head held high and still, a tiny tongue flickering in and out. She could see every detail of its minute feet – they were splayed, and coloured a paler brown than the rest of the diamond-patterned body. She moved her hand slowly forward. Victoria would love to see this; here was a real live inhabitant for their golden bowl. The cloud broke apart high above her head and the sun shone down, bright and powerful. The shadow of the child's hand crossed over the newt, which flicked its tail in derision as it disappeared once again into its dank home.

'Damn!' Bobby slapped her hand vainly down on the stone where a second before she had been so close to catching her prey.

'Does your mother know you speak like that?'

Bobby turned round quickly. 'Good morning, Lady Montford,' she said.

'When I had a little girl, I used to tell her that I'd wash her mouth out with soap if she used naughty words.'

'And did you?'

'No, I never did. But then she had elder brothers, and I always blamed them for swearing in front of her. Not that they did it often, but boys think it's clever to swear, which is silly really because it makes them sound very young.'

'There are no boys here.'

'No. I suppose it's very lonely for you, is it?'

'I have my friends,' the child said defensively. 'John, and Miss Victoria.'

'Oh yes, I have a message for you from Miss Victoria: you can go and see her. And you shall make some new friends soon. Next week we'll be having a big party in the garden and all the village children will come.' She should have thought earlier to introduce Bobby and her mother to some of the village. They were quite isolated in the house.

'A party? That will be lovely.' Bobby could remember a party. It had been for her fifth birthday. Daddy had been there, and some of her friends. Mummy had baked a cake, and put icing on it, and five pink candles. There'd been presents, and Gran and Gramps. 'Can my gran come?' she asked. Gramps had got old and died, just before her daddy went away.

'If she can get here. It's difficult sometimes for people to travel at the moment.' Bobby's mother had said the old lady was poorly, and she might have to go back to the coast for a while to be with her at the end. Isabella had suggested the child stayed on at Pencombe when that happened. 'Why don't you go and see Victoria now? She likes company and it's good for her.'

'Could we have the fountain at the party?'

'Yes, we shall have the fountain. If John can get it working, that is.'

'John can do anything. He's teaching me about the country, so that when I go home, I shall be the best in the class at nature.'

'You shall be going to school here, in September. It's a very nice school in the village.'

Bobby had expected to be back home by the end of the school holidays. She considered the new situation for a few moments before asking, 'Did your children go there?'

'No, Honour was brought up in Australia, and the boys were taught at home, by a tutor, before they went away to school.'

'By a tutor.' Bobby said the words carefully. 'That's like Jasmine, she had lessons at home.' Victoria must want to tell her the rest of the story. She paused for a moment. It wasn't polite to hurry away from grown-ups;

247

her mummy had taught her that. But Jasmine was so lonely, she couldn't be left for long.

'Off you go.' Isabella smiled down at the child. She was such a funny little thing, she screwed her face up in the oddest of expressions. But it was lovely to have a little girl about again. It made her feel quite young. And the girl was nine, or was it ten? The age that Honour had been when Victor came into their lives. She turned away from the fountain and stared out over the garden, which was oddly overgrown now that Isabella had given instructions to cut the lawns only every second week.

Now that Victor had come back into her thoughts it was as if she'd seen him only yesterday. He was a big man, quiet as strong men often are. He'd been so supportive when Michael had his breakdown, and then afterwards. She began to walk, pollen from the golden rod in the flower border making her eyes smart. She would never be truly at peace, not ever. She owed it to Victoria to tell her how dangerous life could be – life and love. When the girl was stronger.

John was ahead of her, bending over a border of mixed pinks. He would enjoy getting the fountain going again, especially if he knew it was at the special request of little Bobby. Isabella smiled. Children were such a blessing.

'We're going to have the fountain, and the baby dragon can go for a swim, and Gran will come, and – '

'Stop, Bobby, stop. If you don't calm down and take a breath you'll end up in bed here instead of me.' Victoria was laughing. It made her cough, but the child was so funny – she was bouncing up and down on her seat in excitement.

'And you won't be in bed any more, you'll be able to make up new stories for me every day, and we'll have a golden bowl here in the garden. We'll . . .' Bobby thought hard for a minute and then continued, 'perhaps we could paint the fountain gold?' But one look at Victoria's face made her understand that that, at least, was not possible. Although everything else seemed to be.

'Tell me about your baby dragon,' Victoria asked.

'He's beautiful. He's brown like mud, with a pattern like your window panes pressed into it. He's got fingers and toes you can see right through, and a tail that flicks backwards and forwards when he's angry. He sticks his tongue in and out, very quickly, just like this.' She demonstrated, pursing her lips to stick out her bright pink tongue.

'I think he should be Jasmine's next friend.'

'I thought that. I thought that first,' Bobby cried. She wanted to jump around the room, but Miss Victoria was coughing again. She would have to sit quietly or there would be no more story.

'So, the next day,' Victoria lowered her voice. Storytelling was a secret, private pleasure, 'a beautiful fairy dragon appeared. It perched on the edge of the golden bowl and looked down at its reflection. Its tiny toes were so delicate that it seemed Jasmine could see right through them.' Victoria smiled at the child's obvious pleasure as her dragon was immortalized in the story. 'The dragon knew many adventures, tales of great daring, about the men who lived in the high mountains and wore the skins of wild animals to protect them from the cold. They ran so quickly that they were faster than the fierce little ponies of their enemies. The stories took a long time to tell because the dragon even had to describe to Jasmine what a pony was, because she had never seen one.'

Victoria smiled. Bobby was gratifyingly amazed at the thought of a girl who had never seen a horse.

'But the spies were watching, and as Jasmine slept the tiny dragon was sent to the land of its ancestors, while the secret friend painted its image close beside the green jewelled frog. The days passed and Jasmine had two more friends who came to her in the May garden. First there was a beetle like a great fat green jewel, with eyes like sparkling diamonds. It too was seen and became nothing more than an enamelled image. Finally a damselfly, with wings like gossamer and a body that shone like mother-of-pearl, came floating gently down. It hovered for a moment above the still water before settling to speak to Jasmine, who was sitting, as usual, by the golden bowl. To this little creature Jasmine opened her heart. She explained how lonely she was and how she couldn't bear that each of her friends had disappeared, leaving her alone with their silent effigies. All around was beauty, yet inside her was pain and despair. She begged the damselfly to leave and save itself. As she at last went into the house, with the sun setting, orange and grey on the far horizon, she saw the damselfly hover in the air, and then disappear into the night. She slept well, thinking her friend safe. But the little creature came back to the golden bowl at dawn, because it wanted to talk again to the beautiful Jasmine. It was captured, and its image recorded for ever by the secret friend. That morning, Jasmine knew that she could no longer bear to be the cause of the death of these gentle creatures. She wrote a letter to her parents – a most beautiful poem that told them how much she loved them and missed her home – and she wrote to Ahwoh, explaining to him that however much you love a creature you cannot capture it, except to destroy its heart. Then she threw herself into the golden bowl.

'The next day, Ahwoh came home. He went straight out into the garden and, not finding Jasmine, he sat down beside the water. He looked down into the bowl, admiring the fine enamel work of the green frog and the jewelled eyes of the painted beetle. Then he saw, in the very centre of the dish, the most beautiful painting of all. It was of Jasmine. She was as sweet and gentle as she had ever looked, and on her lips there was a smile of great joy that he had never seen before. He thought she held her hands out to him, and he wanted to follow her, but he was too big, because the bowl was very small. So he left Japan and roamed the world, but he never found anyone as lovely as Jasmine.' Victoria relaxed on her pillows. She felt tired, spent.

'And what happened to her?' The child's voice was insistent. 'Don't go to sleep. You've got to tell me, what happened to Jasmine?'

Victoria hadn't thought any further. For her the story was ended, but it clearly wasn't for the child.

'Please,' Bobby pleaded, 'you can't leave her in the water.'

'Well . . .' Victoria had to think quickly. Bobby was sitting forward on her chair, listening eagerly to every word. 'Jasmine joined her friends, the frog and the dragon, the jewelled beetle and the damselfly. They all lived in the fields of irises, making a home where the cool water trickled through the white gravel.'

'With her secret admirer,' Bobby said.

'But of course.' Victoria's voice lifted. Bobby was right, there was a happy ending. 'Her secret admirer was a very handsome boy, not much older than Jasmine. He wasn't rich, but he was clever with his hands and they had a beautiful home filled with things that he had made.'

'And they had a pony.' Bobby nodded emphatically. She liked stories finished off nicely.

'Yes, they had a pony, and a bright yellow and black

251

trap, and one day they went to visit Jasmine's parents to show them how happy she was.'

'The end.'

'Yes, the end.' Victoria closed her eyes. She felt as if there were weights on them, she was so tired. 'I'd like to sleep now,' she murmured. It was like slipping into the water of the golden bowl – as cool and as comforting. She slept dreamlessly. In the evening she woke and had a light supper. Then she slept again and in the morning she felt much better. The pain was still in her chest, but her head was clear and she was able to help the nurse wash her. She was well on the road to recovery at last.

'Haemorrhoids, Mrs Banes?' Isabella struggled to cover her smile. She could not treat the self-important wife of the church warden with less than the seriousness that her contribution to the Pencombe collection of herbal remedies deserved.

'Yes, H . . . A . . . E . . . M . . .' Mrs Banes enunciated the letters forcefully. She was hot and bothered inside her best pair of corsets, and the temperature in the small tent was even higher than on the baking lawns outside.

'Do you think we should put "piles" instead?' Isabella looked down at the book on the trestle table in front of her. 'I think quite a lot of people refer to the complaint that way.'

'Well,' Mrs Banes was getting crosser with every inhibited breath she took, 'you can call it what you like, Lady Montford. But I insist that you write down the cure as "wild camomile". I won't have my contribution as "German camomile" even though that's its proper name. I'm not going down as a Nazi lover.'

'Of course not, Mrs Banes.' Isabella was finding the

252

villagers' contributions to the Herbal she was compiling the cause of much competition on their part, and amusement on hers.

'And you've to put down that the sufferer has to sit over the steaming mixture. A sink bowl does very well. The French, I understand, use a thing called a bidet, but it doesn't seem to have done them much good, does it? I don't hold with foreign ideas.'

Isabella wrote down the instructions for use. The loose-leaf sheets were building into a nice pile. 'Thank you so much,' she smiled, and held out her tin for a donation to the church fund. After all, if the likes of Mrs Banes wanted her name included for posterity, then she could pay for the privilege. A threepenny bit joined the sixpences and coppers.

'How's it going, Mummy?' Honour popped her head round the flap of the tent. 'Heavens, you must be cooking in here. I'll bring you a lemonade.'

'How are our littlies getting along?' The small children from the village would be playing the fairies in the play on the lower lawn, while Samuel Brown, leading tenor of the choir, would be Bottom; a very confused elderly retired colonel, Oberon; and a pretty young wife of a sailor would be the Fairy Queen, and . . . Isabella couldn't remember any more of the cast. One thing was certain, there were going to be a lot more laughs than ever Shakespeare envisaged.

'Did you know that chocolate makes more little girls sick than little boys?' Honour giggled. Eli had brought dozens of bars of chocolate and had enjoyed himself immensely, distributing them amongst the squealing children and their equally delighted mothers.

'I have a cure for you, Isabella.' Lucinda pushed the tent flap open wide. She didn't want to spoil her hat by

253

squeezing through a narrow gap. She was wearing a blue georgette dress with matching bolero, an outfit she had bought in Deauville before the war. The skirt was bias cut and floated beautifully on the almost non-existent breeze. Her hat, a wide-brimmed white straw, was trimmed to match. She was using a furled parasol instead of a stick to help her walk comfortably. Isabella thought her sister looked very fine, and very much in her element. It quite clearly suited Lucinda having Isabella hidden away.

'I shall tell you something to help low blood pressure.' Lucinda settled herself as comfortably as she could on the rickety folding chair provided for contributors.

Isabella smiled as she began to write Lucinda's entry. Trust her to choose an ailment so ladylike and Victorian; no period problems for Lucinda – nothing so intimate.

'Gather short sprigs of fresh rosemary.' Lucinda leaned forward to make sure that Isabella was writing as she dictated. 'Cover with boiling water, and allow to infuse for ten minutes. Allow to cool, then mix with cold water to taste. Drink this mixture twice daily. In severe cases . . .' She paused and lowered her voice, sounding quite professorial. 'A bath in rosemary will be most efficacious. One handful of leaves should be soaked in one pint of boiling water for twenty minutes. This mixture should be strained and then added to the patient's bath. The treatment should only be carried out in the morning as it is very stimulating.'

Isabella had an almost overwhelming desire to say something rather rude – to comment that sometimes stimulation was most useful in the evening. But Lucinda was so much the prude, and had so completely discarded thoughts of the flesh, that it didn't seem right. Lucinda put two shillings into the tin; hers was the biggest contribution so far.

'Honour said you could do with this lemonade.' Victoria had watched her mother enter the tent and waited outside until she'd left.

'Thank you, Viccy. Come and sit down with me a minute, if you can bear the heat, that is. How are you? Are you very tired?'

'No, I'm fine.' Victoria felt quite well, she was calm, her emotions limited by her breathing that still seemed shallow, but it was a feeling that suited the day. 'Everyone's having a wonderful time. Bobby is almost delirious at having had some chocolate and several of the other children have been sick already. I shall miss Bobby, you know. It's understandable that she wants to go back with her mother, but I'd grown very fond of her and it was lovely having a child about again. It made me feel quite broody. Still, all in all, it's a pretty perfect day.'

'Eli seems happier than I've ever seen him.'

'Well, he's got Sylvia Vartan with him. Have you met her yet?'

Isabella nodded as she handed Victoria her empty glass.

Victoria stood up slowly. She wanted Isabella to understand how she felt. 'I know he's playing with fire – after all, she is married – and yet it's plain to see she adores him. I can't help but wish the two of them luck. Who knows how much longer any of us have got, and as long as nobody gets hurt.'

'Somebody always gets hurt in a case like that, Viccy. Being thoroughly selfish, I hope it's not Eli.'

Eli stepped in, unexpectedly, through the open doorway. 'Not Eli? What's not to be me?' he asked. 'What are you two schemers doing taking my name in vain? I've brought Sylvie into your web, Isabella. She has her tuppence to throw in your pot and some dark secret brew that her long-lost granny used to inflict on her.'

Sylvia giggled. She was vainly trying to disentangle her fingers from Eli's grasp. It seemed he didn't care who saw them, and even she had to agree how unlikely it was that anyone could spy on them at Pencombe. It was just villagers and family. 'If I'm allowed to,' she said. 'After all, I'm not local and I know the sign outside says it's to be the Pencombe Herbal.'

'You are quite entitled, Mrs Vartan, and besides, we really do want your money.' Isabella had been ready to dislike a young woman who played fast and loose, but Eli was clearly very smitten, and the girl seemed ingenuous enough.

'It's just that when we had colds my grandmother used to give us an elderberry drink. It was a mixture that she kept in a bottle, and she would dilute it with hot water and sweeten it with honey. It was very nice. Bertie always used to want seconds. It used to make us sleepy.'

'I expect it was elderberry wine.' Isabella paused, her pen held over the paper. 'The best way to write that down would be to do the recipe for making the wine – I have a rather nice one – and then I could put how to use it. Do you think that would be right?'

'Whatever you say, Lady Montford,' Sylvia said.

It was on the tip of Isabella's tongue to say to call her by her Christian name, but she checked the impulse. She sensed that Eli was disappointed, but however sweet the girl was, it would all end in tears. 'That will be quite a long entry, Eli. I think you should judge your donation accordingly.' She rattled the tin.

'Oh, Eli's not to pay for me.' Sylvia was delving in her bag. 'Here.' She held out a five-pound note. 'I hope your church roof will be just as good as new,' she said.

The play was nearly finished when the siren went, but nobody moved. The babies still played at their mothers' knees and Isabella poured more glasses of squash to be passed silently around so as not to disturb the actors. It was coolest under the low, spreading beech tree where Eli sat close beside Sylvia. He breathed in deeply. She smelled every bit as fresh as the yellow roses that fell in festoons from the wall behind them, and she was as mysteriously inviting as the honeysuckle bower that shook as two small children, a pair of the fairies, advanced bravely into its perfumed dark.

'I love you,' Eli murmured. He had his lips close to Sylvia's ear. She sighed happily. It had been such a perfect day and the fact that they'd all carried on sitting there, acting as if there was no threat and ignoring the wave of enemy planes that had swept overhead, had been the final touch. The actors had shouted loudly to be heard over the noise of the engines and the children had pointed up, just as they would have at a flight of geese. Somehow they had all managed to steal a day when the reality of war, the nastiness of so much in life, had been submerged.

'Isabella said she wanted your money,' Eli said. 'It's a bit like the highwayman – your money or your life. Will you give me your life, Sylvie?'

She turned to look at him. They were very close together in the cool gloom.

'Will you, Sylvie? I know there's a lot to sort out. But somehow we have to be together – for always. I've never said this to a girl before, but I want you to be mine, mine alone. Will you, Sylvie? Somehow, some day, will you marry me?'

'Eli . . .' There was despair in her voice. He'd brought back the outside world, the dreadful complications and the danger, the seaminess of it all. Compared to the purity of the day that she'd so enjoyed, the thought of going back, playing her role again and being the dutiful wife, the considerate confidante, was unbearable.

Eli leaned towards her, and her lips were parted. They kissed, and she tasted warm and loving. He put his arm around her and she yielded, coming towards him although in her heart she knew she should pull away – she couldn't give him any hope.

Isabella had two last drinks on her tray. She had seen Eli and his friend go under the beech tree, and she thought she would join them for the final act of *A Midsummer Night's Dream*. She parted the copper leaves and stepped into the natural canopy. It took a moment for her eyes to adjust to the light, and then she saw them. They looked very young – that was her first thought. Eli was nearing middle age, but he was like a boy; it might have been his first kiss. She felt so sad. Fate could be so bloody, and suddenly she wished vehemently that things would turn out all right for them. Never mind what convention said, Eli deserved one true love, and perhaps this could be it.

She turned silently and went back out into the sunlight.

'Please, please don't hit me,' Sylvia sobbed. She had her hands up, trying to fend Simon off, but it was like trying to stop the tide.

'Slut,' he said as he smacked her, open-handed across the face. His eyes were red, suffused with blood, but his voice was calm and cold. 'You knew what I'd do.' He gripped her wrist, twisting it viciously.

'Please, please don't hurt me,' she begged.

'Stupid bitch.' He began shaking her, digging his fingers deep into her shoulders. Her head swung backwards and forwards. There was a roaring in her ears and a red mist swam in front of her. 'Enough!' He threw her down, away from him, and she lay huddled on the floor.

Her sight cleared and then she could see the room that was tipped at such a crazy angle around her. The ornate legs of the Louis-Seize chairs mocked her torn dress, the refined silver-grey silk-covered walls sneered at her dishevelled hair.

'I'll never see him again, I swear . . .' She was terrified now, fear for Eli shaking her body more than Simon had ever done. The man she loved was in the most terrible danger.

'Shut up.'

'It was my fault, I led him on. I was lonely . . . I swear I'll never even talk to him again.'

His footsteps were silent on the thick-piled carpet. She watched him coming towards her and with a final convulsive shudder her trembling stopped. The caps of his black shoes were so highly polished that she could see her face, madly distorted in their mirrored surface. 'Move your hands,' he commanded.

She had curled up as she fell, her arms protecting her body, hands pressed over her stomach, and she felt very sick.

'I said move them.'

She lay still on the floor. She could feel her hip bone pressing down through the carpet. Slowly she moved her hands, stretching her arms above her head.

'You could be pregnant,' he hissed. He had been so careful; all their married life he had withdrawn from her before his climax, leaving her trembling with a need that had never, before Eli, been fulfilled.

'Please, Simon, please . . .'

He drew his foot back slowly and she watched, mesmerized – she was the prey of the snake that was poised to

259

strike. He kicked her with all the force of his fury and she cried out, doubling up, writhing on the floor. He turned away and walked to the telephone. Without looking at her he dialled his doctor's number. A few words were enough to persuade the Harley Street physician to abandon his dinner party. After all, he owed his continuing luxurious lifestyle to Simon's ingenuity.

The snooker table in the back room of the Black Lion was elderly but still functional. In mid-July, to stop the constant bickering as to whose turn it was for a game, the landlord had started a knockout tournament in aid of the local children's home. Most of the fliers had paid their half a crown and been in at the start, but after almost a month, only the good players were left in. They were playing best of nine frames. Since things had begun really hotting up in the air, they'd set up a new rule: any game disturbed by the call to duty was left as it was – the balls spread as they'd been at the last shot, the score marked on the oak board. Neil was still in with a chance, as was Percy; their game had been interrupted with three reds and all the colours on the table.

'Christ, I need this drink,' Neil smiled tiredly at the publican as he picked his tankard up off the counter. It was jewelled with cool beads of condensation and gently foaming over. He took the beer to his lips. He'd killed at least one man today, probably more, but he drank deeply and submerged the thoughts of depriving another human of his right to live. He'd been in the air for so many hours recently that he'd given up counting and his head was still spinning from the last skirmish. This was the battle for the skies and no mistake. He looked around the bar. There weren't that many fellows in yet. He went back to his drink. He didn't want to start missing the faces that he knew wouldn't be coming back again. Over the lip of his tankard he caught sight of a girl sitting on her own at the other end of the bar and he nearly spilled the last drops of his pint when he realized who it was.

'What the heck are you doing here?' he called out to his cousin Margaret. He hadn't seen her since the wedding.

She smiled tightly at him; she hadn't wanted him to see her. 'Hallo, Neil,' she said, as she got up and walked towards him. 'I thought I might have a chance of seeing Percy. Do you know if he's back yet?' She tried to put the question casually but it was obvious she was anxious.

'I expect he'll be in here in a tick,' Neil answered. 'We've got a game to finish off, through there.' He gestured towards the back room.

'A game. That's all you ever think about, isn't it? Life's a game to the whole lot of you,' she said bitterly. 'Have you any idea what Percy talks about? When we're alone together, when all I want to do is to hold him close and tell him how dreadful it is being apart, he tells me about your prattle, the jokes that're going the rounds, who's winning at that damned snooker tournament. He can't be serious for a minute. Have you any idea how much I hate that bloody game?'

'Steady on, old girl.' Neil felt awkward. Margaret's voice was carrying and they were attracting attention. Percy wouldn't like his wife showing him up. 'You don't want him moping around like some old duffer, do you? He's got to keep his concentration up, not just his pecker.' He laughed at his joke. Percy would think it was a good one.

'You're just as bad – you make me sick, the whole lot of you.'

Margaret had changed. Neil would never have believed

261

how a few weeks of marriage could have made her into the overwrought creature in front of him. 'Want to come through into the back room?' he asked. He thought it best to get her out of sight; she'd probably lay into Percy something rotten.

They were alone in the dusky room smelling of spilled beer and old woodwork. Neil looked up at the ceiling that was the colour of burnt cream and wondered, as always, how many years of cigarette smoke it had taken to get to that colour. He gestured Margaret to a stool. There was quite a racket coming from the bar they'd just left as the boys were pouring in now. 'Won't be long,' he said, smiling to try and cheer her up. 'Fancy another gin?'

Margaret nodded. She shouldn't have come down, she knew that now, but she had the afternoon off and a whole day's leave tomorrow. It had been so easy to invite herself to Pencombe and then borrow Isabella's car and drive over. She'd watched a handful of planes fighting it out above her head, an aerial ballet performed for the cognoscenti of war. Only she didn't appreciate any of it. The realization that it might be her Percy up there, fighting for his life, made her physically sick.

Neil bought himself a second pint and Margaret a gin and tonic. He stood at the edge of the snooker table, surveying the lie of the balls – they'd each won three frames and it looked as if Percy was going to take the one on the table. He'd have to sharpen up. 'Remember Christmas at Pencombe?' he asked Margaret. 'We all used to play at rolling a ball up the table and running round to beat it.'

'Fancy trying it now?' Margaret asked. She was desperate for something to pass the time. She walked towards the table, reaching out to gather up the balls.

'No, don't!' Neil shouted as her hand closed over the

white ball. 'You've got to leave it until Percy comes back, that's the rules.'

They both turned to look at the door as it swung open and the landlord walked in.

He was a jovial man – the ideal publican. He generally wore a sporty waistcoat and a bright bow tie, and that evening's offering around his neck was red with yellow spots. He had a broad face, with wide-spaced hazel eyes and a drinker's nose. Beneath a handlebar moustache, he had a smiling mouth, but he wasn't smiling as he walked up to the table. 'Sorry, old boy,' he said as he pulled the triangle out from under the rail. He began gathering up the red balls, walking methodically around the table, checking the pockets.

'What are you doing?' Margaret's voice was high with sudden fear. 'Don't touch them, don't . . .'

'Sorry, Mrs Ridley.' The publican didn't look her in the eyes. He hadn't seen her come into the back room, otherwise he wouldn't have cleared the table in front of her.

Neil felt numb. He stared down at the green baize. Not Percy – he couldn't accept it – he'd always been such a lucky sod.

The publican closed the door of the snug quietly behind him. Margaret hadn't moved and Neil slowly became aware of her. She was rigid, her hands still clenched around the white ball. Her face was blank, expressionless. 'Margaret.' He held his arms out to her, he wanted to hold her, to comfort her. He wanted to hide the tears he could feel choking him.

'How could he?' she whispered. 'How could he not come back to me?' She turned to face Neil. 'You bastards, you mad bastards, it's all been a bloody game.' She hurled the ball she held, and it struck him a glancing blow on the temple. He put his hand up, covering the pain as Margaret's face crumpled. She rushed forward into his arms. 'I can't bear it,' she sobbed. 'Dear God, I can't bear it.'

Tom breathed in the welcome cool air sweeping over Reason Hill. He paused for a moment on the front doorstep of his home and looked out over the downland that spread away from him, mellow in the afternoon sun. He had left Isabella and the others at Pencombe with strict instructions to go down to the cellars if things got too bad. Isabella had promised to keep listening for the siren. It seemed that Kent was to be the setting for the battle for air supremacy, and the manner in which Michael was killed had proved that fighters, as well as bombers, could be deadly dangerous.

He wanted to check that there were no urgent messages, and that everything was all right in the house before he went round to see Lizzy. The girls hadn't been working in the fields for the past couple of days. It was all very well for the powers that be to tell the farmers to carry on with their work as if nothing was happening unless there was an air-raid warning. But Tom had no intention of leaving his workers exposed in the open fields while there was such activity above them. He didn't think the crops would suffer from a few days' lack of weeding.

He closed the door behind him, relieved that the sky, for the moment, was clear. There'd been four planes chasing each other over his head as he drove across the river flats by Yalding. The combatants had split into two separate dog fights as he crossed the narrow bridge. They had swooped and dived, leaving nothing to mark their passing but the silver streaks of vapour trails across a clear blue sky. He'd had to keep his eye on the road, so he hadn't been able to see which side's plane it was that had spiralled down. Whoever it was, he thought, must have crashed close to Tonbridge.

'No, I won't come.' Lizzy shook her head vehemently. 'I'm sorry, but I just can't bear the thought of being cramped up in there again with Bert.'

Sally and Anne had been begging her to go back with them. The sirens had gone and it was well past time to get into the shelter at the end of the garden. Tom had made them promise to look after her, as he knew she was just as likely to stand out in the open and watch the enemy planes go over.

'You go on, I'll be all right. No one's going to waste a load of explosives on this dump.' She flung her arms out wide, indicating the miserable living room, with the air heavy from the stink of their landlord's pipe, and the oversweet perfume of his wife's cheap scent. Lizzy was desperate for them to leave her alone. There had been air-raid warnings going on and off all day, and each time she'd felt more uneasy. She couldn't bear to be cooped up. Cooped up – the words reminded her of the night she'd helped him kill the chicken. 'Go on, sod off,' she shouted, turning away so that she wouldn't see how hurt they looked. She was angry with herself for being difficult, and furious that she'd sworn again. She'd been trying so hard not to, for Tom's sake.

Once the house was empty Lizzy sat down on one of the dining chairs – it was hard and uncomfortable. A bluebottle was trapped in a spider's web in the corner of the window beside her, and she watched it for a while, sympathizing with its plight while feeling a revulsion that made her stomach tighten. There was no one outside, the lane was empty, and everyone else had scurried down into their burrows. She thought of them all as a load of rabbits, believing that a hole in the earth would save them. When you saw the size of a bomb crater, it didn't make much sense.

Perhaps she should go back to her family in London. She loved Tom, and she thought he felt the same about her, but it wasn't going to come to anything with his miserable old mother so set against it. This way she was just going to get herself into trouble, because however much of a gentleman Tom was, there was only so much temptation a man could take. She stood up abruptly. The planes had started to come over – she wasn't really frightened of them, she thought. She began to walk slowly up and down the room – five small paces each way. She would go crazy if she didn't get out. There was a lull as she let herself out of the front door.

It was very bright in the tiny garden and the smell of privet was even stronger than the reek of cats. The sound of the planes was distant now. Earlier it had been fighters, but this time she'd recognized the heavy drone of bombers. There were anti-aircraft guns too, blasting off over near Maidstone. She walked uncertainly down the front path. Where was Tom? He'd said he was going over to Pencombe earlier. It wasn't safe, him driving across while all the planes were fighting above them. She imagined him, the car so visible out on the wide, open river flats. He could be strafed – she knew that was what they called it – when one of the enemy screamed down out of the sky, shooting everything he saw. Tom's black car wouldn't stand a chance. She imagined the petrol tank blowing up, a ball of flame. There'd been a car exploding like that in the film she'd seen last week.

'Tom,' she whispered as she opened the gate and stepped out into the road. The few hundred yards to the

266

farmhouse seemed an insurmountable distance. 'Tom,' she shouted as she began to run.

The sound of the lone bomber was low. It started as a hesitant growl, but then, as it climbed the last slope to the ridge of the hill before the slow descent towards the plain, the noise became a threat. Inside the plane, decisions were being taken. There was something wrong with the engines; they were not running smoothly, and that was why they had turned back before reaching their target. The bombs would have to go as soon as possible, then they would have a chance if they had to make a crash landing – they weren't high enough for parachutes. There was no aim involved, it was a simple jettison procedure. The plane lifted as the weight fell away.

Lizzy had stopped to take off her shoes. They were a pair she only wore around the house because the heels were too high to walk far in. She heard the whine in the air. 'Tom,' she moaned. She was so desperately lonely out there in the road, she began half-heartedly to run, as if she knew there was no escape.

Tom was halfway through the orchard when he heard the returning plane. He had been walking only moderately quickly, trying to convince himself there was no reason to panic. He wished suddenly that he'd taken the car as he began to run, one hesitant, reluctant step in front of the other. He felt that to charge full pelt would be to invite danger. But by the time he reached the lane he was flat out, his breath coming in great gulps, his arms swinging. The plane was wheeling over them. He saw it all – Lizzy in the road, her head back, as she staggered towards him, and then the crash, the almighty explosion. He watched as she flung her arms out and then fell to the ground like a rag doll, and then he was blown off his feet as a great wind lifted him and rolled him along like a fallen apple.

When he reached her, she was curled up on the ground, clutching her knees like a small child. She was crying pitifully and he put his arms around her. She leaned against him, then he began to pray. It was a prayer of thanks, of very selfish thanks for their deliverance. There was no more Laburnum Cottage – a gaping hole, like a missing tooth, between its crumbling neighbours was all that remained of it. He could see right through to the back garden. There was no shelter left either, just a smoking crater, edged by a crazy jumble and a fence that tottered on the brink. He picked her up in his arms. She wasn't badly hurt – just covered in grazes and cuts. The one on her arm looked quite deep – it would need a few stitches – but there didn't seem to be anything broken.

'You're coming with me,' he said, his voice shaking as he walked down the road, swaying under her weight. 'Back to Reason Hill, and you're never going to leave again.'

'My father's a flier.' Jill busied herself straightening the bedcover, checking her newest patient's pulse by pressing down through the bandages. She nodded to herself when she detected a feeble beat; it was the only thing that proved the mummified body was alive. 'He learned to fly during the First World War. He envies you boys. Says it was the happiest time of his life.' She walked round to the end of the iron-framed bed. 'Now, let's see who we have here. Oh, my God . . .'

It was one of Nigel's easier patches. When the pain was like this it was almost a friend, sharp but constant. He could retreat from it inside his head and after a while it seemed to lessen. He didn't know why the nurse had sworn – perhaps she'd unwrapped a bit of him and he hadn't even felt it. He had an image of himself, a picture of a man without skin. There was a picture like that in an encyclopaedia he'd seen once. The veins were coloured in a vivid Mediterranean blue, the arteries the same bright red as the lipstick his mother wore, the flesh was the colour of raw pork. That's how he must look – no wonder the girl had been upset.

'It is, it's Nigel, I've checked it all out. He was picked up in the Channel and ended up in a London hospital. He's been sent down here for some specialist treatment.' The telephone receiver was damp and sweaty with the heat from Jill's hand. She was still feeling light-headed. The last six hours of her duty had dragged interminably. She'd been desperate to let them know that she'd found Nigel. But Neil would be on duty, and she didn't want to tell Victoria over the telephone. 'He's covered up from hand to foot. Yes, his face as well. There's nothing to recognize him by, only the name on the chart.' She paused, listening to Honour's questions. 'No, he doesn't know it's me – not that I suppose he'd even remember having met me,' she said shortly. 'He doesn't know if it's day or night or where the heck he is. Half the time his temperature's so high he probably doesn't even know who he is. Yes, yes I'll phone again tomorrow.' She put the receiver down slowly. They weren't really allowed to use the phone in the private office, but Sister had agreed that this was a special case. After all, Jill's cousin was very poorly, and it was understandable that she would need to speak to someone in the family.

Honour ran quickly down the stairs. She was so flustered that she nearly didn't acknowledge the greeting of the old man who lived in the ground-floor flat. He left his door open so that he could wave to any passerby. She slowed herself down and smiled at him. After all, he was old and lonely and it wasn't his fault that the system had broken down and they'd had to find out about Nigel this way.

It was all so unreal. They'd heard nothing except a brief note announcing that he was missing. It was Neil who'd told them that somebody had seen his brother's plane going down over the Channel, billowing smoke and flames – but there had also been a parachute. That was what they'd pinned their hopes on, that and the fact that Neil was adamant his twin was alive. Something had gone wrong with the system – she kept practising the words that she would use to tell Victoria as she hurried along the dark streets. Usually she felt nervous being out on her own at night, even though the blackout wasn't quite so bad as it had been in the early days. As long as there wasn't a raid on there was just enough light to see her way.

She walked quickly past echoing, inky-black stairwells leading down to silent basements – she had so much on her mind that they held no threat. There was a sudden crash beside her as a dustbin tipped over and she thought instantly that it must have been caused by a marauding cat. It was surprising how the anguish she felt at the prospect of telling Victoria about Nigel left no room for fear of strangers.

The house in Cadogan Gardens was as dark as its neighbours. Honour rang the bell twice before she heard any sounds of life. It was Victoria herself who opened the door to her. 'Honour! What on earth are you doing out at this hour?' Victoria was wrapped in an oyster satin housecoat. Her hair was dishevelled, and it made her look younger than usual. She was very thin after her illness. 'What is it, what's the matter?' she asked.

'It's Nigel.' Honour stood in the familiar hall. She was still wearing her overcoat and the house was warm and comfortable, but she shivered. 'He's in Jill's hospital,' she said.

'He's alive! Thank God.' Victoria's eyes glittered brightly with tears, her lips lifted in a faltering smile, then suddenly her expression changed. 'But that's . . .' She stood very still, very upright. 'But that's for burns, isn't it? Awful burns. I mean, that's for the men who . . .' She swallowed convulsively. 'Men who've been burned so badly that they've lost their identity, lost their faces. Is that why they didn't let us know? Is he unrecognizable?'

'It doesn't have to be that bad.' Honour spoke softly. It seemed wrong to speak in more than a whisper.

'I must go to him,' Victoria said, but she stayed standing stiffly, her slim figure elegantly outlined by the clinging fabric. She seemed untouchable.

'Jill says you can't. Not yet. She said that they won't allow visitors.'

'No, I can understand that.' Victoria wasn't looking at Honour, she seemed to be staring past her. 'They said his plane went down in flames, but I hoped . . . When he was a little boy, very little, about three I think, he burnt himself. Not badly, it wasn't much more than a scorch that he got from the towel rail in the bathroom. I put some ointment on it and he cried. He said it was because he didn't like it. The ointment, I mean . . .' Her voice tailed off.

'I think you ought to have a drink, Viccy. After all, you've had a shock.'

Victoria allowed herself to be led through to her drawing room. She stood by the remains of the fire, averting her head as Honour used the brass poker to stir up a blaze. She said, 'I was very careful after Nigel burnt himself that once. I always kept a fire guard up, even when the boys were quite big.'

'Here.' Honour handed her cousin a brandy.

'Is he very bad?' Victoria asked. She held the glass up to her face, breathing in the rich, heavy smell. It made her feel ill and she put it down on the side table.

'He's bandaged all over. Jill only knew it was Nigel by the name on the chart.'

'Then it might not be him.' Hope flared in Victoria's voice.

'No, it's definitely Nigel. Jill checked it all out before she phoned. There's been some kind of muddle in keeping you informed, I expect.'

'Thank God Luke won't know anything about it.'

'Is he . . .' Honour paused. She didn't ask about Luke any more. 'Is he impossible to talk to?'

'Oh no, he's quite easy to talk to,' Victoria laughed in a strained, high voice. 'But he doesn't understand, so what's the point? I tried for a while. I thought it might keep him going, some kind of involvement with the family. But it would be kinder now if he died. That's not heartless. I just think it's so sad – it's not my Luke lying up there, it's a total stranger. And now there are two strangers – because that's what Nigel must be like too.'

'Poor Viccy, poor, poor Viccy.' Honour wanted to hold Victoria, to comfort her, but she seemed so aloof. It was as if she was making herself impervious to suffering.

'No, not poor Viccy – poor Nigel, poor Luke, poor thousands of other souls in torment. I'm the lucky one, I know that.' And she sat down abruptly and cried.

* * *

272

'Your mother sends her love.'

Nigel had known it was Jill in the room with him, even before she spoke. There was something about the way her uniform rustled that was different from the others who nursed him, and he recognized the sound of her shoes on the floor. She moved efficiently but with enthusiasm, her steps quick and light. If he could, he would have smiled.

'If you're a good boy you'll get a visit one day soon.'

How could he be a good boy? he wondered. Was there some hidden sign that showed through the bandages, something that showed he was thinking wholesome thoughts?

'I went out with Neil last night,' Jill continued, 'and he says you're bluffing. Is that right, Nigel? Are you a fraud, keeping out of harm's way for a bit inside your cosy little cocoon?'

She was doing something he didn't like as she chatted, messing about with parts of him that he'd rather she wasn't seeing.

'Nearly done,' she said cheerfully.

What was nearly done? His mind was tired, he understood that. He couldn't think for more than two or three cohesive sentences, then everything drifted away.

'You know Margaret's married to that pal of yours, do you? What's his name?' She was bustling about again and the scratchy, rustling sound of her moving was interfering with his thoughts. Who was Margaret married to? He couldn't remember any friend of his that she'd especially liked. Come to that, what was she doing thinking about getting married at all? She was little more than a baby. Nigel could picture her, all blonde curls and wearing a pink and white dress that had frills down the front. She'd spilt something sticky on it and cried. That had been at a party, a birthday party at Pencombe. There – he'd remembered the name of the house. It had been bothering him, next he would . . . Without warning the pain came back, not the one he could cope with but the threatening, overwhelming surge. It came from deep inside, rolling him over, turning him upside down. He started to shout as his feet went up in the air – here came the bad bit. He was screaming as his head jerked back.

'Well, that's you all neat and tidy.' Jill turned away from the silent bed. The dressings were changed, and tomorrow they were going to have a look at his face. It wasn't her day on, and she was glad in a way. 'See you soon,' she called back over her shoulder as he sank again into the darkness.

'I'll have to go.' Victoria plucked at the tasselled trim of the cushion that she held protectively in front of her. 'Sooner or later, I have to see him.'

'It can't be as bad as you're imagining.' Honour stood by the fireplace. Her fingers seemed drawn to touch the china parakeets on the mantelpiece. She dreaded calling at Cadogan Gardens, but it was her duty to keep an eye on Victoria. Her mother had said so and Lucinda had said so too. Still, it didn't make it any easier.

'How do you know what I think?' Victoria asked petulantly. She wanted to be a girl again. She didn't want the responsibility of grown-up sons, young men who went to war and came back strange, unrecognizable creatures. Someone should have told her that the problems of having children didn't have an end.

'If I can, I'll come with you,' Honour volunteered. 'Jill said she'll make sure she's on duty when we go. So there'll be three of us.'

'What on earth are you talking about?' Victoria

snapped as she stood up abruptly, sending the cushion tumbling to the carpet. 'Three of *us*? It's nothing to do with you. I'm his mother.'

The silence was awkward and Honour couldn't think how to break it. She wanted to go to see Nigel herself. It was frightening to think of him being so hurt, but not as painful as it was to think of him waiting in vain for someone to go and visit him. No one could go until his mother did. Victoria would have to pull herself together.

'I can't leave Luke.' Victoria turned and walked towards the door. 'You understand that, don't you? I can't possibly leave him. He may die at any minute.'

Honour didn't reply. She thought of all the things she could say, such as the fact that Luke had been close to death for months. Or the indisputable truth that Nigel, struggling back towards life, had to be given preference over a senile old man for whom death would be a blessed release. But she knew that to say the wrong thing would make everything even worse. So she waited.

Victoria walked to the bottom of the stairs and stood there, one hand on the curling mahogany banister. She'd had to stop the boys sliding down it when they were small. Nigel and Neil had been inseparable. Neil hadn't been to see her since they'd known where Nigel was. It was as if he blamed her for staying away. Each of the boys had always known the other's thoughts, the other's longings. Neil had known that Nigel wasn't dead. He'd been so desperately sure, even when it had looked certain. She took a deep breath, staring down sightlessly at the camel-brown Wilton carpet. Neil was staying away so that she would go to see his brother.

'Honour!' She stayed where she was, calling the girl to her. 'I'm just going to pack a few things. I'll go down to

Pencombe tonight and drive over to East Grinstead tomorrow. Can you come now?'

'I'm not sure. I'll have to see if I can swop a shift. I'll try and telephone.'

'I'll go anyway. I've waited too long already.' As she started to walk upstairs the door bell rang.

'I'll get it.' Honour was suddenly full of life. She felt a great weight had been lifted from her shoulders.

The man on the doorstep was a man of the cloth. His dog collar was too wide for his thin neck and his dark suit was dusty, but his eyes were so alive, so full of eager happiness that Honour found herself smiling at him.

'Is Mrs Jones by any chance at home?' he asked, and before Honour had a chance to answer Victoria was pushing past her.

'Colin. Oh, Colin.' She stood there, her hands held hesitantly out in front of her, undecided as to how she should greet her visitor. Then she seemed to relax. It was as if the tension of the past few days had gone out of her. 'Colin,' she said. 'It was you I was waiting for.' And she leaned forward and kissed him very gently on the cheek.

The land around Pencombe was baked hard. Half a dozen blue and white striped deck chairs flapped forlornly out on the terrace as the first few drops of rain fell. Isabella was away and there was no one to bother about bringing them in. Eli stood at the window. He was waiting – like the weather, he was in a lull before the storm.

Sylvia opened her turquoise enamelled compact and repowdered her nose. Her reflection in the small round mirror shivered in time with the beat of the car engine.

'That's the third time you've done that.' Simon's voice

held contempt. 'Is it vanity or are you nervous he'll have gone off you?'

'I'm not vain.' Sylvia stared out at the surrounding countryside. It was the first time she had been out of the house since Simon kicked her. The bruising had almost disappeared, and the doctor said that she hadn't suffered any lasting damage – but she had. Inside her mind she would never be the same. She put the compact back in her bag. It was a game they were playing – cat and mouse. Only, she was determined to show that the natural order of things could be reversed. She wasn't going to provide an easy prey.

'This should suit you – visiting the stately home,' Simon continued. 'Your Eli certainly has the right background for your misplaced social ambitions.'

'It's not his home, he doesn't live there.'

'Oh no, I forgot. It's his sister's place, isn't it? His half-sister, to be precise. Same father, different mothers. I don't suppose he told you that his mother was a slut, did he? She was little more than a woman his father picked up off the street. She did them all a favour when she died producing your Eli. There's no real breeding in the family, whatever kind of line he spun you. All this lord and lady stuff, it's just something his sister married into. And I expect she used her body to do it. You're all alike. Sluts, the lot of you.' Simon's face remained impassive.

'I still don't understand why we're driving down to Pencombe. You didn't have to accept Eli's invitation,' Sylvia said.

'But I did, and you will understand, I can assure you. Before long you'll understand very well indeed.' Simon stopped talking. It was raining in torrents and he had to concentrate on his driving. He pulled out around a slow-moving Army convoy. The road ahead was clear but for a

277

moment he almost wished it wasn't and that it could have ended there and then in a twisted wreck. He'd never loved anyone before he met Sylvia, and he should have known she was like all the others. He should never have trusted her.

Eli pushed open the french windows. The rain was bouncing up off the York stone paving in a mad flurry of tiny fountains. A dozen rivulets snaked together, making a stream that ran towards the drain. It was clogged with fallen leaves and a shallow pond was gradually covering up the oblong outlines of the slabs. Eli felt claustrophobic. He couldn't see more than a few yards ahead; it was as if a net curtain cut off the view. The air itself was wet, and even breathing in deeply he felt as if he was suffocating. It had been a mistake to suggest Simon met him at Pencombe. He'd thought it would be a good idea to let the man see how important his connections were. But there was something wrong. Eli hadn't heard from Sylvia since the garden party – two weeks had passed without a word. She'd always managed to contact him somehow. The bell rang behind him. The sound of the rain had covered the car arriving at last. He threw his half-finished cigarette out into the rain, where it steamed briefly and then lay sodden, beaten into shreds.

'Come through to the drawing room.' Eli turned his back to lead the way and to hide the confusion he felt at seeing Simon and Sylvia together. He had seen instantly how Simon hated him, and felt the man's emotion as a red-hot sensation at the base of his spine. Simon was beyond covering his thoughts and there was no need for him to try. There was no one else in the house. Not a soul to witness what might happen beween the three of them.

Sylvia laid her gloves and bag down on the galleried

wine table beside the mustard velvet-covered chair. She remembered admiring the delicate beauty of the table on her last visit. Then Isabella had been in the room and the atmosphere had been of a home. It was grand and imposing but still a place where people belonged. Now it seemed as lifeless as a museum; the objects were too splendid, and everything was on too big a scale. She sat down on the edge of the chair and waited.

'Drink?' Eli proffered the decanter to Simon. He wanted to ignore Sylvia. He'd rather she hadn't been there – this was something between the two men. The woman that they both felt they had a claim to was suddenly superfluous.

'What did you think you were going to do by inviting me here?' Simon asked. 'Impress me with the family silver?'

Eli allowed himself a small, tight smile. 'If you aren't impressed then perhaps you ought to be. If one of the guides had been on duty you could have had the tour with all the juicy details – the dates and makers, the lot. At least I haven't pawned it. That's one small immorality I'm not yet guilty of.'

'Black sheep of the family – that's the role you'd like to cast yourself in, isn't it?' Simon felt the advantage of his size. He was a good two inches taller than Eli and much heavier. He pulled himself up to his full height, inflating his chest and enlarging his voice. 'But it's only a role. In reality you just follow the herd, carry out instructions. There's no more inspiration in you than that.' He snapped his fingers derisively.

Eli kept silent. He felt he would learn more by letting Simon rant on.

'Where's Isabella?' Sylvia asked, and they both looked

at her. Eli's face showed his concern – she should never have revealed that she'd been to the house before.

'Isabella?' Simon's voice was high, mimicking his wife's. 'Isn't it Lady Montford, my dear? Or are you on intimate terms with the rest of his family as well?'

'I told you, I said all about my coming to the fête. You know that I've met Eli's people.' She hadn't had a chance to let Eli know that Simon had found out. Somebody had told him about them.

'And what do they think, Eli?' Simon asked. 'What does your family think of this slut you brought to visit them?'

'Leave her out of this.' Eli's voice was low. He was being careful not to let his temper take over because he understood that was what Simon was hoping for.

'Man to man, that's how you'd like it, is it?' Simon reached slowly inside his jacket. He was smiling, his wide face flushed as if he had been drinking.

Eli watched his adversary. He saw the tension in the white lines that ran from the corners of the fleshy nose to the edges of the moist lips. It was as if Simon had a fever.

'Let's play at soldiers, shall we?' Simon pulled a gun out. It was oiled, and gleamed a dull blue-black. Neither of the men reacted to Sylvia's small cry of fear.

'You'll never get away with it,' Eli said.

'But of course I will.' Simon seemed relaxed now, totally in his element. 'The pair of you will meet with an accident. It will be unfortunate, but with so many going honourably to their deaths, a sordid little mishap isn't going to excite much comment. In fact, in deference to your sister's feelings, I think it will be quite hushed up, don't you?' He reached down and gripped Sylvia by the arm. His fingers dug painfully into her skin but she didn't cry out. She wouldn't give him that satisfaction. He pulled her up, and then pushed her towards Eli. 'Go on, hold her close,' he sneered. 'Hold her as close as you like, because that's all you've got left. Each other.'

The sound of the rain outside was very loud, covering even Simon's breathing. He was panting as if he had been running, and yet he hadn't moved at all since Eli had put his arm protectively around Sylvia.

'Let Eli go.' Sylvia spoke clearly. Suddenly she wasn't afraid. She'd always known it would come to this, but the ending had to be between her and Simon. Eli had no part of it.

'What, and miss the chance of seeing you go to pieces? That's what you'll do, my dear, disintegrate, fall begging to your knees, because I shall kill him first. You can watch him die, while you grovel for another chance, and then I shall take an infinite pleasure in ending your life. I should have done it long ago. You deceived us.'

'Us!' Sylvia pounced on the word. 'You mean you and Peter, don't you? It's always been the two of you. He means more to you than I ever could. You don't want me to die because of what I feel for Eli, you want to get rid of me because I might shame you in front of your beloved Peter. That's it, isn't it?' Her voice rose victoriously. She had to have her say, no matter how much Eli squeezed her arm to be silent. There had been too many years of suffering for her not to speak now.

'Shut up.' Simon took a step towards her and raised the pistol. He would smash it across her face, spoiling what he had once seen as beauty beyond compare. But he saw the flicker in Eli's eyes, and it stopped him. He must keep his distance.

'Get out.' He jerked the barrel of the gun towards the open door. 'Go on, get out of here.' He wouldn't kill them inside the house. They didn't deserve the dignity of such a setting.

Sylvia stumbled over the step. Her open-toed sandals gave her no protection at all as she stepped into the water that now covered the terrace completely. She bent down to take them off and then froze as Simon shouted close beside her.

'Stop that!' His voice was loud and cracked, like a faulty bell.

She stumbled again. 'I'll break my ankle,' she said. She made her voice thin and pitiful. She had an overwhelming conviction that she must take the high-heeled sandals off. She had to be able to run. If there was the slightest chance at all, then they would take it.

'Then carry them. Go on, hurry up.' Simon didn't want the shoes left by the house. He wanted the pair of them to die out in the country – lovers seeking privacy, a sordid adventure gone wrong. He gestured once more with the gun. A warm glow was building low in his stomach. It was like the feeling he so enjoyed when he wanted sex – a raw mixture of power and energy. He laughed out loud at the sight of his captives as they went ahead of him. The rain was beating their hair flat and their clothes were sticking to their bodies, to the forms that so shortly would be twitching in death. Simon had killed before, and he knew how it would look, how he would feel afterwards. He laughed again. He was so hot inside that the rain didn't seem to touch him.

The air was full of the sound of running water. Liquid gurgles sounded from the filling of a warren; summer-fat rabbits crouched in terror on top of a grassy mound as, blind, naked and helpless, their offspring drowned with scarcely a struggle. All of Eli's senses seemed heightened as he scanned the ground around them, the trees dripping

282

with water to the left, the rough, tussock-littered river bank to the right. The Medway was rising.

'Like the country, do you, Sylvia?' Simon asked. 'You always used to say you did. Said you'd like it if I retired there one day. To a house like Peter's. I remember, I remember everything you've ever said to me.' He was striding out. He felt marvellous, young and strong. Even the dull ache in his chest had gone. The doctor had put it down to overwork but the truth was now evident. It was Sylvia who had been doing her best to make him feel an old man. When she died he would live. To serve Peter.

Sylvia was hardly aware of the pain from her feet. They were scratched and bleeding as the path was stony, covered with flint-like chips that cut her at almost every step. There was nothing she could say that would stop Simon, she was sure of that. So she must wait her chance. There had to be a moment, however fleeting, when he would be off his guard.

'Here, we stop here.' Simon shouted to be heard over the low, menacing thunder. Almost at once lightning flashed behind him, a golden, jagged fork that stabbed down into the woods. He looked at his wife. Her dress clung so closely to her body that he could see every curve. The outline of her nipples showed clearly, and he thought he could see the brownness of them through the fabric. 'Take your clothes off,' he said, and his voice was thick and wet in his throat.

'No!' Eli took a step forward. 'Don't do it, Sylvie.'

'Oh but she will. Won't you, my dear?' Simon held the gun out at arm's length. It pointed steadily, unwaveringly, at Eli. 'And what are you worrying about? After all, we've both seen her naked. It's not as if her body's a secret to either of us.'

Sylvia moved slowly; it was as if she was in a dream.

There was no escape now. The rain was easing, falling as a warm, comfortable embrace, and the ground around them steamed. Only the river was a threat – the water and Simon were the dangers. She unbuttoned the top of her dress, slipping it off her shoulders, and all the time she watched Simon's eyes. His face was bloated, swollen with his hate. She pushed the dress down over her hips, stepping out of it gracefully. Her slip clung to her and she took it by the scalloped hem and lifted it slowly over her head.

'Now you.' Simon gestured at Eli, but his eyes kept darting back to Sylvia. Her skin was like alabaster streaked with wet.

'No,' Eli said softly, and Simon had to lean forward to hear him. 'You can't make me. After all, what's the point?'

'Do as I say!' Simon's voice rose to a scream. He would not be thwarted now.

'Simon,' Sylvia said softly as she held her arms out towards him. 'Simon, kiss me goodbye.' Then she laughed, and it was a sound from deep in her throat. 'A kiss before dying.'

'You slut.' Simon stepped towards her. His voice was low with venom, and he spoke for her alone. But he hadn't forgotten about Eli, he kept Sylvia between them. 'Slut,' he whispered again. His mouth was thick with saliva.

'Please, Simon, please.' She took a step back, her arms still beckoning him. She tipped her head back, her lips parting. The thunder began to build. Simon felt it around and inside him.

'Please,' she murmured, and he raised the gun high. Nothing would stop him, he must smash her to pieces. He stepped close and her arms went around him as he began

284

the great sweeping arc to bring the gun down. She spun swiftly, her young strength winning over his unfit, unaware body. They teetered for a moment. The river bank was sodden beneath them, and the dry of summer had eaten into it, desiccating its structure. Without a sound it gave way and they pitched down, clinging together in a tormented embrace. Eli shouted out as Sylvia hit the water. Simon's great body rolled on top of her but she clung to him – he mustn't escape. The water filled her mouth, her nose. She dug her nails into her husband's jacket, wound her legs around him, and the river rolled them over and over, sweeping them away. .

'Sylvie! Sylvie!' Eli sobbed her name. The thunder gave way to mad, crackling lightning, and there was a sudden smell of burning, but he didn't notice any of it. He saw only the obscene bundle floating way out of his reach. 'Sylvie.' Then they were out of his sight. The bend of the river took them forever beyond him.

The rain stopped as it had begun, a few last drops falling desultorily. He stood there for a long time, until the sun came through the clouds and small drifts of midges rose up from the ground at his feet. The river swept past him. There were tangles of hay and a great branch of an oak tree carried in triumph on the broken water, but Eli didn't see any of it. Eventually he turned and went slowly back towards the house. His arm ached, the one he'd lost at Dunkirk, and there was a pain in the fingers of his non-existent hand that was so bad it made him cry.

A chilling spray splashed through the open porthole. Oily water ran down the polished mahogany panelling and soaked into the navy-blue duffel jacket lying crumpled on the bench below. Eli held the wheel steady. It tried to jerk in his hand but he had no intention of following the whim of the tide. A low groan behind him was the prelude to Bella being sick again. Even over the wet river smell the stench of vomit reached him.

'I'm going to die,' Bella moaned. She had never felt like this before. Never wallowed on the hard slippery floor of a boat that was being steered to maximize the destructive potential of choppy water. 'Eli,' she sobbed, 'Eli, have pity.'

'Swear to me you'll never see him again.' Eli shouted to make quite sure she heard him over the throb of the twin-screw diesels. He had opened the hatch beside him and was saturated, but he didn't notice it.

'No.' Bella shook her head. It made the pain in her temples almost unbearable, but what Eli was asking her to do was like asking her to give up life itself. 'Anything else – I'll do anything you want, Eli. But I'll never leave Peter, never.'

A seagull kept course with them for a moment, mewing harshly as it scanned the water for food. It must be rough at sea, Eli thought, for the bird to be inland. Then he smiled. It was a wry, questioning smile. There were sea birds that lived their lives out on the estuary only a few minutes' flying time away, and he was thinking like a landsman. But then, of course, that was what he was. He put his head out through the hatch, scanning the river ahead and then behind. With a grunt of approval he stepped back into the cabin and spun the wheel hard. They would go back. He'd got nowhere with Bella. If she got tangled up in the tightening net around Peter Savage, then she had only herself to blame.

Soon, Eli could finish with telling lies. All the arguments he'd used with Bella had been diluted by the fact that he had to act as if he was going to continue to work for Savage. Thank God, before long it would be over. He began to whistle tunelessly, letting his mind relax into thinking about Sylvia. The thoughts were private, happy ones, memories of times they'd shared together. He had shut out Simon as if he'd never existed. He should hate being on the water now, because it had taken her from him. But in a strange way it was the only place he was at peace.

Isabella watched as the carpenter drilled the holes and then put the long thick screws through the oak door. In peacetime he would have been committing a sacrilege. It was strange how values could change. The family were now totally cut off from the convalescent home. They had been left with the east wing and the gardens on that side of the house. She looked slowly about her. The corridor had never had so much furniture in it. There were three unmatching side tables and a clutter of odd chairs. Only the portraits were as they had been – five elderly oil paintings of Montford ancestors. She wondered what they would make of the chaos. She left the workman to finish his job. From this moment, she thought, life at Pencombe would be very different.

They had made the buttery into a kitchen for the family. There was a refectory table and eight spindle-backed chairs, a wide dresser stocked with cream kitchen ware and half a dozen flower-patterned jugs. The floor was uneven, the flagstones worn by countless feet through centuries of use. A woven rush mat had been unearthed from the jumble in the cellar, and it was almost wide enough to cover the floor completely. Fortunately, the butler's sink had been in good repair; it had a well-scrubbed draining board to one side and a free-standing set of drawers to the other. The old range had somehow been coaxed into a new lease of life. Isabella had the feeling that the room would become the new hub of life for the family on their visits, and she ignored the thought that Michael would turn in his grave if he could see it. There were a lot of changes, and some of them were for the better.

To make a cup of tea she had simply to move the heavy-bottomed kettle forward from the ledge behind the range to the hot ring. Within minutes it was boiling; she'd had just time enough to warm the pot and then spoon in some precious tea. It wasn't much more effort than it had been in the days when she'd rung for a servant to perform the task. She sat down at the table, waiting for the tea to brew. She always left it a good five minutes – that way the smallest amount made a strong potful. She stood up suddenly – she'd forgotten the cosy.

A marmalade cat stretched in its basket and looked warily around the room before deciding to see what was in its bowl. Isabella wasn't quite sure about cats. She didn't like the way they curled around her legs. This one was a visitor, but she suspected it might turn into a permanent fixture. It had been the pet of the couple Lizzy had lodged with. The creature was lucky and it had been out mousing when the bomb struck. Tom thought it would settle better well away from the ruin of its home, and so it had been the first real occupant of the new kitchen. It wanted milk and began mewing softly, exploring the possibilities of motivating Isabella into action.

She stood by the dresser, holding the red and blue Welsh tweed cosy in her hands. The cat was so obviously trying to bend her will. It couldn't have any milk. After all, everyone had to do without something. 'You'll have to wait, puss,' she said. 'You're not due to be fed until supper time.' The cat stretched luxuriously, arching its back in play aggression. 'No,' Isabella said. 'You must learn not to eat between meals.' She laughed at herself. It was rather nice having a friend to talk to, especially one who couldn't answer back. She wondered if the cat was thirsty, and picked up the empty blue and white bowl. The water from the tap over the sink was very cold as it splashed over her fingers. It came from a bore hole outside. She placed her offering down in front of the cat that had begun to purr in happy anticipation. Its tongue flashed out, pink and quivering with hunger, then with an aggravated shake of its head it moved back, its tail swishing irritably, drops of water hanging from its whiskers.

'Oh, poor kitty.' Lucinda came into the kitchen. She was so much thinner that she moved quite differently and looked years younger, and she'd even been able to give up her stick. She walked quickly over to the cat, picked it up and held it against her chest. 'Poor kitty's hungry,' she crooned, pursing her lips to drop kisses on its head. She looked accusingly at Isabella.

'Well, I'm sorry for it too. But it isn't to be fed until this evening.'

'What utter nonsense.' Lucinda placed her cheek against the warm fur. 'Is she cruel to poor kitty? Never mind, Lucinda will save you, my pet.' She walked purposefully towards the larder.

Isabella thought about stopping her, about joining in the argument that her sister was so clearly eager for, but she wouldn't give her that satisfaction. 'Suit yourself,' she said. 'Would you like a cup of tea? I've just made one.'

'Oh, but should I really? After all, it would use up a few drops of milk, wouldn't it? If poor kitty should starve in a good cause, then perhaps I should too?'

Isabella poured the two cups of tea without comment. She opened the biscuit jar and proffered it to Lucinda.

'No thank you, I wouldn't dream of taking food out of

the mouths of babes and invalids. Talking about invalids . . .' Lucinda poured milk into the cat's bowl as she spoke. 'When are our new neighbours moving in? I do hope we're not going to be disturbed by moans in the night.'

'I think I liked you better when you were fatter,' Isabella said. 'You didn't have the energy to be so unpleasant then.' She sipped slowly at her tea. Lucinda was tiring when she was in one of her moods.

'If the day ever comes that we can all have what we'd like, Isabella, I promise I will not trouble you any more. I shall fly away from this godforsaken place like a swallow in autumn. I shall visit Florence and Venice.' Her voice softened as she thought of all her friends she would look up, after the war.

'It won't ever be the same,' Isabella said. 'Nothing will.'

Lucinda stood up silently. She gathered up the cat that had just finished its drink, and walked from the kitchen with a light step. Isabella was a dreadful pessimist, and she was getting old. Lucinda felt that she herself was on the verge of regaining her youth. She was even showing herself to be far more resilient than her daughter. Victoria was beginning to look faded and if she didn't take care she would be a middle-aged frump. Everyone was sorry for poor Nigel, but life had to go on, and it was selfish to inflict a long face on the world.

She made her way slowly to her new bedroom, stroking the cat and whispering endearments in its furry ear. She wanted it to be her especial pet, to follow her around and to miss her when she wasn't there. That would show them. Now that only she and Isabella lived at Pencombe, the cat could show everyone how much nicer Lucinda was than her sister. Animals understood a person's soul. She put the cat down carefully inside her bedroom, closing the door softly behind it. 'Here,' she said, patting the soft, feather-filled eiderdown on her bed. 'Kitty can sleep here.' The cat jumped up. It sniffed cautiously, and then began kneading its feet down into the softness, making a hollow for itself. It turned around a few times, finding the exact position for the most comfort. Finally it lay down and curled up, then it purred loudly until it fell asleep.

'I'd much rather you stayed home with me, Bella.' Adele's voice was high with concern. She had promised Bill that she wouldn't let her daughter out of her sight.

'Look, I'm going to spend the evening with Honour, you know that. And I'm obviously not going anywhere else. I mean, look at me.' She held her arms out wide. She was wearing a pale blue two-piece that was her most staid outfit. It was the sort of clothing eminently suitable to wear visiting an aged aunt, which was exactly what she'd bought it for, several years ago. 'You can't possibly think I'd go to Peter's in this. And you can see I don't have anywhere to hide a change of clothing.' She held her clutch bag towards her mother.

Adele sighed. There was nothing more she could say. Honour had promised not to lend Bella any evening clothes, and they'd done everything they could short of locking her up in her room.

Bella walked slowly down the stairs. She didn't want to get overheated. Next to her skin she was wearing a skin-tight silver sequined sheath – it was just as well that she'd lost a few pounds in weight thanks to the past few weeks' arguing, or the suit would never have fitted on top. The shoes she had on were open-toed black patent – not exactly what she would have chosen normally, but they would do. In her clutch bag she had her evening make-up and, folded very small, a multi-coloured silk square with a long fringe. She would wear that over her hair and shoulders on the trip down. Safe at the bottom of her bag was the key to Neil's car. She had picked it up off the sideboard at Honour's flat. She knew the car had a full tank of petrol because Neil had been boasting about it. He'd been saving it up to take Jill away somewhere for a weekend.

When she reached the pavement she began to walk more quickly. The garage where it was kept was only a few streets away, and once she got there she would drive as fast as she could to get out of town and down to Peter's. She didn't want to get caught as it got dark. Her driving wasn't very good at the best of times, and on dimmed lights it would be hopeless.

Eli checked his black tie in the mirror. It was squint, and with a grunt of annoyance he pulled it undone and started again. Victoria was sitting silently, watching him get ready. She coughed – her chest was hurting – and then she asked, 'Will it be dangerous?'

'It depends,' Eli said slowly, concentrating on the knot he was tying. 'There'll be quite a crowd all set to pour in when I shout. What it really depends on is if Savage himself gives in easily. You can't tell with a chap like that.'

'Be careful, Eli. I've only met him a couple of times, but I think he'll put up a fight. There's something about him that reminds me of someone I once knew, someone I once loved when I was just a girl. He was dangerous too. Watch out for yourself tonight.'

Eli turned towards her. 'There, how do I look? Dressed to kill?' He smiled grimly.

'Yes.' Victoria stirred restlessly in her chair. She was

huddled under a lightweight mohair rug, and beside her a half-drunk cup of cocoa was slowly growing cold.

Eli picked up his evening coat, which he'd brought into the room earlier, as if he was marshalling his forces ready for the attack. 'You're lonely,' he said. 'You need a steady type of fellow – you're too highly strung.'

Victoria smiled sadly. 'I'm still married, you know. Luke could live for years. We shouldn't be discussing any kind of fellow for me.'

'Now isn't the time to talk about it, Viccy. Half my mind's on Savage and his crowd. But when tonight's over, we'll sort things out. You can't give up your life to the memory of Luke; he might as well be dead, the state he's in. And you can't throw yourself away on a cheap affair with a man like Bertie. I'm fond of Luke too, you know, but the only answer is for you to divorce him.' He walked over to his niece and bent to kiss her on the cheek. 'I'll help you through – you can depend on me. And don't forget, you go down to the cellar the minute you hear the sirens.'

Victoria sat unmoving as she listened to Eli letting himself out of the house. Divorce. She mouthed the word soundlessly. Would it be possible? She didn't know how the law worked – was a woman allowed to discard a man who'd simply grown too old? It didn't seem likely. After all, it was old men who made the rules. She picked up her cup and looked at the skin that had formed over the now cold milk. She still had to take her sleeping tablets. There was no staff living in the house apart from the nurse who was upstairs with Luke, so she would have to get herself a drink of water. Suddenly the kitchen seemed a long way off. She was still so exhausted, even climbing the stairs to her bedroom tired her. So why couldn't she sleep through the night? She asked herself the question that had seemed to take up most of her thoughts since her illness.

The answer was painfully simple: the moment she lay down on her bed she began thinking about Luke, about how guilty she felt. There had been Bertie and for a few blissful weeks she had felt no guilt, only a heady joy at being so in love, and then everything had soured. She'd seen her lover for the shallow, worthless creature that he was and she'd felt bitter and cheated. And what about 'her reverend'? She smiled tiredly, thinking of how Eli always referred to Colin as that. Perhaps in a strange way she did love him. She certainly felt she could depend on his spiritual strength. When he came back, on the day she knew she had to steel herself for a visit to Nigel, it had been as if all of life had taken her to that moment, the time of finding that there was someone she could depend on. But she wasn't a woman to make a vicar's wife, even the thought of a mothers' meeting made her smile cynically.

She got slowly to her feet. She would have a glass of water with her tablets, and then she'd go straight down to the cellar. She wouldn't wait for the siren, or she'd be too tired.

The many windows of Peter Savage's house were ablaze with lights. As Eli's car swept up the drive towards them, he wondered just how quickly the blackout screens could be closed if there was a raid. Left as it was, the house would stand out like a beacon, and for a moment he wondered if that was what it was meant to be, a signpost to the enemy. He smiled wryly at his overreaction; he knew that was taking his hatred of the man too far – there would be many other isolated houses flouting the blackout rules for no other reason than bloody-mindedness.

There was a stream of chauffeur-driven cars ahead of him, depositing visitors at the front door. Luxurious fur coats were much in evidence despite the mild weather. It was obviously an evening where impressions would count. Eli stepped out from the car. He was going to make the most lasting impression of all.

He saw Bella as soon as he walked into the drawing room. She was standing beside Peter, greeting the newly arrived guests. Her being there seemed to accentuate the fact that Sylvia would never again be paraded to enhance Peter's image. There was music playing – that was a new touch – and the flower displays were subtly restrained, yet somehow more opulent than they had been in Simon's day. Eli recognized a Degas in pride of place over the mantelpiece – that would be Bella's influence as well.

'Eli.' Peter proffered a hand in greeting. 'Still no word from Simon?'

Eli shook his head. Peter had accepted the explanation that the sudden disappearance of his right-hand man had been necessary after Eli heard his name being bandied about by some of the dockyard police.

'Eli, how nice to see you.' Bella pressed her cheek coolly against his. She smiled with her lips while her eyes were cold. She knew she was safe enough from Eli's lecturing when she was with Peter. Afterwards there would no doubt be hell to pay. But after tonight she was confident that she would be able to run to Peter for shelter from her overpowering family. Without Simon he would be putty in her hands.

Eli moved on towards the centre of the room. He wanted to see who was there, to wait until everyone important had arrived. He had only one chance to catch as many of the network as possible. The party was to celebrate the success of the dockyard organization, and

Eli found it remarkable how many faces he recognized in the gathering. There were men who should certainly have known better than to reveal their connection with Savage, but they and their womenfolk had apparently not been able to resist the appeal of being entertained in style at the Manor. Eli nodded to a dock official who only last week he had heard accepting congratulations on running a tight ship from a high-up member of the Ministry. His job was to oversee the unloading of vital supplies for the war effort. Tonight would bring a sudden end to his dreams of a medal in recognition of services to King and country. Eli sipped his champagne. It tasted flat and sour, but he knew that was only his disillusionment.

Peter came up to him quietly. 'Give them five more minutes and then call them to order, Eli. Just say a few words and then hand them over to me. We'll eat after that.'

Bella was still beside her lover. So, she thought, Eli was to take over in Simon's absence. They would have to come to some kind of truce. If he wanted to play squire to Peter's role of king – and he was bound to – then he would have to come to terms with the reigning queen. She went to follow Peter, but Eli held her arm tightly. Peter walked away from them and joined a group on the far side of the room, where he began chatting amicably. He was being the perfect host. Bella smiled, Eli must have come to the same conclusion as she had about joining forces.

'You have to leave.' Eli squeezed Bella's wrist tightly.

She looked at him in amazement. 'Let go of me,' she whispered. She pulled to get away from him, but he held her more tightly than ever. 'Eli, stop it.' She was keeping her voice low. To make a scene in this gathering would be unthinkable.

'Get outside.' Eli's face was close to hers. 'Did you drive yourself down?'

She nodded. The question had taken her by surprise and she added, 'In Neil's Bugatti.'

'Drive home – go on, get away now.'

'For Christ's sake.' She shook her arm abruptly and he let her go. 'What the hell is this all about? You're involved in Peter's business – you seem to think it's all right for you but not for me. Is that how you see it? And where's your precious Sylvia? Peter might believe she's gone scurrying off after her lord and master, but I don't. Not the way you two have been carrying on. There's something very odd about you tonight.' Her brow wrinkled suddenly. 'In fact, I don't like any of this. I think Peter should . . .' She turned to look for him.

It had never seemed quite right, Eli being mixed up in the black market. When he'd come back the hero from Dunkirk, no one in the family had been surprised. But if they heard he was working on the wrong side of the law they would never believe it. The family was right. Eli was still being a Goody Two-Shoes. She had to speak to Peter. She began pushing her way through the crush towards him. Eli was a cad around women, and a bad influence on young men, but he wasn't the black sheep he was pretending to be. 'Peter!' She raised her voice in a vain effort to be heard above the chatter. 'Peter!' She was desperate – there seemed to be an immovable crowd around him.

'Ladies and gentlemen.' Eli jumped quickly up on a chair. There was only one way to stop Bella. 'Please can I have your attention?' They all turned to look at him. There were smiles on their animated faces, glasses held up in anticipation of a few self-congratulatory toasts. He could see Bella – she had nearly reached Peter. 'Hey, you lot over there.' He forced a laugh as he shouted to the

297

group around her. 'Stop that woman!' He was acting the buffoon and they laughed at him. 'I don't want her to spoil a little surprise I have for our host.' A dozen hands reached out to stop Bella. They were roaring with laughter. Most of them had already had more to drink than they were used to.

'Let me go, I've got to . . .' Eli could hear her voice, but they were shouting her down, telling her to be a good sport.

Eli smiled. He'd done it. He took one last look around the room, at the gathering who'd sold their souls to the man who'd known the price to offer. He put his hand in his pocket. 'Surprise time,' he cried, then he pulled out his whistle and held it to his lips.

It took all night processing their catch, and Eli left Bella until the very end. It was dawn as she was brought into the bleak, yellow-painted office that had been put at his disposal. He was tired of the tears of men and women who'd gone out for an evening of good food and drink and instead had come face to face with the prospect of life in a cell. Bella hadn't taken the waiting well. She looked old and worn, and her silver dress seemed tattier even than the elderly chipped filing cabinets that flanked the wall behind her. She had a thin scarf pulled round her shoulders and was shivering with cold. Eli took off his jacket and handed it to her. There were two other men with him and he quietly told them to go out and take a break for ten minutes. Then he sat, expecting her to break down now that they were alone. When she didn't he realized that she was beyond feeling, her eyes glazed.

'I tried to warn you,' he said. 'Even before last night, I told Bill and Adele to make sure you stayed at home.

298

And I told you to leave off seeing him. You should have done it.'

She didn't say anything, but it seemed she must be listening because she gave a faint shrug of her shoulders as if dismissing what he said.

'There's nothing I can do now,' Eli continued. 'Bill's trying to see if they'll accept your being sent back to the States.'

'They?' She looked up at him, her eyes meeting his for the first time since she'd come into the room.

'The authorities – the men with the power to send you to prison.'

She shivered again. 'What'll happen to Peter?' she asked.

'It depends. If he's lucky, he'll be locked up for a long time.'

'If he's unlucky?'

'There's a war on. What he's done is a form of treachery. What do you think?'

She seemed to shrink, to shrivel in her chair. 'Do you think they'll let me go?' she asked.

Eli stayed silent for a moment. The truth was that he didn't know. He said, 'I'll get you a change of clothes.'

She nodded as the two men came back into the office. Eli cleared his throat and stood up. 'You have to go with them, Bella. They'll take you to a women's prison to wait. That's the form, isn't it, boys?'

He felt chilled. Bella had been foolish, nothing more. He hoped to God Bill could get her off with deportation. Much earlier he had felt euphoric. Sandy had been gratifyingly delighted at the successful raid. Miles and the others had stormed the house, to find their quarry milling around Eli. Savage had been trapped in a crush of his own making and actually watched his adversary blow the whistle that called in justice. Now it seemed a hollow victory. He would go back to Cadogan Gardens – he needed to change out of his evening clothes and there was a nasty taste in his mouth. His stomach had been rumbling on and off for hours, and he had to eat, and then a few hours' sleep wouldn't go amiss. It was all over.

Eli closed the file in front of him on the desk. His job was finished. Sylvia was nothing more than a dream. She'd been laid to rest in a burial plot beside her husband, somewhere in the south of England. That was all he'd been told by the organization, which had kept their deaths a secret so that it wouldn't spoil the operation.

'But it's nothing like as bad as you're imagining.' Jill was on the verge of losing her temper. She knew she was being unkind, heartless in a way, but she'd seen so much worse. There were other patients with vast gaping holes that exposed their inner workings; there were men without noses; men without lips. There were small miracles being carried out every day at the hospital, the pulling together of the edges of life. Nigel's injuries weren't horrific to her as a nurse, and besides, she had a special reason for wanting this particular patient to recover. 'Nigel, you have got to look at yourself sometime.'

'That's not true. The doctor said it didn't matter if I couldn't face it. He understands.'

'He's only saying that today, because he saw how frightened you were. Tomorrow he'll start a little gentle pressure, the next day a bit more. You can save him so much time and effort. Don't be selfish, Nigel. You've got to start getting used to it sometime. Go on, look.' She held the small mirror out towards him.

'I can't,' he whispered. 'Please.' He turned his head away. 'I'll try tomorrow, I promise.' But he was lying, simply buying time. He would never look at his face. He'd seen some of the others. Dear Christ. He struggled to keep himself under control. He wouldn't cry. He mustn't disgrace himself, and more than that, the salt tears would begin by stinging his face but then dry and tighten, making him want to claw his cheeks to ribbons as the itching became unbearable.

Jill came out of the front door of the hospital to meet Honour and Carl. She looked very pretty in her starched uniform, calm and in control of herself. That was why it surprised them so much when she suddenly broke down in front of them. 'I'm sorry, so sorry,' she kept saying as she buried her face in Carl's quickly offered handkerchief. Her narrow shoulders were heaving. 'I'll be all right.' She turned her back to them as she struggled for self-control. At last she was able to wipe her eyes, blow her nose and turn pale-faced towards them.

Honour held Carl's arm tightly. Nigel must be dead. She felt giddy, light-headed with shock. He'd been getting better, that's what they'd been told. They'd come down to ask him to the wedding. Jill had suggested it over the telephone, as a way to make him look towards the future. But now it was all too late.

'Whatever must you think of me?' Jill managed a faint smile. 'I'm so sorry but I've just had a horrible morning. Much, much worse than usual. And Nigel . . .' She paused. 'Nigel's just being silly.'

'Silly?' Honour's voice was shaking. 'You mean he's not dead?'

'Dead? Good Lord no. He's had the bandages taken off his face, all of them. His chest is still under dressings, but most of his legs are fine. Both his hands are still suppurating, and he's lost a few fingers, of course.' She was so matter-of-fact that it took a few minutes for her words to sink in.

Honour flinched. She hadn't heard about his hands. 'How many fingers has he lost?' she asked.

'Two on the right hand, three on the left. Well, actually it's more like two and a half on the left – he's got quite a long stump.'

Honour swallowed. She felt sick. She forced her eyes to stay open, knowing she was close to fainting.

'Let's go and see him,' Carl said. 'It sounds as if he could do with some friends.'

Jill turned to lead the way. 'He'll probably tell you I'm heartless,' she said. 'But the sooner he faces up to how he looks the sooner he'll get out of here and start living again. It's not the end of the world for him, and he's got to understand it. He'll be out of here in no time. We need his bed for patients in a much worse state than he is.'

It wouldn't be surprising if Nigel found Jill unfeeling, Honour thought, because that was just how she sounded. Whatever she was having to do, whatever horrific injuries she was seeing, was hardening her.

'I thought you'd come to tell me Neil had bought it. It's bloody murder lying here thinking about him flying.' Nigel lay back against his pillows and closed his eyes.

'I'm sorry. We should have written to say we were coming, but we didn't know we could both get time off until late yesterday.' Honour found she could look at Nigel's face now that his eyes were closed. The worst thing about it had been the awful haunted expression in his eyes.

'Not that I'd have believed you.' Nigel carried on as if Honour hadn't spoken. 'I know he's all right. We always know about each other – hope he doesn't understand how

302

I feel right now though.' He opened his eyes suddenly and caught the look on Honour's face. It wasn't the revulsion he'd expected, it was pity. 'Sorry for me, are you?' he shouted. 'Let's all be sorry for poor Nigel. Well, you needn't be. I've got it all planned out. I'll get out of this bloody place and then I'll go away. So far away that you'll never see me again. That'll suit the lot of you, won't it? Never having to look on poor, frightful Nigel.'

'Pack it in, old chap.' Carl's voice was quiet but strong. 'It looks to me as if there are a few other chaps in here who might feel like that too. But some of them won't be going very far.' There was the man in the corner bed with no legs, for a start.

Nigel lay silently staring up at the ceiling. It had been easier, he thought, when he'd been covered in bandages. His mind was being kind to him and he no longer remembered how desperately he'd wanted to tear the covering off his face. There was a day when the pain in his eyes had made him claw at the bandages and they'd tied him in some kind of straitjacket. He'd thought he would go mad then. 'Got a mirror?' he asked suddenly. He felt detached. It wasn't him lying there; he was visiting some other chap who'd been so nearly cooked alive.

Honour reached into her handbag and brought out her compact. It was the one her mother had given her as a going-away present when she'd left Pencombe to go and stay in London. She ran the tip of her fingers over the red enamelled lid with its painted pattern of tiny pink roses. 'I'm sorry, it's not a very big one, but it's all I've got on me,' she said as she opened it and held the mirror in front of him.

It was the colour – that was what shocked him at first – the mixture of purples and pinks, that looked like a seventy-year-old peasant after a lifetime's hard work in the fields. In the tiny round mirror he could only look at a small piece of himself at a time. The expression in his eyes was frantic and he stared at them for a long time. He couldn't really look like that, could he? It was the look of a trapped animal. He'd once seen a terrier caught in a gin trap. It had been throwing itself about in a frenzy, and then, just before it died it had lain very still, as if its suffering had stopped, but its eyes were still wild, as his were. That was how he looked now. He tipped his head. He wanted to see if he had any hair left. He had no eyebrows and he wondered if they'd ever grow back. There was silvery scar tissue criss-crossing his forehead among the livid patches. Most of his hair had gone and what was left looked moth-eaten. The more he saw of himself the more it seemed he was looking at someone else. He academically studied his right ear, or rather, what was left of it – there wasn't that much. His left ear, on the other hand, was amazingly perfect. He admired that even though it made that side of his face seem even worse in comparison. His mouth was still surrounded by stitches, and it looked like a very bad needlework sampler.

'I think even you might have done a bit better than this, Honour, and we all know how much you hated needle-work.' He tried to gesture towards his lips with his hand, but he was still clumsy and the weight of the dressings made his actions slower than his words.

'It could be worse,' Carl said. He wanted to leave. He hated the hospital, with its calm self-righteous air. He'd rather be dead than lying there like some kind of decaying monster in one of their orderly beds.

'Want to buy a green Bugatti, Carl?' Nigel laughed bitterly. 'I can't even hold a lady's compact, so I'm not likely to be able to handle my car.'

304

'Don't be silly.' Honour knew how he felt about the car that had once been his father's. 'You'll be driving again before you know it. We came to invite you to our wedding. Why don't you drive us away from the reception, how about that? Why don't we make it a date?' Honour's voice sounded very bright. She loved Nigel; he had been her friend since they were babies. She didn't look at Carl. He would have to let her try this, if it would be something to make Nigel want to start living again.

'You don't want me there on your wedding day,' Nigel said, but there was a kind of desperate hope in his voice. 'I'd be the ghoul at the feast. No, you two go ahead without me. Anyway, I've got no idea if I'll ever be able to drive again, or, come to that, when I'll get out of this place, and I don't expect you'll want to wait indefinitely.'

'We'll wait.' Carl leaned forward on his chair. He didn't want to have to postpone the wedding, he wanted them to be together as soon as possible. But he loved Honour too much to go against her. She was so taut, so on edge, willing Nigel to come to terms with himself.

'You'll have to hurry and get better, you know,' Honour laughed nervously, 'because we're so much in love that every day we wait seems an age.'

'Trust old Nigel, I'll extract the digit. Tell you what.' The stitches at the corner of his lip pulled painfully as he smiled. 'Get someone to drive my beauty over here. Park her outside the window where I can see her. That'll make me better, if nothing else does.'

It was Jill who suggested that Neil should visit Nigel before taking her to the cinema. So far she had made very little of the fact that she was going out with his brother, but she wanted it out in the open between them. The relationship of patient and nurse had inevitably become a

305

close one, and more and more Jill was finding herself wanting Nigel fit and well. She knew that the time would come when she had to choose between the twins.

'How are you, old man?' Neil stood uncertainly at the foot of the bed. He hated hospitals, they made him realize how fragile the human body was and it wasn't a good feeling for a flier.

'I'll be out of here soon.' Nigel felt the atmosphere between them. Jill wasn't there in the ward, but the thought of her was in both their minds. 'I don't know what kind of job they'll be able to give me but I think I'll be flying a desk from now on.'

'Lucky devil,' Neil said, and they both knew he didn't mean it.

'Funny thought, you know, not being able to fly any more. It's not so much the fingers I've lost, but the fact that my grip's gone entirely. That's something to do with the tendons.' He looked down at his hands. Now they were unwrapped they looked like the scaly claws of some giant bird. 'Still, they're doing some amazing things.'

'About Jill.' Neil couldn't stand it any more. 'I'm serious, you know. I've never felt like this before.'

'Not even with the girl in the car?' If Nigel's face could have let him, he would have looked cynical.

'It's not like that. I wouldn't dream of trying it on with Jill. I respect her. I . . .' He swallowed, and then lowered his voice. He didn't want anyone else to hear. 'I love her, and I'm going to tell her so tonight.'

'Good luck then.' The bitterness was clear in Nigel's voice. 'Not that you need it, you've got a clear field.'

'Have I?'

'No, by God you haven't!' Nigel was suddenly full of life. His voice, which had hardly risen above a whisper since he'd come to the hospital, was now loud enough to be heard down the corridor. 'Jill!' he bellowed. 'Jill!'

She came running. She'd been waiting for Neil, undecided as to how she felt, but when she heard Nigel's voice, she knew.

Remember all the details, Neil thought. Notice the little things – that was what his mother had asked him. Her words seemed to fill the cockpit of his Hurricane. He thought about how the flight had started – had he told her the way the dead weight of the parachute thumped up and down, banging your backside as you ran out to the aircraft? He couldn't recall. He was scanning the sky, part of his mind consumed with the search for enemy fighters, while he thought of other things she could put in her book. He would take her up for a flight one day, he decided, but that would have to wait until the bloody war was over. He had a headache, an absolute blinder that felt as if the top of his skull was being forced down towards his collar. He was drinking too much – they all were.

Nigel would have Jill to himself now. He mustn't think of her. He clenched his hands unnecessarily tightly on the controls. His palms were sweaty but he wasn't nervous – at least, not more than usual. The clouds beneath him were a carpet of snow and where the sun touched them they sparkled with gold. It was like the rare clear days he remembered climbing the mountains above Aviemore. Snow like icing sugar – Christmas cakes like they used to have at Reason Hill.

Christ, his mind wouldn't stay still. Nigel deserved her, and something deep inside him knew that it would end up that way. Jill had said that she wouldn't make up her mind until Nigel was back at work, but she would marry

307

his brother, because . . . because this was the trip he wouldn't be coming back from. The certainty of it hit him hard in the stomach. He gasped, feeling as if he was suffocating. It was impossible to breathe, but he knew it was only his heart beating too fast. He would have prayed, but he'd seen too many good fellows die, chaps who didn't deserve to go out in a cartwheeling fireball. As far as he was concerned, there no longer existed a God to believe in. There was no pattern, no destiny, nothing was pre-ordained. He pulled off his goggles and rubbed the back of his hand across his eyes. Then how was he so aware that he wouldn't be going home? How did he know he wouldn't have time to smoke that first, precious cigarette standing beside the cooling plane, waiting for the truck back?

A staccato hammer of sound cut across his thoughts and a ragged line of machine gun bullets ripped into his craft as he reacted instinctively. A new fear flared at the thump of heavy cannon shells clawing their way towards his frail body. There was a sudden stink of cordite. He rolled over and down, hurtling towards the cover of the clouds. The controls kicked at him and he straightened the instant before he disappeared into clinging white candy floss. The stink of petrol burned his throat and eyes but for the moment he was safe, hidden in the clouds. How long could he stay in there? What were the odds against his colliding with the searching enemy, or even with one of his own side? He was scowling, working out what to do next as the fire blossomed. He began to cough as black stinking streamers caught at him. Oh Christ, he thought, why me?

He dreamed he was tumbling to earth. He had to be dreaming because he was falling so pleasantly. His head rolled comfortably, leisurely, over his heels and he was turning a perfect somersault – he'd been good at them at school. He couldn't breathe, but it didn't seem to matter. His hands began moving by themselves, following some instructions long submerged in his muddled brain. There was a hard jerk – he was a puppet on strings – and then suddenly he was floating. The earth wobbled, and then it was the right way up. There was an unnerving loosening in his bowels as he realized that it was all for real, and he gulped in air, tightening his muscles, pleading with them to function.

He must remember everything for his mother. The fields beneath him were a patchwork, a French pattern of green and bronze. He longed passionately to be able to stop falling and to stay where he was, suspended in both time and space. When he'd practised tumbling out of the sky, he hadn't been able to wait to get down to the ground. But this time the earth wasn't his friend and it was rushing up to meet him. Everything was very clear: there was a road and the glint of a river. There were lorries parked, with ant-like figures swarming out across the biggest patch of green beneath him. The ants grew swiftly until they were dark grey figures, German soldiers in an uncut French hay field.

He reckoned he was over Brittany. He knew the country – he'd holidayed there with a pal of his from school, and Nigel had been there too. They'd cycled every day and he understood the lie of the land better than any bloody Kraut. He could have gone to earth, then pinched a bicycle, as they had all said they would, if it was their turn to go down.

Somehow he could have escaped the bastards if they hadn't been waiting for him. But of course – he laughed out loud at his stupidity – if he hadn't been so concerned with not messing himself he would have worked it out.

He wasn't going home, not for a long, long time. That was why the Jerries were waiting for him.

The field threw itself up towards him, much more quickly than he'd expected. He felt his leg crumple beneath him. 'Roll as you land,' he thought as the lights went out. '*Hände hoch*,' he heard dimly.

'Will you take care of it for me for the next few days?' Carl held the brown cardboard box towards Honour. Inside, on a soft bed of straw, a tiny leveret slept peacefully. 'I'm not sure if I'll be around enough to look after it, so I'll give you the pipette and a bottle of goat's milk.'

'Of course I'll take it. I used to be quite a dab hand at animal rescue, you know.' Honour was smiling brightly although she wanted to cry. They were saying au revoir for a week at least, while Carl was confined to the base. The only good thing to say for the whole silly incident was that he'd promised never to do any of his out-of-bounds aerobatics again.

'I am sorry, you know, and embarrassed. It's a bit like being a boy at school, kept in after lessons.'

'I should take it as a compliment.'

'I didn't tell my CO the truth. He kept on asking what was my excuse, but I didn't think I should give him it.'

'I would never have forgiven you if you had.' Honour leaned forward to kiss his cheek. It was because at last they were lovers in the fullest sense of the word that Carl had 'bombed' the mess; he had thought it a romantic gesture.

Honour kept the leveret in the flat. Carl had shot the pregnant mother on the outskirts of the airfield, and when he'd picked the carcase up he'd felt a kicking in its belly and cut it open, giving the tiny creature its life. Against all the odds, the baby hare had survived for a week before he gave it to Honour. She had to get up early in the morning to drip the milk patiently through the pipette into its tiny mouth. The moment she came back in the evening she fed it again, and then once more just before she went to bed. After four days it had become a routine. There were still three more lonely nights until Carl could visit her. They would have such a reunion.

Carl received the telegram at three-thirty in the afternoon of the fifth day. For some inexplicable reason he glanced down at his watch as he took the envelope. There was only one reason he would be sent such a missive. His brothers were together, serving in a ship on the Atlantic run, and he was their next of kin. The words swam before his eyes: 'We regret . . .' There was a mist and he had to struggle to see the name. As he read 'Leopold' the telegraph rider came back. 'Sorry, mate,' he said. 'Didn't think you'd be gettin' two of them. I was nearly . . .' But he didn't bother to finish his sentence. He'd seen the look too many times before, the sunken eyes, the sudden ageing round the mouth. The kind of bad news he brought never did have a silver lining.

Carl was desperate to fly. He felt tied to the earth, weighed down by a grief he couldn't even begin to face. Honour would have to be told, he had to speak to her. But he couldn't bring himself to tell anyone. Pictures of his brothers kept surfacing. They were giants of men, fair-haired, blue-eyed – 'The Vikings', they called themselves – they couldn't be dead. He was the baby of the family, he'd always had them to depend on. When his father died, they'd cushioned the blow, taking it in turns to sit with him through the nightmares, and then when their

311

mother took her own life, they had tried their best to explain. She had been a wife first, a mother second. They were grown-up enough to survive on their own, and the wife in her had had to follow the man she loved.

He was so desperate to fly out his grief that he couldn't sit still, but he'd promised Honour – and more than that, he'd promised his CO. He'd listened to the words that had spelled out how selfish he was being to risk an aeroplane when the war effort needed every one available. Eventually he couldn't stand it any more and picked up the set of keys that were waiting to be sent to Margaret.

Eli came to the flat to tell her. It was just after six. She'd done her chores and was settling down to listen to the radio.

'Come in.' She was pleased to see him – a bit of company was just what she needed to get her through the last evening but one.

'Honour.' He stayed outside the door, as if frightened of stepping into the flat. 'It's about Carl. I'm afraid you've got to prepare yourself for some bad news.'

'Has he crashed?' The words came out quickly, because she'd been poised to ask them ever since they'd first met.

'He wasn't flying.' Eli was hesitant, stumbling over his words.

'What's happened? You must tell me.'

'Carl's dead. He killed himself on Percy's motor bike.'

'Killed himself?' She couldn't understand it, couldn't believe what Eli was saying.

'Not on purpose, I don't mean on purpose. It was an accident. He'd just heard that his two brothers had gone down with their ship. He got the telegrams this afternoon. And he was grounded – you know that – or I suppose he

312

would have gone out and beaten up the sky.' Instead he'd tried the same on a country lane, careering round a blind bend at seventy miles an hour, with the wind blowing the hair into his eyes. No helmet, no goggles – he hadn't stood a chance. 'I think you should come with me.' Eli was surprised when she nodded acceptance. She just reached out blindly and picked up her handbag from the chair beside her, then stepped towards him, pulling the door closed behind her.

After two days at Cadogan Gardens, leaving to go to work as usual in the morning and returning tired out in the evening, she remembered about the leveret. She cried about that, but she didn't cry about Carl. That part of her had died with him.

'Eli.' As she spoke, Honour slowly poured tea into the three cups on the tray. 'I'm sorry if this is going to shock you, but I don't think there's an easy way to say this – Dr Groak says I'm nearly three months pregnant.'

Victoria stared into the crackling fire. It was comfortably warm in her drawing room, despite the wind outside.

Eli sat very still. His expression didn't change as he took in the news. Dr Groak was the name of the doctor at Pencombe, and the significance of Honour going to see the family practitioner hadn't escaped him. 'You mean, you've already decided to have it?' he asked.

Honour nodded. 'How could I do anything else? The baby will be mine and Carl's. It means a part of him lives on.'

'Have you told your mother?'

'No, I only found out for certain a few days ago. And I wanted . . .' She paused, and glanced at Victoria. 'I wanted to make sure I put it the right way. I need her to want the baby as much as I do. I don't think I could stand

313

her being shocked – I mean really shocked, scandalized. I'm sure she'll understand as long as it's put to her properly.'

Victoria reached out and put her hand on Honour's arm. 'I think the truth has to be that none of us have any idea how your mother will react. Now, if it was my mother,' she laughed, 'I can tell you right off how she would behave if it was me in your boat. But I'm not going to act holier than thou. I was foolish with Bertie, and I'm not going to start throwing any stones.'

'Do you want me to tell her?' Eli asked. He couldn't decide how he thought Isabella would take the news. After all, she was so fond of Honour. He thought that her most likely reaction would be to blame Carl, but that was just what Honour didn't want.

'No, I'll tell my mother. That's only fair.'

'We thought you might come down to Pencombe with us,' Victoria told Eli. 'The more the merrier, and all that. Besides, my mother's there, and you could get her out of the way for a bit.'

'Thanks very much,' Eli grimaced. 'You know, I wish you hadn't seen old Groak, not right off. If it had been someone in London . . .'

'I didn't trust myself,' Honour said. 'Truthfully, I was so frightened that I felt I might give in if you all ganged up on me. To have an abortion would be the most terrible thing – to destroy Carl's child.' Her lips began to tremble, and Victoria gave her a quick hug.

'It's all decided now. You don't have to worry about what might have been. You've got to look to the future. You know, it's only a week to go to Christmas, and we're all down at Pencombe for that. Why don't you wait? Nothing's going to happen between now and then. Dr Groak won't say anything, will he?'

'No, he said I should tell Mother myself. I don't have to see him again for four weeks.'

'Then we'll all go to Pencombe together for the holiday,' Victoria said. And so they would, she thought, but she would go down first, on her own. She had remembered something Isabella told her, something it would be useful to follow up.

'So, how's the book going, dear?' Isabella was looking forward to reading the account of their lives. She felt that she could trust Victoria not to let too many of the family ghosts out of the cupboard.

'Much better now that I've decided to make it fiction.'

'Why on earth are you doing that? I wouldn't mind your using my name and I don't suppose any of the others would. Is it your mother?'

'No, for once it's nothing to do with her. It's just that fiction gives me more scope. And it's fun to be able to imagine how things might have happened differently. I've got so much I want to write about that I'm splitting the story into three parts. The first is about how you and Mother met Michael. And there's all about your father and things that I've heard about Eli's mother, Lavender. There's a lot in it.'

'I always felt bad about Lavender. I could have been far nicer to her. Perhaps it's just as well you aren't using our real names, if you're getting as deep into our beginnings as that.'

'There is one name I'm using, and that's Honour's. To tell the truth, I tried not to. But I needed a title for the second part, and it was the only possible word, because honour is what it's all about. I mean the word, not the name, although it ends with her being conceived.'

'Good Lord, you're not putting sex into it?' Isabella

315

showed the horror she felt. 'Conceived' was such a graphic word.

'It's part of life, isn't it? Just as much as living and dying. None of us would be here without it.'

Isabella sat silently. There were days when she felt that she had outlived her time. She wasn't all that old and she could have a good twenty years of life ahead of her, but when she listened to Victoria she realized how outdated her own views were.

'I came to ask you for some more help. This is for the last part,' Victoria said. 'A while ago you promised to tell me about your time in Australia. You said once that everyone had their "moments". I have the feeling a lot happened out there that nobody in the family knows about.'

'A lot happened that I wouldn't want them to know. And I'm not sure any more if I should tell you, Viccy. I wouldn't want it written in your book. The only reason I mentioned it was that I was concerned about you and that Bertie fellow. But that's all over and done with now, isn't it?' She looked sharply at her niece.

'Bertie? Yes, he's long gone. Eli has this mad idea that I should divorce Luke and get myself free in case I fall in love again, but I don't know, I don't suppose I ever will.'

'Love can strike at the oddest times, Viccy. But I don't know about divorce – I mean, how long can Luke . . .? It's disgusting, isn't it, having to talk about him this way? I find myself wishing he'd just die in his sleep, and yet he was such a good husband to you and a good father to his sons. I don't know if Eli's right or not, but you're young and you can't stop falling in love just because it's inconvenient.'

'Was it inconvenient for you in Australia?' Victoria kept her eyes averted from her aunt. She was determined

316

to lead Isabella on into revealing whatever her past held, and she felt that she was on the verge of success.

'I . . .' Isabella stood up uncertainly and then sat down again. 'Very well, I'll tell you, Viccy, but only as a warning to you. Fortunately your mother won't be back until late. I don't want her finding out what I've said. And you must promise me, absolutely, not to use it in your book. I know Michael's not with us any more, but . . . well, I simply wouldn't like it. Fictionalizing our names won't fool everybody. Will you promise me at least not to write anything about Australia until after I'm dead?'

'I promise, Aunty,' Victoria smiled. 'You look pretty healthy to me, so I won't make my publishers any promises that I won't be able to keep for years and years.'

Isabella smiled fleetingly and then began. 'It really started when we made all that money. Michael had invested in a small mining company, and it went from success to success. We were tremendously excited, and then there was a new mining company set up on a totally different site – it also needed investment and they were so desperate that they were offering an enormous percentage of the company. I thought it was too dangerous to take the risk with the profit we'd already made, but Michael was like a man with a fever. He was so sure that we would succeed again.' She sat very still, her cheeks flushed, remembering the tingling thrill of waking up every morning to see what the day would bring.

'And did you? Did you succeed again?'

'Yes – however much against the odds it seemed, we went from strength to strength. We were rich, and all the penny-pinching ideas for the house here could be torn up. And then – well, then Michael went over the top. He'd

317

always been so proper, so in control, but I suppose it was suddenly having all that money. We went on a mad round of Sydney, we entertained in such style – everyone said that there'd never been anything like it. The mad Lord, that's what they called him for those few weeks. He'd buy anyone a drink – champagne was always on the house. He was like . . . well, I suppose he was like his brother, Johnnie – he always was wild. It would have been all right if he hadn't met a woman, quite a nice woman, in a way. She wasn't very beautiful; at least, she didn't seem so to me. But she was only in her thirties and I was fifty. I had my birthday party in the middle of all the gaiety. Michael thought it would be fun to have a professional singer to entertain us – a little light opera. And that was how she came into our life.'

'What was her name?' Victoria asked.

'I can't tell you that, my dear. You see, she became very famous. I think Michael's money helped there. He wanted the very best for her, he was so eager for everyone to admire her – even me. He wanted me to say how talented she was. And then, of course, I got jealous. I never knew if I really had anything to be jealous of – I think perhaps I didn't. Goodness only knows what would have happened if Michael hadn't had his breakdown. Perhaps it wouldn't be me sitting here now.' She sat quietly for a moment, considering that possibility, and then she continued. 'Then Victor came into my life. I knew him already, we both did. He owned several thousand acres bordering on the mines and we'd been to dinner with him a few times. When Michael collapsed, Victor stepped in to help me. He was wonderful. He organized everything, even down to that singer, whom he sent on a tour of Europe. That was what made her international reputation – and got her away from Michael.

I didn't think . . . all the time Victor was helping, it never occurred to me that he was doing it for me. Then, when Michael was recovering in a convalescent home, Victor took me out for a drive. The country was vast, the sky a great dome above us. It was so different from here. Michael and I were booked on a passage home. That was why Victor had to tell me how he felt. He wanted me to stay, and to keep Honour with me – he adored her and she was very fond of him. He'd been a widower for a long time, and had no children of his own. He was such a strong man, I hadn't realized how much I'd grown to depend on him. Suddenly I saw the future – how could I face it without him? I went back to his house, to where he wanted me to stay for ever. We were lovers – it's so long ago, it's as if this all happened to someone else. I find it impossible to imagine how I could have let passion rule me so entirely. That was what I wanted to explain to you. It does pass. I can't remember the passion at all.'

'That's not true, is it?' Victoria said softly. 'What you mean is that you can see so clearly why you shouldn't have, now. But you can remember how it was, can't you? How you get swept along, how nothing else matters.'

'Yes, yes, I do remember that. But I also remember the pain of having to live without that feeling afterwards. I knew my duty was to Michael and the children – Honour would have been all right in time, she was young, but the boys would never have understood.'

'Have you ever heard from Victor?'

'No, I told him when I left that I wouldn't be able to bear it. I don't know if he's alive or dead. But I still regret it.'

'Why? Why do you regret the fact that someone you loved loved you in return?'

'Because it hurts, that's why.' Isabella put her hand to

319

her breast in an expression of pain. 'That's what I want you to understand. It would have been so much easier never to have known that I could have had a different life. And the deceit – I never told Michael; he always thought that he was the only man I'd ever loved.'

'If you could blank it all out, rub out that part of your mind, so that it was as if Victor never existed, would you do that?'

It was something Isabella had never thought of. Would she give up her memories, how it had felt to be with Victor, how much he had loved her, how she had loved him? 'No,' she said. She spoke slowly, consideringly. 'I wouldn't. And I suppose that says it all, doesn't it? All that pain, but it was still worth it. But please, Viccy, take care of yourself. Don't go looking to get hurt.'

'Don't worry, I intend to take care of myself. Thank you for telling me about your past. It's good to know there's someone in the family who appreciates that there are times when the heart rules the head.' She stood up. 'I think I'd like a bath before supper. I'll see you later.'

'Could you manage a slice of goose, dear?' Isabella held a small portion of the rich Christmas meat out towards her daughter. Honour had said that she didn't feel too well, and she certainly looked peaky.

'No, thanks. I think I'll just have some vegetables.' Honour didn't want to eat anything. She felt as if her skin was going to burst. She was bloated and her red velvet dress pinched uncomfortably around the middle. She knew that she could only be three months pregnant, but her waist had already thickened considerably. For the past two days, since coming down to Pencombe, the sickness hadn't just been early in the morning, but off and on throughout the day. Victoria had said that she ought to see the doctor as soon as she could after the holiday, but first she had to tell her mother.

'I've got a little something.' Eli delved into his pocket like a magician about to pull a rabbit out of a hat. He was wearing a green smoking jacket, a yellow waistcoat and a red bow tie that echoed perfectly the table centrepiece of berried holly and Christmas roses. He placed a small grey tin on the table and reverently lifted the lid. 'Now that should put the colour back into your cheeks,' he said as he exposed the tiny black seed pearls.

'Caviare.' Lucinda whispered the word. How long was it since she had tasted her favourite delicacy? Her mouth watered in anticipation.

Honour smiled weakly. A faint fishy smell drifted towards her. 'I'd love some Eli, but perhaps for tea.' She stood up unsteadily. 'I think I'll just go upstairs and lie down.'

Victoria pushed her own helping of goose to the side of her plate. It was too cold for her at Pencombe. However high the fire roared up the chimney, the cold walls still made a chill in the atmosphere that struck deep inside her. But it was Christmas, the time to go home, and Cadogan Gardens would never again be that for her; Luke and his nurse were in possession of the spirit of the place. She had made no decision about a divorce, and she wasn't going to think about it until after the holiday.

Isabella left the room with her daughter. It was cold everywhere except in the family rooms and she pulled her cardigan around her. She was concerned at how pale Honour was. If they had to fetch the doctor Eli would have to go on foot because there was a good six inches of snow on the drive. It was as well that it wasn't far to the village.

Honour lay down on her bed. It took the strain from

321

the small of her back, and she felt suddenly much better. 'Go and have your own lunch, Mummy,' she said. 'I'll be all right.'

Isabella hesitated. She didn't want to leave the family to fend for themselves, but she sensed that Honour had something on her mind. 'You really don't look well,' she said. 'Have you been looking after yourself in town? Eating properly and all that kind of thing?'

'I'm fine, really. We'll talk later on. Go downstairs and join the others. They need you more than I do.' Honour was close to tears. She wished she'd told her mother before she'd started to feel so unwell. She didn't have the energy to cope with a scene now. All she wanted was comfort and reassurance.

'What's it all about?' Isabella sat down slowly on the side of the bed. She took her daughter's hand in her own. 'Is it so very dreadful?'

'I'm pregnant, I'm going to have Carl's baby and I wish – oh, I don't know what I wish.'

Isabella sat silently. After Victoria's visit she had been uneasy. She knew that her niece had encouraged her to talk about Victor on purpose. There had been a reason for reminding Isabella of her own fallibility. Yesterday morning – the first time she heard that Honour had been sick – she wondered if it might be a baby. After all, such things happened in war time. But then when the sickness lasted all day, she thought she'd been mistaken.

'Are you very angry?' Honour couldn't bear the silence. A new wave of nausea was making her hot and sticky and she wanted to sit up, but she wasn't going to move until her mother spoke.

'No, I'm not angry, darling. I'm just sad. Sad that your child won't have a father, sad that you won't have a husband. But you're young, you have a whole life ahead of you. There will be someone else one day.'

'Never.' Honour turned and buried her face in the pillows. 'There'll never be anyone else.' Her voice was muffled.

'Honour.' Isabella took a deep breath. She was being forced to look at life very differently, her values were having to change. 'You do want this baby, don't you? I mean, there are doctors who . . .'

Honour twisted up suddenly, and threw her arms around her mother. 'Please, please help me,' she whispered, 'I have to be brave, but it's so difficult.'

They came downstairs together and Honour's sickness seemed to have faded. Isabella suspected it had been anxiety that had made it so bad, but she thought she would probably call Dr Groak in after Boxing Day.

Isabella stood at the head of her festive table. 'I have an announcement,' she said. She suspected that Victoria and Eli knew already from the way they had looked at her as she walked back into the room, but Lucinda was most certainly going to get the surprise of her life. 'I am delighted to be able to tell you that I'm going to become a grandmother. At last I have a valid reason to stop calling Honour the baby of the family. Come on, Eli, break out the champagne – only none for the mother-to-be. She has to take great care of my future grandchild.' Lucinda's obvious horror was ignored as Victoria jumped up to kiss Isabella, and Eli busied himself dealing with the bubbly – he had to concentrate to produce a flawless performance.

Albert and Maggy arrived early on Boxing Day and Tom and Lizzy were expected at lunch time. Lucinda had been awake most of the night, trying to decide how she would react to Honour's condition. She had gone up to bed early on Christmas night, so no one yet knew how she felt. Her natural inclination was to appear disgusted. On the other hand, she knew that Isabella's acceptance of the situation would encourage the rest of the family to make the best of a bad job.

Victoria brought a beautifully laid breakfast tray into her bedroom. Mother and daughter exchanged nothing more than light chatter. Lucinda still hadn't made up her mind. Later she descended the stairs slowly, contemplatively, and the first person she saw in the hall was her son Albert. 'I'm positive the girl's carrying twins,' he said by way of greeting. 'I've told Issy to get old Groak in. She's puffing up, and she'll have to watch herself.' Albert, the instinctive stockman, was so matter-of-fact that Lucinda had no choice but to follow his lead.

'I thought there was something wrong myself. I shall be glad to hear the doctor's opinion,' she said. 'For all Isabella's Herbal, she doesn't appear to have noticed anything. Dear Albert, did you have a nice day yesterday? It's such a pity we weren't all together, but there will be quite a crowd at lunch, and Nigel might be here within the week. Have you heard about that? It's wonderful, isn't it, how Christmas brings us all together.' She walked with dignity towards the drawing room as her son followed, lost in amazement at his mother's charitable attitude to the family in general, and Honour in particular.

Eli and Albert went out together to fetch the doctor. They entered a silent, shrouded world. More snow had fallen during the night and the drive was virgin white. There was little activity in the village. Plumes of grey smoke drifted up from the cottage chimneys to join a low, grey sky. Two children ran silently from one front door to

324

another, scuffing up snow as they went. The doctor was out on his rounds, and the telephone lines were down, so they had the choice of trudging in search of him or leaving a message with his housekeeper. Albert doubted that his mother's new-found kindness would last, so he suggested they tried the last two calls on the doctor's list before going back. They were lucky and found him at West Lodge, so they all trudged back to the house together.

Honour was dozing. Her ankles were puffy and uncomfortable, so Victoria had suggested that she should rest on her bed until lunch time. There was a cheerful fire flaring in the duck-nest grate and the room was cosy and warm. She rested her hands lightly on her stomach. Carl had made love to her only once – it was as if God had ordained that she should carry his child.

They had made love . . . Her eyes were closed, and she could see the room at the inn as if it were yesterday. Carl had wanted to go up to Scotland, but leaves hadn't worked out, and they didn't have enough time. Instead they drove out of town for a day in the Sussex countryside. They planned to get back for the evening, but they were so close, so happy together, that when they stopped for a drink it seemed only natural to ask if there was a room for the night. The landlord and his wife assumed they were newlyweds – Honour smiled as she remembered how she'd twisted her engagement ring round on her finger, so that it looked like a wedding band. She was trembling as they followed the landlady up the narrow, winding stair – she was on the verge of changing her mind, but Carl held her firmly by the hand. 'I love you,' he whispered as they paused outside their bedroom door, and suddenly they were alone.

The inn was old, seventeenth century it said on a plaque

by the front door, and the floor of their room was made of wide polished oak boards covered with loose rugs. Narrow strips of rose-patterned wallpaper had been painstakingly fitted between the multitude of honey-coloured beams that ran up the walls and across the ceiling. Honour walked towards the bed, her hands clutching at the cool of the iron bedstead. She looked around her, wanting to remember every detail – there were pretty pink curtains that matched the coverlet, a fringed cream lampshade swinging gently in the breeze from the window. It was early evening and she could hear birds singing outside.

Carl put his arms around her. 'I won't hurt you,' he said. For a moment she wanted to tell him about James – she had never even mentioned his name, but then Carl moved his hands down from her shoulders. He brought them together to cup her breasts for a moment before running them down to her waist, and on, to feel the curve of her hips. She moaned softly as he bent his head and kissed the pulse at the base of her neck, then he began slowly undoing the buttons of her blouse.

'Honour!' Lucinda stepped into the room. 'I'm sorry, were you asleep?'

Honour opened her eyes wide with surprise, and the vision of Carl faded. 'No, not asleep,' she said. 'Just resting.'

'Good, I want to talk to you.' Lucinda settled herself on the low chair beside the bed and carefully arranged the folds of her grey wool dress. She looked at Honour to make sure that the girl was paying attention. What she had to say to her was most important.

'She wanted you to do what?' Victoria couldn't believe what Honour was telling her.

'Your mother said that I should pretend the baby is

James Sullivan's. She said that she had it all worked out. In her opinion the only reason James went back to Ireland was to raise the money for his shops. She thinks that my mother should lend him the capital he needs and that he and I should go to America, where he could start up in business immediately.'

Victoria's face showed the amazement she felt. 'I can't credit it. Honestly, I just can't. I know she believes in sweeping any family misdemeanours under the carpet, but that has to be the most . . .' She couldn't put how she felt into words. Her mother had been in an ebullient mood over lunch, and Honour so quiet and subdued that it was obvious something had happened between them. 'What did you say to her?' she asked.

'Nothing – I just thanked her for the interest she was showing in my welfare. The most upsetting thing was that I realized as she was speaking that James would agree to an arrangement like that. It didn't make me upset at her for interfering as much as I felt miserable at seeing right through him – he's totally money-motivated, I can understand that now. Anyway, I don't suppose Aunt Lucinda will be the last to want to run my life for me. Albert and Tom were wonderful, but Maggy started going on about how I should get away. She acted as if it was to keep clear of the bombing, but I think she wants me out of Kent. She's terrified her reputation gets tarnished.'

'She's got nothing to boast about. We all know how she seduced my brother in the first place.'

'It doesn't matter how they started off, they're married and that makes everything all right. If Carl and I hadn't decided to wait for Nigel, so would we have been. I would have been a respectable widow and that would have made them all much happier.'

'I'm sorry.' In a way Victoria felt responsible. Carl and

Honour had stepped in to give her son a reason to recover – as a mother, she had failed to provide that for him. The only time she'd visited him at East Grinstead he'd said not to come again. At least he would be at Pencombe soon, and perhaps then they could heal the rift between them. He would need somebody, especially now that Neil was in a prisoner-of-war camp and Jill had been promoted to ward sister – she was so busy that he hardly ever saw her.

'Let's talk about something different,' Honour said, 'nothing to do with the baby. How's the book coming?'

'Surprisingly well, considering. Over the last few days I've even come up with the title for the final part of the trilogy and you can be the first to hear it. In fact, I think you're probably the most suitable person to comment. I think it should be *Heroes* – it's the part about what's happening now. About William and Eddy at Dunkirk, and Eli on his *Bunty*. Then there's Nigel's accident, and Neil and Percy in the Battle of Britain. It's about the men of the family, and how their lives have been altered beyond any possibility of mending.'

'They're not the only ones.'

'You mean us women? I know life's altered for us too, but we always go on, don't we? We go through all sorts of trials and tribulations, and somehow we survive, to still be here when the men come back – if they do. That's what it's going to be like now. Can't you imagine it? There'll be your mother and mine, and you and me – that's two generations. In fact, with the age difference between you and me, it's almost three. When the baby comes it will actually be three generations, all living together, getting on each other's nerves, waiting for the men to come home.'

'I've got nobody to wait for now. When I've had the

baby I'll go back to work. I want to do my bit, for me and my child. You've said it yourself, there will be quite enough aunts and a granny wanting to babysit, even if it's for two. Dr Groak said there was no way of knowing yet. He said the fact that you'd had Nigel and Neil didn't necessarily mean twins ran in the family.'

'I think you ought to have a second opinion. I'm sure they can tell by now. When I go up to London to pack up my things, you can come and see a gynaecologist in Harley Street, the one I had for my babies, if he's still alive – he was marvellous. But I suppose he must be nearly seventy. My goodness, doesn't time fly?'

The two women sat cosily together in front of the fire in Honour's bedroom. Victoria felt happier now that she had decided to accept Isabella's invitation and move down to Pencombe. It was cold, but she didn't think that would kill her, whereas the stifling atmosphere at Cadogan Gardens might well do just that. With the baby to look forward to there was a purpose in life, even if it was only protecting Honour from Lucinda.

Isabella dressed carefully for dinner. She put on a maroon woollen dress that had been a favourite of Michael's. It required a strong effort of will to take trouble with her appearance. She would very happily have stayed in her room. She had known that this would be a difficult Christmas – it was the first since she had become a widow and the first since she had lost her elder son. Her face looked strained. It was a long time since she had worn lipstick, but she felt that a little would give her some colour. She looked dispassionately at her reflection in the wardrobe mirror. She had kept her figure, and her hair, which was almost white, was pulled back into an elegant roll. The pearl stud earrings that she was slowly screwing on matched the long rope of pearls around her neck. She checked her watch; it was coming up to seven.

Eddy had written to say that he would try and get home that evening. It would be the first time she'd seen him in almost six months; he hadn't been back since his father died. A friend was giving him a lift as far as Sevenoaks, and Albert had promised to drive up and collect him – the main roads should be clear enough. The telephone line had been repaired that morning, but when the operator phoned through to say it was working, she'd warned that it might not be for long. There was a fallen tree pressing on the line and a gust of wind could bring it down, then they'd be cut off again. If only Eddy had given her his friend's address – they were completely dependent on his call.

Isabella fingered the pearls at her neck. If she had Honour and Eddy together, it would really feel like Christmas. She believed she was on the verge of coming to terms with her life as it was. Having talked about Victor had exorcized his memory. She had been a good wife to Michael, and a good mother to her children. One slip shouldn't be allowed to spoil her final years, which suddenly were to be full of life.

She heard the phone ringing in the hall – it must be Eddy. The others were changing for dinner and there would be no one to answer it. She ran to the door, throwing it open wide as she hurried through. Three, four, five, she was counting the rings – please let him hold on, please, she thought. By the top of the stairs, she had reached nine. It must be Eddy, only he would keep on trying to get through. 'I'm coming, I'm coming, darling,' she called as she began to run down the stairs. Suddenly she pitched forward. Her heel had caught on the carpet, and she realized fleetingly that it was the stair she'd tripped on running towards Michael. And then she was falling.

Eli found her lying very still. She was twisted awkwardly and her face was ashen, but she didn't look as if she was in pain. 'Issy.' He bent over her. 'Issy, can you hear me?' He glanced up as Victoria came running down the stairs. Honour was close behind. With her hair flowing loose and unrestrained, she looked very young.

'It's all right.' Isabella's voice was faint and they had to bend close to hear it. 'It doesn't hurt at all.' She tried to lift her hand to beckon her daughter closer, but it wouldn't move, so she smiled instead – a gentle, crooked smile. 'You must give my love to Eddy. I'm very proud of you both, my darling. No one could have asked any more of their children. Victoria will take care of you and the baby – she understands things today far better than I ever could.' She looked at her niece. Viccy was developing into a woman with strength who could hold the family together and make a future for herself. 'You can write what you want now,' she whispered. 'The whole of the truth about the family – about the men who all fought to be heroes, and the women whose greatest victory was love.'

The births of Carl Michael and William Eli Montford were recorded on 12 May 1941. Ten days later, they were christened at the Montford family font in the parish church of Pencombe in Kent; Mrs Nigel Jones was godmother to the firstborn child; Victoria Jones godmother to the second; Edward, Lord Montford and Eli Bradbury stood as godfathers to both boys.

For tens of thousands of real-life RAF heroes the fight for survival continues.

From July to October 1940, an epic struggle for survival filled the ies above London and the Southern Counties.

Thanks to the dedication of the Royal Air Force, the Battle of itain was won.

But amongst those who participated – and many of the 1.75 illion men and women who served in the RAF and organisations sociated with it – the struggle for survival did not end with the war.

TODAY THEIR FUTURE DEPENDS ON US

Tens of thousands of surviving veterans have reached the age hen they and their dependants desperately need a helping hand.

So they turn to the RAF Benevolent Fund. As a result our sources are under unprecedented pressure.

JCH IS THE SCALE OF THE PROBLEM, £20 MILLION IS RGENTLY NEEDED. THIS IS WHY WE'RE ASKING FOR YOUR SUPPORT. PLEASE TURN OVER.

We must raise £20 million in 1990.

The RAF Benevolent Fund recognises the debt we all owe to the men and women of the Royal Air Force. For their service during the war and the performance of their duty since.

To help them in *their* hour of need, now and in the future, the "REACH FOR THE SKY" Appeal must raise £20 million in 1990. This will help meet the massive need for housing, residential care and nursing facilities. With your help we can supply vital medical equipment, or educational assistance for dependants.

Your generosity makes it possible for many thousands who face serious hardship to take heart. To be certain their commitment in the past has not been forgotten.

‒ ‒ ‒ ‒ ‒ ‒ ‒ ‒ ‒ ‒ ‒ ‒ ‒ ‒ ‒ ‒ ‒ ‒ ‒

They gave their all. Will you now give them the help they so richly deserve?

YES, I'd like to play my part. My donation will help bring security and peace of mind to men and women who have earned our respect.

Please accept my gift: £25 ☐ £15 ☐ £50 ☐ £100 ☐ £500 ☐ Other £ _____

Please charge my credit card: Access/Visa £ _____

Card No. ☐☐☐☐ ☐☐☐☐ ☐☐☐☐ ☐☐☐☐

Please make cheques or postal orders payable to the RAF Benevolent Fund's Battle of Britain Appeal Ltd. Thank you.

NAME _____

ADDRESS _____

POSTCODE _____

SIGNATURE _____

Please send your donation in an envelope to:
REACH FOR THE SKY, Dept. HH, PO BOX 1940,
FAIRFORD, GLOUCESTERSHIRE GL7 4NA.
The Royal Air Force Benevolent Fund is a registered charity, No: 207327.

REACH FOR THE SKY
THE RAF BENEVOLENT FUND'S
BATTLE OF BRITAIN
50TH ANNIVERSARY APPEAL

ADHOC2